AMERICAN MYSTIC: THE LIFE, DEATH, & REBIRTH OF JIMMY WONDERFUL

by Coyote Wallace

Nightmare Press
Shepherdsville, KY

For Those I Love (A Coyote's Dedications)

To Faith and Kelli for making the future bright.
To Satyr for being my mentor and brother.
To Christiane Truelove for cookies, a bard's wisdom, and a friend's comfort.
To Steven for being my little brother and reminding me to laugh.
To Gemma for being the pixie that put me back together.
To Marguerite Reed for a good book, and a fine friend.

For all of you who have been thrown away, doubted, and still found the courage to dream of worlds brighter than the ones outside your window.

We're all a little Wonderful now.

AMERICAN MYSTIC: THE LIFE, DEATH, & REBIRTH OF JIMMY WONDERFUL

by Coyote Wallace

AMERICAN MYSTIC

THE LIFE, DEATH, & REBIRTH OF

JIMMY WONDERFUL

COYOTE WALLACE

NIGHTMARE
PRESS

COYOTE WALLACE

America has always had a love-hate relationship with magic. We, at our heart, are a technologically oriented people; one who has wrapped themselves in the warm glow of computer monitors and long ago exchanged faerie roads for horsepower and highways. We are beasts ever in search of new horizons, drunk on freedom and dizzy with our own arrogance, ready to rip apart anything that frightens us – while coveting anything we do not already have. Our nation was birthed, at least in part, with the help of masonic rituals and indigenous spellcraft that sent the British forces back to King George III and his court wizard with their tails between their legs.

We promptly killed those indigenous allies, developed a deep distrust of their masonic counterparts to the point we burned their temples, and proceeded to steamroll our way ever westward. The battles were bloody, hellish, the sort of thing that words do no justice for the shame is too great. Men and women with abilities and knowledge gained from mystical understanding clashed in open warfare with those who wielded The Word (as it is known in the circles that may wield it) like a bludgeoning club and enough firepower to stain the sky black. There are places out there, places where only the coyotes and the wind dare tread, that the ground itself still hums with spent power and spilled blood.

When we Americans first encountered lycanthropy in the indigenous peoples, our European sensibilities called it a disease. When our explorers first stumbled upon pixie nests in the redwood forests, they tore them down and ate the damned pixies. When we filled our mines with poor Irish tinkers, we also filled them with wide-eyed members of the Bean Sidhe and naïve Brownies eager to make new human friends – but terribly unaware of the dangers of silicosis.

You want a horrifying idea of what kind of people we are? Here is one for those record books, Bubba: When

Houdini contacted his wife from beyond the grave to confirm the existence of an afterlife, it was exactly two days later that the first 'Post-Death Debt Collection' legislation was presented before Congress. We let Muhammad Ali fight a Promethean golem made from the spare parts of Rocky Marciano in Madison Square Garden because we wanted to see a man beat a monster, with no care to the sloshing of the man's brain in his skull.

Our history is one that is intertwined with capitalism and mysticism. This relationship is not now, nor has it ever been, a harmonious one. The American Dream, at its core, holds that all men are created equal and are owed the right to pursue their own life, liberty, and happiness.

The Night Folk, however, are a blatant contradiction to this dream. They are bestowed with abilities, powers, curses, and knowledge that by their very nature sets them as the opposing force to notion of men being created equal. There must always be the shaman, the wizard, the spiritual guide, a pope wielding a flaming sword, or some timeless would-be king who seeks to lead their people through what they believe their majorities cannot understand.

Unfortunately for those born under such strange auspices as the Night Folk, America has a tendency to destroy anything that it finds too strange to absorb into the patchwork of its great fuel-injected dream.

The machine of capitalism, the iron fist of the authoritarian, the blank-eyed stare of the badge-wearing brute, and the empty smile of the politician armed themselves with their own magic and learned to speak their own spells. These words, while more easily understood than those spoken by what modern parlance has dubbed 'Namebreakers' (I know, I prefer wizard too), were no less potent. Words like: Preemptive Detention, Ad Campaigns, Mineral Rights, and Standing Warrant. They armed themselves not with wands, blessed swords, conjured staffs, or ceremonial daggers, but with riot shields, automatic rifles, and tear gas.

When at last man discovered the ability to harness Dynametrium, he also discovered a way to, at long last, rid himself of his fear of what I call 'The Big Weird'. Magic, vampires, ghosts, and stranger things still – are all much easier tolerated when humanity believes it holds the leash. This comfort, addictive and deceptive in equal measure, helped turn a people who once cast their eye to the westward horizon and held the throttle wide open, into cowards (of which I have been counted), whose greatest fear is a tomorrow they cannot predict.

This is who we are, this is who we may well always be, and this wound only continues to fester the longer it is left untreated.

The heart of the American Dream is tearing itself apart, pulled in too many directions at once by forces that all claim to be owed a piece of the swirling melting pot. There are those who see this division as a great opportunity; they line their pockets with money made from fear of the different and unknown, pandering to the worst elements of our hearts. They are joined by those who, in The Night Folk, see opportunity for exploitation. Debates rage constantly about the rights of everyone, from the living dreams that are the fairies to the corporate-owned dead who have been fighting to exist since Henry Ford figured out dead men need fewer breaks than living ones. We in the media, obligated as we are by notions of objectivity, make our bones no longer on the singular truth, but in the art of giving each person their own unique truth that confirms the biases they've always suspected.

Soon, that heart will cease to beat, and we will skid headlong into Nightmare Country where the empires of great nations are thick with fear; and those who once taught us there was more than what we could see or touch are consigned to existence on the page alone. Our most basic primal selves no doubt find this strangely comforting; a world without the unexplainable certainly has its own appeal, but also its own steep cost.

What sort of world would it be without the Night Folk?

I do not have the answer and have long run from anything that even remotely smells like prophecy.

Something in my bones tells me we are going to find out. Hopefully not in my lifetime, but soon enough. With the discovery of the 'Chaos Gene,' parents now have a choice in whether or not their children will grow up to develop the ability to use those magic words. With the implementation of the Orlock Protocols, the federal government now has the addresses of every person who has been treated by vampirism. There is seemingly a 'cure' for every type of Night Folk that exists, and those for whom there is no cure – our society is rapidly finding ways to exploit into non-existence.

Few things are sadder than watching a dead man work himself to the point where letting go of all that tethered him to this world is preferable to another moment on an assembly line. There are few things as outright disgusting as watching a family separated by the Lycanthrope 'camps' that are so often portrayed by my fellow journalists as preserves rather than the reservations they are.

Yet, 'few' does not mean 'none', and if there is one thing worse than the attempts to erase the Night Folk, or consume them, then it is those who have thrown their lot in with their would-be oppressors. The American government has its own task force consisting of its own specially trained Namebreakers; the lycanthrope camps have their own spokesman and leaders who, despite their containment, are afforded luxuries for keeping their people in line. Richard Nixon has only recently proven to be the pinnacle of these inward-facing Judases; under the regime of our first undead president, the arrest and containment of the Night Folk has seen an increase of twenty-three percent, in others it's nearly double that.

What is to become of our nation, our dream, and our souls?

What are we without magic?

Jimmy Wonderful, *Editorial Molotov Cocktails: A Mystic Standard Collection*

The End at The Beginning

The Hop N' Happy Burger Bar on the corner of Poplar Avenue in Memphis feels like coming home.

Comfort food always does, doesn't it? If I had to guess why, I'd say maybe it's the faded yellow wallpaper, heavy with the scent of old grease and frying beef, or maybe it's the worn-out '50s décor that feels like a fever dream recollection of a time that never was. The cook and owner, an elderly African American man by the name of Samuel Myron Hayes, his bald head ringed with white hair and from whose mouth, at the time of this writing, still dangles a thin cigarette in admirable defiance of health codes and safety regulations, is as close to a priest as I could want. This place is a dying breed, too authentic to be trendy and too far set in its ways to adapt. Eventually, some well-intentioned kid with a cell phone will walk in, mistaking the Hop N' Happy for the sort of place that has a vegan menu, and then it'll be curtains for old Sam.

Adapt or Die, Sport. It's the law of the wild. This is America, the land of the free for the first month, and home of those brave enough to dream of royalties. Dinosaurs must be hunted, how else are fresh-faced youths supposed to prove their manhood if not by stamping out relics of bygone ages? Poor old Sam doesn't even see it coming. To be fair to Sam, though, neither did I. When they tear this place down and replace it with some trendy chain store, clean, sparkling, and efficient, that'll just be the forward march of progress, or so I am told.

COYOTE WALLACE

This is a fitting place to start the ugly work of crafting the end of my own career.

There were times when I was first starting out that I basically lived on cheap, greasy cheeseburgers and arterial-jamming heaps of home fries. This exact meal was sold with a cold soda for two dollars and fifty cents in half a dozen places like the Hop N' Happy along this charming strip of the Memphis of my youth. Cash is rarely in abundance when one is cutting their teeth on any scrap of opportunity they can find to make a living as a writer. There were times when anything above bologna on hand felt like a victory, and in those early days, I was sustained by those stolen moments as much as the chow. Little dives like this were where one celebrated victory, while the bars were reserved for the more common daily defeat of selling your soul one deadline at a time.

I'm anonymous here, what few patrons that do exist pay very little mind to me, and even less to the little rectangular slice of modernity that I carried in under my arm. I'm free to bury my nose in the glowing screen of the laptop uninterrupted, free to miss my old home office and the trappings of who I once was, and yes, the laptop is a poor substitute for my old typewriter.

Funny, the things you miss when you ultimately have to let them go in favor of moving forward.

However, I know it's more than that. Circles have a way of closing. That's the natural order of things, and no amount of money, power, or time stolen for our own pursuits will ever change that. I've traveled across the face of this country and back again. I've rambled down the dark back roads of America's South and lost myself in her mountains in search of answers and truths. I've danced with faeries beneath the moonlight while drunk on tequila at The Sacred Grove of the Dragonfly. I've slept in the mud outside of the lycanthrope camps like Fort St. John before being dragged away by the police, and I've done my level best to play the Van Helsing to an undead Richard Nixon. You can find all those stories on your own time, and you may consider my token endorsement of public libraries for the day. I do not mind; I once found the fact that becoming some manner of leftist idol paid extraordinarily well – quite amusing.

I don't exactly need the money where I'm going.

What follows is my final tale, the last chapter in a life full of loud music, warm nights, crazy sex, and all the beautiful little moments that make traveling on the margins worthwhile. I cannot say if this will make print; the scandal and the turmoil that have risen in the wake of this story make that an uncertainty. Sometimes writing something is far too much like tossing a message in a bottle into the sea; fame has spoiled me, made my flesh tender to that particular sting. I'd forgotten what that brand of uncertainty tasted like. The best I can muster is a newborn hope, inspired by sacrifice, that the tale gets told, and that both time and truth conspire to undo the efforts of wicked men.

This is the tale of a terrible cancer that grew upon the American spirit, fed by money, terror, and our own worst instincts. This is the tale of those who were consumed by that malignancy, and those who died to stop it from snuffing out that which makes our world special. The tale of the strange, the weird, the beautifully different, and the long-forgotten truth of who we are as a people.

I'm Jimmy Wonderful and this is the tale of the new generation of American mystic.

COYOTE WALLACE

Life

"In a world of the strange, the obscene, and the downright Weird, you learn to take the truth like a shot of whiskey. Fast and without lingering on the fact that it burns you up on the inside." —Jimmy Wonderful, *America: The Strange and The Immortal*

Like every tale in my life for the last ten years, this one began with a busted story, a hangover, and a trip to Chicago. There's nothing quite like waiting outside the assignment editor's office for *The Mystic Standard* on a rainy Monday morning with a world-record-setting headache and the sort of acid reflux that makes you wonder if you're turning into the goddamn Brundlefly; all of which only serves to reinforce the fact that one does not have the ability to light bystanders on fire with their mind, but alas, such is my cursed existence.

According to recent studies conducted by the CDC, there are more than 5,000 active Namebreakers in the United States alone. God only knows how many more worldwide. Labeled 'Persons of Mass Destruction' by the Federal government, testing and screenings have grown steadily more precise since they were mandated back in the late '70s. I still hold out hope every time I'm here I'll suddenly develop the power to be anywhere else, or at the very least set someone on fire with my mind. How can I not? I've always hated being told what to do or what to write, even more so when I'm hungover and only taking the gig to reinvigorate my increasingly anemic bank accounts.

I'm a very good whore, but that doesn't mean I like it. Fortunately, liking "it" and being good at "it" are rarely, especially in this business, both a requirement.

You can learn a surprising amount about people just sitting outside an office waiting for your turn to have a healthy dose of smoke pumped up your ass. A bevy of energetic interns, hungry young wordsmiths, freelance photographers hoping to sell their goods—and then there's me, the old man, the black sheep, the one who threw it all away. A figure to be afforded sidelong glances in between questions about everything from how I manage to find the good stories to what my 'process' is. Poor bastards. If they knew how often I envisioned taking a stapler to their foreheads each time they ask me an inane question, they'd probably keep their distance. I make do instead with the occasional dismissive, 'It's different for everyone,' and when I'm feeling really prickish, I look them dead in the eye and tell them that whiskey and cocaine are more reliable muses than sunsets. The eager little shits always hate that. You can see it crush their souls a little bit.

Maybe I should be a little more grateful. *The Mystic Standard* has become just that: "the standard" for American journalism centering around the extra-human, the outright supernatural, and most importantly the good old-fashioned weird. A once venerable institution that helped make the American public come to terms with the existence of things best left unseen. Robert Kennedy's secret life as a sex wizard? *The Standard*. Yoko Ono's career as a soul collecting Tengu keen on the souls of unfortunate British musicians? *The Standard*. Kim Kardashian sucking the very life force out of strapping seven-foot-tall basketball all-star athletes? Well, that was *The New York Times*, but you get the point.

COYOTE WALLACE

I came along right at the tail end of the glory days, when a man could waste half of his expense account trying to fund Colombia off the lower back of a bronze-skinned goddess while setting the whole damned floor of a hotel in Havana on fire—and so long as the story about the once-a-century return to shore of the goddamn Lovecraftian fish people is on time and moderately coherent, they didn't ask questions.

I believe that is what is called in professional circles, "the good old days."

"Mister Wozynski," Delores purred from her desk,

"Tom is ready see you now."

Too late to run.

Shit.

"Delores," of course, isn't her name. I didn't know it, and I was probably not going to learn it either. Somewhere around 1988, all secretaries for all editors of all shapes and sizes became "Delores" to me. This might seem cruel, callous, or emotionally stunted, and that's good. It should. This particular Delores was in her late 20s, with rings of red hair and skin like fresh cream. She made the most convincing argument to date for reversing my policy about the various Deloreses of the world. I didn't, mostly because in my line of work, the high art of not shitting where you eat was (and still is) a valuable life skill. That, and there's the fact that my wife would have introduced me to the joys of a long and interesting life lived as a eunuch. We men can say what we want, but nobody loves their freedom more than they love their balls, and the only people who say they do are presently not enjoying the existence of their balls to the fullest.

There's a lesson in that which I didn't have the time for then and certainly don't have now. Some things you just have to learn on your own the hard way, with plenty of HPV screenings and a damned good paternity lawyer.

You're the best, baby. The bee's knees," I said, giving "Delores" a wink as I rose from my chair. She responded with a quick giggle and a splash of scarlet on her cheeks.

This sort of ritualistic exchange serves to ward off the dreaded "bad juju" that can snakebite these sorts of meetings, essential for the confidence needed when dealing with any assignment editor. It's not as relaxing as a shot of single malt and a blowjob in a stockroom smelling of printer's ink and old newsprint, but it's enough to put a little spring in the step. When you've been at this as long as I have, you learn to take any advantage you can get, even the ones that are just superstitions you cook up on your own time. Hell, especially the ones you cook up on your own time.

I was trying to be better than I'd been but old habits that hid somewhere deep in my aging carcass didn't buy it; not all the way, and I don't think I could blame them.

I'm not a religious man; I haven't even been to church since I was a child, and yet every time I walked into Tom Mulkey's office, I was filled with the golden, pure certainty that there is, in fact, a Hell—and I was there. The floor was the only thing in the damned office that was still original, and that old wood felt badly out of place, covered by Tom's black modernist desk and several asinine beanbag chairs. His ridiculous Nerf basketball hoop was mounted on the inside of the door. I could still remember when this office belonged to his predecessor, a good man named Mike Hall, who used to get loaded with me after work at the corner dive bar when we were both still breaking in. When this was Mike's office, there were framed stories on these walls. Now, I was bombarded by motivational posters. I silently swore to whatever God listens to the prayers of men like me that one day I would walk into this office with a flamethrower strapped onto my back. I would, of course, being a peaceful

13

and sensible man, allow Tom to get out of the way before I send that kitty that has been "Just hanging on" to the Inferno.

Maybe.

"Yo! Jim-Daddy!" Tom's lame corporate attempt to rake across my nerves felt like Margaret Thatcher's favorite rusty cheese grater. "You know, when you didn't show up the first two times, we were almost certain that you had given up the ghost entirely. Hot damn. I knew the third time would be the charm. The old guard you belong to needs a long rope to run on, I'm always saying that." Tom might have been the assignment editor for *The Standard*, but he'd missed his calling as a game show host, and now he took it out on the rest of us by making us endure a perfect smile that was just too goddamn genuine.

No one likes their co-workers that much. No one. If you think your co-workers do, that means you're the most hated person in the entire office, and you should probably be wary of getting close to any rooftop ledges, open windows, or team-building exercises involving duck hunting.

Tom was the youngest man to ever hold that position, tasked with helping bring *The Standard* into the competitive modern era of blogs, vlogs, and high-digital fuckery. He is an energetic, upbeat, and fashionable young man with blond hair shaved at the sides and coiffed back on his head, aided by some sort of hair wax that he probably thought created the illusion of a natural hold. Of all his traits, though, the most insufferable was, at least on that day, his youth. Setting aside the fact he'd replaced a good friend, I felt not a single common thread with the man, like a dinosaur being stared at by some strange, pink, hairless monkey as the dawning horror that he's just an exhibit sets in.

Over the last twenty years, the U.S. government had managed to accumulate an eight-trillion-dollar bill for The War on Infernalism. Too bad the rat bastards never asked me, or I'd been able to tell them that all they needed to do to identify a Soulless was check for who the fuck was out there buying bean bag chairs for offices. I'm not saying it would be a sure-fire method; I've got no hard scientific evidence to back it up—but I'm telling you. Adults in a business setting with bean bag chairs and the Infernal. There's a connection.

Don't say it. Don't you fucking say it.

"Have a seat," he says as smooth as company downsizing and as genuine as a clip-on tie. "And tell me how you and Jenna have been. I'll get you a drink. Go on, don't be shy. It's been a while since we got to catch up in person." Tom was already up and halfway to his stylish little corner mini bar before I even had a chance to respond.

I edged towards one of the beanbag chairs and gave it an experimental push with the tip of my shoe. One was bright green and the other pink—I suppose to look more energetic but to me they seemed like big squishy clown testicles—and they desecrated the office. This weasel, with his underhanded work, can-do attitude, saccharine-sweet positive disposition, and understanding of modern media platforms, had unjustifiably inherited from Mike. Why did the young have to be equal parts so goddamn smart and Christ-awful annoying? I thought about it. Sitting in one of those chairs would be my first step towards embracing the modern cra— aside from the laptop I had reluctantly fallen in love with after Jenna had given it to me on our anniversary, almost as a joke, without any real expectation that I'd use it.

In with the new, out with the old.

Unfortunately, at least for any hopes Tom might have had of actually getting me to sit in one of those awful chairs, I happened to catch my reflection in the little mirror he kept behind the small bar in the corner. The dark hair was a little grayer around the temples, the frame a bit thinner, and the lines deeper, but it was the same sort of black suit—cheap

15

and wrinkled—that I had worn on the first day through the doors. I wasn't sitting on some damned beanbag no matter what the kid said. Work wasn't supposed to be fun and upbeat. If one wanted to feel fun and upbeat in an office setting, they'd do cocaine or smoke grass in the parking lot like millions of Americans have been doing since they were forced into the labor market.

"Jenna's fine," I said. "Working on a new album. We had a rough patch there for a while, but we got through it..." I tried to downplay the rough patch the best I could with casual tones. Fumbling, I tacked on – maybe a little too quickly – "Make that a single malt, will you?"

Tom turned and looked at me like I'd just proposed the violent fucking of his beloved family pet here on the office floor. Though I did not know the cause for that expression, I was immediately filled with a more genuine pride than I'd felt over anything I'd written in the last nine months. This triumph (like most in my life) was short-lived, as to my horror, Tom's expression of incredulous surprise slowly morphed into a big grin that broke into high, chipper laughter.

"Oh my God, you were just joking; that's so on brand for you!" Tom exclaimed with a grin, his tone a mix of amusement and faux incredulity. "The whole surly alcoholic writer image. I cannot even imagine what that was like back in 'the day.' You know, Jimmy, we even got rid of the old smoker's lounge and replaced it with an on-site yoga studio. Now when people are feeling a little bound up creatively, they just hop down there and, oh, listen to me ramble on! Here, try some of this. It's an artisanal soda with burdock root to give it a nice full antioxidant note. Go on. You'll like it.

Tom's joviality was contagious, but then again so was herpes.

Healthy soda. Even writing it down now feels wrong, dirty somehow. Like I need to go take a shower while guzzling some high-fructose corn syrup with an insulin needle sticking out of the side of my ass. Ever since the government began cracking down on unauthorized Name Breaking, there has been a resurgence in gray areas such as alchemy, herbology, and various forms of spiritualism among the young. It was laughable under most circumstances—people seeking to feel special by clutching a crystal in their hands and hoping it would make a difference.

The reality was that with only 5,000 people remaining with what those trustworthy souls in Washington called "the Chaos Gene," there was very little special left about anyone. Especially when even the most human of the Shadow People, or Mortality Impaired, or whatever the sweet Hell the new term was for them that I'd have to learn this week, were also the rarest. Magic, if that's what you want to call it, was dying off one generation at a time but you'd never know it to look at it. It has never been more fashionable.

"Thanks," I told Tom, but there was no sincerity in it.

I've covered a lot of stories, seen a lot of weird stuff, and a lot of things that are actually pretty normal, but nobody wants to pay attention to those. The standoff in Montana in '79 with those lycanthropes who had decided it was better to risk being hunted down than die as captives, and make no mistake, no matter how many times the government calls them "quarantine centers" – they are reservations; there was the Summer of Ashes in '97 where stupid teenagers infected themselves with vampirism and turned themselves into solar-powered Roman candles all across the U.S., and I'd even written a book about the six months I spent living with the faeries, of which everyone tells me all my other works are derivative.

17

COYOTE WALLACE

Yet, in all my time and all the things that I have seen, I have seen nothing quite as sad, miserable, and capable of making a man contemplate throwing one of his own colleagues through the plate-glass window of an office building as burdock root soda. The liquid was brown and murky enough to have come from an inner-city tap, and what bubbles it possessed reminded me less of carbonation and more of the kind of gurgling horrors that might emerge from the bottom of a swamp.

I knew two things after I took that first tentative sip. The first was that burdock root tasted like justifiable homicide, and whatever good-intentioned human being had first hauled it out of the woods (for what I am sure was a perfectly good reason) should have been flogged and then thrown, perhaps, into a large pit featuring carnivorous beasts of varying shapes and sizes.

The second was that I would never, ever, even at the threat of my own imminent demise or the destruction of all that I hold dear, drink this awful concoction again. Not for money, not for love, and not to be part of whatever new and healthy future awaited mankind with arms full of kale and assholes blown out like old tires by lemon water cleanses. Someone had to take care of all the red meat, cigarettes, and good old-fashioned liver-rotting alcohol. I'm a writer by trade but feel certain I'd make a fine custodian of those old, antiquated ways if anyone wants to start handing out paychecks.

"What do you think, Jimmy? Good, isn't it?" Tom's impossibly white smile, that seemed too big for his face, made it impossible for me to tell whether he thought the horrible liquid was delicious, or whether he simply took some sort of twisted and sadistic pleasure in watching another grown man force down the shit tonic that dared to call itself soda.

"It's fucking horrible. Goddamn..." I didn't respect Tom enough to lie to him. When you create stories for people, it's a bit like being a whore. You don't just "make things up" for people anymore unless you respect them. Everyone else gets two scoops of piss-off and a prescription to go pound sand.

"That's just because you're still used to sugar. You have to go a few weeks without sugar before the taste really 'pops.' You know what I'm saying?"

Nothing says 'delicious and refreshing' like forcing your brain to forget another food that it finds delicious in order to enjoy ass-brown tap water. That's why I often, for relaxation, contemplate shooting speed directly into my eyes and punching a Rottweiler in its dangling testicles. We're living in the glorious chrome-plated modern era, after all! Forget everything good in favor of everything that's supposed to be good for you.

If you don't die from not eating enough fiber, you become a sort of misanthropic burden upon society—*oh, you scandalous deviant!* You indulge in tobacco, relish a juicy steak, or perhaps, on a reckless whim, engage in a clandestine liaison with an adoring undergraduate who's devoured your entire bibliography, and is poised to spill every secret you have to your wife should you fail to elope with her.

How dare you!

As a nation, we do not tolerate the old, nor does stagnation sit well in our bellies. That sentiment, as driven by futurism as it sounds, is also the recipe for our own downfall, at least from where I'm sitting. A final hot dose to erase the past so that we can better enjoy the future. If that means we make the same awful mistakes again, then no one will care because they'll be fresh and new mistakes.

Burdock root soda, Jesus H. Christ.

"I'll take your word for it"

COYOTE WALLACE

I put the glass down on his desk and waited for my tongue to stop plotting a violent revolt, nothing else I was going to hear today would be any more palatable than was that drink.

I'm damn sure Tom doesn't bark 'get to the point!' as much as he drowns folks under a deluge of pointless trends until the weight of mediocrity crushes them into submission. You'd sooner chew off your own leg like a rabid coyote than endure another minute of his hipster sermonizing. The young whip out their 'weaponized new' like it's the second coming, ready to atomize our brains with innovation. But let's face it, we're relics from a time when sex was still sexy, and fun wasn't a felony. This 'weaponized new' is a creature from a future we never saw coming, a wild beast of both wonder and woe.

I'd made my mandatory appearance, descending from the mountain to remind the youngsters that I, *The Standard's* favorite son, still counted myself among their faithful flock. But this didn't mean I had the patience for this meeting, nor did I intend to drag it out any longer than necessary. I'd enjoyed a certain freedom for so long that I'd forgotten the feeling of being chained to a desk, listening to the rapid-fire clatter of keys under the fingers of eager young wordsmiths. They were like trigger-happy soldiers, aiming to shoot the beating hearts out of the world with bylines that burst like bombs in the minds of the shell-shocked public

No one at *The Standard* understood my strange alchemy for producing works, nor did they care. As long as I remained out of sight and out of mind, the results mattered more than the means. This quid pro quo had defined my relationship with Mike, and while I had no such assurances with Tom, I placed a certain faith in the momentum of things.

"I've got a few ideas I've been working on," I began. "Picked myself up a good line on a satyr commune out on the Gold Coast. Going to cost a pretty penny getting in, and I'm sure you know how expense accounts can take a beating on these things."

I tried to keep my tone gentle. It was also best to be gentle when breaking it to a man you wanted to spend his money watching goat people fornicate in supposedly enlightening ways while drinking enough wine that you don't even care you were going to vomit.

Tom was already maneuvering back to his desk and that lone chair, fiddling with a few errant papers that he'd left out. What he wasn't doing was listening – not really. By the time I had fallen silent and was waiting for him to ask me about the details and get down to brass tacks, he was simply looking up at me with condescension wrapped in positivity. As if sunshine and rainbows could make whatever horse pill that lay in store for my throat go down any goddamn easier. He gave his own burdock root artisanal soda a healthy sip, as if he really did enjoy the taste, and then he got down to the business of cutting off my balls.

"That sounds really great," Tom leaned forward on that little piece of assembly-line art that had been mislabeled as a desk. "Interesting stuff, I'm sure. We'll put a pin in that and swing back around to it, okay?"

Whenever an assignment editor tells you he's going to put a pin in something and then circle back around to it, that means you'll never hear about it again. I've got it on good authority that's how they got rid of Hoffa: put a pin in him and circled back around. Amelia Earhart, payphones, pixie dust that hasn't been cut with PCP—lots of pins, lots of circling.

I started to tell Tom that I'd already begun making plans for the trip when he cut me off.

"Just hear me out, Jimmy. Do you know who that Roy Altenhofen is?" Tom's tone of expectation suggested that all further progress hinged upon the possession of this knowledge.

I felt an insidious twinge of pain in my back from taking the stairs and being left standing; a cheeky little reminder from Father Time that I wasn't as young as I once was. Still, that wasn't enough to consider sitting across from Tom on one of those orbs of shame. The question was insulting, and an incredulous little grunt escaped me before I could put the lid on it.

"That's the guy who owns AltCorp," I replied, and like a sea captain glimpsing dark clouds on the horizon, I knew I was in for trouble. "Real Howard Hughes type, and by all accounts he's got every politician on the West Coast in his pocket. He helped cook up that cure for Namebreakers. Likes to sell himself as the reason we aren't all overrun with Namebreakers or wizards or whatever the hell the new term is." I left off the low-income housing for the Shadow People, which only served to create neighborhoods that were doomed to be little more than ghettos, and the donations to the preservation of every facet of "natural" humanity, from the Human First Movement to the Daughters of the Pure Blood and everything in between.

Even the most benevolent king is still a king, and until I meet the billionaire who is prepared to simply give it all away and live like the rest of us in the rat race, my distrust for the fabulously wealthy remains strong and vital. Money makes slaves of us all, whether we are flesh and blood or the stuff of dreams. As an American, I often contemplate the issues of capitalism but find myself unable to hold such thoughts in my head for more than a quarter mile at a time, never looking back while racing to capitalize on my own self-exploitation. I have made peace long ago with the understanding that even counter-culture defiance is just another wheel in the machine, but that does not mean I hold any love in my heart for those who control that machine and crush so many with the callous pull of the invisible levers.

"Exactly!" Tom flashed every pearly white tooth in his head when he laid it all out there. "Now, what would you say if I told you he's got a project? An unveiling of sorts, real hush-hush stuff. He wouldn't even tell me what it was about, but he wants you, and he's willing to break the damned bank to have us give you to him. What would you say to that, huh? Dope, right?"

Some of you who read this, provided *The Standard* doesn't have it burned and the authorities do not seize the manuscript as masturbatory training material for junior FBI agents, may (for reasons incomprehensible to your fellow man) go on to become assignment editors yourselves one day. If, through a twist of fate, you do find yourself in this profession, please understand that every day, every single day, from now until the sun decides to burn out and cold darkness envelopes all of Creation, extinguishing not only civilization but life itself—someone like me will want to kick someone like you directly in the forehead.

We will publicly thank you and tell young aspiring writers that you, like any editor, are an essential part of the process, but this is a lie we repeat to ourselves so we do not go to prison for what would surely be a nationwide epidemic of murders. Though, in the interest of honesty, I feel inclined to point out that it was the split-second recollection of the existence of the security cameras in the downstairs lobby that kept me from transforming into an agent of God's wrath before Tom's eyes.

"I'd tell you that I don't care if he came in here and promised you the moon and complimentary reach-arounds," I said with enough surly contempt to kill a horse. "I don't do

23

fluff pieces on guys who probably hunt the homeless for sport. I'll pass. Thanks for the offer. I'll email you the details about the commune before I fly out."

I was being a little heavy-handed with Tom. Maybe that just comes with the territory. I was the creator. He was the businessman. It'd been a long-damned time since I chased the rabbit around the track. I had no desire to do so once more.

Tom made this little snorting sound of displeasure, like he'd just got popped on the nose, and sat back in his seat, there was a rapid little drumbeat from the tips of his fingers as he chewed his lip and looked at me over the desk. I could almost hear the gears working as he tried to regain his mental balance. Refusing Tom's offer was almost enough to make the hangover go away. Almost.

For a moment, he didn't say a word, just squinted and eyeballed me before leaning over and opening one of the drawers of the desk. The manila file was fresh and new, which meant it was a copy of something that had been sent over from one department or another. Probably the vultures in legal.

A copy of what exactly? That was another matter entirely.

"I feel you, J-Dog," he said. "I feel you. But – and this is a big 'but' here – what if the people upstairs WANT you to do this, Jimmy?" Tom's easy good cheer served as the velvet glove to the iron hand of the shareholders who owned *The Standard*. I was suddenly reminded of another detail I hate about the young.

The impersonal smoothness with which they can dispatch the old.

Tom made a show of having another sip of that godawful excuse for soda, giving his lips a quick smack before carefully placing the glass back down on the desktop.

Fucking someone over might not require much meritorious capacity, but when you do it while sitting across from him, it takes a little more grit and spit, at least if you intend to maintain eye contact.

"What if…" Tom slyly began, pausing just long enough for his eyes to meet mine. "…I'm not asking?"

A cold sliver of duplicitous manipulation lent Tom's fake smile a harder quality I'd previously overlooked. It was the sort of smile that distracts you from the knife that will soon be at your throat.

"See, you know what this is, Jimmy?" Tom held the manila folder up and gave it a little wave back and forth.

"I don't have time for this. I've got a long drive out of the city," I interjected, signaling my disinterest in continuing the conversation. I was in no mood to be handed marching orders by some punk kid, and though I rarely traded upon it, perhaps I was feeling a bit of my own clout.

The problem with clout in this industry, or any other, is that it is a bit like a muscle. If you don't use it, then it begins to atrophy and wither away. This is perilous at best and disastrous at worst. A man may go to put his weight on that clout, only to have it vanish beneath his foot like loose soil on a treacherous mountainside. The last thing running through his mind as he topples into the mist-filled darkness below is the burning question of when exactly the hell he'd become so complacent in his affairs. Maybe that's why I didn't see it coming. I'd grown old, fat, and soft, wrapped in the warm blanket of praise, comfortable in the treading of water and expected sales. I'd forgotten that it was a fuck-or-be-fucked-world, and a reminder was long overdue.

"This is your contract," Tom's eyes slid to the legally binding vice he had around my balls, then shot back to my own. "I bet it's been a while since you looked at that, hasn't it? An old salty dog like you probably doesn't even remember the day you signed it, do you?"

A soft chuckle escaped Tom's lips, and I briefly lost myself to the fantasy of squeezing his throat in my hands.

"The Wild Man, Jimmy Wonderful himself. Terror of expense accounts and hotels across the country. The problem is, Jimmy, those days are gone. Sure, you send us an article and we run it... because of your name."

Names have the power to be both the key that sets a man free or the lock that binds him. At that moment, mine felt more like an anchor attached to my ankle, and it had just been pitched over the side of the Good Ship Wonderful.

"Maybe you don't realize this," Tom leaned forward in his seat as he tossed the metaphorical velvet glove into the trash with whatever hopes I had of the day not going to shit. "But we own you, Jimmy. Everything you've written here according to this piece of paper belongs to us.

Tom flexed the iron hand that had waited so patiently beneath that velvet glove. "What do you think happens if you just storm out of here?"

The weight of my name pulled me down into the dark. I could feel my ears getting hot and my jaw tightening.

"I'm not Mike, Jimmy. I'll be your friend, I'll be nice, I'll tell you how swell you are. But..." His gaze sharpened as it dug into me. "If you try to fuck me, Jimmy - if you try to fuck *The Standard* - you'll be eighty by the time you get your next royalty check. We'll break you with the lawyers so that even if you win - even if you pull some amazing feat of courtroom magic...

He paused to take another smug sip of that godawful soda.

Arrogant little prick.

"...You'll be paying legal fees by taking public speaking gigs, telling high school kids how important it is to 'notebook' their ideas. When you go to push out another few hundred pages of Old-Man-Being-Sad, the critics who take it easy on you because they're in our pocket won't be so forgiving this time." Tom's tone was stern, but not stern enough to hide the pleasure as he forced the bitter medicine of truth down my throat. "Do you understand what I'm telling you, Jimmy? You feeling me?"

"You fuck-faced little swine-felching cock-gobbler" The words hissed through my clenched teeth, and I turned around with the world already going red around the borders.

I'd beat him to death with a stapler and then push his body out the window. When the authorities came, I could claim he'd grown tired of living, tired of being a soulless little vaguely man-shaped hole in the fabric of human decency, and he had decided to jump for the betterment of mankind. I'd watch from the window as he spiraled down to the pavement, out of horror and disbelief, and not at all just to make sure the little fucker landed on his head. That was the ticket. That was what I was going to do. I'd already begun to map out my police statement as I crossed the room, my hands bunched so tightly into fists that my fingernails were digging half-moons into my palms.

He gazed up at me as I loomed over the edge of the desk. I'd seized him by the lapels of his sport coat before I even realized what I was doing. I found myself staring down into his eyes. Tom did not fear me, not exactly, nor did he cower at something as mundane as being grabbed by the coat – instead Tom just smiled up at me like a cat who'd just eaten the canary.

"What?" Tom's voice sounded like his soda tasted. "You're going to hit me? Do it. Go for it."

Fucker.

"This isn't 'the good old days' anymore. You won't be regarded as some outlaw artist living on the edge. You'll be just another D-rate celebrity that gets ripped apart on the nightly dregs."

Dirty Fucker.

"If you're really lucky, you'll trend for a day before people start burning your books to show how progressive they are, and that they stand united against workplace violence."

Dirty Fucker of Filthy Swine and Mentally Stunted Sheep.

Tom just smiled up at me, full of triumphant assuredness, and said, "Go ahead though, if it really makes you feel any different."

That was the worst part. Because looking down into that youthful smug face, I knew in the pit of my stomach he was right.

My fervor vanished like a magician's rabbit, leaving me with the bitter aftertaste of defeat. I pined for the meeting's demise, itching to skulk back to Jenna with my tail tucked between my legs. I'd pocket the cash, deposit the checks like a robot, and keep dishing out advice to the starry-eyed youngsters who spotted me from my legendary escapade through the faerie realm. Yet now, every move would be slathered in a fresh coat of phoniness, and I'd loathe myself a smidge more with each passing sunrise.

I released Tom's coat, and he slumped back into his chair with the fluidity of a snake returning to its glass-walled terrarium, ready to savor a juicy rat that had foolishly believed it had evaded the relentless pursuit of its fellow rodents. A sigh escaped me as I descended with the defeated weight of gravity towards the floor, eliciting a mirrored exhalation from the beanbag chair.

Part of me yearned to battle, to summon Sherman Moscowitz, my lawyer, and wage war with all my might. However, when your marriage is barely recovering from your own foolishness, a man must come to terms with the fact that not every skirmish is worth fighting, especially those that threaten to disrupt the fragile peace of domestic harmony.

"Tell me the fucking details," I growled, massaging the bridge of my nose.

The unmistakable sound of the desk drawer sliding open reached my ears, and I reluctantly opened my eyes.

There it was, sitting innocuously in the center of Tom's desk—a sleek, modern "smartphone," his sickeningly easy smile once again showcasing those unnaturally white teeth.

"We'll get to that," Tom said. "But first, let me tell you about the importance of spontaneous video content to a healthy social media presence." Tom's words held the smug triumph of the deskbound and the institutionalized office workers who aspired to nothing greater than their own climb up the ladder.

Sometimes, the only way through the shit is straight down the middle.

The Devil, The Details, and The Fabulously Dead

"Fuck you, you soulless, goddamn, empty sacks of misery and bad ideas!" I screamed from the parking lot of *The Mystic Standard* into the face of its Chicago office, my words partially muted beneath the drizzling rain.

"FUCK YOU! Fuck your job! Fuck your building! Fuck your mother in her bloated, pale ass, you collection of dog-sodomizing shit-gibbons! You curs! I hope you die with the shit still sticking to your rump, you bastards! YOU STORM OF CUNTS!" I punctuated the tirade by spiking the new smartphone against the pavement as if I'd just scored a game-winning touchdown in the Super Bowl.

The phone shattered with a satisfying crash, and bits of glass, plastic, and circuit board joined the rat piss, pigeon shit, and collective angst of Chicago on the sidewalk. All in all, it was a perfectly reasonable response in my estimation.

Fucking Tom.

I don't know how long I'd been bellowing obscenities at the office and ranting like a madman. Long enough for Gus, the security guard from the downstairs lobby, to shake his head in dismay, like a fundamentalist preacher who'd just stumbled upon his daughter on the cover of *Coed Creampies Eight: Schools of the South*. I was seething with anger, steamrolled (and quite expertly, I might add) by Tom, a man not even half my age, possessing the integrity of bargain-bin toilet paper. But I didn't give a damn about the rain soaking through my clothes, nor did I care that my peers could occasionally peek out their office windows, hoping to witness a grown man having what could generously be described as a fit of pure, epileptic rage. Anything to break up the office doldrums. Even in Chicago, you don't get to witness a coworker lose their mind in the parking lot every day.

Most of them were probably terrified I was going to go out and infect myself with vampirism or lycanthropy then come back to the office for a good old-fashioned spree kill. I wouldn't be the first. This is America, after all. Living alongside the possibility that a man could tear a hole in the fabric of time as you walk down the street or transform into a grizzly-sized wolfman has a strangely numbing effect on our society. It's like we're all walking around in a minefield, and after so much tragedy, we've begun to develop not gallows humor, but a numbness all the same.

Just imagine what it would be like without the Shadow Folk. We'd probably be worrying about guns, or, given that this is America, the insidious dangers of vaping.

Once, long ago, I'd sworn to myself that I would never again be the sort of whore who doesn't pick their own John. I was happy to bleed all over some keys while some young couple from the suburbs, who thought it was forward-thinking to put a "We Stand with Magik" sign in their front lawn, watched and diddled themselves in the safety of their bedroom, as smugly satisfied with their own doings as I was with the price. Unfortunately, part of keeping my sanity throughout that bit of self-prostitution was deeply tied to the exercising of choice. Tom had taken my choice from me, and to suggest that I was pissed off was an understatement.

"Fuck!" I yelled in the face of God and kicked the bumper of my Saturn.

Only the telegraph wire-like chirp of my private cellphone's ringtone cut through that still-smoldering garbage pile of rage. Nothing fancy. I was still operating on flip-phone technology and was more than content with it. By that time, I was on my sixth or maybe even seventh obscenity-kick combo; "fuck" had begun just falling out of my mouth like it was the single occupant of my vocabulary.

Only when I stopped to pull my phone out of my back pocket did I become aware of the young blonde mother and her child hurrying down the sidewalk, her hands thrown over the kid's ears as if to protect him from the very real danger that he might die from hearing an adult say a "no-no" word.

It was Jenna, and she no doubt wanted to know how my meeting with Tom had gone.

"Remember to stay in school..." I began to call out, but my words dissolved into the ether as the young mother fled from the lunatic spectacle of a man shouting obscenities and trying to bludgeon a cheap midsize sedan to death in the parking lot of what was once a thriving publication.

In the peculiar world of literary celebrity in America, fame wears a different cloak than that of reality TV stars or the mythical rock gods of yore. Each time you stumble into public idiocy, there's a safety net of anonymity, a delay before recognition sets in. It's less a fault of the medium and more a symptom of our society's gradual descent into what, in my more inebriated moments, I dub "The Big Dumb" — both the blessing and bane of my existence.

"Whatcha got cookin', good lookin'?" I greeted as soon as the phone pressed against my ear.

I had a tone tucked away in my back pocket for these moments, perhaps a universal tool for all men, a quick dose of upbeat cheer meant to mask actions and deeds that would otherwise bring shame upon our partners. Of course, we never quite manage to tie up all the loose threads, but it's a comfortable self-deception, nonetheless.

Like kicking the living daylights out of the back bumper of my Saturn and cursing the very foundations on which *The*

Mystic Standard stood, or more specifically Tom Mulkey's eternal.

"Don't give me that. How did it go?" Jenna's voice flowed through the phone like a breath of fresh air in a room that had grown stale.

Love, for all its wonders, could also be a terrible burden for a multitude of reasons. I always found it most insidious for the way it made me simultaneously yearn for the sound of someone's voice and resent it for the pain I inflicted upon its owner. My own dalliances, debaucheries, and lapses in integrity had nearly torn us apart before, and now I keenly felt each heartache, a sentinel on watch against the ceaseless horde of my own corrosive nature.

You tell yourself there's always something you won't sacrifice on the altar of your art for the sake of the muse, something you'll hold more sacred than The Truth or The Tale, but for me, that had always been a junkie's lie at best. In the end, there was precious little I didn't offer up to feel alive enough to get the ink on the page. Only now, with so much hanging by mere threads, did I feel the acute sting of potential loss. We had salvaged things and righted our ship, but the hull was still questionable.

"Not great," I began, testing the path forward like a man taking his first tentative steps onto an old rope bridge, its wooden planks and fraying lines promising a long fall.

The satyr trip out west was at least partly Jenna's idea. Her career as a musician had taken her to seemingly every festival, raucous get-together, and gathering of the Weird that had taken place over the last two decades. The Gathering of the Grove was her baby much more than it was mine. On my end, the prospect had been waxing poetic about the nature of revelry and its impact on the American spirit. For Jenna, this was meant to be a shared experience where she would get the opportunity to be among her own.

COYOTE WALLACE

You can't have Rock N' Roll without revelry, that dog just doesn't hunt.

Never let it be said that all creative minds are cut from the same cloth. Though we traveled in similar circles, and we knew similar people, the difference between Jenna and me was like the contrast between a pedigree show dog and an old mangy coyote someone found rummaging through their garbage. Jenna would starve for her art if required, remaining as constant as the North Star even if the world around her shifted taste.

I lacked the courage to starve; my nobility had long been hamstrung by a love of warm beds, good single malt Scotch whisky, and the perverse pleasure I took in slaying giants with my words. I hated being told what to do, but once commanded, I ran on pure spite—a special sort of gasoline that ignited the engine fiercely and for an extended duration, often outlasting wonder, championed causes, or even hunger for fortune or fame. Politicians, kings, even entire religions had been brought down with the right configuration of words; you just had to have the fire to keep searching.

The act of recounting the tale of Tom, myself, and the barrel he royally screwed me over with left me feeling ancient and empty, raindrops pelting my head and seeping into my suit. By the time I fished my keys from my pocket and sought refuge in my Saturn to escape the intensifying rain, I'd more or less spilled the entire story. Slumped over the wheel with the phone pressed to my ear, I was relieved that Jenna couldn't see me.

"Those pricks!" Jenna's language of affection was murderous rage whenever someone threatened or hurt those she cared about.

"Screw them! You don't need them; we don't need them—just come home, and we'll figure it out together. We'll make it, I've got some cash stashed away and..."

Jenna's words may not have brought the comfort she intended, but they reminded me of why I loved her.

I'd always viewed relationships as a weakness, a crutch for those who couldn't stand their own company. My work thrived on solitude, and while there were others before Jenna whom I tried to make it work with, those relationships were always marred by a sense of inevitable doom. Jenna was different—too strong, too stubborn, too smart to fall for my bullshit or let herself be pushed aside by it. Part faerie by way of her mother's lineage, she had guided me through the dark times when Nixon had outlasted Clinton and America had chosen its first Vampire President. I had drowned my sorrows in bottles (more than a few) as I proclaimed for the next four years that democracy had met a sorry end. Jenna was superior to me in every way, a beacon of true north guiding me no matter how far off course I veered.

What choice did I have but to lie?

"We all bite the bullet eventually," I began, summoning the old Wonderful charm. "Besides, maybe there'll be a fat bonus waiting for me. Altenhofen's supposed to be a fan, and you know how much I love meeting my fans..." I trailed off with a chuckle, hoping it didn't ring as hollow to Jenna as it did to me. If it did, though, I wasn't about to acknowledge it until she called me out on it.

Never incriminate yourself.

"You say that, but how many signings have you bailed on early to go blaze up with some college kid dying to know if you really did dive into the ether with those wild faeries *in Terror, Disgust, and Pixie Dust*?" I could practically feel Jenna grinning through the phone, and I yearned to escape these rain clouds and return to the comforting warmth of home.

She was right, as always. I could grouse all I wanted, but the truth was, I was ensnared in a web of vicious addiction.

COYOTE WALLACE

All of us who spend our nights with ink on our fingertips suffer from it. Some quietly endure, while others flaunt their insatiable hunger for attention. But make no mistake—we all crave it. We long to be seen, to be read, and most importantly, to be celebrated for our ability to carve truth and substance from the stone that is language. For me, I was so often at odds with this love-hate relationship that I'd practically adopted another persona just to cope with it

Jimmy Wonderful had been my pseudonym for as long as I had been at *The Standard*, but over time, planted in the soil of my own narcissistic heart and watered with the sometimes-blind adulation of the young, that alias had put down roots and grown into something altogether bigger than just the man who made it.

Had I conjured Jimmy Wonderful from thin air—a fearless and brash seeker of Truth, no matter how bizarre, uncomfortable, or shocking? Jimmy Wonderful, who guzzled liquor like a fish and churned out entire chapters in a single night fueled by Colombian marching powder. He was a sexual deviant, a libertine who leveraged his silver tongue and inability to refuse a challenge into situations that both scandalized and delighted his adoring fans. Love meant nothing to him, for rules were beneath his notice, and as long as the copy was good and the booze flowed ever faster, any criticism would be swept aside like a spring shower.

Jenna had married James Wozynski, the shy and sometimes awkward boy from the hills of rural West Virginia who enjoyed the solitude of their shared home, who was terrible with money because he had seen how it rotted men from the inside, and who had at one point in his life felt so invisible that only the act of building walls out of words like he was a stonemason gave him any sense of substantive weight. She'd never asked for my other half. While I like to believe that she still can see the line between myself and my alter-ego, there are times when I cannot say the same for myself. I could not always be sure where the mask I had made to help sell myself to the American public ended, and where the true man beneath it began.

"I'll drive back tonight; there's a few things I want to take care of in the city first." I told Jenna, summoning the strength to lift my head off the steering column and give my own eyes a quick, hard stare in the rearview mirror.

Jenna had put me back together so many times that I often worried one more breakdown would be the last straw. It wasn't her fault; it was mine. I'd broken enough bonds of trust that her continued patience felt like a miracle. Honesty would have been the best policy. Maybe my life would have stayed its course if I'd had the guts to tell her how deeply the disappointment stung, or how a beast inside me was already salivating at the opportunity to walk back into Tom's office with a story about Roy Altenhofen in hand—not the story he'd wanted, but one so well executed he'd have to swallow it down and print the damn thing anyway. I'd show that young pup the folly of nipping at old dogs' heels, striding out as a conquering hero, a titan whose craft was airtight against the whims of the industry.

In retrospect, I think I downplayed the hurt just to have an excuse to try.

I'd scorch Altenhofen to the ground with my words, ensuring no one at *The Standard* or elsewhere would ever think to pass a fluff assignment my way again.

The swine.

"Bring steaks and beer," Jenna's command was infused with a touch of what my grandfather would have called "moxie," tempered by the playful charm I adored in her. It made me long to be there already.

I envisioned myself devouring prime cuts of beef, savoring cold beer, and surrendering to the passionate embrace of my beautiful wife while vintage records played in the background. In that moment, I vowed not to think of Tom Mulkey, *The Mystic Standard*, or the lingering ember of indignation smoldering within me. Instead, I would drift into a contented slumber with Jenna nestled against my chest, the crackling logs in the fireplace lulling me into the peaceful rest of the just and the fortunate.

That's where the story ended as far as Jenna was concerned. A man's self-awareness is a double-edged sword, and I knew that no matter how comforting my slumber was, I would awaken before the first cold light of dawn could find me. I'd stand on our front deck, leaning against the rail, and indulge in the Marlboro cigarettes I'd been trying to quit for the past two years, one by one. In those moments, my mind would be consumed by thoughts of what lay ahead. Not plans, for the Truth cannot be planned; when one aims to wield the Truth against their enemies, patience is paramount. It was akin to a skilled swordsman waiting for an opening in his rival's defense—the opportunity would reveal itself, and I would seize it. There was no point in meticulous planning; instead, there would be a familiar anxiety, for despite my flaws, I was a thoroughbred, born to race. The anticipation before the starting gun signaled both exhilaration and dread—a unique hell reserved for those of us who sold fragments of our souls, one deadline at a time.

"Then steaks and beer it is. Imported, or shall we stick to domestic?" I inquired as I turned the key in the ignition, and the Saturn roared to life, unfazed by the thrashing it had endured at my hands.

"Imported. What sort of girl do you take me for?" came Jenna's playful retort.

And with that, laughter and promises of a homecoming filled the air—a conclusion every man could hope for.

I had always held a peculiar affection for Chicago, more so than for New York or Los Angeles. The city was grittier than New York, lacking any illusion that success there meant success anywhere else. Chicago wasn't a test to be passed; it took a perverse pleasure in devouring and spitting out unsuspecting souls who dared to think they could tame it. It was colder than Los Angeles, its chill forcing you to prove yourself every morning as you stepped out to confront the day. There was a raw honesty to this demand that I found absent in the West Coast cities. Chicago didn't pretend to be your ally; it didn't feign concern for your rights or individuality. The city offered a harsh form of equality through the enforcement of a single, unyielding rule that disregarded where you stood on the law, whether you believed in the Shadow People, or with whom you shared your bed. This rule was simple yet brutal, and perhaps that's why I was drawn to it.

Fuck or be Fucked.

Despite my personal sentiments, as I pulled out of *The Mystic Standard*'s parking lot, I was swiftly reminded why sensible people avoided driving in this city. Traffic was a complete nightmare, with all of us confined within our metal cocoons, seething at the inconvenience of not reaching our destinations with the swiftness of thought. Though my journey wasn't far, the gridlock showed no mercy. With nothing to do but scan license plates, I reached for a cigarette from the emergency stash in the glove compartment and switched on the radio. If I were to be condemned to the slow, soul-sucking demise of navigating Chicago traffic, I at least hoped to soothe my agony with some good old-fashioned rock and roll. Music had always been a solace for my kind – the wordsmiths of the page – and few among us would deny its significance.

COYOTE WALLACE

Under the cacophony of static and a medley of station snippets, I managed to detach myself enough to ignore how drastically things had changed since my youthful arrival in this old city. Back then, we lugged our damn typewriters on our backs until they screamed, and our eyes stung from watching the sunrise through a haze of cigarette smoke. In those days, I was a young greyhound, reveling in the thrill of the race, knowing there was always another one waiting on the horizon. Now, my joints were brittle, my muscles soft, and my lungs weighed down by the remnants of that smoke from long ago.

The world felt heavier now, gravity more possessive, and each morning a struggle to confront. How many races did I have left in me? One, maybe two? If I were a bricklayer, I might have said the spirit was willing, but the flesh was weak, but in my line of work, it was the reverse. My spirit had endured blow after blow, not just from the demands of my craft, but from the relentless ugliness of the world.

Even my cherished rock and roll hadn't escaped that ugliness. Case in point:

"Up next on our Billboard Top 100 for the eighth consecutive week, we have Taylor Swift and Kurt Cobain's pop sensation 'Bad, Bad, Boy,'" the DJ chirped with such cheer that his listeners were in danger of slipping into sugar-induced comas once the broadcast ended.

The Living Impaired, or the Restless Dead for those inclined to be assholes, may have received a bad rap since the veil of secrecy was lifted, revealing a vast untapped labor market for corporate America. A labor market that, mind you, worked for remembrance and a few kind words since they had nothing they needed to purchase.

However, it was the damn entertainment industry that proved to be the most exploitative. Celebrity had no discernible shelf life as long as you could be dragged in front of the camera and your image milked for a few drops of nostalgia. Despite most of the Living Impaired suffering from severe creative constipation—a phenomenon that even experts trained in unraveling a man's mind have yet to explain—this served as little deterrent. They couldn't create anything new, but that was no problem for Hollywood or the music industry. They had writers, and the dead could certainly follow direction—they just lacked spark.

I often ponder what the world would be like if people simply died and vanished, forcing us to remember them instead of watching them degrade themselves for a scrap of faded glory. No one died a hero anymore, and sacred icons were a thing of the past. It became fashionable to attach oneself to a shade and churn out as much bland, formulaic garbage as possible.

Another jab at the button sent the radio scanning, diverting my mind from that grim train of thought, especially with my final stop in the city before heading home still awaiting me beneath the gray sky.

The Top 100 might have been a death sentence for good taste but it was nothing compared to the offerings of country western and hip hop. I've heard it said that if you cannot say something nice then you should not say something at all. This is wise advice so I will omit from the record my verbal reactions to both rap and the uncut misery of country western. I freely admit that when it comes to hip hop my distaste is not with the spirit but with my own ears and temperament, but country western however is as old as dirt and only half as inspiring.

No thank you.

It's not just the music either. As I drove, I could see the changes in the city from when I first came to Chicago all those years ago. Largely gone are the old Polish, Serb, Troll, and German populations who carried with them the traditions of their homelands. They've been replaced and utterly Americanized with most of their grandchildren scrubbed clean of the Old World so that a fresh bevy of new wide-eyed peoples from new lands can come and the process can start all over again. The restaurants and corner eateries where your tongue can visit places the rest of your body might not ever get around to were slowly giving up their valuable territory to Foodways and corporate-owned chains. She's cleaner too, as mayor after mayor has taken their best shot at making Chicago more visually appealing and less likely to steal the shoes from tourists. Once upon a time it was nothing in certain parts of the city (usually the most interesting) to see a car stripped of its wheels and other vital parts sitting on concrete cinder blocks, or a building that had burned out now left to stand abandoned among its brethren. Now, though, everything has a shiny coat of "new" to hide the old dirt and I even hear that some brave souls go kayaking in the river.

I eventually stumbled upon Tilly's Rest after sacrificing my sanity and stomach lining to the insatiable gods of Chicago traffic. By some twisted stroke of luck, I managed to snag a parking spot that spared me from navigating the treacherous streets in the relentless rain. Alas, even this minor victory was swiftly snatched away as a fat raindrop from the gloomy, slate-colored sky extinguished the cherry of my cigarette the moment I stepped out of the car.

"Motherfucker!" I cursed, my expletive lost in the cacophony of the urban jungle.

With a resigned sigh, I trudged on towards the dilapidated facade of Tilly's Rest.

The number of watering holes in the Chicago area had been dwindling steadily since 2011, when the city boasted over a thousand establishments. Today, that number had dwindled to a mere eight hundred, and out of those, Tilly's stood as a decrepit monument to urban decay. The interior was a cramped, dimly lit cavern devoid of any semblance of modernity. There was no dance floor here—no, this was a place where dreams came to die, and dancing was the last thing on anyone's mind.

The walls, adorned with gangster memorabilia and faded posters from Scorsese films, bore the scars of neglect and indifference. They hadn't seen a proper wipe-down since the days of Mayor Daley. Tilly's was not a place for the faint of heart or the squeamish. It was a haven for the downtrodden, the disheveled, and the disillusioned—a sanctuary where dirty men came to drown their sorrows in cheap whiskey poured into even cheaper glasses. It was a refuge from the madness of the outside world, where politics were left at the door and the only agenda was to drink until the pain subsided, if only for a fleeting moment.

Despite this, I once made a point of living at a corner table. A questionless solitude afforded to all who passed through the doors made it more appealing than its cleaner counterparts. No one wanted to be your friend, no one cared how you felt, no one asked questions about what you were writing and that had suited a young surly version of myself just fine. Right up until Chris had his accident and then I could only bring myself to come here for a single shot whenever I was in town. A forced act of attrition for the part I had played in the derailing of a friend's career. We all had our devil's due to pay and for the longest time I thought this was mine.

The bartender, a short black-haired man with a bulbous nose and hairy arms, was wiping down glasses with a rag that smeared more filth than it cleaned. He gave me a cursory nod to acknowledge I existed but didn't offer me a greeting beyond that. I wasn't worth his time until I shelled out the crumpled bills and laid them out on a bar top scuffed and laden with rings from the glasses of old. Benny was an old hand, he knew me, and he'd been slinging booze here as long as I'd been slinging words at *The Standard*. His lack of charm was just part of his charm.

"Well, well, look at what we have here," Benny's gravelly voice rasped through the smoky air, his grin missing several teeth as he swept my money to his side of the bar with a meaty hand. "Been a while since I saw you. I was starting to think you'd forgotten me and your little friend. You want the usual, or have you finally decided to try something off the top shelf, Shakes?" he continued, his grin widening.

Shakes was short for Shakespeare; a nickname Benny had concocted in his own mind. It never quite caught on, even during my regular visits, but Benny was too stubborn to let it go. Eventually, I'd given up and allowed him to call me Shakespeare, which over time had been shortened to Shakes or Shakey. Part of me hoped each time I made my little pilgrimage to Tilly's that he'd forget about it, but he never did.

"Maybe if you didn't just pour the bottom-shelf stuff into the top-shelf bottles, I'd be inclined to do that," I retorted, matching his sandpaper demeanor.

"How's business treating you?" I asked, though I didn't give a damn. When you've got nothing of substance to say to another man, you can always fall back on his "business." It'll either earn you a quick shutting of the trap or a few lines that no one, other than the person who spoke to them, really cares about.

"You kiddin' me? Fuckin' taxes keep going up on this place and pretty soon I'll be sellin' my blood just to keep my friggin' head above water," Benny complained as he poured the whiskey into a spotty glass.

No sooner had Benny slid the glass over and I picked it up than I felt the temperature drop a few degrees. Benny winced as if he'd just stepped on a tack. Though it was hard, I made a point not to turn to my left and look towards the source of this new chill beating down on my skin. I simply held my drink and pretended to try puzzling out a meaning in the spots on my glass. There was a smell—spoiled meat and copper.

It's terribly rude to stare at or notice such things.

"You know your narrow ass doesn't have to keep coming in here. I know you hate it, and I don't blame you for what happened. Beer me, Benny. Jimmy's paying." The voice drifted up out of nowhere to my left, familiar but hollow.

"Bold of you to assume that I'm the one paying. Bold," I replied, giving the glass one final eyeballing before throwing it back. I turned to look towards the voice as the bartender vanished in search of beer.

"How the fuck are you, Christopher?" The whiskey was the only way I could hold the nerve to talk to my friend. Being here was a forced act of attrition.

I didn't want to, but I was compelled to look. Chris Turner, twenty years afflicted with his condition, was kind enough to keep the right side of his face to me. Looking at him was like entering a strange time warp. He was still as young as he had been when we were hell-raisers fighting our way up from the bottom of *The Mystic Standard*. He had been better than me and yet still took me under his wing when I first arrived in the city, without any trace of the normal cutthroat competitiveness that exists within the ink-stained hearts of our breed. A young, handsome African American wordsmith who had been so far ahead of his time that if one dwelled on the injustice of the fact I was the one sitting on that stool and he was the one sitting on the chilling air, they might just have begun to question whether or not the whole damned game was rigged.

After one of our wild nights at Tilly's in the depths of my youthful ignorance, I left a story sitting on that very table I mentioned earlier. It was forgotten, abandoned in the haze of my intoxicated stupor, the morning before it was due to be handed over to my editor. I was deep in the throes of my own self-destruction, lacking the influence to shield my career from the consequences of my hedonism. Chris, being the loyal friend he was, ushered me to his couch and ventured back with the intention of pounding on the door until ol' Benny relented. However, the Chicago Police Department was more comfortable entertaining the existence of werewolves, vampires, faeries, and ghosts than they were with a young black man knocking on doors in the dead of night.

I drained my glass, my hand steady as a rock. Later, I'd question whether I should be proud of that composure or horrified.

"On the house," Benny offered, his earlier surliness replaced with a sense of submission akin to that of a whipped dog. He couldn't help but cringe when meeting Chris's gaze head-on.

"How's Jenna?" Chris asked, though he had never met her, only heard of her through my occasional sabbaticals that led me back here.

"Better. We've been working things out, finally got things looking a little brighter," I replied.

"How's..." I trailed off. If you ever think you feel like an asshole talking about your life to someone else, try talking about your life to a dead guy.

Chris let out a bitter laugh, a sound I had always liked, but ever since the accident, it had acquired a phlegmy undertone that sent shivers down my spine.

"I've got a new therapist who comes in here once a week to chat with me, lights a little candle, makes me feel important. It's nice. Really. I even picked up a side gig as a proofreader. Doesn't pay for shit, but hey, neither did *The Standard* when we started. And without rent or groceries, there's not much to spend the money on. It's all profit."

Chris's attempt to alleviate my guilt and sense of responsibility fell flat. The truth was, I hadn't come here to see him so that I could feel better.

No one decides when a penance ends but you. Whether that penance is deserved or not is entirely circumstantial, but deciding when it ends? That is up to each of us to figure out in our own time.

The bit about the job was the hardest to swallow because I knew, at least in theory, what sort of Hell Chris found himself in. As I mentioned before, the dead can't create anything new; they simply don't possess the necessary spark. For talented singers or musicians, this isn't the end of the world, only of their integrity—they can always sing someone else's song, play someone else's notes. A dead actor's performances may become flatter, but he can still read a script and play to the lowest common denominator of an audience.

A writer though?

Robbed of our spark and ability to make something new, we became little more than masters of dictation. If anyone ever wonders why I live as I do, then I'll confess now that there's nothing more frightening to me than the possibility of returning to this world once I'm through with it. Unfinished business is the nightmare of all men with gray in their hair, and I'd just as soon not spend eternity with a terminal case of writer's block.

"I should get my head examined working at that place. I knew I shouldn't have signed that damned contract again.

They really got me by the balls this time, man. Cotton candy bullshit... Hey, Benny—get me another, will you?"

Benny complied, and I was already in the process of drinking it down when Chris shifted the full weight of his gaze onto me. I could feel it. It made me want to run screaming from this place, to burn every dollar I ever made, to drag my ass to his grave and sink down on my knees just to beg him for forgiveness on behalf of myself and the whole damned world. I didn't, of course. I've been immunized against such ghostly side effects by virtue of being an incredibly self-absorbed asshole with a Day-Glo streak of self-serving tendencies, but the thought was there.

The dead always remember their potential.

"Don't fuck it up," Chris told me bluntly. He didn't need to delve into my mind, grasp the details of the situation, or even comprehend my assignment—he simply understood me in a way only a true friend might.

For a fleeting moment, I lost myself in his gaze.

I'm no war correspondent, so instead of attempting to depict the sucking black hole where my friend's right eye used to reside, I'll suffice it to say that bullets wreak havoc on bone and flesh far worse than Hollywood's watered-down replications. The dead never heal from the wounds that claim them; they remain as they were upon death, forever immutable. This makes confronting Chris a daunting task, and although I had encountered him countless times over the years, I couldn't bring myself to sustain eye contact for long.

Whatever words I had planned to utter withered on my tongue, and I observed with a sense of paralyzed, instinctual horror as he extended a hand to rest on my shoulder. I despise myself for succumbing to that horror. There's no place for it in a modern world where all that once lurked in the shadows now stands shoulder to shoulder with mankind in the light, but I experience it, nonetheless. I didn't want his touch; I didn't want him to perceive the contrast between my warmth and his perpetual chill.

"Don't," Chris interjected, dispelling whatever desiccated remnants of language lay inert on my tongue. "I've witnessed you flit in and out of that place as if you were God's gift to word processors since I took my last breath, and you were a young man. Thus far, you've managed to evade scrutiny. However, you must have realized that eventually they'd demand something unpalatable from you, my friend. Look at you—you're nearing the end of the race regardless. Just finish it and claim victory. Retire with Jenna and endeavor not to be so fucking despondent. Strive to relish being alive."

As Chris spoke, a trickle of blood seeped from the wound, meandering down his cheek like a twisted rivulet, its crimson path a testament to the macabre reality of his existence.

"What if I can't?" I blurted out, unable to contain the question bubbling up from within.

Asking such questions was akin to inviting disaster.

COYOTE WALLACE

Nobody understood me quite like Chris, my closest confidant, and no one could decipher the labyrinth of my heart like the departed. There I sat, my gut ablaze with fiery liquor and residual fury from the altercation with Tom back at *The Standard*'s offices, staring into the grotesque visage of my past mistakes. Chris, devoid of all the intricate details, still grasped my predicament with an eerie precision.

"You're like chewing on tin foil? You know that?" Chris remarked, his spectral voice cutting through the thick, smoky air. "How long have you been dancing around that edge, man? Long enough to make a habit of returning even after swearing off of it more times than quitting drinking. So, what's the deal? They want you to trail after bloodsucking Nixon on the campaign trail and churn out a bestseller about it? Let's see..." The banter flowed between us, his ghostly presence serving as a stark reminder of our enduring friendship. Yet, in an uncharacteristic moment, Chris faltered, his gaze vacillating as if lost in a fog.

"Blood Drunk: The Fall of the American Empire," I interjected, completing his jest with a somber tone, my attempt at transforming self-deprecation into self-preservation. Dwelling on Chris's condition, marked by the gaping hole in his face, was a discomfort I preferred to sidestep. Who wouldn't?

The frozen mask on Chris' face dissolved into laughter that never reached his solitary eye. I joined in, and for a fleeting moment, the weight of years seemed to thaw. In that brief laughter, there lingered a temptation to forget, but beneath the surface of memory, and despite our attempts to bury it, there remained an enduring chill. No matter how hard we tried to ignore it, to drown it in alcohol and smoke, the cold persisted, immutable and relentless. Even if the dead could escape their past, the living were bound to theirs, shackled to the waking world.

"Damn, that's brutal...I... I'm glad you're here, Jimmy." Chris confessed, his words laden with unsaid emotions.

"Yeah...Me too, buddy. Me too."

America, the land of liberty, knows all about ghosts. Our modern empires rise from the ashes of history. Yet even the departed fade away eventually, compelled to release their regrets—or so they say. But this truth doesn't hold for everyone. Anyone who's harbored resentment toward a former lover or been entwined in the drama of a faerie princess and her furious suitor knows the enduring grip of bitterness and unresolved grievances.

I can't help but wonder why it took so long for people to acknowledge the existence of the departed. Imagine a world where Bess Houdini's code remained unsolved. Where the mystery lingered, and we were left with only fuzzy images from grainy videos on the internet, shared by attention-seeking adolescents.

Where Chris was merely a photographer, a nameless figure in a report on gun violence statistics.

The thought always sends a shiver down my spine.

COYOTE WALLACE

Those Bloodshot Baby Blues

The journey back to Utica on Interstate 80 turned into a relentless battle against the unyielding rain. Despite this, with Chicago fading in the rearview mirror, I sensed Jimmy Wonderful's grip loosening around my throat. His hold had steadily tightened ever since I stepped back into *The Mystic Standard*, that Frankenstein's monster of my own creation, part man, part myth. Jimmy Wonderful was relentless in his pursuit of the Great American Truth, refusing to compromise or negotiate. He demanded fire upon the page, even if it meant watching the world burn in its wake.

He was too eccentric to be tamed, too enigmatic for those who fancied themselves enlightened enough to give orders, and too damn good at his craft to be silenced. Loved by the anti-establishment and secretly envied by those in starched white collars, Jimmy was a symbol that surviving life's madness without compromise was possible.

While he wouldn't be of much help in what lay ahead, the faint echo of his voice might serve as a guide for one last ride before the true, sad version of myself rode off into the sunset, pretending the corporate bastards hadn't finally broken me. Crossing the finish line, even with a limp, offered some solace, though not as much as drowning my sorrows in alcohol—a plan I might have entertained if not for Jenna.

Distance became my sanctuary, a refuge from the familiar stomping grounds, the city's pungent stench, and the biting wind. Another hour and I'd be home, with Jenna wrapped in my arms, the scent of sizzling steak filling the air. I'd bury my face in her hair, inhale deeply, seeking a brief respite from my relentless pursuit. She was my anchor, and the monstrous myth I had woven around myself was too destructive. There was no space for both of them, and whenever I worked—now with a much gentler approach to fueling my creativity than in my youth—Jenna was always scarce.

She insisted it was to avoid disturbing me, but deep down, I suspected she could sense him lurking within me. Waiting. Waiting for the moment when the craziness became intolerable, when I would be compelled to decide whether to unleash him from his cage or lock him away forever. Retirement was meant to be my escape from that decision, or so I fooled myself, envisioning a life of ease and enjoyment before my alter ego vanished forever.

However, Tom had doused that plan with gasoline and set it ablaze.

My foot slammed down on the accelerator, and the Saturn's speedometer surged steadily. There's a certain clarity that comes with hurtling down the highway at breakneck speeds, a forced immersion in the present moment. When you're chased by the ghosts of your past missteps, escape is found only in velocity. Though Jimmy's grip was weakening, I could still sense him lurking, as if he perched in the back seat, grinning at me, waiting for my gaze to meet the rear-view mirror so he could revel in the certainty of my downfall.

I hope Jenna can bring herself to read this one day and understand I battled to halt that descent.

When I pulled into Nina's Market and purchased our dinner, I still clung to the belief there might be a way to conquer it. To keep that devil in his cage. To go through the motions and appease both Altenhofen and Tom. If you want to fathom the devaluation of artistic integrity, you need only observe how many of our kind end up with a gun barrel in their mouths—there's a fun statistic.

The problem, of course, for those who lack their own caged little devil, is that choice doesn't always play the role we wish it to. Explaining this to those who don't instinctively grasp the lesson is like teaching a fish to fly or advocating for sensible gun reform to a Texas congressman.

Steak. Beer. Ten minutes spent sitting in the car as it idled in my own driveway, scrutinizing the reflection of the man in the rear-view mirror for signs and symptoms of his Hyde-like companion. It was as if he could be spotted peeking from behind my eyes like a desperate dope fiend emerging from a three-day coke bender.

We purchased the house in Utica years ago, one of the first things I truly splurged my "fortune" on. It's a modest two-story with wood siding and a spacious yard surrounded by thick trees, nestled on the shores of Lake Shannon. In the summer, one could lounge on the front deck and listen to the crickets' serenade to the night, inhaling the crisp air in deep breaths and reveling in its sweetness. This is where Jenna and I sought refuge when the world spun out of control — a sanctuary of warmth amidst the frigid American storms, a fortress where we could escape the rat race and simply exist.

Paradise feels like an inadequate term now; its usage would only serve to mock the concept.

By the time I reached the front door, the music wafted up from her studio in the basement, a melodic backdrop to my arrival. Calling out would have only disturbed her, so I silently placed the beer in the fridge and set about preparing the steaks for cooking. The routine motions of domesticity held a peculiar power, reinforcing our peace through repetition.

No matter how fervently you pursued the elusive rabbit, it was all too easy to succumb to The Still: that tranquil space where the relentless drive to progress was suspended, and where one found solace in rest and reflection. There was no moral judgment attached to it; it simply existed as a state of ennui, gently guiding us toward the conclusion of our journey. Perhaps 'The Still' was an essential evolutionary adaptation designed to ease individuals into the twilight of their existence — buy a house, raise some children, promise yourself you'll return to your dreams in a few years, and then never quite manage to do so — classic salmon mentality. I had experimented with a plethora of substances, from pixie dust to the blood of the damned, yet none proved as effective in quieting the insistent voice within me, demanding the pursuit of truth and the surrender of the last vestiges of my soul to the page, as the idea of a long rest.

I left my shoes by the door, craving the sensation of the creative engine pulsating beneath me, its vibrations resonating through the wooden floorboards. Jenna's music straddled the line between the dulcet tones of old protest folk and the raw aggression of punk rock. I dubbed it "Electric Infused Get Off Your Ass," though I readily admitted to staying in my lane when it came to such specifics.

Some would argue that two souls with artistic inclinations are destined for failure in matters of love. They claim there must always be one grounded individual to balance out the madness we peddle to the masses. Perhaps there's some truth to that. Jenna, in many respects, was more pragmatic than myself, yet also fiercely uncompromising. She could coax melodies from almost anything she touched and offered music lessons to children whose parents stumbled upon her advertisements online or in the local paper. With a quick assessment of their parents' income, she adjusted her rates accordingly. Despite her talent, she steadfastly refused to create for the sole purpose of commercial success.

There were no commissions in her world, no pandering, no sacrificing artistic integrity for the allure of fame. What sold, sold; what didn't, didn't matter. All that mattered was the act of creation itself. I could relate to that sentiment. Even as I stood there tending to a steak on the grill, feeling the birth of new music reverberating underfoot, I understood the necessity of etching truth into the grand stone wall of the American psyche.

The distinction lay in my insistence on being recognized as the one wielding the chisel.

That's the difference between a devil and a muse, at least in my book. We're all tasked with creating something new, something that previously only existed within us, but not everyone requires acknowledgment to validate their efforts. The common thread, however, is that there's never a choice. Those who have the luxury of choice all too often flee when the going gets tough and the opportunities dwindle. If the ink isn't already flowing in your veins, you'll never understand, and you'll never be able to comprehend.

Like the Namebreakers, Mystics, Wizards, Magi, or whatever other label you want to attach, we're driven to shape reflections of the world from nothing but our own determination and perceptions. You might scoff if you'd witnessed the real deal, perhaps even accuse me of taking a liberty or four, but to me, the transformation of a blank page into tangible text remains the purest form of magic. There's no destruction involved—only creation. Whether it's ugly or beautiful, clumsily executed or painfully perfect, it's all the same.

The steaks were just about ready, and I was on my second beer when Jenna emerged from her den of instruments and recording gear.

A decade my junior, she boasted hair as dark as the midnight sky cropped into a pixie cut, and eyes that shifted from blue green to stormy gray when she was upset. She was, and still remains, the most captivating woman I've ever encountered—not for any single physical feature, but for the way she carried herself. Despite her petite stature, she strode through life as if she were a colossus, unstoppable by anything the world could throw at her. Clad in baggy T-shirts and worn-out jeans, she rescued me from the depths of my own despair and kept me whole when my darkest impulses threatened to tear me apart.

How could I have ever hurt her? What was wrong with me that I even considered needing someone else?

Simple.

A man cursed with an addiction to the scent of ink and the construction of worlds upon blank pages will do whatever it takes to sustain his truth. He'll indulge in copious amounts of alcohol, seek out esoteric techniques, ingest mind-expanding substances, and throw everything into the fire. This includes his dignity, his loyalty, and even his last shreds of self-respect. He'll use flesh, powder, and seedy motels to build an engine to propel his Truth onto the page, and most damningly of all—he'll lie. He'll lie to himself, to his lovers, to his masters, and even to the gods themselves, without a moment's hesitation. If the choice boils down to telling a lie and being able to do the work or telling the truth and letting it go, he chooses the work.

That, and maybe I'm just a bastard.

"You should've let me know you were home; I would've taken a break," she said, crossing the floor towards me. I felt her arms wrap around my waist, her soft warmth pressing against my back.

I was home...

...and there was no "maybe" about it. I'm a bastard.

I turned to her, lowering my head to kiss the crown of her head, inhaling her scent. She smelled of sweat and perfume, with hints of cannabis smoke cutting through. The familiar scent took me back to lazy days spent naked in bed, to better times when nights felt shorter, and everything was warm.

"You were having fun. Besides, someone had to chill the beer and start dealing with our bovine overlords," I replied with faux haughtiness, my voice muffled in the soft blackness of her hair.

For a moment, all the troubles of the past and the hardships that likely awaited me in the future were swept away, as surely as the snakes were banished from Ireland. In hindsight, I should have been content to live only in that moment, to appreciate my existence as it was and what I had, rather than longing for some legacy or need for achievement. Perhaps if I had done that, I would have been able to bury Jimmy Wonderful for good, leaving him entombed with no need for final hurrahs or resurrections.

The kiss lingered for a moment before breaking, and then Jenna's hand lightly touched my chest.

"Save it. I'm starving, and those steaks smell delicious," she said, her mouth still close to mine, her breath warming my lips. Then, she was gone, leaving me to plate dinner while she headed into the living room.

I heard the click and hum of the television set, followed by the voice of a man so white he smelled of lemon Pledge and had a name like Chip Blankenington. I could envision his coiffed brown hair and his sixty-grand implant smile without even being in the room. Jenna and I had different tastes in decor—I favored old motorcycle pictures from the mid-'50s, while she went for symbolic depictions of capitalism's demise at the hands of hockey mask-wearing lunatics—but the news was always on.

Coming from a long line of newspapermen, much of Jenna's work was influenced by current events. Some people found it impossible to relax while bombarded by bad news, but for us, the idea of burying our heads in the sand would have only heightened our anxiety. It was better to see the oncoming train that threatened to splatter us, as we both agreed.

"The trial of Latisha Green began today, with the prosecution laying out its opening arguments..." Chip Blankenington read from his teleprompter with the faux sympathy of a coffin salesman.

In case you've been living under a rock, Latisha Green's upcoming trial has dominated the news cycle almost as much as Nixon's goddamn undead rise to power. The difference is they're selling Nixon's blood-drinking and open evil as heritage, while Latisha Green prepares to have her whole life ruined for being a Namebreaker, and a financially destitute one at that.

Earlier when I said that there were maybe 5,000 of their numbers left, I wasn't lying. For years, the government has been taking steps to curb the birth of those with so-called active "chaos genes," and if you were to look at the data, you might believe that they were even successful. The ability to change the world around them is treated like a disease, and though the United States hasn't gone so far as to round the Namebreakers up, they do come down on any mistakes with the wrath of an angry god.

The public may be entranced by the magical, while corporations view it as an opportunity for profit, but when it comes to the government? Let's just say Uncle Sam takes a grim view of anything that threatens the status quo.

Labeling Latisha Green a Namebreaker would be a gross miscarriage of justice. She's a 16-year-old girl from Dorchester in Boston—scared, confused, and by all accounts, horrified by the havoc she's wrought. The fact that her stepfather's arms were burned and cauterized up to the elbow, and his eyes erased from his face as if he'd never had them at all, tells the tale of the trauma that triggered the "activation" of her chaos gene.

I think it's safe to say I speak for the majority of the American public when I say that had it ended there, even The Man would struggle to find charges that would stick. Hell, I'd nominate her for a medal if I could, but that's beside the point. It didn't end there. Whatever manifestation her "breaking" took, it not only incinerated her target but also managed to ignite—the entire apartment building, likely by way of a flailing eyeless asshole.

Seven people died. Two of them were children.

So now the nation watched, us included, as men tried to decipher justice from the murky waters of misery. In a country infatuated with the notion of shoot first, ask questions later, fueled by conceit with its chrome fuel-injected heart, people grappled to make sense of the entire sordid affair.

Whenever Nixon or his cronies at the Justice Department paraded one of the unfortunate souls captured in The War on Infernalism, they ensured they had a certain look. It wouldn't do to have John Q Public suddenly sympathize with the enemy; this is America, and empathy for the enemy is the first sign of a diseased mind infected with the dreaded affliction known as Sensible Thinking. Most of the time, this strategy worked; you don't question why someone would sell their soul, you don't ponder if they had a sick child neglected by the system, you don't care how many nights they went without food or warmth before they made their choice—because what you see is usually a hollow-eyed husk who learned one truth too many.

They were also easily mistaken for Namebreakers.

"This is ridiculous," Jenna remarked, turning up the volume with the remote.

Latisha had the look of a sweet young girl, but her demographic was poorly suited for receiving mercy from judges, police, or those who usually profited from the systemic misery of the downtrodden. However, her situation had reopened the debate. Crowds gathered like storm clouds outside the courthouse, and you could see it in the worried expressions of the police officers tasked with holding the divided mob back. Fear and the thirst for justice mixed like a forest fire and a windstorm; individually they were bad enough, but combined, they created something far worse that consumed all in its path, leaving behind the burned-up and broken remains of delusions of freedom.

"You know she was just defending herself and look at how they're treating her. You'd think she was a monster the way they're behaving towards her," Jenna continued as I settled down beside her, balancing our dinner plates in my hands.

"Yeah, they have some new kid at The Standard covering the trial. Jenkins, I think that's his name. A goddamn mess is what it is. Poor bastards," I grumbled, my usual acidic tone dimmed by the simple enjoyment of the meal as I spoke with a mouthful of steak.

I attempted to keep my thoughts on Latisha Greene to myself and focused solely on my steak. There was nothing I could contribute to this conversation that would ease the rest of my night. Jenna had her principles regarding the Namebreakers—those afflicted with lycanthropy or vampirism, even the faeries struggling to preserve their culture from being trivialized by well-meaning parents who adorned their children with wings. Musicians could encapsulate terrible events just as we wordslingers could, but they often only held onto it long enough to regurgitate the horror back into their work. For us, however, sometimes you simply had to allow the darkness to settle, to digest and permeate through your being. Then you could carry it with you indefinitely, another weapon in your arsenal against ignorance and empty pages.

For all my searching for the Truth, my own self had always felt the hardest to know, and the answers that I had found rarely neatly squared with the man I wanted to be. I was not callous or unfeeling; I sympathized with Latisha and her situation and her fear. I sympathized with those like her, born with just the bad luck of having your whole life turned upside down by a simple fluke of genetics that landed them under the government's thumb. Sympathy, however, did not necessarily mean that the other side did not possess points of its own though.

One of the most popular arguments against what the government was doing was that magic was a natural force and that by removing those capable of wielding it from our population, we were setting ourselves up for a sort of mass metaphysical blindness. That we would lose some vital part of ourselves, be it good or bad, that had carried us to this point. I'd held that position myself through much of the work of my younger years, but as time had passed, I'd begun to lose faith not just in The American Spirit but The American People. We were greedy, quick to anger, slow to learn, and easily led by fear.

For me, the debate always boiled down to one question: "Would you trust your neighbors with a nuclear bomb?" I'd never progressed beyond that. Too many people lay dead, not from Namebreakers or any of the Shadow People, but from good old-fashioned human hate, ignorance, and cruelty. It wasn't supernatural monsters who killed King; it wasn't magic that dropped the bomb on Japan; there were no vampires on the grassy knoll, and while Yoko Ono was an

Oni of some sort, she had not killed John Lennon. We did. Good old-fashioned regular American Joes.

We'd long surrendered whatever claim we had to the big 'M' word, like children whose parents were forced to take away their Red Ryder BB guns because they kept shooting at the neighbor's dog. It was possible that once, long ago, we had been worthy of such gifts. It was only through the constant bombardment of fear and the ingraining of a compulsion to always want more that we'd been somehow warped and changed, not unlike the domestication of the pig, with which we as a species shared so much in common. I somehow doubted that was the case, though; the times may change, but people remain fundamentally the same—shitty to each other.

Namebreakers have always been intertwined with our history, even if it took governments until the late '60s to officially acknowledge it in a legal sense. The bloody battles fought with the rightful indigenous owners of the land, ingrained in every schoolkid's education—even those raised as backwoods hell-raisers like me—served as moments where our Manifest Destiny collided with righteous rebuke. Magic, and those who wielded it, mirrored the diversity of America itself. Some were heroes like Gustav Schröder, the captain of the cruise ship St. Louis, who successfully hid more than 900 Jewish passengers from the Nazis using light distortions on the sea. Others were outlaws like Bonnie Parker and Clyde Barrow, who thumbed their noses at the law with their abilities, while still others were monsters like The Zodiac Killer, haunting the nightmares of a blood-soaked American populace.

For a long time, those in power did their utmost to keep us blindfolded. But eventually, everything comes to light.

You can call them wizards, magi, Namebreakers, or Keepers of the Word—the name has changed as often as public opinion, but at the end of the day, they were us and we were them. I didn't distrust magic; I distrusted mankind. This was a distinction that Jenna and I sometimes clashed over; she always gave the benefit of the doubt, but I had long since found my stock of such benefits in short supply.

The steak was great though.

Later, with a procedural police drama and the rest of the beer between us and Latisha's tale, we made love. Naked and cooling beneath the air, I lay with her head upon my chest, watching the blue-gray smoke of my cigarette haunt the ceiling. The evening had been perfect, and I dared to hope that maybe she had forgotten.

"Tell them you won't do it. You'll be miserable if you do and then you know how you get," Jenna's words were pressed against me, her breath warm, leaving my skin greedy for it amidst the prickling coolness.

"How exactly do I get?" I asked, mistakenly wearing a grin as I continued to watch the ceiling, oblivious to the thin line of her lips or the deepening of her brow. What I called (privately) 'cut the shit' face.

Jenna's response was a sharp, quick plucking of one of the hairs from my chest.

"Ouch! Fuck!"

"Well, don't be mean!" Jenna warned. "You'll try to just get in and out, I don't doubt that…but you won't be able to let it go when it doesn't set right with you. You won't be able to let it slide, and you'll go off the rails. This Altenhofen guy, he's a very rich and powerful person, James. I don't want to have to come bail you out of a jail in the middle of God knows where or worse…find you like I did last time living out of a motel, stinking of sour beer and death…"

I didn't let her see my flinch. There was no small part of me that had been optimistic enough to believe that enough time had passed for the scars of the past to be healed. Maybe they were, but the memory of the pain that had come with those scars remained vivid for Jenna, and there was a bitter jab of shame and frustration.

Naturally, I deflected.

"I didn't smell that bad," I said, offering a half-smile, attempting to lure her back from the edge of worry. It was the tone of a man who knew he was already in the red and probably wouldn't see the black for a long, long time.

Another hair, another pluck. At this rate, I'd be aerodynamic and divorced by the time I got around to the story.

"Be serious."

I sucked in air through my teeth to keep from letting the yelp of pain escape me. Having given my lungs a dose of the pure stuff, I felt inclined to dirty them up with the next breath. The ash from my Marlboro grew long and perilously perched as I pulled in the sort of desperate drag with which only the true nicotine fiend is intimately familiar. As if the poison smoke might have an answer, or maybe I was just stalling for time. It was all the same in that moment; all the delay in the world doesn't make the dirty deeds any less dirty.

"Altenhofen's company has been making a mint off the Shadow People situation since before either of us were born," I explained, straining to reach the ashtray. "His company makes the test that they use to determine active chaos genes, lycanthropy, and even those injections that are supposed to keep the vampires from looking at us like Happy Meals with legs," I grumbled out.

"He just wants someone that he's sure his detractors will listen to so he can point and crow about how noble he is. The rich bastard is probably a goddamn blood drinker himself," I grunted, stretching to knock the ashes away.

COYOTE WALLACE

Woe be unto the fool that drops cigarette ashes in a woman's bed.

Woe.

"Don't talk like that, the infected are just sick—they aren't murderous fiends, James," Jenna scolded. "That's what the injections are for. Besides, you like Larry, don't you? He's one of the infected," she said, reminding me as she did something far worse than pluck at a stray hair; she untangled herself from me and rose from the bed.

Larry Schtoppe had married our nearest neighbor Sue Reed, giving her the unfortunate name Sue Schtoppe as well as a stay-at-home stepfather for her two boys. Nice enough people and Jenna wasn't wrong: I did enjoy Larry's company. I had a deep appreciation of anyone who could do such a spot-on impersonation of a very famous bowtie-wearing conservative news host performing fellatio on an equally noteworthy U.S. Senator. If, crude though it may be, such an appreciation marks me as juvenile then so be it. We shared similar politics, and both our wives happened to enjoy each other's company. It was easy to forget that he was infected, easy enough, that is, until a year into his moving to the neighborhood I'd begun to notice a distinct lack of squirrels, cats, and other small creatures.

I'm sure it's coyotes and not cases of the injections failing.

There was a certain base but honest appreciation of watching her move naked to the bathroom, but it was tempered by the cold that crept in with her absence and cooled whatever brooding justification I had been working myself towards by talking about Altenhofen. She knew I wouldn't turn it down; tanking it or towing the line were up for discussion, but any notion of quitting and just walking away was only posturing.

It wasn't the money, it wasn't the loss of all those stories whose ownership would default to the bastards at The Mystic Standard, and it wasn't even the delusion of my own devotion to the Truth. That I had framed so often as integrity for praise or peace of mind as the situation warranted. No, it was because Jimmy didn't back down, Jimmy Wonderful did not bend his knee, Jimmy Wonderful—if he were to go out one final time beneath the banner of The Mystic Standard— had to go out on his shield.

Pride was a motherfucker, and Jenna knew which way the cards were going to fall even before I did.

"He just wants to show off, you know how rich bastards are when it comes to their egos. Probably some sort of school for kids his mighty cure couldn't save or some sort of monument to the prick he wished he had," I called to the facing of the door while gingerly swinging my legs over the edge of the bed and beginning the process of finding my pants.

When did this start to hurt? Jesus, getting old was terrible.

"Don't make jokes. I'm not worried about you getting hurt, I'm worried that with some billionaire footing your bill and with this fight with Tom sticking in your craw you'll…"

Behave poorly? Drink heavily? Purchase narcotics and do them to an excessive degree? Only stumbling to my laptop under the near black-out conditions with which one must find themselves to summon Jimmy?

Fuck anything that moves and sleep in puddles of my own making?

There is so much for you to choose from.

"…have an episode." Jenna sighed out in the end before turning on the shower, the hiss of the water let me know that if I had anything else to say to dispute these worries, it would have to wait.

COYOTE WALLACE

I didn't push it. It might seem strange to hear coming from a guy who makes his living with them, but sometimes, words can't change a damned thing. Jenna had been able to lie to herself enough to give me comfort, hoping I'd choose to call the whole thing off, show a little of her kind of integrity—but in the end, it was my kind that had won out. Nothing I could say was going to fix that, and only time would ease the sting.

Naked from the waist up, I slipped from the bedroom under the cover of a fantastic shower head and a large hot water tank (in all matters of spousal stealth, I recommend this) and walked barefoot down the hall to what can loosely be called my "office." Here among the trophies of past glories and on ground where I had taken to the Truth like a mad blacksmith with hammer and anvil, beating and banging from that Truth not only my fortune but the identity and mythos of the degenerate roaming wild man that was Jimmy Wonderful, I sought peace from my own troubled thoughts.

I had one more fight in me, one more time into the fray where I might be as good as I once was, maybe even better. I could feel it, I could feel it in the pit of my stomach and feel that potential, as if it were a wild charge of electricity, passing along my limbs and dancing in my fingers. Even before I turned the doorknob, with its brass scuffed by countless passings of my palm, I knew that any pretense I might have had of letting go was gone; any hope of doing Tom's bidding would not survive the act of opening that door. No, behind that door was the first step to becoming Jimmy Wonderful.

For a moment, with the door open, I just stood there, my eyes familiar with the shapes beneath the shadows arguably better than I knew the bedroom I shared with Jenna. I'd fallen over chairs drunk in my little writer's den, but I'd never stubbed my toe in the dark—there was something to be said about that.

With the flick of a switch came the guilty rush of pride and not always hollow accomplishment. I had kept souvenirs and tokens of what I considered "victories" over the years: photographs of the places I had been, whiskey bottles from nights drinking with men and Shadow Folk alike, a sword supposedly forged from moonlight itself (though I highly doubted this, for some of the silvery finish had already begun to chip away over the years after I had used it to slice open a watermelon on a particularly warm Fourth of July)— gifted to me by a faerie duchess who Jenna had every reason to hate, and I desperately hoped would not show up in a few years with an all-too-familiar looking child. Books that I loved, books that I had never read, and newspapers (I had a steady supply of them delivered to the house from across the country) all littered every conceivable shelf and open space, strewn about like the remains of valiant knights who had perished to the hunger of some terrible dragon.

Me.

The desk I had saved from a garage sale in my first years at the Standard. The old Sauder had nearly broken my back carrying it up the stairs to the tiny apartment that I'd had in the city (and nearly crushed me when I'd finally moved it), but its acquisition had marked a defining point in my destiny. The surface was scuffed to pieces, and around the keys of my computer, and on the desk itself, there was a fine layer of ash from where countless cigarettes had perished, riding upon my fingers as I had built my kingdom with paragraphs for stones and arching tales of my exploits for mortar. That hunk of wood had served as Frankenstein's table as I had brought Jimmy to life, first as a joke to perhaps keep some of the heat off of the Wozynski name and then later as a sort of mask that let me speak to truths that I might not otherwise have had the courage to.

Bit by bit, word by word, success by success, that mask had morphed into a full-on identity that was either who I had always wanted to become or who I had always been on the inside; the answer changed depending on how far into the spiral of my own bullshit I was.

I crossed the room, letting my fingers brush across the keys with their letters long worn away, their identities known with a familiarity that made my eyes redundant.

Goddamn it.

I was going to be a bastard.

The Only Way to Fly

"**B**onneville? What the hell is in Bonneville, man?" I yelled into my phone. "For God's sake, can't the rich bastard at least have a private island with half-naked girls serving us rum? Bonneville! That's the Salt Flats, you pasty-faced, shark-smiling bastard. Damn you!"

Ranting with indignity and rage had not come easily to me. I was once a fairly laid-back guy, but years in this business had erased that.

I'd called Tom to shamefacedly accept the job. Even if the shame was largely manufactured, I didn't want him to suspect that I was going to take a large, angry journalistic shit upon Altenhofen and all his money. My plan was as simple as it was farfetched, ill-conceived, and driven by spite—I would play nice to the face of the rich and those who imagined they would handle me. I would smile to their faces, nod to their statements, drink their booze, do their cocaine, sleep in their fine beds (though not after doing their cocaine, obviously), and they would suspect nothing.

Their years of buying men with money and promises would make their senses dull and their minds eager to accept their own victory over yet another greedy American whose pursuit of his own dreams and fame mattered far more than the preservation or purity of any vital truth. Then, in the dead of night when they least expected it, I would cut their throats upon the page, I would etch their secrets in ink on the psyche of my readers, and the absurdity of the pomp that the powerful afford themselves would be used to stitch the guilt of their own corruption right on their chest for all to see.

It was a shit plan, but it was at least noble, and it lasted right up until Tom told me where I was to go.

That goddamned young, smugly happy sonofabitch!

"Look, Jimmy-Jam, my man. It's going to be alright..." Tom soothed like a man giving a lethal injection.

"...The tickets will be waiting for you at the airport, and once you touch down, they're going to take good care of you. This guy has more money than the government—shit, most of his money came from the government! You'll be fine. You can't just drive out there from your little cave in Utica."

"The fuck I can't!" I knew I was defeated, but that didn't mean I was going to make it easy.

I had my own way of doing things and was willing to bet on my own value. If that meant The Standard had to eat some expenses, then so be it.

"Jimmy..." The wall of silence that followed Tom's exasperated use of my name marked the end of my hopes that I wouldn't be trapped in a metal tube hurtling through the sky. There is a tone that those who sit above our newsrooms and studios wield when they have had enough of our artistic impudence, and Tom had just used it to say my name.

I had never been a fan of flying. Though I could endure the nastiness of the process, I sought to avoid it when possible. To me, there was no charm in being ferried across the heavens by a man who had likely been drinking since noon and hadn't slept in three days. If anyone was going to drink until noon and then rocket through this world at speeds that meant certain fiery death, then I wanted it to be me, goddamn it!

There were also very practical reasons for my dislike of aviation, chiefly among them a distinct lack of opportunities to partake in any number of chemical salvations that I used to settle my nerves, or at least get the "creative juices" flowing. Throw in the fact that most flight attendants these days were trained to spot a man who had partaken of more alcohol than his legs or liver could withstand, and you had a recipe for a mostly sober trip. I'd never been a total craven criminal; I only dipped my toe into the cool waters of heroin-fueled oblivion and amphetamine-laced genius on rare occasions, sensing perhaps that there was something predatory in the sort of love those drugs offered. However, I had never felt more like a wanton drug fiend than while trying to hash it in my head how I would smuggle my own personal stash of "creative supplements" through the modern airport system.

"Fine. Just send the goddamn car before I change my mind," I damned near bounced the phone off the receiver with such force that Jenna shot me a look.

Had she been speaking to me; I might have even gotten a warning and a reminder not to take my foul mood out on the phone. Unfortunately, the failure to sway me into just letting it go had settled over the night into an icy layer of preparation. Whether she was preparing for my departure and absence or for the potential of my hurting her, I couldn't tell, but my gut told me that I wouldn't have liked the answer even if I had it. The whole morning, Jenna had been distant, and now she stood by the window looking out over the lake with her morning coffee and barely speaking.

There were few sins that I believed to be unforgivable, but hurting a woman that had already been hurt before was surely one of them from which a man had little hope of returning. That was the sort of stain that lingered on you over the long days of your life, a mark that you had to carry each step of the way. You might pretend you can lay it down with whiskey or drugs or sex, but the truth is that it sticks there in the back of your mind like a splinter of glass. And if you have even a dash of soul, it will remind you, even in the wake of all your triumphs and victories, that you are, at least in part, a no-good sonofabitch.

"They're sending a car..." For a man who made his living as a firebrand on the page, the words felt lame and anemic as all hell coming out.

This earned me an arched eyebrow and a moment's consideration as she sipped her coffee. Then she turned her face back to the window, where the lake lay swaddled in morning fog. From hard-earned experience, I knew she did not want an apology, not if it lacked sincerity, so the offering of one was off the table.

Bad small talk was sometimes all you had in your hand when playing out matters of the heart. And though I loved Jenna with all my being, a certain caged restlessness was eager to escape. Not because I longed to be free from her presence; I could have spent all of my days silently soaking up her essence. It was because I didn't want to inflict further pain upon her. I was like a hound starved before the hunt, already feeling the sick anticipation building within, despite the grousing I might have directed at Tom.

One more rodeo, old man. One more fuck you.

This wasn't the swan song I wanted with The Standard; it wasn't the end I had hoped to make for myself, but my end it almost surely would be. I'd long ago made a promise to myself that I would not become one of those aging relics, milking their life story in the end for a few extra pennies. I might have been The Standard's whore, but I wasn't a dirty one. I needed her to understand that. I needed her to be behind the idea of fighting with every means at my disposal, because if this was to be the last piece that I ever did, it had to be better than good. It had to be not just a piece of my soul but the whole damned thing.

I just didn't have the courage to say it.

"I gathered. Do you have everything you'll need? Don't want to change what you're packing now that you know... What?" She must have seen my eyes light up, for she trailed off into the question without prompting.

"You're beautiful standing there, you know that?" I meant it, too.

That's why it hurt that much more when she shook her head and pushed away from her spot by the window. She didn't say anything at all to me as she slipped by me and into the kitchen. I could hear what was left of her coffee splashing into the sink.

"Jen. Does it have to be this way before I leave?" Seemed a reasonable question at the time."

I, like many men before me who lay littered on the various battlefields of marriage, made the mistake of following her into the kitchen. I took up position in the door frame, and though I said nothing, she must have felt my presence there. She turned, and her eyes narrowed, seeing me far clearer than I saw myself and knowing me in a far deeper way than I even had the capacity to fool myself. All trickery and lies were deceptions of the self, first and foremost, and Jenna had long since gotten over fooling herself when it came to me. I didn't want to leave with bad feelings in the air, and she didn't want to lose me to my own less-than-sterling history of behavior.

"You don't have t–" and then she stopped herself, and the storm clouds that were her eyes narrowed as she looked at me. "If you come back strung out, I won't be here. I'm not doing it again, not after all the other times. If your plan is to go out there and try to be some counterculture...thing. A thing that isn't even real, James. That you just made up to sell some stupid books…" The words came from Jenna's lips tight and boiling, and tears had gathered in the corner of her eyes.

I hazarded a few steps across the kitchen tile that may as well have been no man's land. Her assessment of Jimmy wasn't flattering, nor was it entirely accurate, but it was close enough to wound. The raw hurt made reaching my hand out for her shoulder feel awkward, but I had to try. She was in pain, and it was my fault.

Justifications don't stand for shit against the tears of someone that you love.

"Jen," I started to say.

"No! It isn't fair!" She yelled in my face and slapped my hand away, turning her back to me. In the movies, this is where the lead would ease up behind her and hold her despite that slap, but this wasn't Hollywood, and Jen didn't hurt like the women on the silver screen.

"I know it isn't fair," I tried to say with as much comfort as I could muster.

"Don't just agree with me like that makes it all right. Jesus, knowing that you're a piece of shit doesn't excuse being a piece of shit!" Jen snapped; she had my number. She always had my number.

"How many times, James? How many times have we done this? How many times have you come back fucked up, strung out, your head full of weird shit and shut down? Every time you say that you've learned your lesson, every time you say that you're going to go easier—for me. For US, James!"

Jenna's words battered me like the hard rain from a storm, and I made no attempt to shield myself from them as she steamrolled on.

"Every time, it's me that picks up the pieces, me that takes care of EVERYTHING while you lay in bed, me that cleans you up when you're so fucked up you piss yourself, James. Me. No more. I won't. Do you understand me? I won't. Come back the person I love or…. please…Just stay gone."

She didn't look at me for that final ultimatum. Just as well, I didn't need to see her face to know that she meant each word.

"I'll, umm, just wait for the car outside," I said with a little more stiffness than I had intended. My bell had been rung.

I'd managed to scrape together the remains of a prescription for Xanax that had been resting comfortably in my medicine cabinet and now fished the bottle from my pocket as I waited beneath the cold morning sky for my car. The little football-shaped pills were technically a gray area in the modern world. If you just threw down a brick of heroin in front of a man and started going to town, he'd look at you like you were a depraved, drug-addicted fiend of the very worst sort.

HOWEVER, if you swap out that same brick with a bottle of pharmaceutical happiness, then you were just another average Joe doing his best not to let the world crush him beneath its heel. This was America, after all, and we only like our drug addicts when Uncle Sam is getting his kickback. If you think that the common North American Drug Addict (Medicamento addicta) displays a certain grotesque amount of fear at the prospect of missing his fix, then I suggest to you the prolonged observation of a U.S. Senator. No down-on-their-luck fiend has ever been so willing to sink to their knees in front of their fixer and gobble down his cock like the American politician when confronted by a pharmaceutical company that has made generous campaign donations.

COYOTE WALLACE

It was important that I controlled myself, that I not let the argument with Jenna spurn me to some initial act of degeneracy that would then color my entire trip. I did not wish to become my wife's self-fulfilling prophecy, at least before I'd even gotten out of the driveway. Two of the pills would be more than enough to calm my nerves and allow me to pass the trip with a deep sense of calm. Two and absolutely no more.

Too much Xanax can lead to all manner of poor behavior and spoken truths that are better left on the tongue, a degenerate loss of self that leaves the afflicted with all the charm of a man lost beneath the tides of ether and all the subtlety of a gorilla that has recently suffered a catastrophic brain injury.

I fished the bottle out of my pocket and began to shake two of the Happy Footballs into my palm when I made the mistake of looking back over my shoulder at my home. I could see Jenna watching from the window, and for a moment I felt such a strong urge to turn back around, go inside, and surprise myself by taking her advice. This pull toward choosing domestic happiness over my own legacy was so strong that the only counter that my convictions—flawed and soaked in alcohol as they were—could come up with was anger. Anger at myself for loving her, anger at myself for hurting her, anger at myself for being this shameless addict to my own line of bullshit. The angrier I got; the more pills found their way into my palm.

I popped ten of the pills into my mouth and chewed them as if they contained the cure for cancer and written clichés.

By the time the car that Tom had sent finally arrived, I was cold from being too stubborn to go back into the house and wait, but I was beginning to slip deep beneath the waves of an alprazolam high. Put on the back burner were my concerns about my marriage; gone was the anxious energy that had pervaded my every cell since I found out about this, my final story, and gone were any concerns that I might have had about flying.

In their place was now a warm blankness that would occasionally lap at what remained of my emotional spectrum like a tide that was coming in to wash away the sandcastles I'd made from my worries. It was not an unpleasant high, though it was one that lacked a certain degree of personalization. A weightless warmth that was to be the cocoon for a familiar chrysalis.

Jimmy Wonderful was stirring.

Even through the settling fog of my perfectly legal and exquisitely American acquaintance with Fun Time Pharma-Candy, I was surprised to find that I was still capable of lamenting the demise of the taxicab. Gone were the days of yellow cabs smelling faintly of smoke, vomit, and cabbage with colorful drivers who might, with gentle prodding, disclose to you the hidden wonders of a city or a town. The cabby with his knowing grin who would gleefully point out to you the sort of massage parlors where you might affordably contribute to the human trafficking problem, what neighborhoods you could buy pixie dust or good old-fashioned Ronald Reagan-endorsed crack cocaine, and where you might reasonably buy new underwear at 3 a.m. after shitting your pants from drinking too much tequila.

His replacement in the modern era was the "Independent Transportation Service Industry Representative"—in my case exemplified by a young man in his late 20s with blue hair that had been neatly styled into not a duck-tailed pompadour, but the essence of all pompadours, valiantly struggling against good taste and time to avoid oblivion. The glasses looked as if they had been pulled off Buddy Holly's corpse, and the green button-down shirt had, at a glance, made it through the horrible practice of living without knowing either vomit nor spilled cigarette ash.

The cabby is, at his heart, a ferryman for the traveler. This? This is a kid working a side job, and his interest in me ends with my money. His thumbs were on his phone before I even loaded my suitcase into the trunk—undoubtedly texting with the broken, bastardized form of US English (already a twice-removed bastard itself) about the horror of potentially being engaged in conversation by an old man.

Twenty years ago, I would have masturbated in the back seat while licking the poison off the back of a toad just to give brats like this a lesson in the unpredictable nature of The Weird. That all attempts to remain clean and comfortable are delusions in the face of the big, hungry Fuck-God that was America. Doomed children who think that the way to solve being made uncomfortable by water while on a sinking ship is to plug the holes rather than learn to swim in that big, filthy sea. Noble in intention, certainly, but annoying in delivery. As hopeless in their generational naiveté as the hippies had been all those years ago when they preached tuning in and dropping out as a solution. We'd at least had faeries then and notions of dreams that lay beyond men—what did they have? TikTok? Followers? The idea that if you told bad men not to say bad words, that the bad words would magically vanish from the face of the earth?

I called him Billy. This was not his name. I did not care.

"Airport?" Billy asked from the front of the car as I settled into the back of his small foreign sedan.

I craned my neck to look back toward the house, maybe I was hoping that Jenna would come running down the steps of the porch and offer me some sort of goodbye that would taste less like ashes in my mouth than the one that I'd received. There was no such luck, and the world felt as if it was slowly sinking into a tub of cold molasses. The muscles of my shoulders, neck, and back were beginning to politely excuse themselves from the company of my bones. The possibility that I had taken too many of the All-American Cure-Alls grew, bloomed, withered, and died in my mind. All of it in the amount of time it took me to turn my head back to Billy.

"Would I have gotten into the car if I wasn't? Does that happen often? Is there an epidemic of strange men hopping into your ride and taking lifts to someone else's destination?" I meant the question as a joke, but admittedly having asked it with one eyebrow hitched high up over a suspicious eye and beginning to lean forward like a leering menace, that may not have been how it came off to Billy.

"I...uh...I don't think so?" Billy glanced at the rearview uneasily.

"Good. Good. That's good..." I eased myself back into the seat, my eyelids felt heavy, I'd spent too much energy wasted flapping my gums.

My home was behind me. I felt like I was falling.

"Are you okay, man?" Billy asked with the frightened concern of a child who'd just watched Daddy take a header off the roof while hanging Christmas lights.

The blinking of my eyes seemed to take an inordinate amount of time to complete; the question posed by the boy about my welfare was worrying, though. Damned pills. Didn't they know that I would have to endure the questions of Billy the New Age Boy? I had to ride it out, fight my way up from the bottom of the scummy pharmaceutical pond. While the idea of thwarting Tom's assignment for me by ending up in the local hospital having my stomach pumped certainly had its own charm; Jenna would have tracked me down and killed me if I didn't make it at least past the state lines before I succumbed to every bad habit and started breaking promises with the care of a rampaging bull in a china shop.

"When we get there, roll me out of the car. I'm fine, just having a little trouble with my legs, dear boy." This is what I thought I said, quite clearly.

Xanax though…

What I actually said was…

"Fuck…Legs…Fuck. Legs."

Did Billy answer with a reply that would shake me from my stupor and make me reconsider that bevy of questionable life choices that made it seem like a good idea to eat half a bottle of Housewife's Chemical Helper? I can't say. The narrative became spotty and lacking in detail as gravity pulled me down into the deceptively soft back seat of the perfect stranger entrusted with my safe travel. It is possible that from the lips of young Billy's mouth came the wisdom of the ages and I, by virtue of having consumed an unconscionably large number of pills, out of both spite and fear, simply couldn't tell. That was part of the forbidden charm of such modern all-American delights. The giant potholes in awareness that made traveling seem a little less monotonous, or at the very least made you too numb to care.

"Hey…uh…Old guy? Are you awake? If you puke in my car, I'll put you out on the side of the road. The charge already went through; I don't need this." Billy's words were like driftwood in the warm black sea of my diffusing consciousness.

Not exactly kind perhaps, but then again, I had taken an irresponsibly large amount of prescription-strength anxiety medicine in preparation for a soul-crushingly dull flight. His concern that I might disgorge my lunch upon the backseat of his car was warranted, and when you are drowning in a sea of your own almost predictable bad habits, hitting all the best notes on your worst behavior, anything that will keep you afloat will do. On the upside, I couldn't even feel the fact that my last chance at real happiness was burning like Rome behind me.

"Not in my constitution," I managed despite my still-thickening tongue.

"I didn't ask about your politics. Man, why do I always get the weirdos?" Billy's question might have been rhetorical, but the youthful eyes peering at me were full of the righteous judgment only those who feel their futures are stolen by the one before can ever properly manage.

Did he really just say that?

I had heard the secrets of faeries, watched the undead corpse of Richard Nixon rise once again to the highest office in the land, and until twenty-four hours ago was going to close out my career with beings of dream made flesh who had turned wine and music into a religion. Now I was halfway between trying to decide if my inner disdain and jealousy for youth was manifesting itself the way a drunk might manifest an insult when spoiling for a fight...OR...The American education system was the sort of horrifying dumpster fire that led English professors to throw themselves from the highest building and angle themselves headfirst into the pavement.

I was leaning towards becoming a weeping lawn dart myself, but my motor functions were already breaking down beneath the cold tide of The Perfect Numb.

Abruptly the world faded to black.

Fuck.

"Come on man, get out. You said I could just roll you out, but you can't just be dead weight" Billy? That was Billy. Somewhere out in the black.

"Phhhhhh...cun walk...Just need legs, Billy." That would show him, teach him to speak to a wordsmith like me in such a manner.

"My name isn't Billy," my driver says with such dryness it's almost enough to pull me from my stupor. "Get out of my car. Come on, just roll out the door." Billy-Not-Billy was clearly unmanned by my insightful critique of the importance of legs because he pushed just a little bit harder.

Light beat against my closed eyelids, revealing to me that I had, in fact, had them closed. Who knew? The parking lot pavement was wet beneath my hands, and dampness was steadily soaking through the knees of my pants. Now I wasn't just a clearly intoxicated degenerate; I was also a dirty, clearly intoxicated degenerate who was about to do his level best to walk his way through Rockford International Airport. Who was expected, somehow, to pick up his ticket and find his way to his gate all while avoiding being arrested or detained for being (as I've said) a filthy, clearly intoxicated degenerate.

THUNK!

That? That was my suitcase. Billy hadn't forgotten after all!

I wobbled up to my feet as Billy slammed the trunk down and rounded his car, glaring at me from over the black frames of his plucked-from-Buddy-Holly's-corpse glasses. It was always good to connect with young people, and some dim memory of propriety compelled me to start digging for a tip. That or I just didn't want to meet his eyes because I knew the pills were hitting hard. It was a coin flip.

"Get help. I don't know what your deal is, man, but get help. You're old enough to be my dad." Billy-Not-Billy told me in no uncertain terms as he slammed the door that I had fallen from closed and began to climb back into the driver's side.

"I'd never fuck your mother; you've been too good to me. Money? I have money..." I offered in a half mumble as I dug for the bills.

"Screw this job, I'm a fucking engineer and this is the shit I deal with," Billy groused with a shake of his head. "Fuck you, old man. Fuck. You." Billy-Not-Billy shouted the last bit at the anesthetized shell of a man that might have been me; I couldn't tell. Then he hauled ass from the Chicago Rockford International Airport parking lot like the devil himself was coming to repo the four-cylinder sadness machine that Billy used to make his living.

Fly free, little bird. Fly free until the student loan debt collectors, social media moguls, and warmongers come for you and yours. Veal for the ever-hungry American Beast that once every few generations likes to feed the young, fattened on small victories and changes, into its thresher-like mouth. Communism, Oil, The War on Infernalism, I wonder what altar you shall be sacrificed upon?

It is no trouble for me to spare you the indignity of stumbling my way through the airport, mostly because I have no direct memory of it. It is impossible to feel shame when under the influence of Xanax; at best, you can remember the motions of shame and might poorly parody those motions. I have instead snippets, snapshots, and the hazy memory of exhausted frustration and chemical apathy.

That, and a small note of what was still, as of then at least, breathing regret. The last bit of James Wozynski clinging to his existence as Jimmy Wonderful stirred from his slumber. You can't raise a demon or please a fickle god without sacrifice, and I'd spent so much time putting the better parts of myself on that altar that I might as well have owned summer property there.

Fortunately, I am an old hand at piecing together chains of events from the broken memories of a narcissistic drug fiend's mind. I have had, after all, a great deal of practice. This is an acquired life skill picked up from the rough and tumble living of a word-tramp rambling from story to story, one that is often necessary for the survival of any aspiring degenerate wordslinger's sanity at that.

There was the tall (or was I sinking?) African American woman who had dispensed to me my ticket while looking at me as if I were some sort of strange boneless animal from the bottom of the sea. There were the security agents, arms crossed and faces sullen, who could not see me, not the real me. Instead, they unwittingly perceived only the aging meat that could have belonged to a perfectly respectable businessman on his way to maybe sell some aluminum siding in a town like Plainview, Iowa, or Big Cedar, Missouri. Crowds. Blurring faces.

Somewhere in the distance, my own numbed laughter, as if I were coming up from a dose of the good stuff at a dentist's office.

Waking up on an airplane already in flight with no actual memory of boarding, checking your luggage, or finding your seat is an experience. Whether that experience is a rock bottom that you pay attention to or a moment for reflection on whether or not this might be what it is like to die, or both, is entirely dependent on how much of the chase you had in your blood. I'd done something 'bad,' I'd stepped off the straight and narrow that was supposed to be my redemption and it felt amazing; especially with a pharmacy in my bloodstream working overtime to make sure I didn't feel much of anything else at all.

Tom had not booked me first class, and if you haven't ever taken a commercial flight to Utah, then I can only say that it has all the charm of a bus stop with absolutely none of the personality. I'd rarely seen so many bland white people crammed into such a small space, and I had once tried to record conversations in the bathrooms of the Republican National Convention.

Beside me sat a powerfully ordinary but robust woman with short, bottle-blond hair that had been pulled back from her face and fastened into place with two small cat-faced hair clips. She was clad in shapeless gray sweat clothes that only hinted at the rest of the fashion-forward beauty of the K-Mart clothing lines. Neither ugly nor beautiful, she was a cross-section of the unremarkable—aside from the fact that the man beside her on the commercial flight was suffering a near-total form of sleep paralysis brought on by too many pills and a powerful disdain for flight.

She was reading a dog-eared copy of one of the cheap romance novels you often see aging housewives burying their noses in on the beach. The long-haired shirtless bastard on the cover, undoubtedly the hero who would be thrusting his lance for Lady Goodbritches before the second act was over. I'd always preferred actual degeneracy, but who was I to judge?

Despite what you may think of me, I've always had a certain respect for romance novels. We in 'the biz' consider it to be the lesser form of literary porn star, which is considerably more respectable than tabloid journalism. Never present 'The Adventures of Lusty Sir Morrowind' to your English professor as a favorite though. He will throw the book at your head, and the corners can be unforgivingly sharp. Acceptance only goes so far in the smoking jacket circles.

Romance novels, with their heaving bosoms and throbbing members, are the forbidden fruits of literary escapism. They offer a glimpse into a world of passion and desire that many dare not explore in their everyday lives. It's a guilty pleasure, like sneaking a peek at your neighbor's lingerie drawer or indulging in a pint of ice cream at midnight. However, don't mistake it for highbrow literature;

it's more like a steamy rendezvous in a cheap motel than a refined soirée at the opera.

With no prompting at all, my neighbor looked over at me from over the pages of her book, and her brow scrunched up as if she had just stumbled upon some smashed-beyond-recognition piece of roadkill and was trying to work out what sort of poor beast it had once been.

"You're a very strange man, aren't you?" she said, almost conspiratorially, and reached over to wipe a little of the drool from the corner of my mouth.

Come on body, snap out of it. Lips? Tongue? Pinky finger? Ok, nothing. Great. Just fucking great!

"You've got a very sick soul," she said with faux sympathy that reminded me of the plastic plants some people keep in their offices.

"I don't usually tell people that because it's a little rude and with all the political hoo-hah these days…" She licked her finger and turned a page on the book, speaking to me but no longer bothering to look.

The drugs kept the panic down. Mostly.

My thoughts, however, still raced.

How the fuck does an Infernalist end up on a commercial flight? Isn't this why we put up with having to step through salt circles and splashes of holy water at the damned airport? Isn't dealing with this very problem why America bent over, grabbed its ankles, and presented its rosy upturned rear to the vampiric overlord that was Richard Nixon? For that matter, why wasn't it at least one of the sexy demonesses that the Lord of All Cocktail Weenie Genitalia himself, Tucker Carlson, was always warning us about?

"Unbaptized baby blood on the heels is a pain in the ass to get. The rest? Don't be a pig. There are already enough pigs in the nine Hells," she stated simply, plucking the thought from my mind as easily as she might have picked a ripe blackberry from its vine. "We have an overabundance of pigs in my particular Hell. Here, you're missing the inflight movie," she said with a smile that would have made my entire body shudder in revulsion had I possessed the ability to move or speak, or anything other than lay there like a fish that had been stunned out of the water.

The American legal system defines an Infernalist as any man or woman who willingly trades their soul with an incorporeal being of proven malicious intent for purposes of power, wealth, or personal gain. It is a wide net by intention, a perpetual conflict with an enemy that has no uniform, borders, or even physical manifestation in some cases. This means he can be anywhere and that the government, in order to protect us, must be everywhere. Ever vigilant, unless the good old USA slides into steep moral decay and makes the whole business easier for them.

I, however, now define the term, on a personal level at least, as anyone who would position an immobile grown man so that he was forced to watch "Mary Kate and Ashley Take the Lost Kingdom of R'yleh".

In a world of vampires, ghosts, werewolves, and Namebreakers (why can't we just call them wizards?), the Infernalist and, by extension, anything classified as a demon, were public enemy number one. They beat out the Namebreakers and those infected with lycanthropy two-to-one when it came to who got the righteous fury. This is because while the lycanthrope may be dangerous and the Namebreaker may be uncomfortably powerful, it is the Infernalist with his conducting non-taxable transactions that is the greatest threat to the American way of life.

You can sell your soul to the Devil (or at least a devil) but you will pay sales tax or Uncle Sam will make the Inquisition look like a goddamned cakewalk.

You vile sadistic bitch! If you're going to kill me, please transform into a beautiful succubus! I've had some ideas about my death. There's no need to torture me further than your presence.

"Oh, aren't we a cutie-patootie with our hurtful stereotypes and assumptions of self-importance." She gave my cheek a pinch as she settled back into her seat, satisfied with her awful work.

I had managed to get one eye open and now desperately wished I could close it. Where the Hell was one of those blank spots of memory when I needed it the most?

"If you must know..." she began.

No, I mustn't. I'd genuinely rather not. Truly. Choose between making me watch this horrible visual torture or speaking to me. Goddamn it, She-Devil just smother me while I can't move and be done with it! I got into this condition partially to avoid airplane small talk. Please, have mercy on me!

She fixed me with a stare that reminded me I had just asked a demon for mercy. One eyebrow thrown high above a blue eye that twinkled with delight, as I was forced to absorb the horror of two spunky teens averting the apocalypse by showing him what was really important, your dad's visa card. Who would have guessed that the way to an Elder God's heart was through shopping, a makeover, and telling your parents how their divorce makes you feel sad inside?

"...I am going to see this meat...I mean...MY sister and her husband and her perfect three kids that she somehow managed to have and just bounce right back from. Bitch. You know I thought about feeding them all to a woodchipper, but I think I'm just going to introduce them to some Deep State literature. What do you think?" she asked, as sweet as apple pie.

Over the rim of the seat in front of me, I could see the doorway that led to the rest of the plane and in it stood an attractive brunette flight attendant. Salvation. In a desperate attempt to escape the soul-obliterating torture in which I had awoken to find myself, I called to her. Using all my willpower, all my strength, even all my loathing for this conversation and the two giggling morons having a montage about rollerblading in a sunken city.

"Uuugn.." The sad sound of a dying walrus was the best I could manage.

Help me! For God's sakes! Help me! I renounce all my former subversive tendencies; I have been broken Daddy America and I need you now. Send help! Send help for your poor wandering son who has long last seen the error of his ways!

"Do you really talk like that? Goodness, if you aren't a strange one, mister-mister," my flight companion gave a little shake of her head and pushed on. "I'll tell you what, since you're a fussy-gussy, I'm just going to keep my own company. Lord Blackmoore is just about to confess his feelings for Lady Petalkiss in the old tower anyway..." she paused and leaned in close...

"...and if you try that again I'll eat your fucking face and use your soul to clean the meat from my teeth." This was not the voice of a mortal woman, but something old and terrible that had missed its calling in talk radio.

Just like that, she returned to her previous position and gave my shoulder a little smack with her book. I could only see her out of the corner of my eye, but I could feel the smug and satisfied smile. The screen in front of me continued to kick out colorful upbeat adventures for the hollow-minded who the rest of us had to make sure didn't drown while looking up each time it rained. A small divine mercy was brewing; however, the dark tug of the Xanax was once more starting to pull me down, but even the pills couldn't entirely dispel the combined horror I was faced with.

Down. Down in the dark. Down to where the dreams you hoped you didn't remember come, the light of day waited for you.

When I awoke, the plane had landed, and the seat beside me was empty. A tired-eyed flight attendant, who seemed much less attractive than the one I recalled, was standing over me. She was exhausted but genuinely concerned. Nothing takes it out of a person like dealing with the entitled, the ungrateful, and the in a hurry—basically, most Americans in any form of transit.

"Sir, we've arrived at our destination. I had a little trouble getting you awake, are you ok?" The glittering brass name tag told me her name was Wendy, and Wendy sounded like an angel after my experience.

Was it a dream? A fiction conjured by a mind riddled with guilt and controlled substances? The ambiguously empty seat beside me contained no clues, and even if it had, the flight attendant's patience would surely not have tolerated my dawdling. Besides, what would I have told her or security anyway?

"Fine. I mean, I'm fine. Just a deep sleeper, thank you," I said as I rubbed my face to re-familiarize my nerve endings with successfully sent signals from my brain.

I was in Utah, and as was the case for every other person ever to travel from anywhere in the world to Utah, nothing good would come of it.

The Gathering of Years

As expected, the quest to reacquire my luggage was encumbered by both the checked baggage screening process of the TSA and a smooth, blank wall of oblivion that stood in for details a sane, well-adjusted person might deem necessary for such a task. Fortunately, I was an old hand at picking up the pieces left behind by my own foolishness. Recovering luggage from an airport with a memory shot full of holes turned out to be substantially easier than repairing my life if all this went off the rails as I expected it to.

That last thin silver chain of dignity and self-control holding Jimmy Wonderful in his rusty cage behind my heart, keeping James Wozynski with his tidy framed diploma from the University of Miami (Go Hurricanes) strapped into the driver's seat, lashed to the wheel like a ship captain facing down a storm—that chain was about to snap.

Eventually, two baggage handlers, heads spinning no doubt from jet fuel fumes, found my wandering suitcase, but until then, I was left standing there with the other strange wayfarers, consigned to reflect on just what in the Hell I was doing here. This was the last moment of sanity where a man or woman, as a traveler, can choose to tear up the ticket and go back home. For me, though, the ugly truth was that I couldn't just set aside a fiction, a mask of my own creation that had persisted until it had become at least a partial truth.

Over the years, I've encountered those who could loosely be described as fans of the works I've produced. Most of these works came through my association with The Mystic

Standard, and there was always a certain flattery in young minds believing I was some American trickster god with a pen. If nothing else, the money was nice enough to allow for the soothing of guilt or artistic integrity, with large quantities of booze and fine things to please those I loved.

I had received letters, copies of occasional theses, underwear (Jenna did not like that one), keepsakes, and joints in every conceivable container that could be used to fool the postal service, and more. Invariably, there was a compulsion for people to tell you which of your works was their favorite. I was never inherently comfortable with this sort of praise; the adulation felt hollow and only half-earned. All I'd written was meant to encourage my fellow Americans (and those readers who dared to wonder about the spirit of this strange and fabled land) to go out and embrace both the good and bad of all that was Weird. Instead, it was too often the vicarious livers and the voyeurs who marveled at these deeds of debauchery and pursuits of the strange. Still worse were those who, instead of forging their own paths, sought to replicate my own, who too often ended up discarded upon the side of the path like so many spun-out automobiles in a race they were ill-equipped to win.

Do you know how many of those, however, cited the works of James Wozynski—one of which was published just two years past—that featured neither Jimmy's name nor the usual adventures associated thereof, as their favorite?

Not nearly enough.

Corner any one of us in a bar and fill him with enough liquor and we might tell you how it feels. Like the song says:

'Who made who?'

"Sir? Is this the one?" said a pudgy male baggage handler whose carefully constructed tone of cheery helpfulness jarred me out of my musings like a splash of cold water.

He had the cold dead eyes of a man that spends each day fantasizing about taking tack hammers to his coworkers only to return home and spoil his cats rotten. I was just the latest in a long line of travelers who served to make his life a little more bothersome. I'm sure he was contemplating even then the dark joy that would bloom in his heart if he could but wrap his stubby sausage fingers around my throat and give it a good squeeze. I know that had I been standing there in his position that I would have certainly given the matter some thought—after all how long could you choke a man before security pulled you off as you frothed at the mouth and cursed your enemy's heart?

Inquiring minds wanted to know.

"Thanks." I half mumbled as I took my luggage and deftly avoided further eye contact.

When I turned around and saw what those poor bastards working here must have had to endure each day I nearly wept in pity for humanity. I cannot imagine the mind that must have chosen the design for the Salt Lake City International airport. It is too diseased, too frightening, and too strange for even me. The sort of thing dreamed of only in madness.

The walls were adorned with what I've come to recognize, in this disquieting era of human history, as kinetic sculptures. They were illuminated by LED lights spewing colors of the obscenest and decadent variety: deep blues, purples, pinks, and lively racing greens all cavorted across surfaces devoid of any discernible pattern, save for perhaps that resembling Satan's anus. The polished floors only served to amplify the horror of this faux-organic art piece plucked from the bowels of corporate Hell.

I can only assume the intention of the man who purchased it was to make every visitor to Utah feel as though they were being expelled by a unicorn into the most desolate, soul-obliterating part of America, outside of Hollywood. My bet is on the artist being a demon or one of those faeries you definitely don't exchange names with; especially if you value your sanity or credit score. No other explanation holds water.

"Fucking madness," I muttered to myself, the disbelief akin to Dante laying eyes upon Hell or a cultured European entering New Jersey.

I made a dash for the doors, desperate to flee, suddenly craving clean air and natural light if I hoped to retain my sanity. I knew my driver awaited me somewhere, and that I should be on the lookout for him, but the colors pressed against my eyes, and the Xanax hangover reached its crescendo. I barreled through the double doors at the front of the airport like an all-star running back, shoulder first and at a dead sprint, while my stomach danced the Cha-Cha and the whole building spun around me.

A spin move that would have earned applause from championship caliber athletes for the Indian girl in her smart suit who was chatting on her phone. A high hurtling leap for an ugly baby in his carriage while his overwhelmed mother desperately tried to wipe what I hoped was chocolate pudding from the hands of an equally hideous child by her side. Nothing was going to stop me from getting out there into the air, nothing was going to make me endure this place for one second longer than I had to.

Moments before my shoulder collided with the doors, they swung open of their own accord, and I went tumbling to the curb. My suitcase careened across the concrete, bouncing and skipping like a stone, but it didn't matter. I was free now.

For all of three seconds, I was the happiest man in the world to be in Utah. Then again, that's a bit like winning a popularity contest in Hell or the Republican National

Convention—whichever my editor can get the rights to use later for the purposes of this story.

"OH GOD FUCKING DAMN IT!" I screamed into the blacktop as my composure unraveled and my lunch splattered messily across the ground.

This was not the graceful vomiting of a supermodel after a dinner of iceberg lettuce nor the quick upchuck of my college years. I am an old man now, and my body does not cling to dignity as it once did. I found myself gripping the curb with both hands while on my knees, my neck extended fully. I emitted a sound akin to a cat grappling with a difficult hairball—a very old cat of questionable health at that. More than once, I silently beseeched every god I could remember, or thought might hear me, from every religion I have ever encountered, for the violent expulsion of pills and old coffee from my stomach to cease. That I would be spared this humiliation, which was at least partially of my own making.

"Look, Daddy! A sick man!" A boy, perhaps six years old, with the flaxen, whitish-blond hair of a goddamn albino, yelled as his father led him from a taxicab towards the airport doors.

"Stay in school. Read a book." I croaked out as I wiped my mouth on the back of my sleeve.

The boy's father pulled him along a little faster, and they vanished through the automatic doors, into the swirling, offensively kaleidoscopic madhouse that is the Salt Lake City International Airport. It was always important to me that, when possible, I gave the youth of today a positive message. The kid's life would be hard enough when someone pointed out to him that you don't get hair that color unless your mother and father have substantially lied on their marriage records.

"I'll never understand why'n high Hell rich folks do the things they do," drawled a rumbling voice from behind me, the voice chased by the scratch of a match head on the face of its book.

"I'll settle for figuring out why I do the things I do," I half-panted as I hauled myself up and arched my back as if all the stretching in the world could get out the soreness that time had put in my lower lumbar.

"You're James Wozynski, aren't you?" The owner of that voice, which reminded me of the low echo of thunder in the mountains, asked, and the question bid me to turn around and face its owner.

For a moment, though?

Just a moment.

I stood there and drank in this place as I did with all the new lands I encountered. I had purged myself messily on the pavement, and now my head felt much clearer as my lungs sucked down what felt like their first gulps of fresh air in hours. Unlike the lands from whence I had traveled back east, the sky here was blue and free of the seemingly ever-present rain, and the sun was unabashedly bright in its golden hues. There was a tingle of old wildness in my belly and the hit of anxiety mixed with excitement with it that accompanied any journey into strange territory.

I'd always, and still do for that matter, equate the sensation to the burn that comes with a shot of fine bourbon. The experience, even if it could be had without it, would not be the same. It was all part of the savoring, and I would have that moment. Question be damned. Name be damned.

I tilted my face towards the sun, letting my eyelids slowly fall as I welcomed the day's warm light to seep through and cleanse the migraine-like aura of the airport behind me. Surprisingly, my interrogator did not press and allowed me this moment, a small mercy for which he had my gratitude, short-lived though it may have been. When I opened my eyes and turned, I felt the strong impression that the man before me was a man out of time, a product of some bygone era like me. It was not his clothing, no, the suit was gray and while lacking in all sense of fashion or taste, it was modern enough. Nor was it the silvered toes of his cowboy boots, which while demonstrably tacky and suggestive of long nights drinking to the sound of a man yodeling about his wife leaving him, were still within the realm of modern possibility. The hair and sideburns, long and afflicted with a hint of unruly curl that robbed it of the ability to lay flat? Possibly. Though there was always the chance he was some sort of Western reenactor in his spare time.

No, it was the vintage of his stare. Something not brewed in this country (for damned good reason) in far too long. Eyes that saw a man at his weakest moment and held him there for all time without ever bothering to wonder at the greatest. Eyes that had fastened themselves Westward and raped, pillaged, and plundered until they reached the Pacific.

"Guilty as charged," I confessed. "Goddamn, you're a grim looking bastard. Care to throw a drowning man a lifeline?" I nodded towards the cigarette dangling from his mouth.

He gave a little laugh, dry as the arid air and hard as the stony hearts of those who had tamed the land we stood upon. For a moment, he seemed to ponder the humor in my words before fishing out both a cigarette and doing the dirty work of lighting the carcinogenic heaven for me.

There were rough calluses on the insides of his palm and across the pad of his thumb. Maybe someone else would have missed it, but I was still at least a half-decent news hound.

"I'm Ulysses Hawthorne," he introduced himself with simple forwardness. "Mr. Altenhofen sent me to make sure you find your way to the compound in a timely manner." Hawthorne didn't bother offering his hand; it wasn't a greeting but an explanation.

Despite the earlier politeness, I did not get the sense that this Ulysses Hawthorne cared much for me, whether by reputation, first impression, or simply the inconvenience of his task. Fortunately for me, I had very little concern for the opinions of men who would fashion themselves into the guard dogs for the rich. One of the many unspoken secret thrills of American culture is antagonizing "The Goon." If there were an Olympic sport for it, I may well have taken the silver. Not the gold; I'm too humble for that.

The Goon, while not singularly an American phenomenon, is nonetheless found here in a wide variety of shapes and sizes. The Goon can take the form of the policeman, the national guardsman, or the common security guard. However, The Goon, though cursed with limited intelligence and an absolute lack of imagination, can breed with anything, especially common Drunken Louts, Closet Racists, and The North American Big-Bellied, Small-Penised Ammosexual. This unnatural crossbreeding produces strange and horrifying hybrids that litter the landscape of this once-proud land. Though bitingly stupid, never give your book to The Goon, and only approach with great caution or when the numbers are in your favor.

Place no faith in the system, for it is part of The Goon's arsenal, along with the billy club, the tear gas canister, the Taser, the riot shield, and the gun.

"I would have drifted in eventually," I assured him. "I don't really like to be overly managed." I blew my smoke into the air as I spoke, watching the gray smoke fade into the blue of the sky to avoid the dead-eyed stare of the man before me.

This Ulysses Hawthorne, with his silver-toed boots and his suit the color of the London sky and a face like hard granite, seemingly found no joy in my humor this time. For a single breath's worth of time, he kept the weight of his eyes on me as he tamped down his disdain. He then turned and walked over to my suitcase, picked it up from the ground, and halfheartedly dusted the front of it off with the back of his hand.

"There's a car waitin', if you'd be so kind as to follow me, Mr. Wozynski." Then he turned and headed towards the parking garage, walking off with a surprising confidence that I would follow him for a man supposedly so informed of my reputation.

There was a certain wild temptation to instead hail a cab and flee into the city. To lose myself in the dive bars and the filth. To breathe in the whole place and soak it up through my skin. Jimmy Wonderful had made meals of more remote and repressed landscapes than the one before me. That last little chain that held Jimmy snapped and I was already beginning to raise my hand when I glimpsed Hawthorne halt his progress out ahead of me, not yet turning back to look over his shoulder to see if I was coming—merely stopped.

I was no longer the young man I once had been. Hawthorne, on the other hand, was a walking menace and even worse, if it all went to shit and I was in some bar and that got back to Jenna then I would have burned my last chance to go out on my terms for nothing.

My hand lowered and I followed Altenhofen's pet sentinel as he resumed his step.

When I saw the limo waiting on us, I couldn't help but laugh. I hadn't realized that I would be sitting and staring at Hawthorne's ugly mug the entire ride out to Altenhofen's compound and there was something ridiculously amusing about the idea of the man sitting there across from me in the back of this expensive gas-guzzling display of wealth with his arms crossed like an angry parent chaperoning a prom.

"You have to be kidding me." My own echoing voice, distorted by the parking garage, made me question its real owner.

Hawthorne handed off the bag to the driver and turned to look over his shoulder at me. He seemed to scoff at the disapproval of the finery.

"Don't worry, the man made sure the whiskey was stocked too. Reckon that'll soothe your soul about bein' comfortable?" he asked as he flicked his cigarette to the ground at my feet.

I lingered before committing to climbing inside, I was not afraid of the journey or even the destination but having endured the vagaries of commercial flight my body was not ready to give up on the slender stick of nicotine trapped between my fingers. I took my drags with the ravenous insistence that can only properly be birthed from repression. The cherry burned bright all the way down to the filter.

"Can't hurt." I spoke around the stub of the cowboy killer between my lips.

What else was I to say? My cigarette now burned down too low to provide a plausible excuse for lingering now joined Hawthorne's on the ground.

I have always suffered from a peculiar compulsion to behave badly when enclosed in finery, a perverse pull towards walking across a fine carpet in muddy boots or seeing a priceless vase smashed upon the ground. This compulsion, this willful inner entropy, intensifies most when I sense a distinct lack of sincerity in the offered beauty before me.

There was very little sincerity to be had in the back of that limousine.

Hawthorne busied himself securing a bottle of Blanton's Blue from the stock that Altenhofen had provided, as well as two glasses. I would like to tell you that I was able to sit despondent and surly across from Hawthorne based entirely on principle as we left the airport behind. I would like to say that as a man who makes his living carving Truth out of thin air onto the blank white expanse of a page, I was above being swayed, impressed, or set at ease by something as petty as a bottle of two-thousand-dollar bourbon that I myself, even in my most debauched moments, would not have burned the money upon.

That would make me a liar, though, and I am a terrible liar. I accepted the offered glass from Hawthorne and endeavored to at least try to make conversation until we arrived at our destination.

"How long?" I asked before taking that first belt and swishing it around inside my mouth like it was Listerine before sucking it back.

Just because I liked it didn't mean I was going to instantly become the sort of blue-blooded bastard that could afford such libations. An appreciation of fine things does not mean one must be a slave to the ritual thereof. There would be no slow sipping and savoring of notes for me, at least not before that bastard's eyes.

It was a sublime bourbon though.

"What do you mean? Till we get there?" Hawthorne sipped his drink, not savoring it but not taking it like it was jet fuel like me either. There was no fondness in his tone, only toleration aided by the drink.

"Not really, but that would be nice to know at some point. I mean, how long have you been alive? You're one of the Enduring, aren't you? An alchemical? Nah, you don't seem the type. There's usually a change around the eyes..." It was my chance to turn the screws a little. I had been playing along with the polite strong-arm act, even endeavoring to pass the time with conversation. However, I would have the playing field level.

Hawthorne didn't respond at first, but his lips pulled into a tight smile, and I succeeded in driving his hard, contemptuous gaze from myself. He instead looked down at his drink, swirling it in the glass as his jaw clenched and unclenched reflexively.

"Good stuff, isn't it? Little rich for my blood, but if we're going to eat the swine at the top, then let's at least start with their liquor cabinets." I chuckled, trying to lighten the tension.

"No, it isn't alchemical." He lifted his eyes from the drink and dug them into me like claws, having all the warmth of the Diamondback and none of the charm.

"Most counts place the Enduring as numbering less than twenty," I said, tugging at the thread. "Most of them are alchemical, and you're telling me that you're...?" I downed another gulp of my drink, this time to keep the fear and curiosity out of my voice.

"Cursed, Mr. Wozynski. You can say it," Hawthorne spoke from behind a bitter smile.

"I ain't lived this long without a nice, thick skin, and 'The Enduring' is just a word that some fancy feller like you came up with. I'm over a hundred and seventy-six years old." There was a quick wisp of his tongue over his lips, gathering what bourbon dared to linger there before he did me the mercy of lowering his gaze to the glass in his hand.

"Not bad," he tacked on at the end like a bit of inedible garnish for a steak.

There are those who theorize that our fear of the Shadow People is born of an ingrained instinctual aversion that our ancestors developed back when we were all still dwelling in caves. That a solid millennium or more of cruelty, abuse, and predation have instilled within us a call to either flee the room or destroy anything that pushes too forcefully at what our world should be. This reaction stands as the justification for why the Shadow People spent so long hiding from humanity before everything came out in the open.

What then does that say about men and women, who like me, feel not the compulsion to run away but to run towards? The gleeful abnormal swimmers of dark waters who, when the sun becomes but a silver dollar on the surface, choose to push deeper into the unknown. I should have been afraid, or at the very least disgusted at the implications of the man across from me, but instead I felt only the old thirst for answers.

"That's a long time for a Word to last," I began, picking at the facts he gave me, moving them around in my mind. "Someone must have hated you a great deal, but you look as if you're doing pretty good for yourself. Must feel pretty good to turn a punishment into a profit," I told him around the edge of my glass as I snagged another drink.

"If you're not going to learn your lesson then you might as well get paid for it, right? Too much faith in humanity, or at least in you, is that it?" It was impossible to keep the fact that I was beginning to see the puzzle pieces come together from my tone. A predisposition towards honesty in the face of those with bloody boot heels can be its own special brand of curse.

Hawthorne's eyes narrowed sharply, and what had previously only been mild disgust and contempt was now transformed into a spike of anger that I long ago learned to recognize on the face of those quick to violence. His lip threatened to curl into a snarl like that of a dog who had just received a good hard yank on his tail. I had touched a nerve, and everything in Hawthorne's brawny composition seemed to cry out for him to strike the verbal blade I had slid into his ribs from my mouth with his fist. When you're on the losing end of the Truth, there is always the option of a good hard smack in the mouth. Sadly, this has not been codified into collegiate debate rules.

I have high hopes for the next presidential debate, however.

"I facilitate the needs of powerful men, Mr. Wozynski," Hawthorne answered dryly. "That is what I have always done, and I imagine that I will continue to do this until the sun itself burns out." His head cocked to the side. "A lesson? Well, the lesson that I learned, Mr. Wozynski, is that the world keeps right on rollin'. It keeps right on rollin', and it is always paved with blood." As he spoke, Hawthorne's composure settled a little. I might have been able to prod him, but I didn't think I could break him. I didn't know if I wanted to.

I was rather fond of having all my teeth.

"Someone has to do all that killing in the name of progress, right? Bet you thought you were a regular hero," I had not yet realized the mistake of my earlier assumption.

I was not sharing a car with a particularly pure species of The Goon.

"Almost correct, Mr. Wozynski. Yes, someone has to kill in the name of progress. Someone has to do the cruel and awful things that men like you might fancy themselves worthy of speakin' on necessity," Hawthorne sat down what remained of his drink and continued.

"You're a learned man, you've read what this world was like before Mr. Altenhofen's medicines and treatment. Now you try to imagine a people who do not treat the chaos gene like the affliction it is, you imagine instead those folks embracin' it. Weaving it into everything. Imagine the fight they might put up..." The weight of more than a century of life gathered behind Hawthorne's words as he spoke to me, and he'd begun to lean forward in his seat.

"Good God, man. What did you do?" Good bourbon or not, my hand shook as I asked.

"I provide the method to which those with means have always shaped the world, Mr. Wozynski, and it has cost me dearly, I can assure you of that. The regret that it was supposed to inspire though? No. Men like me do not have time for regrets; we push on, we do the job," Hawthorne replied, his voice devoid of emotion. I did not blame him. Devil or not.

I was sharing a car with a bad memory, maybe the worst of memories, given flesh and an off-the-rack suit. A relic of blood, gun smoke, diseased blankets, and shame that clung to the fabric of America like a dirty stain.

"A dog that always returns with the stick is no less a dog than the ones that chase the mail truck. Besides, if you're hoping to intimidate me, then you'll have to do more than vaguely confess to being a rancid-souled bastard," I retorted, my words having grown thorns on my tongue. "I've the advantage of being wanted, and you, my sour-faced traveling companion, are still just the help." The last bit required all the mustered bravado that I had in me, and I quickly polished off the last of my drink.

Just to be something of a prick, I shook my empty glass in front of Hawthorne. Even though I was confident that he could break every bone in my aging body, I even managed a wink.

There was a little nod of Hawthorne's head as if to acknowledge my point. He took the glass from my hand, but his lips had settled into a contemptuous sneer. Outside, the landscape had gone bitter and increasingly rural; what greenery there was began to appear less and less. We were approaching a land without water or kindness—an interesting choice for such a rich bastard to make his home.

But I didn't have time to think about it with Hawthorne there across from me.

Looking back, that was probably intentional.

"Don't get your whisker biscuits in a bunch, Mr. Wozynski. These days, mostly my job is seein' that Mr. Altenhofen's indulgences don't get the better of him," Hawthorne gave a little snort of the air like a horse that disapproved of the bridle.

He must have seen what he took for doubt in my eyes, for he explained further.

"That's the sort of 'help' I provide, ain't like the ol' days at all. No men gettin' set upon by every beast in the land like it was out for his blood, no fire rainin' down from the sky. None of that." Hawthorne shook his head with what almost looked like regret. "There's just men like you, Mr. Wozynski. Men who might seek to profit from the generosity shown to you in unkind ways." Hawthorne's grim face was made worse when the near snarl melted into a small smile that hid in the corners of his lips like spiders in an untended nook.

"If you're telling me not to write anything unfavorable about your boss, then I should probably warn you. For a journalist, I'm a terrible listener, especially when it comes to authority," I had no intention of breaking this news gently. "You might say it is something of a staple of my work." The drink helped with the nerves, but I had the sinking suspicion that Hawthorne was seeing through my own posturing.

He made me just as angry as I did him; neither of us cared for the other, and neither of us could have acted upon it even had we been inclined to do so. I was bound by the passing of years, and he by the exchange of the coin.

Self-preservation and greed, what a fine pair we made.

"I'm familiar with your work, Mr. Wozynski. You tilt at windmills, stir folks up about things that ain't worth rightly gettin' stirred up over it. Fancy yourself some sort of modern explorer, don'tcha?" Hawthorne's question was quick and sharp – he gave me no time to answer.

"I know your type, Mr. Wozynski. They used to ride the trains from out East, come to see the wild Indians and their shapeshifting Namebreakers or the men that fancied themselves quick with the iron. All jus' bullshitters lookin' to make their names off the deeds of other men." Hawthorne's eyes narrowed down to slits, and through those slits, I could see only the disgust that was made manifest in his words. "The only difference is you're the sort of prick who writes himself into the dime novel. That sound about right, Mr. Wozynski?" Hawthorne laced the dagger of his words with Truth, a poison that I was too intimately familiar with.

James Wozynski was undone.

Deep inside me, there was this boiling, a heat that I had not felt with such intensity since the days of my youth. It spread, aided, I believe, by the alcohol and the remnants of the sedatives I'd devoured before my flight. The heat was armed by long, uncomfortable travel and the fresh craving for a cigarette. This fire pushed against the poison that Hawthorne had filled me with, washed over the fear that came with being old, and gathered around my heart.

A little laugh escaped me.

Giving no warning and myself no time to take hold of my senses, I lunged forward, fingers darting into the front breast pocket of Hawthorne's suit. With the skill of an orphan pickpocket, I liberated his cigarettes and matches before he could react, then settled back into my seat.

Hawthorne stared in mild disbelief for a moment, then shook his head as if trying to shake off a punch.

"Mr. Wozynski, in case it wasn't clear earlier, Mr. Altenhofen does not allow smoking in any of his vehicles, even for guests," Hawthorne said, devoid of humor.

I retrieved a fresh cancer stick, placed it between my lips, and gestured for Hawthorne to shove it. Not with words, but with the striking of a match.

"Mr. Wozynski…"

I took a long drag, savoring it with eyes closed as if baptizing myself in the Bush family pool.

When I opened my eyes, Hawthorne regarded me with the warmth of a Gila Monster, and I suspected the same predatory appetites. Perhaps I was wrong. Maybe the leash Altenhofen held on him had snapped, and he'd unleash hell on me. But the fire raging inside me didn't care about bruises, blood, or the battery of my person. Hawthorne embodied the ugly face of a Killer America that had infiltrated the very essence of who we could and should be.

"Stop calling me that," I declared firmly.

Hawthorne cocked his head, momentarily puzzled.

"Excuse me?" he asked.

"My name is Jimmy."

Thirty Thousand Acres of Nothing

T he car ride to Bonneville continued, the driver spared the jabs, japes, and thinly veiled swipes exchanged between Hawthorne and me in the back. As we traveled, civilization's trappings fell away. Streetlights, sidewalks, and corner markets faded, replaced by an older, more natural, yet unforgiving landscape. The flats stretched for twelve miles and were nearly five miles wide, surrounded by a painfully remote area devoid of man's need to pave everything over. Few examples of life survived in this brutal slice of America, where tenacious creatures resisted the sun's heat and sulfur-heavy waters that stung the eyes.

Counterintuitively, the eye was drawn to the absences as surely as to any strange beast or colorful flower. The land lacked color variation, its soil composed mostly of sodium chloride, barren, hardpacked, and often forming a crusty exterior that snapped beneath one's step.

A land watered with the blood of men, yet still thirsting.

A few homes dotted the landscape, and the road grew treacherous. I felt every bump, every jolt, and every piece of hardtop succumbing to the flats' endless hunger. Even in the limousine with Hawthorne, I felt the loneliness of the land, where one might seek true isolation. Not even coyotes favored such a place, and those who entered unaided risked discovering its cruelty.

Despite all the strangeness I'd witnessed in my lifetime, I wasn't, by any conventional notion, a religious man. Divinity and I had long been in opposing corners, and I never acquired the taste for self-delusion common in those who embraced organized worship.

Yet, there was a sense about this land, a stillness beyond the windows of the limousine that lent itself to terrible thoughts and despair. I couldn't help but wonder if perhaps the salt flats of Bonneville were what it must have looked like when God, the same one we'd been taught about in Sunday school, got his shorts in a twist and decided that something or someone needed a good smiting. There's no other proper way to describe that much nothingness with only the mountains serving as a distant backdrop. A sprawling expanse of white death that forces the observer to turn inward, for there is as little for the mind to draw from as there is for the body. This was The Big Nothing.

Wrath of God country.

If one believed in intelligent design, then it was impossible to deny that some force had long ago hung a sign in a language old enough for the scorpions, snakes, and coyotes to understand it. Only men, with their dogged determination to claim, conquer, and exploit, would dare to travel into The Big Nothing. Only man would pretend that he could not read the sign that nature had carved into this place.

Stay the fuck out.

As I said, the only ones dumb enough to ignore it were men. The foolish and the rich were indistinguishable at a certain point, and looking out that window, I remembered Hawthorne's remark about failing to understand why the wealthy do as they do. I didn't know either. Why would anyone with the resources that Altenhofen had go to the trouble of building their fortress of solitude out here? He could have had a private island or some ridiculously phallic examples of architecture in any number of cities that catered to the whims and debaucheries of the wealthy and the powerful.

113

COYOTE WALLACE

He had instead chosen this place, a land of salt and emptiness. A land where even the small amount of water that could be found was toxic, and every element seemed filled with hostile intent when it came to matters of the living.

What had some thirty-two thousand years ago been a respectable body of water was now a playground of sorts to those who craved or found need for all that nothingness. Tourists chasing the beauty of the Milky Way against the hard-packed white clay, runners who wanted to test themselves against the elements, and of course my lost kin— the speed freaks. The salt flats wove a siren's song to those who were forever chasing the shot of pure adrenaline that can come only from going fast. Very fast.

Somehow, though, the flats had resisted the ambitions of man and our all-consuming desire to spread out over the landscape like locusts. The earth here was too hard, too inhospitable, the wind sharp, and the winter rains could send large portions of the whole area beneath the water of flash floods. I did not question how Altenhofen had managed to wrangle a little slice of what was supposed to be protected land for himself. It is common knowledge that politicians are bought cheaply in America; there's no mystery to it, they're just, by and large, immeasurably stupid.

How Altenhofen had managed to tame this otherworldly terrain was much more of a mystery.

Some indeterminable clue in the landscape beyond the tinted windows of our limousine must have told Hawthorne that we were getting near our destination, for he polished off the last of his glass of whiskey. He was still surly from our exchange, and judging from the scowling, downward pull at the edge of his lips, I had little doubt that my smoking had only further aggravated his foul mood. Good. This did, however, seem to leave him with little patience for any sort of politeness.

"Almost there.... Jimmy... I'm going to need your cellphone and any other recording devices you might have on your person," Hawthorne demanded, relishing the discomforting implication that came with it.

"You know, most of the time, if someone wants to take away my phone and any way to get them on the record, it means that they want to put a scare in me," I said, playing it cool as I could in the situation. "A demonstration that they control their environments rather than be controlled by that environment." I was complying as I said it.

You can get away with nearly any remark to a figure of authority so long as you are complying with their demand.

I pretended not to notice the notification on my phone's screen from Jenna. No doubt she had calculated the time of my arrival and was now wondering why I hadn't checked in to let her know that I hadn't been eaten by coyotes, sold into the world of underground old man fighting, or was drinking tequila with a beautiful woman half my age. All fair concerns. All of which would have to wait for now. Though I couldn't know how much of my life Altenhofen, and by extension his pet sitting across from me, had familiarized themselves with, I knew I didn't want him to know about Jenna. This instinctive protectiveness was unexpected in the forcefulness of its rising to the surface, but it lent me the strength to hand over the phone with what I would describe as my "easygoing fuck you" smile.

"Try not to take it personally, Jimmy. Mr. Altenhofen did choose you to do the accounting of this little visit, didn't he?" Hawthorne flashed a wolfish grin.

Hawthorne held up my phone between two fingers. "Naw, this is just to keep you and anyone else from getting too caught up in unimportant details. Distractions, Jimmy. Can't have that."

COYOTE WALLACE

There was a gradual drop in the vehicle's momentum; we were slowing down, but I couldn't see ahead of us. The barrier that separated us from the driver and kept our conversations private also blocked out any notion of what might lie ahead.

Having already decided that I cared little for the man, I was ill-inclined to mind the snappiness of tone that I had taken. "This rule goes for everyone or just the sort of people that you don't like?"

"The rest of the guests aren't the sort of people that need phones; besides, you'll get it back," Hawthorne sneered. "Your room will of course have a phone, and you can use that to contact your loved ones or employer."

Hawthorne tucked my phone away, and with it, my lifeline to the outside world was severed.

I was now, at least in part, at the mercy of those whose wealth rendered them immune to little things like the law and basic decency. An often-overlooked bit of fine print in the social contract is that, like any contract, it can be bought out if one's pockets are deep enough. Everything is negotiable in America; everything can be bought.

That is, as I understand it, the purpose of anonymous campaign donations.

There was the faint sensation of transitioning onto an incline, and outside the windows of the vehicle, I saw at last what must have been some sort of exterior wall. At first glance, it appeared to be made of rough black volcanic stone; the stones had been fashioned in a strange mockery of a brick. They were shot through with threads of gold, silver, and opalescent purple that twisted into countless unfathomable patterns. Objectively, it was beautiful, but somewhere deep inside, I could not shake this creeping sense of dread. Passing through the gate revealed that the beauty was only superficial. The lovely stones were only an exterior shell, and when observed perfectly from the middle, one could see the layers of steel and concrete that reinforced them.

Hawthorne snapped my attention back to him with a clearing of his throat.

"Do not attempt to make a fool of Mr. Altenhofen," he said, as whatever annoyance or perceived stings from my earlier barbs drained from Hawthorne's eyes like water leaving a tub. "I'll step on you like a strikin' snake if you try.

We finally came to a stop.

We had arrived.

"Wouldn't want that, would we?" I said, still too distracted by my new surroundings to have paid much mind to Hawthorne

I was glad to be free of the car and out into the dry but clean air. I had been ferried around too much as of late, and my nerves were jangled and raw as a result. Coming out of the limousine, I had expected to once more take stock of the hard-packed stretch of forgotten American Oblivion that were the Salt Flats; instead, I got something else entirely.

Altenhofen had, through unknowable means and incalculable fortune, managed to erect what I could only describe as a mad modernist fortress. It was perched atop a raised artificial mound of transplanted earth, encircled by high walls seen from afar. The courtyard and front lawn flaunted audacious greenery; an oddity given the barren surroundings. The soil here supported nothing, leaving me to guess the intricate methods Altenhofen must have employed. Topsoil airlifted, placed with meticulous care, nurtured against the harsh elements—a necessary labor for anything as fragile as greenery to thrive in this desolate realm.

As I took in the scene, I started to grasp the essence of Altenhofen. There were few reflections of a man's soul like his dwelling, and it dawned on me that I faced a man who would go to extraordinary lengths to feel the earth beneath his feet as he greeted the morning sun. This was the same man who controlled the very company manufacturing tools to "manage" the chaos gene.

Figures.

The structure itself, slate gray and towering three stories high, spread its expansive wings on either side. Front walls crafted from polarized glass, the rest of the architecture exuding the sharp angles of modernity. Yet, it wasn't the home that struck me most (though later I'd liken it to the deflective plating on armored vehicles), nor was it the greenery. It was the sheer scale of the "compound" nestled within those walls. Off to one side, nearest the far-right wall, stood a series of bungalow-like domiciles, their hyper-modernist design mirroring the main residence. A manufactured comfort pervaded the place, not born of familiarity but of cold, hard cash.

I could sense it, just standing there moments out of the car, the sickening arrogance of it all washing over me. This place was clearly a favorite, but it wasn't the only one. You don't get the audacity to carve your own paradise out of the desert without first leaving a few less intrusive marks upon the world

"Mr. Pringle, if you would be so kind as to take Jimmy's bag and show him where he'll be staying, I'm sure he would appreciate getting some rest after his trip," Hawthorne said, nodding to the somewhat pudgy driver who had exited the vehicle and was now coming around to the trunk. The hot sun did not agree with him, and I watched as he dabbed his face repeatedly with a handkerchief fetched from some indeterminate place on his person.

"The man himself isn't going to give me a welcome?" I asked Hawthorne, partly to keep busting his balls and partly because I was genuinely surprised by Altenhofen's absence.

One of the immutable truths of the wealthy is that with the accumulation of monetary means also comes the slow gathering of vanity. For many in the cutthroat game of capitalism and the chrome-plated, fuel-injected demolition derby that was American business, success meant very little if there was no one to appreciate it. I had pegged Altenhofen to be no different—his self-serving monument to his own hubris suggested as much—yet he had not come to see my reaction. Given the considerable expense of bringing not only myself but whatever other guests Altenhofen had arranged for, I had suspected he would feel a compulsion to witness our expressions upon arrival and surrounded by his strange, enclosed paradise.

Maybe I was just unlikeable.

I was relieved to be rid of Hawthorne, and though I felt a bit silly having the portly Mr. Pringle carry my bag like some tourist valet, I was too elated to be free of all modes of transport to dwell on it. I followed behind at a leisurely, long-legged stroll, taking the time to appreciate the vaguely prison-like vibe of the architecture. It was well hidden beneath the veneer of modernity, but it was there—a domicile meant to keep the unwanted out, while reminding those within that leaving might not be so easy.

"Dinner at six sharp," Mr. Pringle announced, his nose tilted slightly upward as he walked ahead of me.

Like Hawthorne, his disdain was palpable, but there was nothing menacing about Mr. Pringle. No, I had a feeling he was only a danger to himself, and even then, it would be a few more years before the lack of exercise, stress eating, and the typical American diet took him off the board.

There were no signs of any of Mr. Altenhofen's other guests. Only a few tangled notes of guitar, muted and dimmed by the walls of the neighboring structures, hinted that I was not alone. The tune was bluesy but infused with spiderwebs of Spanish guitar and a rock musician's sense of time. Too slow for cruising down the highway with the wind in your hair and your worries at your back—no, this was music for drinking cold beer on a hot beach while fleeing the wreckage of a bad relationship. Music for sunsets and forgetting.

"Who else is here?" I managed to ask before Pringle could fish the key from his pocket.

"You mean aside from the staff?" Pringle pretended to ponder the request. "Well, it is not my business to know who they are. I only know the names I am to address them by, just as I do you, Mr. Wozyn–"

"Wonderful," I cut him off.

"What?" Pringle's correction completely derailed him, and he stood there with the key to the door of my bungalow pinched between two thick fingers, wearing an expression that suggested some critical misfire in his brain.

"When I'm on the clock, it's Wonderful; Jimmy if that's easier. So, what are their names?"

Confronted with the choice between using the name "Mr. Wonderful" or Jimmy, Pringle seemed to gain a new level of dislike for my presence. The realization that he could only go with the absurd or the informal stuck in his craw. Even though I was in a strange place, generally disliked by most of my host's help, and still feeling the warm wooziness of the high-grade bourbon from my ride with Hawthorne, I was beginning to fire on all cylinders. I was not at peak performance yet; I needed more fuel and a clearer line of sight on the sort of man Altenhofen was, but I was getting there.

"Well, there's Mr. Allerton next door and Ms. Tekakwitha on the far end, though I couldn't tell you more than that. You'll just have to meet them on your own time," Pringle said with the sort of smug smile that one would expect from a house cat whose constant whining had finally paid off with a can of tuna.

After acquiring my key and watching as Pringle made his way back to the main house, jostling in his cheap, For-The-Help suit the entire time, I stepped inside.

The air of Bonneville's Salt Flats is filled with the sort of dry heat that strips a man of all his precious fluids and leaves him as brittle as old, dry rotted wood. The moment I opened the door, I was hit by a wall of cool air. This was a shock to the senses and made me hurry to close the door behind me as I had not realized how deeply I wanted the relief of a good old all-American freon. Only after the door had closed and I was free for the first time from the prying eyes of Altenhofen's people or the public could I breathe. I needed a piss, some sort of food, and while it hurt my pride to admit—a long and undisturbed nap.

Altenhofen had spared no expense when it came to the comfort of his guests. The bungalow was much finer than most of the rooms The Mystic Standard had ever put me up in, even in the golden days when I didn't have a reputation for their destruction. Though only a guest home to Mr. Altenhofen, the bungalow was larger than the apartments of most of my city-dwelling friends and any home I had ever owned until very late in my career. The floors were covered with wooden tiling, their multitude of colors born of the natural shades of the timber from whence the tiles were fashioned, forming a strange and intricate design whose meaning I did not recognize. Maple came together with ash and kempas, while walnut and Brazilian cherry seemingly swirled together to make up the lines.

Despite the modernity of the architecture, my bungalow was remarkably homey and strangely comfortable. The furnishings were those you might have expected to find in the home of some late '60s playboy, including large comfortable chairs, a fireplace, wooden tables, and shelves filled to the brim with books. The walls were heavy with paintings and pictures, almost all celebrating some strange part of Americana and its relationship with the Shadow People. Dead rail workers posed with picks in hand over the defeated corpse of the American West in one, William Jefferson Clinton shaking hands with the late Billaboo Hornswoggle at the 1998 Fair Folk Summit for Wonder in another, and both were outshined by a photo of Hendrix passing a jug of wine to a satyr who probably had some perfectly American name like Marty, John, or Phil. These were the sort of photographs that many young photographers (and no few of the older ones) would have gladly committed open murder in front of their own families for.

The whole place felt like my Writer's Cave back home, expanded and taken to its most absurd and flagrantly excessive levels.

There was a faux wood-framed television, demurely hidden against the wall, but it could not hope to compete with the real prize. There was a record player with a wide selection of old vinyl enticing enough to derail any thoughts I had of further exploration until I was free to browse through them, my fingertips gliding over the paper jackets that had at first been replaced by hard plastic and then finally by nothingness as the digital age came rolling through.

Hawthorne had not lied, though. There was a phone, and I made a mental note to return to it as I finally left the records behind and ventured into the bedroom. I had not forgotten about Jenna or the fact that she would still be waiting on my call, but curiosity had always been both a saving grace and a terrible curse—especially when it came to relationships.

The circular bed hinted at comfort with its promise of a firm mattress, soft sheets, and pillows ready to transport a man to dreamland the moment his head hit the pillow. But, true to Altenhofen's style, there was a surprise waiting for me.

Drugs. A veritable treasure trove of drugs.

As Jimmy Wonderful, I didn't measure substances in grams or ounces; no, I assessed them in something much more personal—TIME. I didn't see mere quantities on the bed—no grams, ounces, or dollar amounts—instead, I saw how long those substances could keep me in my own twisted reality.

Like any true fiend, I knew the amount mattered far less than how long it would last. A seasoned fiend like me could consume astronomical amounts of foreign substances in pursuit of escapism or inspiration. The medical community was left scratching their heads, and any visit to a rehab facility would yield tales of fiends defying both science and sanity, surviving what should have been a lethal dose of "good time."

There was a baggie reminiscent of the one Jenna kept her confectioners' sugar in, alongside a solid brick of what I presumed to be the finest marijuana the West Coast had to offer. Two bottles of pills stood guard in front of the coke, and there, on the pillow, sat a small vial filled with an entirely different kind of key to unlock human consciousness.

Faerie Dust.

The other drugs? Legal debates, histories, failures under prohibition. Faerie Dust, though? It danced on the edge of experience, a potent hallucinogen swirling since the early 1600s (unofficially, of course), its appearance akin to red sand, its effects infamous for their mind-melting intensity, surpassing most conventional methods of excess. Yet, its true reputation? Born from the bones of actual Faeries, a process utterly demeaning to the fallen beings when undertaken by outsiders.

The last time I encountered the stuff was nearly thirty years ago, back when I was a young man earning my stripes for The Standard. It's entirely possible, even probable, that Jimmy Wonderful's creation, my creation, my very success, owed something to that initial wild experience that opened my eyes. It was a glimpse into the true face of our country, a revelation of the crisis of soul as we trampled all that was Weird, Strange, and Free beneath our boots.

What revelations awaited me this time?

I snatched the vial from its resting place on the pillow, feeling that familiar surge as if reaching a critical juncture in my journey. Options lay before me: turn around, find Hawthorne or Pringle, demand they take me back, hop on my airplane, and return home. They might be put out, maybe even angry, but it'd keep me on the straight and narrow. Alternatively, I could sidestep these blatant attempts to lower my guard, luring me into a more favorable view of

Altenhofen and his agenda. But James Wozynski hadn't penned a hit in ages, and when faced with creating something loved versus something forgettable, any writer worth their salt chooses love. Consequences be damned.

"You pay for the ticket, you take the ride," a wiser man once said. If you didn't like it, there were always openings for hotel reviewers, medical equipment hucksters, or maybe a cozy spot writing for the AARP magazine. All akin to dental work and a diet of tapioca pudding.

I headed for the phone to call Jenna. She'd be worried sick by now, her concern brewing into righteous anger if I didn't act fast.

Shoving the vial into my pocket, I knew I'd see it again soon. You can outrun a bad marriage, a bad job, even your own dark past, but you can never escape who you truly are, deep down.

Besides, the party was just getting started.

COYOTE WALLACE

Introductions are in order...

"Why aren't you on your phone?" Jenna's first question hit me like a freight train.

Her inquiry followed my greeting, and the discontent in her tone was palpable. In my mind's eye, I pictured her standing in the kitchen or her studio, phone pressed against her ear, her entire world momentarily paused. Damn caller ID, always ratting me out. I felt Jenna's intuition sense the unraveling of my hard-earned redemption, leaving me dangling over a vast, dark chasm, with only her voice on the other end to tether me to reality.

Later, I'd curse that little voice urging me to hang up and get back to business.

"I dropped the damned thing coming out of the plane. Broken. Pieces all over the tarmac. I'll have to get another one." It was the first substantial lie of the trip, and though I should have felt worse for telling it, justifying my questionable behavior had become second nature.

I firmly believe women are the superior sex, harboring an innate mysticism and cosmic attunement that us men, with our dangling bits and penchant for football brawls, can never hope to match. A young man might scoff at this notion, but it's a truth he'll inevitably come to realize either after his 30th birthday or his first divorce. Armed with this wisdom, he might navigate the world more wisely—or descend into the dark abyss of the internet to find solace among his fellow lost souls. It's always a coin toss.

Jenna knew I was up to something, but I wasn't giving her any loose threads to tug on. Not yet.

"Uh-huh, is that so? Is the place at least nice?" Jenna's question forced me to take another look around the bungalow. My addled brain, still reeling from the Xanax and high-octane bourbon I'd shared with Hawthorne, scrambled for a description to ease her worries and throw her off my trail.

"You should see the floor, I can't tell if I'm on the dime of a pompous businessman or Turkish crime boss..." and for the finishing touch, a touch of dismay, "...and the bed is round. Who the fuck has round beds that isn't a fourteen-year-old girl? My ankles will hang off the edge." I grumbled.

This was another lie. I'd seen the cocaine, and I was still holding the vial of Faerie Dust in my hand, rubbing it with my thumb like it was some sort of good luck charm. There would be no sleep, none taken willingly at least, and when sleep did catch me—running me down like a cheetah chasing down some particularly nimble game—it would take me down in a strange and unconventional place, never a proper bed. I was a veteran of many mornings waking up in the bathtubs of other people's hotel rooms with no memory of how I got there and this burning fire in my brain to be quenched with an expulsion of thoughts onto the page.

"What about Altenhofen?" Jenna asked, trying to goad my better spirits into making an appearance, "Eating babies and washing himself in the tears of the poor?" There it was, the benefit of the doubt, delivered with a wry smile and a faint cocking of Jenna's head to the side.

I didn't need to be home to see it, but I already wished I was.

The stab of guilt and pain that came with the mental image of my wife believing in my better qualities was so powerful that I nearly popped the cap on the vial and lined the whole thing out right there. There was still just enough of James Wozynski inside of me to feel awful about the fact that I fully planned on tackling the assignment with every weapon at my disposal.

For some the process is like coaxing a beautiful lover into bed, others it is like capturing lightning in a bottle, but for me, it has always been a down and dirty street fight. I would have my story, I would break all rules, laws, and conventions. I would use every underhanded means at my disposal, just to bring the beast down and wrap myself in its pelt. The question was how many scars would I collect along the way, and how many more could I endure? Most importantly, could Jenna withstand them?

"Haven't met him yet, but that sounds about right," I quipped, pivoting and deflecting like a seasoned pro. "You should see the goons he has working for him. How are things there?" I led Jenna away from further questioning my condition like the degenerate Judas goat I was.

"I just got the cover art for 'Roses, Wine, and Anarchy,'" she shifted the conversation, a more merciful soul than I ever deserved. "If someone hadn't broken his phone, I could send it to him." There was no scolding or doubt now; she believed me about the demise of my cell phone.

Victory, as it turned out, could indeed taste like bitter ashes on the tongue.

"Khali knows his shit, what can I say? When I get back, you can throw me a savage beating with the album cover. Make me regret ever trifling with the likes of you," the warmth and hint of laughter came easily to me. Jenna was my heart, and I would have gladly died to keep her safe or happy. The problem, of course, was that while my heart belonged to her, my soul had long ago been sold to the story.

"Don't hold your breath. Hey, I'm getting another call. Call me back, okay?"

I suddenly did not want the conversation to end. I sensed, somehow, that once it had, I would resume my free fall. The things I would need to do to fly and avoid a messy beating at the hands of gravity would border on unspeakable, and I no longer was sure of the amount of unspeakable left within me. There was the mad desire to confess that I was already slipping, already descending into the depths of myself where I kept what a more poetic man might have called "the fire." At such depths where Jimmy Wonderful operated, the very rules would become malleable, and moral integrity would take a back seat to the integrity of the pen. Only after I surfaced from those depths would I be able to ascertain the damage done to myself, those I love, and the world around me.

But I would have my goddamn story.

"Love you, missing you already," I told Jenna, and there was no lie there. Some truths were too precious for fiends, degenerates, and the willfully mad to touch.

There was a little smoky laugh on the other end of the phone, and if it were in my power to do so, I would have reached through the line to kiss her then and there.

"Love you, too. Call me back, ok?"

I made my promises that I would and hung up. For a moment, all I could do was stand there, holding the vial in one hand and the now lifeless phone in the other.

Jenna was the best part of my life, and it was at moments like this that I felt afflicted by a curse of my own making. One that would surely consume everything I touched from the inside like a bad case of rot. Silently, I made the old junkie's promise that this would be the last time, that no matter what happened, no matter the fallout or what else was to come; Jimmy Wonderful would die in this godforsaken salt flat. He would go out in a final blaze of glory, but that blaze of glory, no matter how intense, would not diminish nor dissuade the fact that he was done. I would throw my laptop into the lake, break every pen in the house beneath my boot heel, and even take a hammer to the old 1916 Olivetti that I kept in the cave until it was nothing more than the broken bits of a bad cliché.

The deal was struck, and though I was exhausted, and the weight of age made the temptation to simply crawl into bed more intoxicating than any lover, I knew that I was not done. That I could not be. All the comfort was meant for indulgence, relaxation, and fawning—or so I suspected. One of the unsung blessings of graduating from abject poverty to a starving writer in my youth was a fine distrust of anything that the general public might have considered "nice" or "fine."

It was my experience that if anything looked too good to be true, it usually was. As flattering as the notion might have been, I doubted that Altenhofen truly gave a damn about my work. His extravagant hospitality felt like a ploy, a distraction meant to disarm and delay. By dinner, Altenhofen would have the upper hand, and we'd all be operating on his time. Advantages were needed, and I didn't have the luxury to dwell on my flagging energy or marital concerns.

My suspicions only deepened as I scoured the kitchen. The small refrigerator was stocked with a variety of delicious yet unhealthy choices that I would have purchased myself, had I been sent to the market. This could be written off as coincidence, but the two cases of Tecate cerveza were too on-the-nose to ignore. My suspicion morphed into eerie unease, bordering on violation. I didn't even bother to close the fridge before I started opening the cabinets, finding more confirmation in the form of greasy potato chips, barbecue-flavored pork rinds, and three bottles of Macallan 18-year-old double cask Scotch.

Was Altenhofen expecting a passive recovery from jet lag? Not today, Mr. Swine. Not today...

I snatched a bottle and a glass from the cupboard, skipping the ice, and poured hastily. My hand trembled not just with eagerness to defy expectations but with the distinct terror of being known by someone I couldn't know back. It felt like I was trapped in a roach motel, designed to ensnare, and the urge to break free spread like wildfire through my tired mind. Drastic action was called for.

The first glass disappeared far too quickly, liquid spilling messily down my chin. The second was smoother, calming my nerves in the decadent embrace of the booze. I still clutched that damn vial, briefly considering emptying it onto the countertop and indulging right then and there.

But I knew better. I'd be a wreck by dinner, likely doing something insane like setting the place ablaze or showing up completely naked, ranting about dragons. No, that was the last resort, a weapon of mass distortion for when reality became too goddamn real and weird at once. Using it now would be a mistake, one I had no intention of making. I had the booze for the jitters, but I needed something to give me the audacity to believe I wasn't in over my head.

The intellectuals among us might cite income inequality, healthcare disparities, or home ownership as examples of class disparity in America. But for me, nothing illustrated the chasm between the rich and the poor quite like cocaine.

After crossing a certain threshold in the golden sands of wealth, you left behind the small corner baggies that had been stepped on countless times. No more subjecting yourself to the side effects of excess, like having to take an unsexy dump in a dodgy bathroom due to an overdose of baby laxatives. Meetings with strange and sometimes shady contacts, oscillating between insisting you stick around to prove you're not on the man's dime or hurrying you out the door, their minds ablaze with paranoid delusions of a narcotics division raid, became rare.

COYOTE WALLACE

Instead, they were replaced by pool boys and high-class dope dealers, skillfully hidden among the high-society art scene. I knew several musicians, a few writers, and at least one painter who had weathered monetary droughts that way, and the story was always the same for those at the top.

Wealth meant no sacrifice. All the glory, none of the scars.

Not that I could judge anyone at that moment. Lofty morals must be set aside when one thumbs his nose at exhaustion, age, and good sense. Altenhofen's stuff was top-notch, and though later I would pay the price in self-loathing, in the immediate aftermath of drug consumption, I felt only a clean streamlining of thought. There was a burst of confidence that obliterated both the effects of alcohol and any lingering shame James Wozynski might have had at letting go. The aging wordsmith was gone, replaced by the maniacal chaser of Truth, known on the page (the only place it really counted) as Jimmy Wonderful.

I strode out into the sun, leaving my suitcase by the door, a discarded relic of a life I could no longer afford to dwell upon. My attention was now fully consumed by the mystery of Altenhofen's plans and the identities of the other guests. Chosen for my supposed fondness in Altenhofen's eyes and my potential to silence his leftist critics with a glowing endorsement, I pondered the purposes of the others. Were they selected based on merit, preference, or utility? Perhaps a blend of all three?

I slipped the vial of Faerie Dust into my pocket, standing in the doorway of my bungalow, gazing out at the unnaturally green island that Altenhofen had sculpted behind the walls. The grass was so vibrant it nearly stung the eyes, the architecture a triumph in its extravagance, yet it all felt displaced, unnatural. The harsh sun and arid air were the only reminders of this within Altenhofen's opulent compound.

Running my fingers over the vial in my pocket brought a strange comfort, though I knew now was not the time to dip my pen into that inkwell. No one wanted to succumb to a heart attack while their mind collapsed under the weight of universal knowledge or be driven mad by invisible tormentors under the scorching desert sun.

Thankfully, there was no sign of Altenhofen's "staff" in sight. I assumed Hawthorne and Pringle had retreated to the main structure, leaving me feeling like a lost traveler in a foreign land. Yet, the sound of music persisted, the lazy drift of guitar notes defying the constraints of man-made walls. Like a hound on the scent of a hidden creature, I followed the melody until I stood before the door of my neighboring bungalow.

There are only two ways to knock upon a door when you're high on cocaine, and both come with a small dose of paranoia. First, there's the speedy, high-powered bang of the unfettered optimist. The worry, of course, is that such exuberance could be mistaken for the demand of an authoritarian - a mix-up that could prove unfortunate in certain company. The other, which I opted for, was the experimental soft rapping of knuckles against an overly pricey wooden frame. There was no mistaking it for authority because there was no genuine demand behind it. That demand is a necessary ingredient for all authoritarian figures, be they hired help or skull-cracking police. While there existed the worry that the occupant would not hear, a seasoned degenerate with a history of self-delusion was nearly impossible to sway. Such a degenerate could happily parlay that into salve for his own bruised ego as he gave in to the urge to keep moving and walked away.

COYOTE WALLACE

The playing was so sweet and rich to the ear that I had half expected it to stop when I knocked. There was no cessation, though, and when the door came open, I registered no small degree of surprise at the sudden appearance of the figure waiting on the other side. I like to play it cool, but sometimes life throws you a pitch that you're ill-equipped to hit, and you end up just swinging at the air.

That is to say, the woman who answered the door was beautiful to a degree that threw me completely off my game. She might have been 5'4" or 5'5" with an obliviousness to her own beauty that only made her dark hair and dark eyes even more captivating. Her skin was the russet brown of the dusty roads of rural misspent youth, and despite the finery of Altenhofen's habitat-like homes that he'd had prepared for us, she dressed as if she were one of the young street musicians that Jenna sometimes offered her patronage to. The jeans were ragged and torn in places, exposing tantalizing swaths of dark terracotta-hued flesh, and the sleeveless black T-shirt she wore left both arms exposed. The tattoos on the skin along her arms were as intricate and lovingly crafted as they were narrations of the trickster gods of old.

I recognized the coyote, raven, and rabbit, but in doing so, I stared too long in silence and made the moment awkward.

"Can I help you?" This mysterious woman with the dark hair and eyes of a midday fantasy asked me

Neither cocaine nor strong alcohol lends a man charm. It, in fact, does the opposite, and an overabundance of both or either can spell disaster for the unwary and unseasoned. What it does provide is the confidence and poor judgment needed to utterly and completely ignore one's own lack of charm, malfunctioning sexual magnetism, or physical failings. A good rail of Bolivian marching powder can transform a man from a self-doubting emotional wreck to the second coming of James Dean, and I knew more than one writer (and several editors) who found the substance to be an essential anesthetic for the messy surgery of the drafting process.

Despite the awkward stumble, I quickly recovered.

"No one has been able to yet," I threw in a wink. "I thought I might take the chance, though, and see who the other poor fools Mr. Altenhofen has wrangled for this little rodeo are."

There was a moment when the only response I had to go on was the arching of a dark eyebrow and an expression that could best be described as the summary judgment of all bullshitting men. I could only assume that this was the Ms. Tekakwitha that Pringle had spoken of, and it was clear then that she had more experience dealing with seasoned bullshitters and the silver-tongued than her years belied. She leaned to the left just a little as if trying to peer around me and make sure that there was no trick, that Hawthorne and the rest of Altenhofen's creepy gestapo were nowhere to be seen, and only when satisfied did she speak.

"You're that *wasicu* writer, aren't you?" The question was followed by a quick bounce of her eyes up and down my frame before she muttered something under her breath that I could not hear and turned to go back inside.

I followed the unspoken invitation. Only after I had closed the door behind me did I realize just how different Ms. Tekakwitha's lodgings were from those assigned to myself. Here, there were no monuments to the American Dream, no photographs of past accomplishments or supposed triumphs over what was once the supernatural, now simply a different flavor of ordinary.

The walls of this bungalow were adorned with handcrafted, spiritually functional works of art that belonged to the original owners of this land. The general shape of the dwelling was the same as my own, but just different enough to confirm that Altenhofen had, in fact, tailor-made each of the guest houses to placate us; using our own tastes for the nails and desires for the wooden frame.

The only thing that remained the same was the bookshelf. But in Ms. Tekakwitha's case, that bookshelf was filled with an entirely unique collection, nothing like the one provided for me. Upon the spines of this tailored collection were names like Momaday, Campbell-Hale, and Harjo. There was a strange faux intimacy to the room, and I wondered if she had felt the same sense of violated privacy upon her arrival that I had.

"That's what they tell me anyway. Jimmy seems like less of a mouthful though." The words came quick and easy, fueled by the high-end cocaine coursing through my bloodstream. "What about you? Feel like giving your name and why you're here to a near-total stranger you just met?" I lingered by the door as I asked, seemingly ready to make my escape at any moment.

There is nothing more terrifying to the married man than a beautiful woman with dark hair and eyes. If she also possesses a good taste in music and a sly, knowing grin, then he may consider himself doubly terrified. Not war or the wild beasts that roam the jungles, nor the unknown terrors of the night, can instill trepidation, worry, and unease so effortlessly. He is forced to face the fact that his inner traitor is never more than a warm breath's distance from the surface, often far closer than he would have liked to believe. There was a certain earthy magnetism to this woman in her torn denim and ink-marked brown skin that pulled the inner compass of personal dignity in strange directions. The line between old fool and philandering son of a bitch was easily blurred with the clashing of such energy against my own inner weakness.

"Tek," she answered, with a little laugh and a shake of her head as she drifted towards the kitchen while the record player kept on with its sad, melting Spanish guitar. "That's as close as you're getting to a name." The way she said it left little question as to whether the matter was up for debate.

I caught a brief glimpse of the interior of the refrigerator that had been provided for her, customized to her taste as mine had no doubt been to me. Green vegetables, bright colorful fruits, and crystalline bottles of water were a far cry from the "you-don't-really-need-your-foot" fare in my own. She plucked a bottle of water from the bottom shelf, closed the door, and turned to reach for one of the glasses resting on the top shelves—the same ones I had filled with overpriced Scotch to even out.

Rather than deal with the small skip of my heart at the sight of the small of her back, I drifted instead towards the music.

Much safer waters.

"Pleasure's all mine just the same." Names were tricky things, and I did not hold this against her.

Much like the setup in my own temporary dwelling, the records were kept in neat crate-like cases extending out from either side of the record player itself. Each record was, of course, preserved in what I could only hazard to be their original jackets, and the whole affair summoned recollections of a youth that was almost non-existent in the modern era. The hunt for a good tune in a record store had been replaced by the instant gratification of digital media, and the exchange was not one that I was entirely happy with.

It was impossible not to feel the weight of years as I let my fingers glide across the cardboard with its old paths worn by the touch of countless others. Names like Tárrega, Segovia, and de Lucia dominated the collection, yet they were strangers to my eyes. Among them, I found a few familiar faces in the auditory crowd, unexpected nonetheless, like Jennings and Nelson and even an odd Ramone.

"You like Tárrega?" she asked dubiously enough that I turned away from the record collection at the sound of her voice.

She had poured the water into one of the glasses, and standing there with it in hand, she looked like a goddess of the desert stepped from legend. A woman born not of this time or for this time, and though there was no quantifiable difference in her in that moment and the one in which she had opened the door, no change that the glancing eye could find, there was a knowing in the darkness of her eyes.

"Not until today," I replied honestly. A lie would have sent me tumbling into the darkness of her eyes to never return.

Tek gave up a little laugh that almost but not quite broke through the facade of seductive strength and casual lack of given fucks. It is fortunate that Jenna did not know the dark joy that it brought to my heart to make such a young and beautiful woman laugh in such a manner. If she did, my fate would be messy and likely involve strangulation with an Ernie Ball bass string, which is much thicker and better suited for the job of removing an unfaithful writer's head from his neck than the thinner guitar string, for those who may be wondering or who may need to know for their own purposes.

She lifted the glass as if she were to bring it to her lips for a sip or a drink but paused midway through. Her head bent forward, and the dark ribbons of her hair dared to spill over like a black veil into the realm of her eyes. Somewhere deep inside me, down in the pits where my more instinctual elements lived and played, I felt a faint but perceptible pulling. A gathering that one might only hope to replicate if he were to stand beneath the very spot where a tornado was to touch down or where lightning would soon strike the earth.

The Word, sometimes called Magik (or magic), sometimes called Forced Totality Adjustment (if you were in handcuffs and facing a federal judge), was how, at least in theory, Namebreakers exerted their will upon the world. In the hands of a good soul, the lame could be made to walk, the hungry fed, and the blind to see. In the hands of the wicked, mere mortal men could be turned into paint with a whisper and mountains leveled with a shout.

Magic, like hummingbirds, has a way of stealing your breath away when it reminds you that it exists, no matter how rarely it is seen. The Truth never needs eyes to validate its existence, and Magic and the Truth had always been part of the same distant family. Sometimes for the better, and sometimes for the worse.

What began as a sound leaving Tek's lips became moonlight before it found the water. That light broke upon the surface of the liquid and before my eyes became something else entirely, yet its shimmering composition did not appear to change. Instead, it drifted like food coloring down to the bottom of the glass before it spread throughout. By the time Tek had straightened back up, the glass once more resembled nothing more than water, at least at first glance, but there was now the faintest of shimmers. The idea of water versus reality of what water was, only now the idea had been given precedence over the actual.

I did not hear the Word; indeed, as I did not have what the medical community dubbed an "active chaos gene," I could not. I heard sound but the distinctions needed for attempts at replication or imitation were beyond me. You may as well ask me to tell you what the rivers sound like in the last place undiscovered by man.

"You're out of your head, I can see it all over you. Try this," Tek said, the sly knowing creeping into her words, making the only option for refusal to run screaming out the door.

There are some in this world who would have thought better of drinking a glass of clearly altered water offered to them by a strange woman in the bungalow of a ludicrously rich potential madman. It was unsafe, foolish, and potentially a bad case of being taken in by a pretty face. No self-respecting man of any merit with his own safety or well-being in the forefront of his mind would have done so. None would have blamed them for their wise refusals.

None of them were Jimmy Wonderful chasing a story.

I took the offered glass and eyed it dubiously. My nerve threatened to give under the weight of that pesky tagalong to any wild time known as good sense. The memory that I am not the young hellraiser that I once had been swum to a surface laden with doubt and fear, a rising tide that even the cocaine had trouble holding down.

"What the hell is it?" I asked her while giving the glass a little swirl.

Despite the prevalence of the American Namebreaker in the media and the terrifying tales spun by the white middle-class male, the surreal sensation of holding any item of mystical or supernatural origin has never quite left me. My mind, electrified by the finest Colombian happy dust that money could buy, spun with all the possibilities contained within what was once a mere glass of water. To the naked eye, I held a liquified form of moonlight itself in a glass—something that any scientist would have vehemently declared impossible before sticking his own head in the oven and turning on the gas.

There was no response, only the intense gaze of Tek's dark eyes as the music transitioned into what I would later learn was Tárrega's "El Carnaval de Venecia", the Spanish guitar pouring into the air like molten lava. There was no escape now, no lifeline being thrown my way, and the melodic guitar evoked images of a summer storm raging over barren, towering mountains. Though it may sound crude, one of the most profound pieces of wisdom I'd ever received boiled down to this:

Sometimes you either shat or got off the goddamn pot.

With twice the ferocity I had for the alcohol, I gulped down the water. I wasn't parched, but I felt almost goaded into it, secretly hoping this was all part of some grand plan to remove me from the game. If I were to be shipped back to Chicago with flying monkeys tearing out of my asshole, at least I'd have a plausible excuse for my retreat—one that didn't require me to compromise. Retreat or demise were both more enticing outcomes than appearing "lesser" in Tek's eyes. A young man might have declined the dare, confident in the knowledge that there would be other dark-haired, dark-eyed beauties in his future. But I was an old fool, akin to the mythological coyote—I'd accept any challenge and laugh regardless of the outcome, my days numbered and my shame toothless.

Despite the shimmering luminescence of the water, its taste remained unchanged. Yet it felt colder, crisper than it had any natural right to be, having been recently plucked from the fridge. With a swipe of my hand across my lips like an unschooled, barn-raised heathen, I returned the glass. I felt no different, but now I pondered: if the lights suddenly went out, would I glow?

"You're a peculiar man," Tek remarked, her eyes once again assessing me. "You poison yourself, and even you don't know why. Do you have any idea what Altenhofen has in store?" There was no malice or displeasure in her voice; it was determined yet smooth and strong.

I let out a little laugh, but inwardly, her mention of poison put me on the defensive. I'd been through too many debates about opening my third eye, cutting out red meat, and the therapeutic benefits of yoga. Dismissing the crystal-waving fools of the world eventually backfires when you encounter the genuine article, and they can sense the toxins and red meat lurking in your colon.

Tek was the real deal.

"Fuel, not poison, sweet cheeks," I retorted, feeling the inner asshole emerge, no longer swayed by beauty or mystery.

As I wiped the sweat from my brow and brushed away a tiny droplet forming at my nose, Tek took the glass back.

It was only when I saw her smile that I became aware of the sweat's persistence, despite the chill in the air and the icy sensation blooming in my stomach. Surprise flashed across my eyes, but Tek spared me the indignity of collapsing in front of her. Instead, she set the glass aside on a nearby coffee table and caught me beneath my arms, guiding me back until I settled into a wooden and wicker chair that was deceptively comfortable.

A weakness spread through my legs, and my head spun like a runaway train. Despite the shock, my heart didn't race; instead, it felt as if it were slowing down. A disturbing thought in any circumstance, but downright terrifying in this one.

Slower.

Slower.

Slower still.

"What...?" I felt as if I were tumbling backward, my fingers desperately clawing at the chair to halt my descent.

"It's okay. It'll be over soon..." Though Tek's tone remained benign, my mind veered toward paranoid fantasies. How could it not?

Slower...

All stop.

"Huuuzaahfukaaaah!" is the sound a man drifting into his 50s made when he believed he'd just experienced a magical heart attack, followed by his first breath of clean, sweet air afterward.

I knew because that was the sound that I made as I tumbled out of the chair with a thud, and limply sprawled out on the floor as if I had no bones.

For a moment, I lay there, an unmoving and shivering lump, but slowly the cold passed, and with it, a great many things. The jitters of cocaine were gone, the faint nausea of booze vanished, and the ache in my joints disappeared. That first breath was sweet, carrying the faint hint of Tek's perfume that my cigarette-dampened nose had missed, along with the scent of some night-blooming plant reminiscent of sunset in the Southwest desert, and beneath it, the subtle notes of her sweat. I could taste my own breath, not nearly as pleasant as Tek's scent, but altogether I felt better than I had since I was a young man. A lifetime of red meat, cigarettes, high-test booze, and degenerate exploits seemed to have been scrubbed clean.

I didn't need to be told; I felt it.

Tek rolled me onto my back with the toe of her boot and peered down at me. Each of my muscles was relaxed, my mind drifting in warm, soupy peacefulness. I knew neither addictive craving nor unnatural burden. I was dead sober, but it was the good sober, the clean sober, the sober that existed before the demon got its claws into you and the monkey built a condo on your back.

"I was hoping you would tell me what he had planned," I managed to say with a smile, still drenched in sweat and in a state that would have certainly raised questions at Tek's feet, as she walked back to the kitchen, leaving me sprawled on the floor.

"*Waslolyesni…*" Tek muttered under her breath as she shook her head and began to walk back to the kitchen, leaving me where I was on the floor.

I sat up, pleasantly surprised, for I believe it was the first time in several years that I had done so without muttering a curse at God and my own failing body. I had no idea what "*waslolyesni*" meant, but on the off chance that it meant "degenerate old man on my floor," I didn't want to live up to that reputation, at least not under her gaze.

"Let's try who you are, not your name but what you're doing here," I said sharply, my words punctuated by a hiss of irritation. "I'm easy enough to figure out. I'm the scribe meant to record and chronicle the whole mad affair for Altenhofen's ego. What does that make you? For that matter, what is a Namebreaker doing here of all places?"

I posed the questions to Tek's back as she put the glass away. They were rapid but feeble, mewling things that surely would not penetrate Tek's defenses.

My clothing was beginning to soak through with sweat, but as I made my way to my feet, I could feel the effects of what Tek had done to me far more strongly than I had on the floor. I was thrown completely off my game and the only means that I had at my disposal for getting the ground back under my feet were questions.

Never make a statement when you still can ask a question.

"Have you ever heard of the American Lost Word Society?" Tek countered with a question of her own but at least it was an easy one.

"They're separatists that believe the chaos gene is a birthright and a fundamental building block of a swathe of North American cultures that has been steadily fucked over

145

by the Man since the founding of the country." I rattled off by rote memory alone, you don't swim in weird waters without learning the names of the fish.

"Jesus, what did you do to me?" I exclaimed, my words a crude oversimplification of the complex sensations coursing through my newly scrubbed clean senses. They were more of a shock than any drug could have induced.

Tek's features seemed to darken at my words, and for a moment, I feared that my statement had unintentionally ventured into inflammatory territory. She turned back to me, her dark hair shifting upon her head with the suddenness of the movement. She reminded me of a cat who had just discovered that some smug bastard was holding its tail. It was an expression not of surprise but of contemptuous discovery. There was a nerve there, poorly hidden in the talk of the American Lost Word Society. This was not unusual in human experience; there was always some league, group, or assembly that brought together those on the margins. Once together, it was the outcast's natural inclination to form the bonds that had otherwise been denied to them by fate or cruel society. When one speaks of these hand-assembled chosen families, one must tread carefully, for no group so vehemently defends its own as the outcast. No one messes with family. Especially the ones we choose.

"We're not separatists. We just don't drink the water or eat the garbage that Altenhofen's poison infects," Tek corrected, her tone firm and unwavering. "Not everyone is 'okay' with giving up who they are just because someone else says it's progress or for the betterment of man." She paused here, and some of the brooding mood left her, replaced by a slight twitching smile as she looked me up and down. "And don't start thinking you're too sprightly just yet. The years will start creeping back in, and something tells me you don't intend to stay away from the shit."

I wasn't as ignorant of the affiliates Tek claimed as my own, despite playing it up for effect. There were, in fact, several sizable groups with the same motives. Some argued from the position of culture; others, from civil liberty; and a few—regrettably receiving the most attention—argued from a sense of superiority.

In my many years, I'd seen these groups clash against the state more times than I cared to remember. Often, their ranks weren't actually filled with Namebreakers but rather the young and sometimes misguided. It was a regrettable truth when considering most police departments' response was as if facing a full-on Namebreaker uprising, of which those in power and much of the populace lived in constant terror.

I'd crossed paths with those who would have debated Tek's position, but I'd never actually taken part in that debate with an honest-to-goodness Namebreaker. Especially not one who didn't seem stunted or limited by the efforts of Altenhofen's advancements or his so-called gifts to society. It felt a bit like standing in a room and talking to a hungry lion.

"You could always go work for The Man, three squares a day and all the regimented culturally bastardized interpretations of birthright that you can stand. If you don't mind the explosive collars or the whole living weapon thing." This, of course, was a bullshit solution at best, and I knew it even before I said it.

The American government was a fine example of how to be irresponsibly wasteful while managing to pleasure absolutely no one. The handling of Namebreakers was grim business, but that didn't mean Uncle Sam would pass up a good deal if he saw it. More than one of their numbers had taken the government's dime and now served to police their own. Those who, for whatever reason, had proven resistant to efforts to remove them from society were now tasked with

147

rounding up others who showed flagrant disregard for the status quo and the laws of man, to say nothing of those pesky laws of Creation itself.

One could, as I grasped it, carve out a decent living if they dared to seize what passed for the king's ransom. These souls usually hailed from humble backgrounds and insular communities, shunned by their own kin for various reasons, often fueled by good old American dread of the unknown. All that self-loathing, twisted and molded into a cudgel wielded by the state.

They were fitted with explosive collars that just a short while ago would have been believed barbaric and inhumane. Yet today, they were peddled to the masses as a form of righteous problem-solving, a symbol that The Powers That Be had everything under control. Nobody quite understood the process by which the good ol' U-S of A churned out these living weapons of mass destruction, how they were indoctrinated or truly kept in check. But in my experience, their cold demeanor and relentless focus on mastering the Word stood in stark contrast to Tek's essence.

"A person shouldn't be damned for their potential deeds, and no one should be coerced into forsaking their identity or betraying their own kind," Tek retorted with the classic defense against the government's stance on those with access to the Word.

Decency and my old pal, the Truth.

"And Joe Schmoe should just count his blessings with the possibility of his home being rent asunder or the heavens themselves igniting as he fetches his kids from school; maybe a delightful firestorm during a cozy evening with his paramour." This was the layman's defense, a barricade forged with fear, deflecting any attempt at empathy with the timeless refrain: What If.

The problem was that fear was not always wrong. One was not a bad person if they did not wish a tiger or a lunatic with a rocket launcher living in their apartment building. This was not a condemnation of tigers or rocket launchers, only the prevailing theory that nothing good came of fat, slow moving Americans mixing with tigers or rocket launchers. I was not lacking in imagination and while Tek was beautiful it was impossible for me to think of any justification that would matter if I were one of the people who had lost someone who was of importance.

I willingly confess that it was easier to put myself in the place of the distraught husband whose wife was reduced to ashes because some angry child had been refused candy and her chaos gene awoke than it was someone who had seen enough goodness in the human heart to believe it might be otherwise. Skepticism had always served me well, especially when it came to matters such as the goodness of humanity. It was alright to believe in the better natures of man, just never to bet the farm on them.

A small dry laugh escaped Tek's lips and for a moment she seemed amused by the fight in me, as if my ability to get up off the floor after having every toxin in my body violently expunged and keep chasing had earned some modicum of respect. I was glad for it. Any man who tells you he doesn't care about the opinion of a woman like Tek is lying even if he holds no attraction to her. She has a magnetism and a drive that compels moral testing and fuels the desire to be better than we had previously been. A measure up to which he will not wish to find himself lacking if only to avoid disapproval or worse a tired lack of surprise in those dark midnight eyes.

"Is that how you go through life? So paralyzed by fear of the apocalypse that you can't even dream up the possibility of glory?" Tek edged closer with each word, her chin defying gravity, her eyes blacker than the abyss.

"Not exactly. I've mastered the art of ensuring every surprise is a damn good one by prepping for the worst-case scenarios." The raw truth slipped from my lips; a feat not easily pulled off in Tek's presence.

The urge to embellish my legend and spin tales was irresistible. It's not exactly dinner party conversation, but it's a trick I've deployed in the past. The dubious quasi-fame from my earlier works had left a trail of women in my wake, lured more by the myth than the man.

Navigating fidelity became an intricate dance when you morph from mere wordsmith to a symbol of rebellious lust and a prized trophy. The collapse of several relationships taught me to inoculate myself against what could only be described as "starfucker" behavior—yet all the literary stars in my sky had long burned out. Nothing kills the vibe quicker than discovering your partner is penning their thesis on your early writings.

At a certain juncture, it's just a vibe killer.

"Some might call that hedging your bets," Tek had a knack for exposing the hypocrisy in any man or system, sparing none from her piercing scrutiny.

Like a rat navigating a maze, I sensed a dead end. We'd tread the same ethical ground, worn smooth by those who'd come before us. Every direction led back to the same circular argument, leaving us in a perpetual loop. But I wasn't ready to throw in the towel just yet. I owed Tek for her mystical detox, but I wasn't about to let the expulsion of cocaine and booze slow down my quest for answers.

"So, why you? More importantly, what's our host's game?" I posed the question, striving to maintain composure as my system adjusted to the recent reboot.

Tek's eyebrow arched, a shadow cast over her dark eye as she offered a noncommittal shrug, her shoulders rippling with toned strength. She was no delicate flower; her life, wherever it lay in the sprawling depths of America, was one of labor and grit. Yet, she exuded a dusty allure, a feline knowingness.

Reaching into my breast pocket, she retrieved the cigarettes I had brazenly snatched from Hawthorne earlier. With purloined tobacco in hand, she turned and drifted back to the record player, where the melancholy strains of Tárrega's 'Oremus' filled the air.

Her mistake was turning her back to me. Freed from the weight of her gaze, my newly purified mind began to work its angles. As The Scribe, it was my duty to chronicle the madness Altenhofen hoped to unleash. But I couldn't fathom him caring one whit about the American Lost Word Society or any other group. If magic were to become integrated into culture, rather than dismissed as genetic happenstance, his entire operation would be jeopardized.

The state had long deemed the matter closed, dismissing recent protests and hopeful calls for change as mere blips on their radar. In their relentless pursuit of quashing dissent, the government had perfected a rope-a-dope strategy that would make Muhammad Ali proud.

Big business, personified by Altenhofen, operated with a chilling detachment, showing traces of humanity only when it fattened their profit margins. The fatal error of past Namebreakers, those who preceded Tek, mirrored the fate of countless others devoured by the voracious American machine since its violent inception.

The playbook was crystal clear: take down the corporate titans first, then deal with the government. To believe otherwise was to imbue the government with a divinity it sorely lacked. Governments, in all their forms, were human constructs, available to the highest bidder. The question wasn't whether a system could endorse murder, oppression, or genocide, but rather how much money it took to tip the scales. No one received fair treatment when someone with influence profited from their suffering.

"What makes you think I know more than you?" Tek's question hung in the air, weightless and indifferent.

She never glanced back, her hands deftly extracting a cigarette from the pack, studying it withobvious disinterest as she awaited my response—whether it held significance or not.

"Rushing headlong into chaos in search of a story is my modus operandi, but for someone like you?" I paused, theatrically assessing her, "You're well-versed in the issue before even opening your mouth. I doubt your comrades at The American Lost Word Society would approve if you took Altenhofen's blood money to be here..." I tried to suppress any hint of smugness, a repulsive quality best left unacknowledged.

The sharp bark of her laughter, tinged with surprise and bitterness, signaled my partial failure.

Tek held a cigarette between two fingers, its tip pointing skyward.

"There are over seven thousand chemicals in this cigarette. Four hundred of them might kill you, another three hundred will, and over seventy directly cause cancer cells to form in the human body. I can see every one of them, and I can change them any way I like." Her gaze shifted over her shoulder, black hair sweeping across her back with the motion.

The deserts of New Mexico or Arizona might rival her eyes at dusk when the moon rose full and fat in the sky, and the coyote sang his song. But they would find no fair competition in the depths of my memory. Not against her.

"If I do, though, it just doesn't taste right. No matter how good you are, no matter how well you replace the old Word with your Word. It's Death that makes this what it is." She shook the cigarette for emphasis. "You're the same way. I can see it on your flesh, on your soul. You have to burn out. If you didn't, you couldn't do what it is you do, could you?" Tek had been amusing herself with me thus far, perhaps even toying with me. I had no way of knowing how much of myself was truly visible to her eye.

For all I knew, all my secrets were glowing in some strange mystical script written across my forehead.

Now, with a certain steeliness, she warned me that some grounds were not safe to tread.

"You really don't want me probing your motives for being here, do you?" I might have taken the hint, but I wasn't going to take it lying down.

The world breaks down into two types of people when dealing with someone who can theoretically scatter your atoms across most of Utah: Those who know when to shut up and those who may soon come to know afflictions such as Spontaneous Combustion, Acid For Eyes, or in the case of one Alabama state trooper turned GOP congressman—a bad case of the Dick Nose. The latter sounds quite comical until you consider the long-term biological implications of switching a racist Alabama state trooper's crooked and diminutive penis with his nose, and then leaving him that way for the rest of us to deal with.

His poll numbers among the GOP are through the roof.

Tek brought the cigarette forward and almost seemed to kiss the white cylinder of paper and poison, but my eye detected no discernible contact at all. There was a faint rustling that I still cannot swear was not the wind simply moving over the barren wasteland beyond the walls of Altenhofen's little artificial paradise. The contradictory element of that description, however, one that only the mad and the inappropriately high will understand, is that it also left the faintest ringing in my ears. Power without volume. A sound whose frequency is not heard entirely by the ear but by something buried deep within our very DNA.

The cigarette yellowed then blackened with small holes opening in the paper like the mouths of hungry pixies. The paper walls collapsed and for a moment, the tobacco stood pressed as it had been in the casing before it leaned and fell, the brown leaves curling on the floor until they were but small black specks and then nothing at all. A flick of her fingers, and the filter went sailing in my direction. Instinctively, I caught it, and as I did, the thicker paper of the cigarette's filter split and its cottony insides, already going from white to light green and black, were laid out in my palm.

It lasted but a moment longer than the rest and was no more than a fine film of dust against my skin.

"What do you think?" Tek's tone suggested that this was entirely a rhetorical question, and Tek might well take offense if I pressed the issue.

The withering-away-to-dust sort of offense.

A whole new and utterly self-destructive temptation was born in the heart of the ruthless but bullshit list of excuses I called my "process" almost at once.

An angry Namebreaker ejecting me from her room, with dramatic effect and a great deal of thunder, would make for a much finer story than dogged-by-the-numbers journalism. Governmental warnings aside, I did not believe that Tek would do me real harm even if I pressed her buttons. She was determined and strong, but I could not then, with an imagination that was in hindsight too tempered by her beauty and the outlaw wisewoman vibe she exuded, imagine her hurting someone outside of her own defense. A calculated risk for the sake of living up to a reputation that I had never wanted but now had to own.

Payback is nothing; it's the consistency of self-fulfilling prophecy that is a universal motherfucker.

Maybe it was because I couldn't fathom Tek obliterating me from the earth for probing her motives that I didn't do it. Instead, I opted for a more cunning strategy: shifting focus to a common enemy. For me, it was a bloated capitalist who fancied himself a savior. For Tek, it was a grotesquely affluent scumbag whose rise threatened her kind across North America.

Even though entire faiths had waged war over lesser differences, I believed we could unite in our disdain. The devil's face always looks the same once you strip off the mask.

"So, you abstain from tap water, fast food, and even those damned Dynametrium pills. You're an enigma, a force to be reckoned with. If anyone asks, I'll say you were a fiery redhead named Matilda, riding a colossal battle corgi around the room. In five or ten years, you'll be inked on some clueless college kid's ass." I tossed out the old diversionary tactic, half joke, half serious.

"Give an old wordsmith a hint, though. What schemes does that wealthy prick have up his sleeve?" Despite the drugs and the focus on myself, I remained a journalist at heart. And there was nothing that ruffled the feathers of the ultra-rich more than being caught off guard by a nosy journalist.

Well, apart from guillotines and socialism, that is.

"Why should I spill the beans, even if I know? You're practically on Hawthorne's payroll yourself." Tek's response was sharp, a fair jab at my compromised integrity. But I couldn't blame her for her skepticism.

"Maybe I'm chasing something grander than mere cash, just like you," I suggested, my words dripping with the honeyed allure of possibility. Crafting a narrative, whether spoken or penned, was an art form, capable of rivaling the seductive charm of a well-crafted lie.

"But money's still in the mix," Tek countered sharply, her words piercing the air like a blade.

Sometimes, the art of spin failed, and you were left grappling with the raw, unvarnished truth that life hurled your way.

"Maybe stirring up trouble in the name of the American Dream pays better than expected. Or maybe it doesn't," I shrugged indifferently. "I outgrew writing for myself in my twenties, back when I learned what it felt like to survive on a diet of bologna for six straight days. Just because I agreed to pen Altenhofen's story doesn't mean he'll appreciate the tale I'll weave." I laid it out bluntly, opting for brutal honesty. Now, it was all about letting the chips fall where they may.

For a moment, silence hung heavy in the air, punctuated only by the soft strains of Spanish guitar wafting from the record player. The melody evoked the gentle patter of raindrops on parched soil, a harbinger of a storm's arrival after a long drought. While I could be persuasive under the right circumstances, I had no insight into the inner workings of a woman's mind, and uncertainty gnawed at me.

I had resisted the urge to provoke, banking on a modicum of decency. But trust, particularly among those who had weathered life's harshest blows, was a currency not easily earned, even in the best of times.

"We have supporters from all walks of life, including some within Altenhofen's own ranks," Tek revealed, her voice tinged with disdain as if she had just stepped in something foul. "When Altenhofen extended an invitation to the Society for this... event, we began digging."

Now, she had my full attention.

"Whatever this is—it's not the only venture he's embarked on in recent years. He bought an island off Nieu in 2015, and another near the Isle of Bouvet. This one's actually closer to civilization than the others... and smaller too," Tek added, her tone laced with bitter disbelief, echoing my own disdain for extravagant displays.

I circled the newfound information like a ravenous hound eyeing a rare, bloody steak on the floor. Mentally, I prodded it from different angles before cautiously ingesting it. Hard-earned experience, delivered in the form of life's unexpected beatings, had taught me not to dive headfirst into questionable intel. Bad information was akin to poisoned meat for a journalist, capable of not only bringing him down but decimating an entire colony of his kind—what the uninitiated referred to as newspapers or, increasingly, "information outlets."

I'll confess, I didn't perceive the looming threat in those puzzle pieces as sharply as Tek did. I, debauched and degenerate to the core, bore some resemblance to the wastefully hedonistic tendencies of the obscenely wealthy and tyrannical elite. I understood the allure of indulgence until one was completely detached from the harsh realities of existence.

For those seeking to understand the sensation of boundless wealth, a mere three days in the company of someone irresistible, interrupted only by feasting and indulgence in the finest tequila, would suffice. The difference lies in the ability of the wealthy to satiate ever-expanding appetites. It spoke volumes about human nature that hosting an orgy of beautiful people or bathing in luxury chocolate from the House of Knipschildt eventually paled in comparison to the thrill of purchasing a new car—except amplified to psychotic proportions when that car was a twenty-million-dollar mansion carved in flagrant defiance of the divine into the very fabric of Creation.

Empathy, wielded by the well-meaning degenerate, allowed him to converse fluently in the language of swine.

"How do you know it's not just one of those rich people things? I mean, he could be like that cellphone guy, or the electric car freak with the wax museum skin who likes building rockets. That would be more ominous than building houses out in the middle of nowhere," I blurted out, trying to inject some semblance of reason into the surreal conversation. But Tek's gaze bore into me with a piercing intensity, making me feel like a fraud even as the words left my lips.

"You're kidding me, right? Look at this place. Really look at it. Those walls outside, that's conjured stone. You would have to break the Word of whoever put it there. That grass means that he's built his own water supply here and that house?"

"Could take a shot from a tank," I chimed in, feeling the gravity of the situation sink in.

"Exactly. This isn't someone's house, it's their fortress." Tek remarked with a grim chuckle, her eyes flashing with a mix of suspicion and dark amusement.

I chewed on that information, figuratively licking my chops clean of the blood and the juice, when an equally unsettling thought crossed my mind, leaving me suddenly craving a cigarette, even though Tek had purged my body of even the hint of a need for nicotine.

"Or their jail."

Futures Bought and Futures Sold

I left Tek's bungalow feeling no better about the situation. I had pieces of the puzzle, but not enough to clearly see the picture before me, and there was nothing worse than the feeling of only half-knowing. I still had some time left before Altenhofen summoned us for dinner and another guest to poke my nose in on. A sane man might have found some corner to curl up in and reevaluate his life, but I was far from sane. All the drugs, sex, acts of debauched lunacy, and frightening mania were but pale shadows of my real weakness.

I always craved speed when chasing a story.

None of my plans survived the first few steps into the sunshine; all thoughts of the story and Altenhofen were laid to waste. Even the missing of my home, nagging my heart and growing in the pit of my stomach already, was obliterated by the sight before me. My mind was unprepared for the scope of what Tek's gift really had been beneath its surface demonstration of her ability.

The sun was setting in the west and was still visible despite the high walls. The sky, the blameless light blue of childhood memory, now surrendered itself to a cavalcade of color. Deep purple clashed against a border of dark, stubborn red, separating it from a sea of orange stolen from every campfire man had ever made to push back the creeping shadows. All that color worked its way down to a furnace of molten gold, surely the beating heart of all creation.

It was a ferociously beautiful sunset, and I saw it with eyes sharper than they had been in two decades.

COYOTE WALLACE

My lungs caught on that first dragging inhalation of the evening air, already beginning to cool. A two-pack-a-day habit had long ago stripped me of most of my olfactory capabilities, but after Tek's restorative efforts, I was, at least temporarily, freed of the burden of all those years of supporting Big Tobacco with my hard-earned dollars. All of which would have been well and good if the air in the Salt Flats could match the sunsets. Unfortunately, the air in the Salt Flats was anything but pleasant. The odor was a combination of burning diapers, rotten eggs, and what may well be the ass sweat of the American Spirit itself.

I lit my cigarette and tried not to gag on the smoke beneath that beautiful sunset Tek and nature itself had conspired to give me. Hawthorne's brand of lung poison was not my own, but it was enough, chemically imposed death or not—anything beats the smell of rancid ass conjured by Mother Earth herself. There were lesser scents, the chlorine of the pool and the sharpness of the grass that Altenhofen had spent a small fortune cultivating inside the walls. None of them could quite push down the stench, and I was forced to stand there puffing away at my cigarette, almost immobile under the sensory assault.

There was, in fact, an upside to killing myself with those coffin nails for all those years, as it turns out anyway, and that upside was not being able to smell Utah. Which, at the risk of giving the rat bastards in the tobacco industry a good idea, should be the slogan and natural counterpoint to any surgeon general's warning.

Tek had used the Word to cleanse me of all my twelve-step sins, but she could not (or at least had not) rid me of whatever dark hole inside myself felt the compulsion to fuel my work with a steady diet of wanton hedonism. There was a pull, as if I were caught in the perfect middle between two large magnets. On the one hand, my bungalow was right there, and inside, Altenhofen had gone to the trouble (with considerable expense) to provide me with everything I needed to keep me distracted and pleasantly inebriated for the next several days. It would be easy to duck back in, line out some more powder, or simply try to unwind and digest my meeting with Tek over some good old-fashioned California green gold. I had a blank, clean canvas of indulgence to work with, a brand-new chance to sink my teeth into experiences my flesh would only recognize as first.

The need to chase, though, was not so easily undone.

My eyes flitted to the last guest house, separated from my own by both Tek's quarters and a small stretch of that out-of-place and obnoxiously vibrant green grass. This was the other source of that near-invisible pull. I only had so much time before we would be called up by Pringle or Hawthorne or some other poor bastard on Altenhofen's payroll. I'd come away from talking with Tek with a few precious scraps of information but not enough of it. Knowledge was power, and Altenhofen would undoubtedly have researched all of us. Whatever secrets our backgrounds held had already been thoroughly investigated, and I aimed to remedy that disadvantage.

Learning more about what he had planned was essential to meeting on equal footing, and equal footing was essential to not being swayed by anything that he might throw in my path. You may be able to argue that you cannot always fight fire with fire, but you damned well better always fight information with more information.

Retreat may have been the better choice, but with time working against me, I chose instead to drift towards what I could only presume was Altenhofen's domicile. There was a distinct sense of being watched, a weight of eyes that clung to me like the stink of the Flats. I drifted from the front of

Tek's door and down onto the small stone walkway that threaded between the pool and the neat row of guest accommodations—the obscenity that they might have served as small homes for two or even three families in the poorest parts of the country worn like a badge of honor by their owner.

That sense of being watched intensified, and it wasn't merely the feeling of someone aware of my presence, like a hotel manager keeping an eye out to prevent you from urinating in the lobby fountain. No, this was a deeper and far more primal awareness. I didn't need to be a Namebreaker or a young man for that—my lizard brain still worked just fine. My mind, still adjusting to its hideous new cleanliness, conjured the mad notion of walking along an immense spider's web.

Something nagged at the back of my brain, a thread of detail becoming clearer in the plumes of smoke that I threw up from my cigarette. The name that Altenhofen's quivering, large-jowled man, Pringle, had given was Mr. Allerton, but at the time, it had meant nothing. Allerton was an old name, common in the wilds of New England culture since the nation's inception.

My mind gnawed and tugged at the threads following my encounter with Tek. Altenhofen had not only welcomed a Namebreaker but one vehemently opposed to his ambitions into his sanctuary. Why? I began a mental cross-referencing exercise. Years of gigs that most conventional journalists would have considered 'strange'—reporting on the domestic troubles of a rap mogul and his wife or some empty-headed politician's retirement—had left my mind cluttered with a sea of obscure and downright bizarre facts.

Allerton felt familiar because somewhere in that jumble, I knew I'd heard his name before. I had reached the door and was still mulling it over when it struck me, just before my knuckles met the door.

A significant portion of the current climate regarding Tek and those like her could be attributed to the testimony of Conrad Allerton in the late 1980s. Allerton had been one of the last multi-generational Namebreakers; individuals who could trace their lineage of Word manipulation back across oceans and the courts of kings.

Their teachings and training were often as structured as those adopted by the government for its arsenal of living weapons but unregulated in content. Secrets and techniques theoretically passed down since the dawn of time in the enigmatic language of Creation itself

Old Magic.

A man of considerable public standing and a potent voice of reason during the rampant era of spirituality-consuming commercialism in the 1980s, he had been summoned before Congress to testify about the perils Forced Totality Adjustment (and its practitioners) posed to the American people. For twenty years preceding, the average American had grappled with their new reality, wrestling with the fact that burying one's head in the sand was no longer an option. The Shadow People were among us, and without a veil of secrecy to keep the public calm, the government had to take visible action. If there's one thing all governments, politicians, and industry leaders share, it's a fear of appearing powerless more than actually being powerless.

It was expected that he would deliver a stirring speech and shift the tide of public opinion. Even in a world where filling internal voids with possessions was the norm, there remained a desperate element of the American people yearning to believe that Wonder wasn't all bad. The Shadow People were emerging into mainstream society, and commonality was slowly but surely winning over division.

The Strange could be wonderful, the Weird could be beautiful, and not everything lurking in the night was horror.

Then came the question, posed by a stodgy old senator from my own native Tennessee: Were the Word and Namebreakers themselves a threat to the American people and their way of life? Did the institutions of law and governance have reason to fear the Namebreakers and their kind?

'Absolutely' wasn't the response those who had put their faith in him had been expecting. It was a betrayal, another nail in the coffin for the opposition to the grim work that would enrich Altenhofen.

Allerton had vanished from the public eye with as much adoration from his followers as Judas likely felt counting his silver. He was the last true magus, if such a term still held meaning, of the American way of life—a towering figure anointed by those who attended his rallies and devoured his editorials in *The Times* as the savior of his people. Perhaps he was the final hope to steer the movement away from the national disgrace it had become.

Nothing puts a cause in the ground like having one of its staunchest supporters switch sides.

I hesitated, just shy of knocking.

The door swung open anyway, revealing not the vision of the near-historical figure my imagination conjured, but an entirely different creature. The young man before me was the antithesis of the bushy-bearded, dark-browed tower of a man immortalized in history books. Conrad Allerton, with his commanding presence in photographs, almost made one believe he could part seas with a tap of his cane, or at least clear the occasional interstate traffic jam.

This was the opposite.

He couldn't have been more than twenty-one, and if he were lucky, he might have weighed a hundred and sixty pounds soaking wet. He was shorter than me by a few inches, but his confrontational posture exuded an aura that dared you to make a joke about his height, just so he could punch you in the mouth. His smartass demeanor seemed genuine, not just an act or a facade of bravado.

His hair was shaved short on the sides but badly in need of a comb at the top, straddling the line between purple and pink in a messy, unnatural bush atop his head. Metal piercings adorned his ears, nose, and left eyebrow, gleaming in the sun. The barest hint of a tattoo peeked out from the collar of what had once been a fine dress shirt and slacks, now stained and rumpled.

If looks could kill, I might not have been dead, but I'd have been bleeding on the ground.

"No," Allerton said dryly, showing no surprise or hint of being caught off guard, in response to my presence at his door.

"I'm sorry, what?" I was momentarily taken aback, not just by his sudden appearance but by the intensity of his gaze and the preemptive refusal to a question I hadn't even asked yet.

Once upon a time, in what felt like an eternity ago, I'd been quick on the draw and able to roll with every punch. A sharp wit could work wonders for a man who was otherwise built like a heavy reader and had the sexual prowess of a chain-smoking librarian. A silver tongue was a necessity for becoming a forgettable disappointment in someone's long line of letdowns. It was also, fortunately, a great way to gain access to places where you'd otherwise have no business.

That had been the case during my time with the so-called Fair Folk many years ago, and it had been the case on the campaign trail as America embraced the idea of an undead Richard Nixon. But now, I stood there like a stuttering idiot, my wit failing me, all the words that had once supported me now fleeing for the hills and leaving me flabbergasted.

This was not my finest hour, and I firmly blame Tek's removal of all proper motivational chemicals from my system.

"No," he said again, his tone firm but impatient, before finally letting out a heavy sigh and elaborating further. "I won't answer your questions. I don't care what that old fuck wants you to do. Vamoose!" Allerton made a little flipping gesture with both hands in front of him, as if to shoo me away.

The cigarette bobbed on my lips as I compulsively bit down on the filter. Like I said, I firmly believe that no one can hate the young more than a man in his late fifties who has been forced to live in a society with a rapidly declining education system. This hate wasn't fueled by the vibrancy or even the boundless energy of the young, though in recent years both had begun to make me increasingly jealous to varying degrees.

No.

It was naivety. Naivety and a sort of nihilistic whining that seemed to suggest that social media uproar was in any way a good replacement for voter organization or, failing that, bricks through windows and some selective turning of tables. They'd seen the hippies and the dreamers in their textbooks, and now one look at their parents was all it took for them to decide the fight wasn't worth it. It was better to let the old die off and just hope the world survives until then.

That or they just made up their own damned rules for fighting The Man that seemed strange and alien to the wild chaser of Truth that was trapped in my aging flesh. I laid the odds at 60/40 at best.

"How do you know what I was going to ask?" The question seemed fair enough, but standing out here with that awful, watched feeling, I can't say that I was happy at the stonewalling.

"Did I not just say that I wasn't going to answer your questions?" Allerton tilted his head forward, his chin nearly touching his chest as he looked at me like I'd grown another head. "You heard that right?" He asked with no intention of letting me answer.

"I didn't just ignore you at the door because you kind of have that sad English teacher vibe, who might give me an A if I let him work out some issues he's been carrying around since college in my bed, but that only gets you as far as me sparing the energy to tell you—Fuck. Off." The Purple and Pink Allerton spat my dismissal at my feet.

I could see over his shoulder—hell, I could see over his head, he was so short—and behind him, the room was a wreck.

Unlike the neatly organized and still clean accommodations provided for me and Tek, the whole thing looked lived in and badly in need of a visit from housekeeping. The floor was littered with wrappers, paper plates, and empty aluminum cans for drinks that promised energy and had names like 'Brain Blower', 'Breakneck', and 'Nitro'. The layout was different too; no record player or neat counter to divide the kitchen. There was only a wide-open box-like room dominated by a couch in the center and an army of serpent-like cables that fed not one, but three different screens affixed to the wall.

There were no books, no pictures, and the only other furnishing besides the screens, game consoles, and that filthy purple couch was a coffee table. The poor thing was so covered in headphones, controllers, and garbage that the surface was no longer visible. It was no longer a table; it was an altar to filth.

"You're a real peach of a young man, aren't you?" I countered his surliness with my own. "Can I at least have your name, or should I just call you Baby Huey Allerton?"

I had only one card to play, and it was that I did already have his last name, and few angry young men starved for attention can stand the idea of the public thinking of them in any sort of mocking light.

Magic could let you turn a man's asshole into a ring of solid gold, but it did not inherently instill a thick skin, or the self-awareness truly needed to not care about the opinions of others. Only time gave you those sorts of calluses, and if I had one advantage over the young man, it might have been that I was older and could have cared less at this point in my life what sort of figure I cut in someone else's story.

Once a man has faced proctologists, publishers, and the first familiar glimpse of his father's reflection staring back at him in a mirror, he is long past the point of giving a tinker's shit about the role he is cast in on someone else's stage. The kid was just that under all his surly pushback—a kid, one who might still fluster at the prospect of the greater world thinking him 'uncool'. You use what you have in this line of work, and what I had was an accumulation of years.

The wisdom of high mileage.

Definitely-Not-Named-Baby-Huey came forward then, chin thrown upwards and a little curling snarl on his lips as if he meant to back me down in some seedy barroom. His eyes dipped into squinting lines, and I could feel the air around me tingle ever so gently, pulling the hair on the back of my arms and neck to attention. The feeling was hauntingly like what I had experienced within the confines of Tek's own bungalow.

"There's a thirty-six-point-six percent chance that you'll eventually shoot yourself, and then a bunch of people who will mostly just remember the drugs and the craziness will fire your old ass out of a big cannon or maybe a catapult," he declared, lifting his right hand, keeping it palm down, and giving it a little wobble followed by a shrug of his shoulders.

"The timeline gets a little fuzzy on the details, grandpa," he added, a bitter twist of emphasis placed on the end—time was the preferred insult of the very young and the very old. "Just thought you'd like to know. Might make your day. Give you something to think about since, you know, you're not fucking off. Oh, and the name is Moxley. Not that you'll be using it much because, again, I'm not talking to you or answering your fucking parasite questions." The newly minted Moxley Allerton made such a show of his disdain that I half expected a bow when he finished.

Besides, that tirade was a little on the nose.

"And there's a hundred percent chance you'll still be a miserable little shit when I do," I retorted, relishing the dry smartassery.

Despite the boy's confrontational and prickly nature, there was some intangible quality about him that, while initially insufferable, was also infectious. You wanted to see him kick, fight, and rip at some unsuspecting but deserving bastard on the streets, and it was easy enough to imagine him doing so. He had all the qualities of the sort of young agitator that Jimmy Wonderful should have been, had he not been trapped within the flesh of an old man with debauched legends for blood and tales of the American Dream for his bones.

I wanted to like him, and maybe he wanted to like me, but it seemed he compulsively tried to make that as difficult as humanly possible.

My gambit had flopped like a fish out of water; I had squeezed nothing out of him that Tek hadn't already spilled, except for the wild idea that he might be a spawn of the original Allerton or just some Namebreaker who'd hijacked the name for kicks. My moves were dwindling, and Moxley would soon sniff out my desperation if he hadn't already.

Defeat was a familiar taste, like ordering Trippa alla Romana in the only Italian joint in a backwater Idaho town—failure with a side of watery marinara

Then, as if Lady Luck had taken pity on this sleepless journalist and favored the fool, two things happened at once. Firstly, The Golden Girls' iconic intro blasted from one of the room's large screens, reminding me of the unyielding resilience of four old ladies living large. That was my cue, a small window of opportunity in the chaos.

Simultaneously, on the middle screen beside Blanche and the Girls, the manic frenzy of virtual gunfights that had kept Allerton occupied before my arrival kicked off its second round. A macho, British-accented voice declared "Kill Confirmed." and the canned cacophony of gunfire tried to outshout the upbeat '80s sitcom theme song.

The reaction was as immediate as it was profound. Moxley Allerton, if that was his real name - and who knows with these characters - for a split second wore an expression that was very much like a man who had just had matchsticks lit between his toes. His eyes grew wide as saucers, and he whirled around, all but completely forgetting about me, except, of course, to curse my continued existence and my inconsiderate interruptions.

"You fuck!" he shouted. "FUCK! No, no, no, don't kill me yet! DON'T FUCKING KILL ME!" With that, he turned and bolted back into the bungalow, leaving the door wide open behind him, and me just standing there.

I glanced over my shoulder and then over to the main house where Altenhofen would soon be dragging us off to dinner. We were to be subjected to the horrors of fine wine and exquisite food prepared by a five-star chef. What worse fate exists for those who hope to maintain any sort of objective purity than decadence and heady luxury?

For a moment, I considered being courteous and at least passably polite, returning to my own room and leaving the boy and his secrets to his own devices. But then I remembered that I have a profound affinity for reckless choices, so instead, I pushed ahead, ready for whatever madness this night would bring.

The initial glimpse through the doorway over and around Moxley hadn't done justice to the mess within. I fancied myself a connoisseur of filth, akin to a mountain man deciphering the tracks of creatures in the woods. While the room lacked the telltale signs of a heroin addict—no discarded spoons or melted candles—it exuded an unwashed rankness. The stench of days seeped into the walls and floors. Though every shade was pulled, it did little to mask the dirt, and I couldn't ignore the crunch of old corn chips beneath my step.

Moxley had covered the walls and ceilings with writings—computations, formulas, sprawling strings of numbers that made my eyes pulse and throb with pain in the gloom. It was an intricate spiderweb of knowledge, yet I didn't understand any of it. Some of the markings were made in pen, some in pencil, and some might have been old ketchup or even blood...

I glanced back at the doorway I had just come through and watched as a translucent apparition with my features shrugged before turning to walk back to his bungalow. It was exactly what I had contemplated doing myself before throwing caution to the wind. My brain stuttered and tripped over itself like I was having a bad acid flashback. I could do nothing but stare with my mouth agape until the ghostly version of myself vanished back inside. I'd rarely been dumbfounded in my life, and the experience was far from pleasurable. Men like me should never be left wordless; it's a destitution that our pride rarely recovers from.

The Road Less Traveled, indeed.

Moxley sprawled over the back of the couch, clutching the controller with his rear in the air and his feet kicking childishly. His face twisted in a mask of snarling rage as he dispensed quick and messy digital death to his foes. Amidst the chaos, he chanted a litany of curses and filth, pausing only between reloads to glance at The Golden Girls in all their glory.

"Fuck Nuggets! Assholes! Screw your Papa and make him bring me a sandwich, you corner-camping cock-stain!" Moxley bellowed at the screen with such intensity that little flecks of white foam escaped his mouth.

"What the...?" I barely managed to start my question before Moxley, still half draped across the back of the couch, interrupted with an answer to a question I hadn't even finished asking. I began to suspect this was his favorite trick.

"Temporal Displacement Ward. Do not mess with it," he gritted his teeth and bore down on his controller with even more intensity. "We will die, and I will lose, and I refuse to lose. I'll make this quick before you completely screw up my aim..." He paused; teeth bared in a snarl of determination as he focused on the war game that bathed his skin in its pale glow.

"...so, I expect you to follow along. I know it's hard. My ass. You being old as fuck. There's lots working against you, and you have my sympathies. Don't speak. My way is faster and since I don't care if you understand or not, things will go smoother if you just roll with it. Ready to roll with it? You're ready."

I was not, in fact, ready, but Allerton the Younger was on something of a roll, and he showed no sign of letting up anytime soon.

"A Temporal Displacement Ward pushes back against the natural flow of time and splits it as if it were light going through a prism, creating branching paths between the IS and the COULD BE." The screen flashed with gunfire as his score climbed higher, and he continued.

"Yes, my father was Conrad Allerton. I have a recurring profitable relationship with Mr. Altenhofen, the nature of which I will not be disclosing. Yes, I'm the best in the world at what I do. Not an overstatement. Aaaaaaaannd we're done. Bye now.

The most uncomfortable thing about the way that Moxley rattled off the answers was not the speed, though they were like burst fire from machine guns. No, that was not the worst of it by far.

The epiphany struck me like a sledgehammer amid this twisted carnival of chaos. These weren't just answers to questions I hadn't even formed yet; they were like glimpses into a twisted, predestined play where every move I made was already scripted. It was like staring into the abyss and realizing it was staring back, mocking my feeble attempts at free will

"This is madness..." I muttered to myself, the words reverberating in the dimly lit chaos of Moxley's lair.

The screen Moxley was gaming on suddenly flashed red, a digital countdown ticking away the precious seconds until he could resume his virtual massacre. In that fleeting moment, he rolled over the back of the couch in a frenzied half-tumble, rising back up with the controller still clenched in his hand. His eyes burned with a manic intensity, like a mad scientist who had just discovered the key to unlocking the secrets of the universe but was too distracted by his own brilliance to care about explaining it to mere mortals.

It was a scene straight out of a twisted acid trip, a surreal blend of chaos and absurdity that left me questioning the very fabric of reality. But there was no time for existential pondering; I had to keep up with the madness unfolding before me, lest I get swept away in the tidal wave of temporal insanity.

"Why is it that every wet end struggles with basic instruction? No talky-talky, you..." Moxley stopped, sighed, and rubbed the bridge of his nose between his thumb and forefinger.

He was roughly the same age as any son I might have had, and I would be lying to you if I said that the mere memory of Moxley Allerton was not enough to make me question every debauched encounter I'd ever had. There was nothing that drove home to me the cold terror of parenthood; of being face to face with a 20-something asshole who reminded far too much of your younger self, like seeing a reflection of your best and worst traits assembled before you. Not how you were, no, but how you once saw yourself through the lens of possibility and as of yet untrampled optimism.

Moxley was cocksure, arrogant, and utterly convinced that he and he alone could walk between raindrops and pluck down stars from the sky.

Part of me instantly loved that about him, though I had no intention of letting him know that.

"It doesn't matter," Allerton said at last as he dragged his hand away from his face and turned his head toward the door.

Pringle was already wobbling and careening down the walkway with a gusto that defied his rotund frame. He was a rotund man, but he moved surprisingly spry when the occasion called for it, and by "occasion," I meant when his master snapped his fingers;

It was dinner time.

The Pieces on The Board

I finagled ten minutes out of Pringle by spinning a yarn about a fiery bout of the trots, courtesy of the airline slop. It might sound crass, but when you're in a bind, needing just enough time to dial your publisher's office because the hotel bill's looming and you're flat broke, the trots come in handy. No one wants a mess on their conscience, so deals for snippets of time are easily struck when minutes could otherwise be a rare commodity in the open market

It was going to take me six weeks and a crate of tequila to shake off the horrors of Moxley's room. The cryptic scrawls and equations etched into the walls, which even now send shivers down my spine to recall, stubbornly haunted the recesses of my mind. Ten minutes was all I had. Ten minutes on the dime of a man capable of buying and selling small nations, who'd turned both dreams and nightmares into cash flow to fuel his ambitions. Ten minutes to ditch the sweat-soaked shirt. Ten minutes to splash water on my face and slap on deodorant. Ten minutes to roll and hotbox a joint, ensuring that the lingering lack of appetite, even after Tek's detox, didn't make food downright revolting. No grizzled truth-seeker who's ever earned his keep pounding the gritty crime beats, or worse yet, chasing feel-good stories while struggling to make rent in the city, ever underestimated the importance of a free meal.

None who've attempted to pry truth from another has undervalued the significance of making at least a moderately favorable first impression.

I managed the shirt, deodorant, and a quick splash of water upon my face; all that it cost me was the violent shaking of my suitcase over my bed. The rolling of the joint was similarly accomplished by way of unthinking rote memory and near feral desire. There was no time to unravel the neat plastic wrapping around the green brick by the pillow. No, I tore at it with the hungry determination of a rodent chewing his way into dry goods. I didn't get the whole thing, and I wished I had Moxley's strange capabilities at my fingertips, but I got enough.

My hands had stopped shaking, a minor victory in the grand scheme of things, but I'd take it. That is until the wine started flowing.

Whether Tek's detox had obliterated my tolerance or Altenhofen had obtained the finest of substances, I found myself immensely stoned. To some, this might seem counterproductive, but those people haven't witnessed a ghostly temporal doppelgänger waltzing before their eyes. Sobriety was the enemy, always, because the mind-blowing was imminent. I had little fear of the Shadow People or the Namebreakers; my terror was reserved for POWER. It didn't matter if it came from magic, politics, firearms, or obscene wealth; it always turned sour.

There was an intimate familiarity in Tek's words, reminiscent of my encounters with faeries in my youth or the rare meetings with the so-called 'Shadow People'. Moxley's applications, however, were a different breed. His manipulation of something I considered linear had a foreign quality, unsettling me on a profound level. What use did men capable of dancing between raindrops and grasping the secrets of time have for the constraints of an orderly world? I couldn't fathom it.

Not yet.

COYOTE WALLACE

Maybe this was all part of the cosmic joke, the twisted puzzle that every Namebreaker faced, contributing to the surreal gap that made acceptance feel like a mirage in the desert. Fear was the lifeblood, fueling the fevered scenarios and paranoid whispers. We understood it, the powers-that-be wielded it like a scalpel, carving out our autonomy and fashioning it into a leash to yank us back in line. There was no universal playbook, no foolproof formula to decode and defy. Americans craved predictability; it was ingrained in our psyche to chase certainty while shunning the unexpected. Even with this self-awareness, we remained vulnerable, especially in the face of Namebreakers.

Stepping out of my bungalow, I was living on the edge. Tek and Moxley had already rendezvoused with Pringle on the walkway, and the crisp night air seemed to sharpen our senses. The sun had long bid its farewell, unveiling a sprawling canvas of indigo sky adorned with a shimmering tapestry of stars. While the Flats below were harsh and unrelenting, their sky was a celestial sanctuary, a cosmic symphony unmarred by the city's smoggy symphony.

Tek had swapped her usual garb for a white blouse and form-fitting black pants, a subtle yet potent transformation. Though her blouse offered a tantalizing glimpse of décolletage, there was an air of calculated restraint in her demeanor, a silent challenge to underestimate her at one's peril. She shot me a disapproving glance as I approached, as if to say, "You're late, and you're not nearly as prepared as you should be."

"Not even an hour," Tek said, her disappointment tinged with a hint of amusement that tugged at the corners of her lips, rendering her disappointment ineffectual. The scolding had a teasing familiarity to it, reminiscent of something Jenna would have said

Allerton, thanks to a combination of my stalling and his own peculiar ways, had managed to do more than just change his shirt like me; he emerged showered, shaved, and completely rejuvenated. Clad in a white suit with a vibrant pink undershirt, along with his purplish-pink hair, he resembled a corrupt and utterly insane young Southern minister. A foul-mouthed, antisocial prophet of a new age, possessing the patience suited for fifteen-second clips on glowing screens, yet wielding the power of a petulant god.

Moxley Allerton, petulant god or not, found amusement in tormenting Pringle while we waited. He had subtly maneuvered behind Pringle, reaching around the round man's flabby arms and theatrically pinching Pringle's man-breasts through his shirt. He jiggled them up and down to a hideous rhythm only he could hear. The spectacle seemed to unsettle Tek, yet her disdain for Altenhofen, Pringle, and the entire damnable affair likely suppressed any inclination to intervene on behalf of the pudgy yes-man.

My mind twisted like a pretzel, grappling with the fact that this grungy recluse was the same guy I'd just faced. I hadn't probed or been given a chance to ponder just how far Moxley Allerton could stretch time's elastic boundaries. Was there a limit? Could he lounge indefinitely between four and four-oh-one?

For believers in the Namebreakers and all things "Shadow Folk", here's a brutal truth: wielding The Word didn't necessarily deck you out in desirable traits. Magic couldn't sprinkle maturity, compassion, or altruism upon you. It was a grim reality check that these wielders came from the mishmash of American cultures, both virtuous and vile.

Call it magic or Forced Totality Readjustment, the Namebreakers footed the bill for the ancient fib that power led to enlightenment. Their own worst foes, they lashed out,

179

rebelled, and dug deeper into Altenhofen's pit of lies with each skirmish.

Power didn't enlighten; it dragged souls farther from the truth that we're all in this mad ride together. In the sea of life, if you can swim while the guy next to you flounders, you might just choose to save your own hide instead of lending a hand.

Who am I kidding? We're all just passengers on this wild trip, holding on for dear life, hoping for the best while the universe throws curveballs like it's in a never-ending cosmic game of dodgeball. And guess what? The Namebreakers? They're the ones who get smacked the hardest because they dared to think they could rewrite the rules of reality itself. So here we are, caught in this crazy whirlwind of power, deception, cosmic uncertainty. All we can do is ride the wave and see where it takes us.

The rest of us must learn together or end up feeding the sharks.

Watching Moxley torment Pringle as he did, I couldn't shake the feeling that this was the final nail in the Namebreakers' coffin in America. They were us, and we were them, and that was downright terrifying. The scariest monsters are the ones who, under the right circumstances, blend seamlessly with humanity. The more familiar the devil was, the more personal the Hell.

Pringle's face reddened like an overripe strawberry, then exploded with frustration. His piggy eyes squinted, and his meaty fingers curled into hammy fists, shaking violently like a discount two-for-one special on a Greyhound bus. He stomped twice and let out a shrill shout.

"Stop it! Stop it now! He's here!" Pringle roared, his limp black hair flailing as he reached the peak of his tantrum.

Tek's attention shifted from me, and while I couldn't imagine her having much sympathy for anyone on Altenhofen's payroll, the loud noise and Moxley's maniacal laughter made her flinch ever so slightly each time they reached her ears.

"Will you knock it off?" Tek snapped.

Moxley yanked his hands back and flung them up to chest height, palms out towards Tek and me. Only then did I spy the inked palms, a thick line emerging from his sleeve near the heel of his palm, spiraling upwards, forming a half-circle just below his fingers, then cascading down the other side. Squinting, silently cursing my old-man eyes, I realized it wasn't a mere line; it was a chaotic jumble of numbers crammed so densely that, at first glance, they seemed like a solid, impenetrable block.

"You caught me, sheriff. I confess it all. I was just killing time to stave off terminal boredom while waiting on our aging scribe here." Moxley flicked me a wink, too cocky to be genuine. "Will you spare me from the gallows if I promise to behave?

Pringle huffed a lengthy breath through his nose, he seemed a bit like a deflating balloon in that moment, then he spoke up. He had no intention of allowing Tek and Moxley to bicker, and I couldn't blame him. Keeping tempers calm was paramount, especially with the imminent dinner with Altenhofen looming like a storm cloud.

"Are you..." Pringle paused, as though choosing the wrong word might undo him, "...Feeling better? Mr. Altenhofen does not like to be kept waiting, and we've dallied long enough, Mr. Woz—"

"Wonderful." I cut him off and lit a cigarette, though they tasted vile without my addiction to soften the blow. They forced me to suppress the urge to cough, but at least they masked the stench of the Flats.

A scowl fought against Pringle's attempts to force a strained smile; his cheeks still flushed from the fiery exchange with Moxley. He struggled to maintain his composure, valuing his job too much to give in to the anger. Compared to Moxley Allerton, I seemed like a beacon of virtue, a lesser evil in the grand scheme of things.

I wasn't sure how I felt about that.

"Yes, my apologies, Mr. Wonderful," Pringle muttered, as if he'd just stumbled upon a cesspool of chaos, before pivoting back toward the house.

"Please, follow me, and try your darnedest to avoid laying hands on any of Mr. Altenhofen's sacred relics. Mr. Hawthorne takes a dim view of any blasphemy against his treasures, and it's best not to awaken his wrath," Pringle warned, attempting to infuse his words with a touch of mystical dread.

"Aw, you don't have to remind me of the rules, and they aren't about to abscond with the silverware. Spare us the Sunday sermon," Moxley quipped, lacing his hands behind his head and sauntering behind Pringle, leaving Tek and me trailing at the rear.

As we trailed Pringle down the walkway, the mansion Altenhofen had erected in the middle of nowhere served as the sole beacon of artificial light for miles around. There was something vulgar and audacious about electric light when it vied with the stars. Man-made illumination was simply too tarnished to harmonize with those celestial sparks that punctured the velvety void of the universe. The contrast was almost profane, like inviting a hedonistic reveler to a sacred ceremony, akin to the Pope crashing a cosmic carnival.

I was engulfed by a sudden surge of primal energy, a raw frenzy that hadn't coursed through me since my wild youth—an overwhelming urge to demolish it all. To systematically dismantle the opulent mansion, wielding sledgehammers to shatter stone and hurling bricks through the gilded windows. Once the edifice lay in ruins, to unleash a furious assault on the generators powering the abominable artificial light. I envisioned myself collapsing, spent and frothing at the mouth, but utterly fulfilled. In the depths of my slumber, I would dream of guillotines and a world where hope reigned supreme over mere financial tips.

"Pen names are usually reserved for actual writing, aren't they?" Tek remarked, a playful glint in her eye as she addressed me by my chosen pseudonym, 'Jimmy Wonderful.'

"I've been informed there's significance in a name," I retorted, the words flowing effortlessly, eliciting a musical laugh from Tek.

The name 'Jimmy Wonderful' conjured images of various personas—perhaps a shadowy mob enforcer from pulp fiction, a shrewd sports bookie, a flamboyant glam rock frontman, or even a trucker's swaggering CB radio alias. It was a name fit for a renegade, a wanderer, or a vagabond— certainly not for a man in pursuit of truth, yet somehow, it had intertwined with my own identity. Once a guise for camouflage and protection against the mundanely sane, it now burdened me with its weight.

Eliciting laughter from Tek was a modest employment of my own, albeit less ostentatious, brand of magic. Wit may lack the spectacle of lightning bolts, but as long as it could provoke laughter in a woman, there remained a glimmer of hope for wretches like me. Granted, younger and unattached wretches, but wretches of the written word, nonetheless

As we reached the front door, trailing behind Pringle in a duckling line, he pivoted to face us once more, as if conducting a final inspection. His beady eyes darted up and down our trio, hungering for trivial details, hinting at the demeanor of a man who would call the hotel front desk over a missing mint on his pillow. Behind him, Altenhofen's front door stood wide open, resembling the gaping maw of a hellish robot from a late-night Japanese animation, glimpsed through a haze of intoxication and drowsiness.

As we approached the front door, trailing behind Pringle in a duckling line, he pivoted to face us once more, as if conducting a final inspection. His beady eyes darted up and down our trio, hungering for trivial details, hinting at the demeanor of a man who would call the hotel front desk over a missing mint on his pillow. Behind him, Altenhofen's front door stood wide open, resembling the gaping maw of a hellish robot from a late-night Japanese animation, glimpsed through a haze of intoxication and drowsiness.

"You'll need to extinguish the cigarette before we proceed inside, Mister Wo–" Pringle paused, catching himself mid-sentence. Instead of mustering the courage to utter 'Wonderful', he cleared his throat and settled on "...ahem...Sir," a feeble attempt at preserving his dignity.

I didn't blame him. Between Moxley and me, a seasoned Yes-Man like Pringle likely dreaded what awaited him.

"Of course, naturally. Wouldn't dream of keeping it," I assured him, sensing a twinge of pity for his predicament.

With a flick, I sent the cigarette soaring in a high arc, landing in the overly green grass. Normally, Pringle might have frowned in disapproval, but time constraints and eagerness to be rid of me overrode any such inclinations.

I had been in fine homes before, including a few that were simply blatant declarations of wealth to be compared to those of their peers. However, the home of Roy Altenhofen was neither simply an expression of means nor was it truly a home. The floors alternated between spaces of rich, almost red cherry wood, and spaces of smooth, polished marble tile that had been flown in from the far corners of the world just to be trodden upon beneath our feet.

The layout resembled a labyrinth, a twisted maze designed to ensnare the unsuspecting, with only the center room beyond the door offering a semblance of orientation. The double staircases leading upstairs served as passable landmarks, but it was easy to get lost in the intricate web of corridors and hidden alcoves, each beckoning with its own peculiar allure. Some men adorned their homes with trophies, others with art, but Altenhofen's abode was a fever dream of eccentricity, an homage to the bizarre and the inexplicable. It exuded an aura of collection and homage, as if each object held a secret story waiting to be unraveled. Strange, transcendental music oozed from hidden speakers, weaving through the air like tendrils of smoke, casting a spell upon all who dared to enter.

"Son of a bitch..." Tek's voice trailed off as she broke from the line, much to Pringle's dismay, and gravitated toward a large portrait on one of the walls.

Hawthorne's grim countenance stared down at us from the painting, his eyes seeming to follow our every move with an eerie intensity. The only change over time was the switch from army blues of the 1880s to a cheap suit, but the air of malevolence remained unchanged. He stood with a hand in his jacket pocket and his chin slightly elevated—a man caught in the throes of his own sinister machinations, forever frozen in time. The painting did him no favors in my eyes either. How could one man accumulate so many years and still remain a miserable bastard? How could one face eternity and decide that living off the scraps of the wealthy was the best course of action? I had no place to judge; I had accepted my payment to be here, yet I liked to entertain the notion that I could have concocted a better plan.

"He looks like he sat on a pinecone," I quipped as I joined Tek, craning my neck to get a better look.

"Yeah..." Tek confirmed, her response cut short with a hard exhale through her nose.

Moxley, lingering behind Pringle, spared the painting a glance, his discomfort palpable, a detail I filed away for later probing. Both of them seemed eager for us to move along, albeit for different reasons. Pringle appeared to dread the thought of arriving a minute late and having to answer to Altenhofen. However, it was Moxley, typically a bundle of confrontation and fire outside these walls, who now seemed strangely muted, as if the oppressive atmosphere of the house had sapped him of his usual bravado.

I couldn't care less about their patience in the face of discovery. I had a few moments I could stretch before it drifted into rudeness, especially with Tek still planted in front of the portrait of Hawthorne. I drifted from the painting to a softball-sized sphere supported by three golden legs on a small wooden table. The sphere appeared to be made of glass but had been coated in gold in such a fashion that the metal resembled the landmasses one finds on a globe, save for the fact there was no familiar geography that I recognized.

I was just beginning to reach for it when Pringle spoke up.

"I'm sure that Mr. Altenhofen would appreciate it if you could resist the urge to touch his things until after dinner," Pringle's voice had regained its tightness now that he was so close to being rid of us.

Failure is never more frightening than when you are almost at the finish line.

I drew my hand back, and Tek was already drifting back to join them. She saw what I was looking at, spared a little half-smile of knowing, laced with amusement, and stopped on her way, leaning over my shoulder a little to see for herself. Her hair smelled of night blooming wildflowers. I felt the gentle resting of her fingers upon my arm.

"*Mundis Animarum*. Maps of the spirit world were all the rage once upon a time," Tek said, her tones warm despite her rough attitude and the foul mood Hawthorne's grim countenance on the wall may have provoked.

She enjoyed teaching, even if the student was an old dog like me who could never learn new tricks but kept signing up for lessons anyway.

We rejoined Pringle and Moxley before drifting deeper into the house. I was thankful that our excursion wouldn't be taking us up the stairs, not because of the hardship of the trek up, but because I could only imagine going up them behind Pringle would be slow work, and Moxley would undoubtedly begin to complain. The rest was oddly impersonal, a vase here and a strange sculpture there; once I saw two lovers, one clearly a demon, locked in a stoney but passionate embrace for all time. Altogether though, it felt detached from any intimate value, as if it existed only to fill the spaces because it had to. This may have been a home that Altenhofen owned, but it was not a home to Altenhofen himself. Not really

Maybe no place really was.

COYOTE WALLACE

There was one last element we encountered on our way to the dining room that challenged my notions of Altenhofen's detachment from the place. Upon the wall of a spacious hallway, defiantly contrasting with the shrewdness of the other furnishings, hung a smattering of old photographs. The black-and-whites were neatly framed, leaving us guessing whether they were originals or copies, but they depicted a young Roy Altenhofen. Handsome and fair-haired, with a strong jaw—a prototype upon which all young and ruthless men of means seemed to base themselves each year. The archetypal blueprint from which all future swine would be fashioned.

One photo featured him on an airfield, smugly standing by a plane ready to take off. Another showed him with hands on hips, sternly overseeing the breaking of ground on what might have been a home or company headquarters on blank, muddy ground. In the final picture, he was a little older than the previous two, paunchier and with thinner hair, yet seemingly happier. One arm looped around the waist of a striking dark-haired woman with eyes that threatened to swallow me up from fifty years back, and his hand clamped on the shoulder of a wide-eyed, smiling boy who could have only been Altenhofen's son.

I barely had a moment to glance at the photographs; Pringle was already heaving open a wooden door adorned with a carving of some monstrous shade tree. Its leaves were coated in shiny metal—could've been silver, could've been gold, but who cared? My focus was on those photographs, each one a glimpse into Altenhofen's past, guarded tighter than a dragon's hoard. Everyone knew the public record, but that wouldn't help me now, or later when I'd have to write the story. No, this was diving into the belly of the beast, and knowledge was the only comfort in such grim situations, rubbing shoulders with the filthy rich and disgustingly powerful.

The dining room was a grand spectacle, just like the rest of Altenhofen's palace. Windows lined one wall, offering a view of the stony perimeter of the grounds, adorned with moonlight and stars. Everything reeked of luxury, from the fine silverware to the crystal chandelier and enough silver to make a small fortune. The table stretched like something out of The Last Supper, fit only for kings and those who hungered for crowns. Empty chairs surrounded us, a silent testament to Altenhofen's solitude.

Altenhofen himself sat at the head of the table, a faded relic of his former self, like an ancient warlord defying time and enemies. His hair, once a robust mane, had turned snow white, neatly trimmed into a flattop that even J. Edgar Hoover would've applauded for its lack of imagination and expression.

He was dwarfed by his suit, and though I'm sure it had been tailored to him, it still seemed to make him appear smaller and more skeletal. His face reminded me of the girders that appeared in the months before a new building rose up in the Chicago skyline—narrow and bereft of the necessities for beauty or even emotional connection. His lips did not pull into the permanent scowl that Hawthorne's had; there was no standing cruelty in Altenhofen, only a thin line of grim dispassion.

Hawthorne waited just behind Altenhofen, dressed in the same bland suit he'd been wearing when he'd plucked me from the airport. However, now he was in the presence of Altenhofen, and like a well-trained but mean-natured dog, he watched us with eager distrust. His cigarette, in the presence of his master at least, had been replaced with a toothpick which he chewed compulsively. The subtle working of

Hawthorne's jaws sent the little sliver of wood bouncing up and down on his lip.

These were two different breeds of swine, part of the same genus but not the same animal at all.

At a glance, I had the impression that Altenhofen had not smiled in a very long time. That this world provided for him very little in the way of true pleasure save for the substitution of profit for victory. Hawthorne? Hawthorne's scowling mug was probably only broken once a day by something as unnatural to him as a smile. The opportunity to inflict pain was much less elusive than whatever stirred his employer's heart, though.

Altenhofen kept Hawthorne around not just for his efficiency at what those of gentle tongue might call "dirty work" (and those of us cut from rougher cloth call "shit kicking") but for the statement it made to have a cursed man on a leash. He wanted him seen, he wanted us to know, and in this bubble where Altenhofen controlled every aspect of his environment, his presence alone made that impossible to ignore.

"I'm glad to see you've decided to join me at last. I was beginning to wonder if I might not have to send Mr. Hawthorne out to find you," Altenhofen's joyless blue eyes dug in like fangs, though his tone was perfectly pleasant, if humorless.

Pringle certainly knew there was no humor to be found in it; he flustered and wrung his hands before him as he sputtered out an explanation.

"They were very interested in the furnishings, and Mr. Woz-- I mean, Mr. Wonderful..."

Altenhofen cocked a white eyebrow upwards, his patience draining out with the slow downward turn of the corners of his mouth. I could already hear the gears turning in Altenhofen's head as he no doubt weighed the pros and cons of dismissing Pringle right then and there. Altenhofen did not look like he suffered fools, and it was possible that after so many years of having nearly everything he wanted in the exact manner he wished it, he'd simply lost the ability to tolerate imperfection. On the other hand, it would make him look a complete tyrant and asshole. It was hard to pretend that you would find commonality with the 'little people' when you were making a display of making a rotund coward pack his bags.

I had no love for Pringle and no reason to like the man. He'd shown me no particular kindness, and I was almost positive that if Altenhofen asked him to do so, he would eagerly enough accompany Hawthorne to bury a body in the desert. He may have lamented at the digging, but he'd make no objection. Pringle was a coward through and through. More than that, he was a coward who had clearly, over a considerable amount of time, taken on the general vibe of an often-whipped dog

The difference between Pringle and Hawthorne was that Hawthorne would never flinch, and Pringle seemed to be perpetually flinching under Altenhofen's gaze.

Something about it reminded me of a man kicking a cowering pet or shouting at a wife that saw no escape for herself; though Altenhofen had barely moved and had certainly never raised his voice, his gaze alone seemed to burn the round man before him. It was Pringle's wilting and wringing of his hands, the beads of perspiration on his brow, and the nervous begging flick of his eyes to me and then back to Altenhofen that made it so intolerable. The slow torture of unspoken implication that only the rich and those assured of their own influence can ever stomach.

Luckily, Jimmy Wonderful never goes anywhere without first strangling his shame in a closet with a thin cord made from his dignity.

"The shits. It's my fault. Never eat airplane chicken, and if you do, don't ask for seconds. You're a man of the world, I'm sure you know how it goes. The rat bastards probably gave me something undercooked!" I exclaimed, throwing my hands out with a sheepish grin.

Surely even those rancid with wealth occasionally had to cling to the edges of their toilets and pray that their butlers, maids, and landscapers didn't hear them being human. All those oysters and caviar that the rich gobble down constantly on the silver screen would lead one to believe that every wealthy person in the world was perpetually shitting their brains out.

Maybe that's why they spend so much time on social media.

Altenhofen did not default to mortification as I'd hoped, but his attention did swing from his portly servant to myself. I had a sense that I had taken a blind leap onto unsteady ground and, like a man navigating an ice shelf, at any moment, the ground might slide out from beneath me. Altenhofen's cold gaze was almost like a physical slap when it hit you. Brutish men, when they look upon you, may contemplate how best to break your bones or crush the air from your lungs, a grim fate but hardly the worst. However, it was men like Altenhofen, the dangerously rich who bought politicians the way regular people bought stamps, who contemplated not your pain but your moral bankruptcy. I would have been more comfortable under Hawthorne's gaze because he simply seemed to want to knock my teeth out.

Altenhofen wanted to buy my soul.

"Well then, I certainly hope you're feeling better," he gestured towards the chairs that ringed the table. "Please, sit down. I think we still have a few moments before everything is ready." Altenhofen said with his lips pulled into that tight line. The dose of crassness only put me in the same crosshairs that Pringle had been.

Yay for me.

I pulled the chair out at the other end of the table and took my seat opposite Altenhofen, while Tek and Moxley filtered around either side. Altenhofen gave a little cant of his head, and Hawthorne moved to pull out Tek's chair for her. Tek seemed to allow this politely enough, standing back a little with her dark eyes boring into the back of Hawthorne as he eased the chair out from the table. One could almost feel the tightening of her muscles in his presence; her whole-body language subtly shifted in his proximity through the alchemy of contempt.

Hawthorne seemed to notice the stare, or maybe just the general shift in energy around him. He paused with his brawny mitts still on the back of the chair and looked over his left shoulder. That same patiently malicious smile that I had dealt with on the ride over, the same one that had provoked me towards his antagonization and even then, made my skin crawl, was back.

"Problem, sugar?" Hawthorne asked, but it was no question; it was an invitation for trouble.

Hawthorne might have backed down hard men; he'd no doubt certainly killed his share and was familiar with the application of blade, gun, club, and fist in the pursuit of his wants. One look at the man might have told one all of these things, but when he came face to face with Tek he encountered a foe that did not flinch, buckle, or bend. She lifted her chin a little, met his eyes, and for a moment that seems longer in memory than it truly was, she only responded with silence.

Tek looked towards Altenhofen, and it was the only time that her eyes left Hawthorne.

"I'm not going to stay in the same room with him." Tek told Altenhofen with the sort of hard determination that left little doubt as to the likelihood of the follow-through.

Tek stood less than a foot away from a man who could not die and who gladly looked as if he might disjoint a fellow human being while wearing a happy grin. She was in the home of, and facing down, a man who had, for all intents and purposes, purchased the United States government and now probably kept the receipt in his back pocket should he ever want a refund. Moxley had slid around to the other side of the table and watched with the mute horrid amazement of a surly teenager seeing a disagreement between parents unfold.

Hawthorne turned his head to look at Altenhofen and, with a sneering mockery that was only half related to a smile, asked, "Aww, h'aint hurt nobody. She can't be serious." Hawthorne's drawled words were like the growl of a sleeping, ill-tempered hound, more incredulous than upset, but maybe only just barely, and certainly only for now.

I watched as Altenhofen regarded both, his expression somewhere between contempt for the tedious and mild amusement at Tek's defiance. His head fell to the side just slightly, as if he may have gleaned some new knowledge of the situation simply from the angle with which he viewed it. The lid of one eye sank down into a squinch, and his lips drew into what an optimistic soul might have called a smile. I didn't doubt the authenticity of the expression then, only the motives that compelled it to surface.

I doubted highly that men like Hawthorne or Altenhofen ever smiled for good reasons.

"I'm sure we'll be able to make it through dinner without the need for your services, Mr. Hawthorne," Altenhofen conceded. "Though, I'd like to assure you, Ms. Tekakwitha, you are in no danger from myself or Mr. Hawthorne."

Altenhofen sounded like he was giving his best impressionist take of a patient grandfather, but the fact he had no soul kept getting in the way. The words were too well-rehearsed and fell too smoothly from his mouth.

Tek's brow furrowed for a moment, and then without a word, she turned her head back to Hawthorne, who still stood before her like some looming statue dedicated to the concept of boots upon throats. He folded his arms across his chest as she stared up at him, and for a moment, I wished that I had brought a camera to capture the size difference between the two and the utter lack of fear that Tek displayed in Hawthorne's presence. There was no backing down, no cowering, or flinching. Not from her. Not now. Maybe not ever.

"That's not what I'm afraid of," she said simply, and the tension in the air thickened that much more.

There was a little shift in Hawthorne, one that I did not immediately recognize but Altenhofen did. Hawthorne straightened a little and shifted his arms back, forcing his jacket to slip away from his waist. This shift in posture, this quiet promise of violence conveyed through the tensing of muscle and the flat deadness of his eyes was cut short, though.

"That will be enough, Mr. Hawthorne. You are dismissed." Altenhofen slid a note of authority into the faux grandfatherly act that he had been using to try to diffuse the situation with the chilly efficiency of a quiet monster placing razor blades in Halloween apples.

Hawthorne gave a grunt, but he did not defy or try to persuade Altenhofen any further than he already had. He instead brought both palms up in front of him in the universal symbol of 'no harm' and edged his way around Tek. He spared Moxley a glare on the way out the door along with Pringle, but he all but ignored me. I didn't rate as

195

anything more than an annoyance to him. Not with the likes of Tek and Moxley on the grounds. They were wolves, and I was but a small yapping dog nipping at the heels of his master with my ink and paper teeth.

Only after he'd left the room did Tek sit down, but for a moment the tension and awkwardness remained.

"Try not to hold it against Hawthorne that he was born without a functioning personality." Moxley said in an exaggerated conspiratorial whisper from his side of the table, he'd already unraveled his silverware from its napkin and was now using it to build what looked like the foundation of a small temple for the sake of his own amusement.

"He's a fucking monster." Tek hissed through clenched teeth, but without Hawthorne in the room the urgency of her anger seemed to be receding.

"That was my impression," I added, and Altenhofen who had been following the conversation along with his eyes was suddenly looking at me, "Is that a common practice of yours? Hiring men like that?" I should have played nice, but a foolish protectiveness was beginning to form; born of admiration and wonder it left me wanting to defend Tek though she certainly didn't need me to do so.

"Are you even aware of the things that man has done?" Tek tacked her own question onto mine.

The grimness that had been on Altenhofen's face when we'd first entered, behind schedule, was now returned. He wasn't trying to defuse or keep the peace any longer, and thus had no need for any sort of kindly play upon his age. No, here he was questioned, and it was apparent from the way he cleared his throat and shifted in his seat that he was not a man that was used to giving explanations. If Congress had hauled him before a committee, he would have simply bought the committee; if anyone in his company questioned him, he would simply fire them, and if all else failed, I had a feeling that was what Hawthorne was for. Still, I wanted to hear it from the man himself.

"I am more than aware of Mr. Hawthorne's questionable past. However, I would remind each of you that the taming of the world requires men like Mr. Hawthor-"

"You mean butchers?" Tek interrupted.

Altenhofen weathered it like a sturdy ship might take the slap of an unexpected wave. There was a little pause, the righting of the 'ship' so to speak, and then he continued on.

"...requires men like Mr. Hawthorne. There is no empire, industry, nation, or people that cannot trace its origins back and find men like Hawthorne among their ranks. None that have persisted into this day, at any rate." He gave a small, dismissive roll of his hand, "Now, please. Is this the sort of conversation we really want to begin with? My hiring practices?" Altenhofen offered us a truce the way one might offer a dog the last bites of a sandwich to spare yourself the trouble of throwing it away.

"What did he do, exactly?" I asked.

"You don't want to know." Moxley quipped before taking a long sip of his water and pretending to study the little temple of forks and knives he'd built by his plate rather than look at any of the involved parties.

"Tell him." Tek with narrowed eyes demanded of Altenhofen in a low voice that reminded me of the wind that sometimes found itself trapped between the buildings back in Chicago.

Altenhofen gave a tired sigh that was born from somewhere deep in the desiccated chamber of his chest, a wet and tired push of air from a failing system that felt the matters of butchery and principle were as ho-hum as I did the politics of northern Idaho. He was not ashamed. If he'd ever known shame, then it was long since washed away by countless transactions. From his expression, I wagered he felt very little at all. Not when it came to these discussions of morality and especially not when it came to the particulars of his business practice.

Mr. Hawthorne and men like him, in the early days of this nation's history, were used to displace those deemed problematic by the government and captains of industry at the time. He was, as I understand it, very effective but not at all what we would consider humane or gentle. So much so, that those who possessed active chaos genes among them did what exactly?" Altenhofen turned the question sharply on Tek, and her eyes darkened.

"They cursed him. Condemned him to walk the earth until he'd mourned for all he'd destroyed." Tek said with a bitterness that I did not think was possible

Altenhofen must have noticed my puzzled expression. His intense blue eyes locked onto mine, and his lips twisted into what might have been the most genuine expression of enjoyment one could expect from him. Money, sex, the subjugation and control of the Namebreakers, an industry built on the Shadow People – all of that had long ago lost its appeal. I realized it then with a clarity that cut deep and made my skin crawl.

Triumph was Altenhofen's drug of choice, and he was a fiend beyond the scope of all known depravity in pursuit of his next fix.

"Precisely. This is, of course, at least partly why I believe it is in the best interest of mankind if the chaos gene is quietly suppressed from our day-to-day lives. Totality Adjustment, or magic if you prefer, is wielded not by gods but by fallible humans. Hawthorne is incapable of remorse. I'm quite certain he's actually some breed of high-functioning sociopath, and I shudder to think what horrors he would get up to if not in my employment," Altenhofen twisted the knife in the guts of Tek's argument without a second thought.

"It would have been simpler, cleaner, and perhaps even better for all mankind had he simply been killed. However, he wasn't, and so now I restrain him by cultivating a taste for finery and the comforts that wealth provides." Altenhofen explained like a doctor giving his justification for breaking out a bone saw.

I never got to hear Tek's response as the door to the kitchen came open and a small multitude of servers and kitchen staff began to filter into the dining room, effectively ending the discussion.

Dinner was served.

COYOTE WALLACE

Dining with The Devil

It should be noted, before I delve deeper into the wild events that unfolded, that I've always harbored a profound and all-encompassing distrust of anything too pristine. I learned long ago that when the object of your deepest desires materializes before you, it often heralds impending doom. This ingrained skepticism, this reflexive aversion to all things bright and dazzling, fuels my restless spirit, propelling me from one adventure to the next. Perhaps this innate wariness is why I remained less swayed by Altenhofen's grand designs than he had hoped.

The servants presented us with silver-domed trays before pouring our wine—a vintage of Gamay that I might have once afforded Jen and myself in the halcyon days of my more lucrative endeavors—before retreating discreetly behind our chairs. Their practiced choreography, the synchronized movements of these servants, possessed an unsettling precision. It wasn't just the unnatural symmetry of their actions that perturbed me (humans, in my humble opinion, should not mimic each other so precisely outside of certain aquatic activities). No, it was more than that; their time had been bought, their very existence molded into servitude for our spectacle.

Can you fathom anything more abhorrent?

My server, a towering, gaunt figure with a mane of oil-black hair cascading over his broad forehead, resembled more a concert pianist than a mere servant. His elongated limbs and skeletal fingers bespoke a potential for musical virtuosity. Yet, here he stood, rigid and upright, as if auditioning for a role in a military parade. Undoubtedly, this display was intended to impress, but I couldn't help but find the entire spectacle absurdly comical. The disquieting realization dawned upon me: this poor, pitiable soul had been ferried all the way out here for this mundane display of servitude. Would he be whisked away under the cloak of night, like some clandestine cargo? Did Altenhofen stash them away in an oversized cabinet, akin to a collection of living steak knives?

Enquiring minds wanted to know, namely mine.

For those curious souls among you, our meal was a subtle threat, served drizzled in nostalgia and executed with a remarkable precision that could only belong to the culinary world's version of a deadeye sniper. Each dish was unique, tailored to our tastes and infused with emotions like a chef's twist on a mad scientist's experiment. They seemed plucked from the grasping hands of time's memory and laid before us, apparently just to soften us up for whatever Altenhofen had planned.

As for my own dish, it was a cheeseburger and a side of fries. But not just any cheeseburger and fries, mind you. No, that would be sacrilege of the highest order. This was a Sammy's cheeseburger and fries, distinguished from its fast-food brethren by a faint indentation in the center for which cheddar may be applied, and a barely perceptible toasting of the bun. All of it originated from a blackened flat grill steeped in no less than thirty years of the conjuring of its artery-clogging brethren. I'd devoured them sometimes twice a day in my youth, when I was hustling to make ends meet on a freelance salary. Cheap and delicious, that was Sammy's Diner for you.

All very intriguing, until you realize that Sammy's Diner had closed its doors long before I could even afford to pay my first light bill. I had cherished that memory in secret, silently comparing all other culinary experiences in my stumbling quest through the gastronomic landscape without even realizing it. If it hadn't been placed before me then, I might never have known just how desperate that search had become.

It was a golden memory plucked from the depths of my past, seemingly insignificant in its size but profoundly influential in shaping my culinary preferences, down and dirty or not. Denying its impact would have been futile. There it sat before my eyes, as if Altenhofen had plucked it from the vault of my own memories while I slept.

The cheeseburger was, of course, accompanied by a heap of golden home fries, no doubt cooked on the same blackened flat grill, each bite infused with a hint of that legacy.

"Fuck me and call me Sally." I muttered in open wonder, more candidly than I'd intended.

My mind was already racing through the possibilities. This wasn't some fact plucked from an obscure reference in a previous work I had written. While I couldn't recall every article I had ever penned, I was certain that none of them had mentioned Sammy's Diner on the low end of Knoxville. The titular Sammy had been a husky African American man who smoked cigarettes as he cooked, listened to Muddy Waters, and grumbled about the youth. He probably tipped the scales at three hundred pounds and was at least fifty years old when I was a young man. There was no way he was still alive.

The initial awe began to wane as my distrust kicked in.

Not so for Moxley, whose excitement and riotous laughter were infectious, pulling me from my cynical theories and astonished musings. A quick glance at his plate would have left any outsider baffled. His meal seemed even less impressive than my standard fare: chicken fingers. Not any special variety either, just something you could easily heat up in a toaster oven or microwave, the kind you could snag for $5.99 at any supermarket.

"Third favorite!" Moxley exclaimed, holding up three fingers. "I've dined with you three times now, and every time you've pulled off this trick. Every time, you get it right – but I still knew I wouldn't need the silverware." he said, plucking a chicken tender between his fingers and chomping off the tip in celebration of what he deemed a victory, or at least a stalemate worth boasting about.

Moxley's excitability and personal dynamism were simply facets of his temperament. However, I found myself pondering the nature of Altenhofen's relationship with him. Hawthorne was the heavy, Pringle a sniveling cur. Where did this young man, who seemed to rebel against everything all at once, fit into the equation? What exactly did Altenhofen have him doing?

Moxley's reaction was loud and animated enough that it had sucked in the attention of everyone in the room like the howling vortex of a tornado pulling in air. The only person who paid no mind to Moxley was Tek. Tek, who sat staring at her plate so quietly that even I only noticed after the dreadful reptilian flick of Altenhofen's eyes in her direction.

I could not be sure, but I did not think that she had even looked up at Moxley's excitement. The features of her face, strong yet feminine and undeniably beautiful regardless of personal taste, had been swallowed by a darkness of mood. Her lips were pulled into a thin line, and the space between her brows had picked up a few furrows that gathered like clouds over the dark sky of her eyes.

"Are you okay?" I asked, all nostalgia and any traces of appetite bleeding out of the wound that Tek's expression left on me.

Tek's plate was no more remarkable than mine, though the choice of grub had undoubtedly required a bit more grease of the elbow variety than Moxley's sad culinary affair or my own stolen memory. The meal appeared to be a rack of what might have been lamb or beef. I couldn't tell from my vantage point, and it would later never occur to me to ask. The meat was slathered in a rich, thick sauce that was almost burgundy in color. Out from the side of the meat where the sauce might have pooled on the white of her plate, island-like slices of potato awaited the skewering of a fork.

"Leave." Altenhofen told the attendants, and they did almost at once, which I was thankful for, but somehow his words felt like they tainted my own concern.

Tek brought one finger over to her plate and very gently dabbed the tip into the sauce before bringing it to her mouth for a taste. There was a juvenile part of me that might have found something lurid in the gesture if not for the gathering gloom around Tek and the certainty that Altenhofen's display was not going to have the intended effect. The lines between her brow that had been like a few gathering clouds earlier now were as heavy as thunderheads. I could almost see her chasing the memory down the hard-packed roads and sharp turns of her own mind. She didn't look up from the plate, didn't bother to hide the small, sad smile that tried to pull her lips upwards but got tangled in bitterness somewhere along the way.

Tek pushed the plate away with enough force to send it clinking and clattering into the wine glasses.

"Not to your liking?" Altenhofen asked with a remarkable glibness for an old man who was staring down a woman who could pull him apart on the atomic level and put him back together again as the world's richest giant living phallus.

"Why?" Tek asked Altenhofen with a certain tightness of tone that only hinted at how hard she must have been holding onto her emotions.

Altenhofen did not immediately respond. Instead, he quietly began to unravel his spoon from his napkin and set about the steady deliberate work of stirring the bowl of brown soup with long thick pale noodles. Tek's anger, stirred no doubt not by the memory that Altenhofen had decided to try to summon up like some hellish necromancer, and compounded by the horrible sense that we had been invaded somehow without our knowledge or consent, burned bright in her dark eyes.

No one likes being under a microscope, there's too many horrible ends that come to those who find themselves under microscopes - just ask bacteria.

A lesson well remembered in the coming kingdom of the single cell organisms after mankind has gleefully and destroyed the world by entrusting it to men like Altenhofen.

"She has a point. What's all this about? For God's sakes man, enough posturing." I had to throw in my two cents. I wasn't going to let Tek fight alone.

Moxley, either by wise choice, his strange affinity with the playing out of events or his own self-absorbed nature ignored all of us completely. Despite all his earlier ruckus, he was as quiet as a church mouse now, all save for the loud crunch of his teeth on the crispy exterior of his meal. An old hand at eating through disputes recognizes the tableside disassociation of their own.

"Flädlesuppe was my son's favorite. Not actually my own…" Altenhofen said with a tired push of air that might have been a sigh.

He let go of the spoon's handle and it fell with a clatter against the side of the dish and lifted his eyes.

"Why?" Altenhofen for a moment seemed as if he might laugh and I could think of nothing worse than that sound.

"To demonstrate to you that there is precious little that your abilities can do that cannot be replicated by men," a lone, bushy eyebrow rose as if in anticipation of how this might be taken by Tek. "There is no trick here. There is no illusion. We live in a world where every conversation is recorded, every email logged, every reservation or review. For matters where no such record exists, well, no man is an island, and loyalty trades at a much lower value on the open market than most consider." Altenhofen said, offering up an expression that could only be confused with a smile by the naivest of men.

He reminded me of a man of very low humor who does not particularly enjoy the company of children explaining how the quarter had been pulled from behind their ear.

"Oh, fuck your desperate justifications for eugenics. Why are we really here?" Tek's cheeks had darkened a little, and her eyes fastened like the jaws of a wildcat on her prey as she asked again the purpose of the whole affair.

I had to admit I was curious too.

"Like most resources on this planet, Dynametrium is not limitless. It is, in fact, quite limited, formed only from the t-" Altenhofen began before Tek interrupted.

"Formed only from people like Moxley and myself who push ourselves beyond our limits. It's made from the Consumed." Tek finished for him.

"The Consumed?" I did not know the terminology.

"Namebreakers who use up everything they have. See, when we start weaving the Word, that energy has to come from somewhere, right?" Moxley had finally deemed to enter the conversation and was now gesturing at me with one of the chicken tenders.

"Right," I agreed, as much as I could, considering how little I actually knew.

"It doesn't happen that much these days. Hell, this is America – it really does take an act of mystical wonder to keep from getting fat. The more you Speak, the more calories you burn," Moxley gave another little roll of the half-chomped chicken tender. "The thing is, it's nearly impossible to do yourself in accidentally. You have to intentionally cross that line, if you catch my drift." Moxley concluded by shifting the piece of processed chicken he was pointing at me back at himself and taking another bite.

Altenhofen must have seen the look of confusion bleeding into disgust because he added to Moxley's explanation, but his words provided no comfort at all.

"Think of it a bit like oil. Unlike most elements, it cannot be conjured by 'the Word.' However, with enough energy, it can be duplicated without the need for waiting for someone like Tek or Moxley to overexert themselves." Altenhofen explained.

"It's ghoulish." Tek said with enough determination to suggest she would not be moved from the position.

Altenhofen's white brows lifted, and he made a short grunting sound of approval that might have been agreement or simply amusement at how often he'd heard that particular line. I could not be certain, but in my experience, men like Altenhofen cared very little for what anyone thought. They cared especially little for those who did not have stock options or a seat on some board of directors.

This condition, a hard-grown and cold shell to keep out any traces of humanity, is a common symptom not just of the greedy but of the successfully greedy; those who believe that such success sets them above and beyond petty things like social limitations or standards. All that becomes inconvenience must be destroyed or paved over. They simply can't help themselves. Their egos are too large to support cohabitation.

For all the work Altenhofen had put into eradicating the 'scourge' of Namebreaking in North America – as much as he'd built his entire fortune on the fear of not being able to keep the American Spirit from entwining itself with the American Dream – he was more like Tek, Moxley, and all those he set himself against than he'd ever be like myself.

"Quite ghoulish. Unfortunately, Dynametrium is the only thing that keeps us, as a people, holding on. Imagine a world without it if you can. Imagine the damage that would have been done if not for the help and relief we've provided." Altenhofen had fashioned his successes into a weapon meant not to bludgeon his foe but to cut their positions to bloody ribbons.

"Vampires on the streets hunting people, dangerous lycanthropic individuals potentially losing themselves in a crowded area, to say nothing of the harm the Namebreakers would do. Most people enjoy their reality being fairly predictable. You have no more right to it than you do their lives." There was a cadence to the words that strongly implied this was not the first time they were spoken.

Anti-Magic Words.

The horrible part was that I was not entirely certain that Altenhofen was wrong. People were wild, crazy, and by their very natures often selfish. The attributes that America espoused to be the high pinnacle of moral pedigree – individualism, innovation, and the pursuit of one's dreams through hard work – could, at the drop of a hat, turn like a half-coyote mix and bite.

There existed a tiny voice within me that argued, with no small certainty, that Altenhofen was hideously right. My time as a journalist had brought me into contact with more elements of the so-called 'Shadow People' than most, and there was a certain fear in them that had been born too late in the Namebreakers, who for all intents and purposes were very much human.

The vampires had to sleep during the day; the lycanthropes looked out (in the moments when they were not afflicted by their curse) and saw the fate of the great beast, be they dragon, white tigers, or the dodo bird, and The Fair Folk recalled the march of Christendom. Cooperation and cohabitation were necessary for their survival. Even in the 'old days', before everyone had stepped into the light, they had policed their own and did their best not to draw down the ire of mankind. The last thing you wanted to do was become the common enemy for a species that spends an extraordinary amount of time murdering itself in the wild throes of a xenophobic orgiastic rage.

The fact that they had shifted, through some strange alchemy of our culture, from the realm of 'monsters' to some form of 'tragically cool', was seen as proof the decision to come into the light was the right one by many or, at the very least, the most profitable.

The Namebreakers, though, were different, for they were tied to us in a way that was far too personal.

One could blame any harm, or even the worst of the behavior of those afflicted with a certain allergy to sunlight or silver, on their respective curses. No matter how newly minted or how many times one was reminded of their origin, the mind simply would not allow for them to be seen as 'us'. There were those who sympathized with them the way they might sympathize with a mountain lion that has found Colorado joggers to be exceptionally delicious. One does not blame a beast for being a beast. However, those with sympathy that was more than surface deep, were few and far between.

The Namebreaker did not have this buffer or barrier in the public eye. Even the most tragic of them, those who came into their abilities through accident or whose harm was no more intentional than a traffic mishap, were still treated as 'Persons of Mass Destruction' by the state. One mistake was all it ever took for the Man to come down on you hard and fast.

All that Altenhofen and men like him had to do in order to sell to the masses and the governments on the notion of his 'quiet solution' to the Namebreaker problem was to emphasize the destructive potential wielded by those for whom nothing was impossible.

Fear, imagination, and what all of us who drive with our doors locked and windows rolled up know to be true did the rest.

"You still haven't told us why we're here. You're dancing around it." I interjected. Whether I agreed with the danger posed by Americans walking around with the abilities of gods at their fingertips or not, I still could not bring myself to tolerate the high stink of the filthy rich's bullshit.

"Would you care to explain to our dear writer friend what a Resonation Amplifier is, Mr. Allerton?" Altenhofen inquired, though it was more of a statement than a question.

"Not really." Moxley retorted as he took a long greedy drink of his wine and wiped his mouth with the back of his hand.

The combined weight of not only Altenhofen's stare but also my own and Tek's did not seem to bring about the slightest discomfort in the purple-haired mad genius. Youth and his own self-importance provided him with a shield which he threw up to ward off the pelting of expectations. Young or not, he'd clearly had a great deal of practice at it, and there was part of me that envied him a little more for that ability. It was one which came to him so easily but had taken me far more years and the creation of a whole other persona to learn.

"They are..." Tek began to explain, and that was enough to finally compel Moxley into action.

"Oh, for God's sake don't mangle the explanation. Informals learn everything second hand and it drives me BATSHIT," Moxley exclaimed, throwing his head back, staring at the ceiling, and shaking his head from side to side in exaggerated frustration. "Look, the concept was first pioneered in sixteen forty-two by Ign–" Moxley began as though from rote memory.

It was his turn to be cut off, though, and I caught a little hint of a smile cross Tek's lips when Altenhofen interrupted with, "I do believe that a condensed version may be in order, Mr. Allerton." he said dryly.

Moxley pushed a quick jet of air out his nose, and his head fell limply forward. I imagined that this must have been what it was like for a nuclear physicist having to discuss his work with a layman. Perhaps he'd brought his car in to have the tires rotated and found himself explaining how a reactor functioned to a man struggling with the concept of complementary air fresheners.

His eyes were closed, and one hand, fingers still greasy from his meal, came up to rub the bridge of his nose.

"Alright, alright - for the stupid people then. Think of them as radio towers for The Word that both project and amplify the signal. You make a field of flowers with one, you make a field of flowers all down the chain. They tap into lines of en–" Even then, Moxley couldn't help himself; there was an eagerness that crept in when he had any chance to show off.

"That will be enough, Mr. Allerton." Altenhofen throttled back for Moxley, though doing so was gradually eating away at his patience and carefully constructed temperament.

"You're going to use them to create more Dynametrium. You've run out of ways to wipe us out using ourselves and you need more..." Tek said, stunned as she made the leap.

"In two years' time, the world's supply of Dynametrium will run out. After that, the governments of the world will be forced to take other more drastic steps to deal with the problem. Your people will not come back all at once but given time, they will become more common, and this is not a secret." Altenhofen's cold stare hit us like an unexpected and lethal blizzard as he spoke.

He was letting the weight of his words sink in.

"Those with the power and means to do so will begin to enact measures to limit the possibility of incident." Altenhofen paused for a moment, but he'd swung the hard blue of his eyes solely to Tek now and showed no sign of relenting.

"There are millions of people worldwide who live normal lives and contribute to society. They take their pills and go on happily with their very ordinary existence. They will, and I can assure you of this, be rounded up and thrown onto trains long before they are given the chance to manifest The Word. Simply put, without Dynametrium, the world will descend into blood and darkness. Instead of quietly and peacefully fading away, you and everyone like you will be hunted down and killed within a decade." Altenhofen was not an emotional man, but he spoke the words with a grim certainty that lent itself to sadness. He reminded me of a doctor giving terminal news to a patient who had bet it all on a positive outlook and healthy living.

"You can't be serious." If I sounded incredulous, it was because my mind staggered at the horror.

"I could be wrong, of course. I am only human..." Altenhofen conceded as we sat before reminders of just how deep his intelligence networks ran on fine china plates.

"You can't think I'll help you?" Tek sounded as slapped and stunned as I did.

Moxley snorted in laughter.

212

"No, you are not here for your talents, I'm afraid. Mr. Allerton is quite capable of the task and is being compensated very generously for assuming the burden of the risk himself," Altenhofen gave a little shake of his head as if the idea just wouldn't do, "Your purpose, despite what you may believe, is to simply take an opportunity. I have invited yourself, one of the loudest and most fervent members of the opposition to my work and a man who, some believe, is an expert on the 'American spirit', to persuade me to not do so."

Altenhofen had finally let the other shoe drop, and for a moment, neither Tek nor myself seemingly knew how to respond.

"What the fuck?!?" Not my finest choice of words, but they seemed to fit given what we were going through.

Once again, Altenhofen seemed to get that fix he craved for now he smiled, and although it was light, no more than the faint pulling of his lips upwards, it was still the sort of smile one might get when they witnessed their dog perform a particularly cute trick, and it still filled my guts with ice.

His gaze had now settled on me as if they intended to pry some valuable commodity from my being.

"It's exactly as it sounds. I am not long for this world, Mr. Wonderful. I have no family, I have no heir, and when I am gone, my company will be picked apart. My empire sold piece by piece until nothing is left at all," Altenhofen's eyes seemed to search my own for a sense of understanding.

Legacy. That was what he was after.

"It will be at least ten years before we, as a species, cross the threshold and momentum does the rest when it comes to the Namebreakers. If that is to be my legacy, it will not be seen by me, and I owe a promise to an old friend to listen, one last time, before I make my final thrust," Roy

Altenhofen explained it all so calmly that you might have forgiven him for being absolutely mad.

I suppose that's the way it is for all madmen. Those without opponents inevitably invent their own rivals.

"Take the night, though, compose your arguments. I am not evil. I am not a monster. I will listen, and if you can persuade me, then we will let the dice roll as they may. If not..."

Tek stood up so violently that her chair went tumbling back onto the floor with a loud bang.

"You're fucking twisted. You're doing all this just so you can feel like some benevolent god? These are -PEOPLE- we are talking about. The Word is part of what makes us people, part of what makes us who we are. You can't expect us to..." Tek spoke with such building fury that whatever control she held on herself threatened to slip. Small cracks were forming in her glass like spiderwebs of crystal.

"You may leave. You're not a prisoner. I'm sure Mr. Wonderful will make a compelling argument all on his own, won't you?" Altenhofen said with all the smug satisfaction of a cat that holds a mouse trapped beneath its paw.

All eyes were on me.

I hesitated.

Shit.

Tek turned and stormed out of the room. For a moment, I remained sitting at the table, and there was no sound at all save for Moxley pouring himself another glass of wine. I cleared my throat and pushed through the awkwardness to find my feet. I had no appetite now, and if I had any more of Altenhofen in one dose, I might well have peeled my skin off while I ran screaming into the night. One could only handle so much exposure to a mad capitalist before you began to lose it, and the only sensible responses were acts of revolution or desperate debauchery in the name of forgetfulness.

"I think I better go talk to her. It's been great. Really. Fantastic," I said so quickly that I don't know for certain if Altenhofen or Moxley heard me.

I was already pushing out the door and going after Tek.

I caught up to her just down the hall and was thankful that Hawthorne did not appear to be anywhere in sight; I wasn't sure that Tek would have been able to hold back from doing something rash and destructive. She stood with both hands against the wall and her head hung low between shoulders as if she had just run a long race and now finally was able to pause for breath.

Though it may seem insensitive now, there was a part of me that certainly understood, that if I surprised her there was a chance she might turn around and lash out. I meant no offense by it, but I did not want to be scattered across the stars or have my arm rendered into solid stone.

"Hey!" I called out long before I was within arm's reach...

Tek kept her head down but at least turned it to look at me, and I could see beneath the anger in her dark eyes was a pool of deep pain. I could approach with relative safety, and I did so with a little more confidence. When I drew close enough to put my hand on Tek's shoulder, I did, and though I felt the muscles tense beneath my fingers, she did not pull away from the gesture.

Still, there was only silence; that silence spoke far louder of her anger and hurt than any words that I knew.

"I say we leave. Fuck him. Fuck the whole thing. The Mystic Standard can sue me, and I'll... I don't know... I'll do shitty podcasts if I have to," I offered up without thinking. "I'm not sure what he gave you to be here, but you'll be better off without it." I was trying to be comforting.

Sometimes it was better to turn over the table than it was to keep playing the game.

"No," Tek hissed low in her throat, and when she straightened up, I saw glittering lines on her cheeks.

"What?" I thought she had wanted to leave, to reject Altenhofen's offer and tell him to shove the whole mad plan up his ass.

"Do you trust me?" Tek asked with a sudden intensity that demanded the truth and gave poor wretches like me no hope of twisting away once the dark pools of her eyes locked on.

"Not really." I answered truthfully.

Tek squinted and stepped forward, throwing both arms around me and locking her fingers behind my back. I could feel the warmth of her skin through my shirt and smell the shampoo in her raven hair once again. This distraction kept my brain from realizing what was about to happen. Her mouth lifted to my ear, and she whispered words to me that slid through the grasping fingers of my memory like water. There was a strange sensation, a bit like the freefall of a rollercoaster mixed with the jarring slowing of time that always seems to happen in any truly destructive automotive crash.

With but a whisper, Tek whisked the two of us away and exposed me to a new truth about myself.

I hated teleporting much more than I could ever possibly hate flying.

Wishes, Luck, and Faerie Dust

Rishel Peak, standing at an elevation of just over six thousand six hundred feet, overlooked the Bonneville Salt Flats like some ancient toad-like deity squatting with the horizon at its back. I had never been one for climbing mountains; my age and love for tobacco had always served as natural deterrents. So, naturally, the best way to celebrate my sudden and unexpected arrival on Rishel Peak was to collapse to my knees before Tek and violently go into a dry heaving fit.

My mind had been assaulted by a myriad of colors that I had no words for, as they did not exist. Smells, tastes, and tactile sensations were all scrambled up in the mother of all sensory overloads. I had been crushed beneath softness, peppered with kisses made of fire and razorblades, bathed in laughter, shame, and joy. The act of having my every atom pulled apart and reassembled over a great distance proved to be a hard pill for a mind inexperienced with such disquieting matters to process. I wanted to remember the "in-between," but my mind just kept pulling up fragments that neither made sense nor fit together in any discernable way.

COYOTE WALLACE

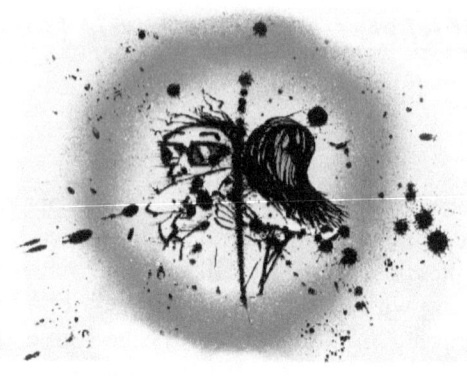

My ears were ringing as if I had just placed my head next to a steam whistle and told the engineer, "Let her rip!" Tek, of course, was doing much better, suffering no ill effects at all. She looked at me with one dark eyebrow pitched upward and shook her head in disapproval. For those of you who are reading and wondering at the best way to court a sorceress, allow me to share a bit of wisdom: dry heaving, like a cat, at her feet is never going to stir the fire in her loins. In fact, I would hazard a guess from the look that Tek was giving me that it had quite the opposite effect.

"You know, I always thought you would be more used to The Word than that. Like, you know - for a guy who wrote about partying with faeries and spends all his time ranting about a blood-drinking Richard Nixon making a political comeback."

It was the dead of night, and the only illumination on the mountain was that provided by the moon and the stars. I was grateful for this darkness because it meant that at least there may be some hope of cover for the raw terror that was still working its way out of my system. I could have argued the nuance of Tek's point, that very few experiences on the planet could rightfully compare with having one's body and soul used to break the laws of physics. However, that would have required more resolve than I had with my stomach breakdancing and my ears full of discordant melodies.

I let my fingers dig small trenches in the stony soil of the mountaintop and closed my eyes. The dark was a merciful balm to vision that had been bombarded by colors too bright and too vivid for this reality; their memory stuck in my mind like small bloody pieces of glass lodged in a cut.

"So, you have heard of me?" I croaked and crawled a few feet towards a rough, irregularly shaped boulder that was some distance from the edge.

I had no desire to find out whether Tek could make me fly.

"Don't let it go to your head." She gave a little shake of her head. "I'm pretty sure everyone who is sixteen and smoked a joint in their friend's car has heard of you. I used to have a boyfriend, when I was seventeen, who had a black and white poster of you on his wall. The one with the motorcycle and the two faerie knights?"

"I know the one." I said with the relief that every fifty-plus-year-old man feels when his heart slows down rather than comes to a sudden halting stop.

The hell of it was, I did know exactly which poster she was talking about. Those early days had been tough on the pocket, and I'd been foolish enough to overlook that The Mystic Standard retained the rights to all unused photographs from my stories. Not that such bitter wisdom served me well now. Call it a hunch, but I somehow doubted that Tek had brought me here to discuss the finer points of being fucked in the ass by contract lawyers.

"I also had a girlfriend in college who said that you didn't really write all that much. You just wrote the same thing again and again. That maybe you believed it all when you first wrote about the American Dream... Which doesn't exist, by the way... Not for a whole lot of us... Then, at some point, you just checked out." Tek carried on, seemingly unaware that I had heard such criticisms before.

Everyone always thinks they're the first to make this observation. Even those with the ability to bend creation with their words are not immune to this law of the greater universe. A side effect of success and being the centerpiece of so much of my own work. It would have been amusing if I wasn't sitting atop a very cold, very dark mountaintop.

I pressed my back a little more firmly against the boulder I'd taken up with and now patted myself down for cigarettes. I'd endured the whole awkward affair with Altenhofen without smoking, and though Tek had purged the nicotine cravings from my system with her demonstration earlier, the jarring of nerves resulting in a mental craving for the tobacco's comfort was overwhelming. I was fumbling about looking for my lighter when my fingers brushed against the vial of Faerie Dust in my pocket.

"Drug habits are expensive, and deadlines are the most insidious of sonsofbitches." I told her as I hauled both vial and lighter out.

This earned a laugh that was beautiful enough in the dark that I reconsidered my position on teleportation instantly. I may well have renounced that position completely, did commercials with a large stupid grin on my face nodding happily in agreement that teleportation, not driving, was the superior mode of travel, if I could have only heard it once more. The laugh was singular in that instance, elusive as a nightbird call that soon fades into the black, leaving one to wonder if it ever existed at all.

"At least you're honest." Tek said approvingly and with the slyest of grins.

There was a faint difference in her features that I could barely pick out beneath the moonlight; she seemed a little thinner of feature, a little more sunken around her eyes. She reminded me of someone who had been awake on a two-day coke binge and completely disregarded the need to eat. There was a toll to what the Namebreakers did, one that slowly ate them alive from the inside out and shunting the two of us to the top of a mountain had done her no favors. Unlike the 'purification' of my tainted flesh, this was altogether a larger matter, and with it came a steeper price. This devil's fee was one that Tek was silently paying and must have deemed worth it to be free of Altenhofen's walls for even a small amount of time.

"Only lie to the ones I love; that way at least I'm going to Hell for a good reason." I said around my cigarette while I cupped my hand around the lighter in a desperate bid to keep out the wind.

Tek turned away and looked out over the Flats and the small glittering jewel that perspective and distance had reduced Altenhofen's compound too. She crossed her arms over her chest, and by her silence, I could feel her thoughts drifting back to the old man and his madman's logic. I tried to understand how it might have felt, to put myself in her shoes and realized instantly that I could not. I would never be where she was standing now; I would never have made the journey or been called to do so. Even if I had been spoon-fed propaganda like everyone else in America, the idea of slowly erasing someone out of fear was fundamentally abhorrent to me.

Then again, so was Altenhofen's predicted alternative, and the cold certainty I had inside me that while he wasn't entirely correct, he was not wrong enough by far.

Somewhere deep inside of me, a voice born of revolutionary tendencies that had been silent for many years began to grumble in its coma-like sleep. The voice had not sunk into insensible slumber on its own, nor had it been placed there by any physical violence or infliction of frightening harm upon my person. No, it had been placed there by the sight of countless others falling beneath the thunderous strike of the billy club, the hiss of the fire hose, and the snarling teeth of attack dogs that only take their commands in German. The urge to flip over any system that only gives you two bad choices and nothing to hope for is like some burrowing insect hidden beneath layers of cynicism and many seasons of bitter observation in the tender meat of a man's soul.

"I was twelve the first time that I saw them come and take someone..." Tek spoke into the dark of the night, the wind upon the mountain scouring the words out of the air the way dunes treat the footprints of those damned to wander the desert.

Beneath the cold beauty of the stars and surrounded by the sort of rough majesty that nature alone seems to wield when it comes to the art of making man feel insignificant, I sucked down poison. My nerves reinforced, but only holding on with every frantic puff of my cigarette. There were no admonishing looks from Tek now, not when she was in the grips of this tale.

There existed stories that went better with poison.

"My father was a roper in the 70s for the All-Indian Rodeo. This was just a few years after the Professional Rodeo Cowboys Association let us in." Tek's tongue slipped out and wetted her lips, "My mom died when I was born, but Daddy... Daddy did his best... It wasn't a bad life, more like an adventure..." Tek's voice had a faint waiver to it that experience had taught me was the trickling of unaccustomed emotion.

I was and always will be a scribe. My life has been filled with an ever-expanding collection of stories punctuated by searches for truth hidden among the tall tales. This alone might have made me worthy of Tek's tale, or I was merely a thing of convenience; I could not say. There are times when a living soul just needs to provide a connection in a moment of doubt and fear.

Sometimes you just had to take the bandage off and let the wound the world left on you bleed a little.

"I didn't know her name. It was at the Fort Hall Legends Tour, and I remember thinking how strange it was that so many police officers were so afraid of one old woman," bitterness crept into every word as she spoke. "She hadn't done anything, of course, maybe what you would call blessings…" Tek hugged her arms around herself just a little tighter, and I was almost certain that she couldn't have looked at me and carried on the tale.

"She was old," Tek stated this as if it were of great importance, her voice little more than a whisper.

I did my best to see it through Tek's eyes, to imagine the late August heat, the smell of horse shit and cattle thick in the air. The people who had been looking for a good time, now staring with wooden hard faces, some whispering as the tension went up and the whole affair was brought to a standstill. A frightened wide-eyed girl watching with wide dark eyes from behind her father's leg or peeking around the corner of a horse trailer as white angry faces with large guns came to throw chains on some old woman.

There were moments that left their mark so deeply on someone's soul that you could almost run your fingertips over them and trace the twisting path of their hurt.

"She didn't fight them; she didn't resist," the bitterness collided with sorrow and produced a warble in Tek's throat when she spoke.

"There were a few who tried to explain that she was doing no harm, and there was some hope that maybe the tribal police, who back then still might have stood up, would do SOMETHING, but... No..." Tek shook her head and pursed her lips before pushing on.

"You know it hurts when they put the Dynametrium collars on, like someone chopping off a limb. You can still feel The Word; you can even sort of still see it - but you can't use it. She barely flinched..." Tek was hard as nails in her own way, but in the neck-deep waters of memory, she softened a little, and traces of who she had been before the world got its teeth into her now seeped to the surface.

"How'd they know?" All those years at The Standard with paraffin wax in my nose and the roar of a busy newsroom in my ears pulled the question out of me before I could stop it.

Tek turned, and in the low soft light of the moon, she reminded me of a statue fashioned by the hands of some great artist whose vision endured past time and elemental outrage. As defiant and strong as starlight in the face of oblivion. The rich browns of her eyes transformed by mood and desert night into the same velvet black as the sky.

The smile that came was bitter, sad, and maybe just because I'm the sort of bastard that appreciates that which is lovely even in the broken parts (especially in the broken parts), beautiful. Not the same beauty of her happiness or even the warm mixture of that beauty with admiration that came from the unapologetic determination she wore on her sleeve; this was beauty that was more like rum and coke, sweetness mixed with well-aged poison.

"It was the first year the contest was open to everyone. Some..." She caught herself before she could say the first word that came to her lips, Namebreakers had words for us, I fancied I knew a few, but Tek wasn't going to use them to my face at least.

I pretended not to notice and puffed on my cigarette. The cold up here was biting, but I was too hooked on Tek's story to really feel it. The chase could swallow you up just as surely as a good dose of smack could, and some fevered part of me refused to let go. The almost sickening need to get down in the cracks of where a thing went wrong and poke where the break still might be tender and fresh was a grueling taskmaster in its potency.

"Someone thought she must have been influencing the results, cheating, or giving riders an unfair advantage. Maybe someone just saw her and felt like being petty and cruel. That's how it is for too much of the world, isn't it? When we don't understand something, the first thing we want to do is chain it up so we're sure it can't hurt us. The next thing we do is lock it away, so we don't have to think about it..." Tek walked a little closer to me as she spoke, her shoes crunching the dirt and pebbles beneath her step.

"And when we do have to think about it?" I asked her in the dark.

"You get men like Altenhofen and their solutions." There was no beauty on her face then, no defiant tragedy in her voice - any talk of 'solutions' when it came to people always killed beauty and all its associates on sight like a trigger-happy cop.

I grasped the fear that would grip them, and that was what troubled me the most. High atop that mountain with Tek, I wasn't alone with a mere 'Namebreaker', sorceress, or conjurer detached from reality.

Instead, I found myself with a tough-as-nails young woman who had clawed her way from powerlessness to the opposite extreme; a soul heavy with its own sorrow, fortified against its weight with hard-won determination and wisdom older than the language that filled my belly.

This juxtaposed the worries and troubles I had mulled over in the back of my poor driver's car at the start of the journey. I couldn't fathom the woman before me rampaging through a crowded shopping center, tearing apart the public. My mind refused that leap, only accommodating it when I removed Tek from the equation. To envision the monstrous frenzy, far worse than the guns plaguing our society (and greatly enriching their manufacturers with fear), I had to conjure a blank-eyed lunatic. Fear made sense only when stripping away the human face, replacing it with something more hideous.

Monsters ceased being monsters once you learned their names, as man had long surpassed them in the dark arts of cruelty, murder, and all forms of villainy.

"You want to play along with the mad bastard, don't you? Do you plan to use the..." I rolled my hand, the cigarette tracing a little orange circle in the dark as my memory momentarily stuttered.

"The Word! That's it. Do you plan to just use The Word on him? Make him agree with you? Jesus Christ on a cracker, woman. Can you do that?" I asked with perhaps a little too much quickness from a dose of fear and doubt.

The cold up here was becoming a real threat; its bite pressed in beyond any defense that curiosity, excitement, or even beauty might maintain. I could feel the little tremble along my arms that would soon lead to chattering teeth as I asked the question. Battling back against the cold was a growing nervous energy that only deepened when Tek did not say 'No'.

I rolled my thumb over the vial in my hand, my emergency escape plan for when things got too heavy.

Tek did not look me in the eyes, and if she wasn't considering the possibility, then I cannot imagine what other thought could have produced such a meditative look.

"No," she said finally but didn't elaborate further.

"Well, what about the other one, Moxley, what about him? What if he can do it?" I asked again, the idea of being able to clean up the world one diseased mind at a time is certainly a heady prospect.

Tek shook her head, and there was a faint purse of her lips.

"There's no persuading that asshole to help. Besides, Altenhofen would figure it out eventually. You can't change someone's mind in a way that goes against their nature, not without them noticing, and once they notice, it all begins to fall apart. Besides, I don't really..." Tek trailed off with a sigh.

"You don't really what?" I asked.

Tek gave a little half shrug and walked a few feet away in the dark before turning her face up to the moon, the wind pushing dark strands of her hair back away from her brow and eyes. Her hands were shoved down into her pockets.

One of the more understated truths about the people who we view as strong is that they, more often than not, loathe the idea of their own limitations.

"I don't know those Words. It's not a one size fits all sort of thing, you know? There are..." she paused, looking perhaps for the right way to frame her words.

"A great many Words, Jimmy."

"Thank God for the thesaurus and kind editors then," I joked as I stole the last drag from my cigarette and flicked it over the edge where it tumbled into oblivion.

This triggered a laugh, too heavy with worry and responsibility to fully take flight, yet I couldn't compete with the moon for her gaze. This matter had far too much gravity, especially considering my married state. Still, even a stifled laugh was better than none in the face of this mammoth situation.

"There were schools once, families, and bloodlines stretching back to the times of kings. Being a Namebreaker wasn't just a personal journey; it was a mark of evolutionary distinction. Maybe that's why, in the old days, they clashed so bitterly with my people. To them, it wasn't just a talent; it was a science exclusive to their elite, a skill to make them indispensable to those in power." The bitterness crept back into her voice, and I wondered if she was speaking to me or the moon.

"Moxley's father?" I prodded gently.

"He was one. There used to be many more, and probably still are. Who do you think the government tapped to train the lap dogs they sent after the rest of us?" Tek glanced over her shoulder at me, her gaze fleeting.

"The thought of others with similar powers, or even greater mastery of The Word, terrified them. For some, not being special is their own personal Hell." Each word dripped with bitter sadness and aged anger.

"That's why he called you an Informal, right?" I seized on a thread of understanding, unravelling pieces and unlocking doors I hadn't known existed.

The Namebreaker was no more a uniform commodity than the species that birthed it. They were divided by politics, religion, and personal values, much like us. Some were good, some were bad; most fell in between, simply trying to survive. There were those like Tek, fighting with the fury of a wounded heart to hold onto their humanity. And then there were others, like Moxley, caring only for their own comfort, indifferent to the suffering around them.

The optimist in me wanted to believe that all people, when faced with the threat of their own extinction, might find common ground. However, history was littered with failed examples that pointed to the contrary. The past of mankind was strewn with the skeletons of those who had learned that lesson far too late.

I wondered (and still do) if there might have been a tipping point somewhere along the way, a moment where it could all have been averted. The problem with villainizing any group of people, and Namebreakers certainly qualified as people, was that it never held up beyond knowing. One dose of empathy obliterated mountains of fear and hate as surely as a raindrop tore a hole in cotton candy. The issue lay in obtaining that first dose of empathy. As useful as common ground was, it was rarely as sought after as conquered ground, which had a sweeter and more comforting taste to the discerning palate educated in comfort.

"Yes, but I don't mind that. It's not the insult he tried to make it sound like. He wouldn't understand how I've learned any more than I could have tolerated learning under his father. No one is more of a dick about The Word than an old Namebreaker with a reputation." A hint of bitter laughter dared to surface in the calm waters of her voice.

"He's actually a lot more stable than most of the ones I know from the old European bloodlines. My life might not have been great, and it wasn't normal by a long shot, but Moxley?" Tek tilted her head, prompting me to fill in the blank.

"Batshit mad." It seemed fitting enough.

Not that I judged; some of my best friends were practically certifiable, as only the woefully insane would willingly chase stories for money.

Perhaps it was the cold, or the bite of the wind and darkness, but Tek took a small step closer to me. We stood side by side, peering out over the smooth night from the mountain top. She glanced down and must have noticed the vial still clutched in my hand; another tired chuckle escaped her. She shook her head and nudged me with her elbow.

The discussions of Altenhofen and Moxley Allerton were inherently heavy, and escaping from beneath their weight, even for a moment, felt like a gulp of fresh air when one is only moments from drowning.

"What's that?" Tek asked dubiously, her skepticism evident enough that I couldn't resist, even in our dire circumstances, summoning a rueful smile.

"All we need is a little peace, love, and faerie dust." I quoted, as solemnly as if it were the words of Hemingway, Melville, or John Lennon, surely the bumper sticker slogan of some soon-to-be-pulled-over-by-the-cops youth.

Never underestimate an old ink hound's ability to bullshit in the presence of a lovely young woman; regardless of the dire circumstance or the minuscule prospect of his success; he may well surprise you. For those in the field wondering when they shall develop this skill, you will find that it is most often packed behind the small baggie of cocaine that comes with your Writer's Guild card.

"How the fuck do you have a job?" Tek asked, shaking her head and doing her best to fight down a smile.

"Skill, luck, a penchant for the weird, a love for the strange, and above all else—the exquisitely poor taste of the masses." I replied with the Jimmy Wonderful answer because it always went down much better than the truth.

No one wants to imagine their aging Statesman of the Weird writing just-the-facts articles for chicken scratch. Any attempt to explain the terrible feeling of slamming against a creative wall, of wrestling with that which makes the very idea of putting words together feel like taking long drinks of boiling poison, self-terminates upon attempt. Typically, those wasted efforts at describing the actual work were met with a blank stare and a nod that was somewhere between sympathetic and oblivious.

I held the vial up, and in the moonlight, the red powder was rendered a much darker shade, as if the shadows infected each grain. I gave it a little swirl, and the old fiend inside of me whispered at the beauty of the view and the old stones. This whisper of the seasoned malcontent was tempered only by some trace of self-preservation and responsibility, held at bay by a sanity that had long grown tattered by my own attempts to make sense of a senseless world.

Survival instinct suggested that indulging in intensely powerful hallucinogens, originating from beings who claimed to be partially woven from dreams themselves, might not be the best idea on the side of a mountain. I would become a parody of myself if that happened, immortalized forever as the lunatic bastard who wrote extensively about chasing the American Spirit and The Shadow People, only to unceremoniously get too high and fall off a goddamn mountain.

I could almost see Tom back at The Mystic Standard dancing around his infernal bean bag chairs, giddy at the prospect of compiling an omnibus of my work and charging an arm and a leg for the whole thing.

"You know that's made from the bones of their dead, right?" Tek, like most unaffected by an inner fiend that wants to burn the whole thing down and collapse in a heap of sweat, booze, and oblivion, threw out the ugly truth like a life preserver.

I smiled and returned that earlier elbow poke with a light nudge of my shoulder.

"Of course. Fortunately, they don't mind. They've moved onto the next dream, and all that remains behind is no more than a footprint. They're nomadic for the most part, and the Fair Folk are a lot less attached to this world than we are. It's why they're so damned bad at dealing with it." As I told Tek this, I couldn't help but remember that picture she had mentioned earlier that had become a cliché part of every young self-modeled firebrand's life.

There were those who found my earlier exploits to be far less about my subjects and more about myself, but I was still a journalist underneath it all. My knowledge was gained almost through osmosis, soaked up through my skin, and sucked down my lungs with every wild and debauched act that had earned me my stripes.

"That doesn't make it less exploitative or wrong." Tek countered.

She had me there.

I'd made quite the living for myself thumbing my nose at expectations, rules, and convention, but beneath Tek's eyes, I felt something that might have been the stirrings of guilt. I sighed and tucked my little escape from The Heavy back into my pocket, where it could provide comfort rather than reprieve. I had never handled temptation very well.

Sometimes, out of sight and out of mind was the best you could do.

Despite the momentary guilt, I still stand by my assertion that mind-altering substances should be treated much more liberally than firearms. I'm not sure if arming every man, woman, and child in America is a good idea, but I'm quite certain that dosing them all up with acid would make things more interesting. It was better to have something to make you melt into a puddle so you could escape through the sewers as some form of sentient slime and not need it than to find yourself deep in The Heavy and not have it.

"Well, aren't you just a barrel of good times," I said, sounding a little petulant, because maybe I was. Moderation was not my native tongue.

Convincing a lunatic, one that had been made near omnipotent through the dark and cannibalistic rituals of capitalism, to let a legacy of quiet genocide (conducted under the mask of control and safety) die on its own seemed unlikely. Convincing said lunatic to do so, only for the man's grim prediction to come true, seemed an awful reward for our success. Altenhofen was a veteran of many boardroom wars, and he knew well that the secret to victory was not crushing your foe but taking away his will to fight.

When the only outcomes that were on the table involved slowly fading into myth like a man dying in his sleep or something too unspeakable for words, it took the wind right out of your sails. The momentary escape with Tek into more lighthearted conversation had been rejuvenating, but one look at the solemn expression that had returned to her features, and I knew that such luxury was no longer within my budget or her own.

This was America, and in America, nothing is free. Even a moment's reprieve came with a cost. Moxley may have been able to stretch time, but Tek and I were at the mercy of a clock that was counting down to something too big for either of us.

The cold on the mountain was getting to my hands and my joints now that the rush of it all had diminished. The whole bloody affair felt like standing on railway tracks and feeling the rumble of the locomotive coming down the line through the soles of your feet. The sense that you couldn't stop what was coming, and if you were foolish enough to try, the outcomes would only be of the life-threatening and blood-soaked variety.

"You know we must do this, right? We can't screw this up," Tek said. In her words, there was the most common of uniting elements: the doubting of self.

"Yeah, I get that," I replied. Though the words felt lame and flat, they were true, nonetheless.

I realized I was no longer an observer of the story but part of it. I couldn't afford inaction any more than I could claim I must remain unbiased. Playing that card would have deprived me of sleep.

"And if he's right about the other half? If he's right about how awful we all are?" I wasn't trying to throw cold water on Tek's determination, but all arguments on the matter circled back to this point.

Tek looked back at the unnatural electric glow of Altenhofen's monument to himself.

"Better to die with flesh in your teeth than with your paw in the trap."

On this, we agreed.

The Night Is Young and The Mind Troubled

"Sweet Mother of God Almighty! Hrrrk!" I valiantly held down the urge to vomit after Tek returned us to my bungalow, but the moment she stepped out the door, my resolve faltered.

I dashed, bouncing off the unfamiliar walls like a wild pinball, and only just barely made it to the small, clean bathroom. I didn't puke; there was nothing left in me to puke up. However, I spent several long moments with my head hung over the toilet and the cool tile beneath me. I'd been sick in many places: truck stop bathrooms, jail cells, the back of an actual vampire's El Camino, and even a faerie mound or three. Yet, it is with regrettable modesty that I confess that dry heaving in the unused bathroom of a mad billionaire may have topped that list.

I shambled to my feet like one of the zombies they use to make expensive running shoes since the labor crackdowns. The thing that looked at me from the mirror over the sink certainly looked as if it would work twelve hours a day in a sweatshop till its fingers fell off for a bucket of rat heads. I turned the water on and splashed my face, but that only replaced the walking corpse in the mirror with a tired old man who was in too deep, and he knew it. It was one thing to live inside a projected armor of fearlessness and acidic Truth; it was entirely another to have lives potentially depend upon that supposed wit I'd used to make a name for myself.

This was too heavy, and I knew it.

COYOTE WALLACE

The urge to run sprang on me and dug its teeth in deep. I needed to hear Jenna's voice; I needed to be back home in my warm bed; I needed to get away from this place and the thrust upon responsibility that came with it. I was a writer, damn it, not a lawyer or a statesman. My arguments were only made after careful editing, parsing, and in neat single-space type. One may as well have asked John Wayne to go wrangle some goddamned cattle. It was ludicrous—a madman's game where I was just a piece waiting to be moved along the board.

My anointing as the voice of the meeting point between The American Dream and The American Mystic had always been more brand than truth. It helped with sales. I was good at the job, and it had been kind to both me and my bank account. Now that the crown was made real and placed upon my brow, the weight of it was horrifying, and I found myself wanting no part of it. I would gleefully rocket down a highway on a motorcycle at speeds that threatened to melt the brain or swallow all manner of narcotic fun, but this was the sort of heavy that killed your buzz cold and left you too paralyzed for music or sex.

Scared shitless was no more my natural state than sober. I was hopelessly out of my depth facing men like Altenhofen, who moved their pieces across the globe as if it were their personal chess board. They bought the dead at a discount from the impoverished, putting them to work in factories with no concern for safety expenses; animated corpses rarely complained about work conditions. With the other hand, they selectively cut pieces of the Shadow People's culture out from beneath them, selling it to those with wide eyes and romanticized notions, while cultivating fears and misconceptions to feed their industries, supported by paranoia and bloodshed.

Running really was the only sane option. I would run and shout the whole thing from the rooftops, contracts be damned. I would strip naked and yell it as I ran down the streets if I had to. Surely the people of America would rise up once the truth was laid before their eyes. They would see Altenhofen for what he was, they would see all the Altenhofens for what they were, and the whole thing would be torn down brick by brick. The mob would be eclectic and wild with their newfound unity, bound not by race, religion, or creed, but by the simple, decent principle of America itself. That crazy notion that said despite all our differences, we could come together and overcome all adversity. Our differences strengthened us, and our collective Weird was the thread that connected us all.

Altenhofen and his ilk would scream and squeal like the swine they were. They would fight and claw to no avail as they were dragged off to the guillotines. When the sun finally rose, we'd be standing in a glorious new era of Truth and common cause, one where acceptance would spring forth from the same scorched soul that was once only suitable soil for the weeds of fear and hate to grow.

That was the ticket.

On my way to the phone to call Jenna and tell her I was coming home early, I turned on the television set, mostly just to facilitate the lie that I had been in my room the entire evening. I paid no mind to the channel, and the volume was so low that whatever was coming from the speakers was muted in comparison to the increasingly hectic rumblings of my mind. Had the layout of Altenhofen's accommodations that he'd provided us with been a little different, then perhaps I would have done just as intended. What can I say? Fortune favors fools.

The phone was on the wall in the kitchen, and to reach it, I was forced to go around the small counter that separated the living room from the rest of the room itself. I already had the phone off the receiver when my eyes caught sight of what was unfolding on the screen... The trial of Latisha Green had devolved into a riot on the steps of the courthouse on its second day. Policemen armed with billy clubs, riot shields, and snarling angry dogs clashed with protestors, mostly the young with a few scattered older sympathizers from the suburbs. A chaotic dance that could only end in a bloody and violent entanglement. The sight was as morbidly fascinating as a train wreck and heart breaking for what it said about us as a people all at once.

I stood there with the phone in my hand, the dial tone humming, as one young man, holding a shirt over his face, ran up, grabbed one of the canisters of tear gas that had been lobbed into the midst of him and his fellows, and sent it hurtling back at the police. The poor bastard may as well have painted a bullseye on his chest or openly lobbied for stricter body camera laws. They were on him instantly, beating him with a wild abandon one would have more aptly ascribed to cavemen than officers of the law. The camera cut away too slowly to hide the flurry of blows and the savage, maniacal smiles upon their faces—a stark reminder that there was very little as American as good old-fashioned police brutality doled out to those who would balk at the status quo.

In that moment, I had a realization about Altenhofen and the malignant world that had grown in his shadow. He was not a bluffer; he was a man who hedged his bets and calculated his odds, a man who entrusted as little of his life to fate and luck as possible. The end that he warned us about, even if he threw it all away, was not a flight of fancy, nor was it a tactic simply concocted to tamp down our fires or make us doubt ourselves. Altenhofen believed it, and as I watched the riots playing out on the screen, I began to feel that belief take root in myself as well.

I hung up the phone, and it was as if the gravity around me increased tenfold. The idea of collapsing into the bed and closing my eyes against not just the task, but the whole damned world, was suddenly very tempting. The prescription for a bad case of sudden clarity was always a good night's rest. Nothing helped reapply the blinders to a man's eyes like a nice long sleep; this was essential if he hoped to convince himself that the truths he'd learned were merely flights of fancy. This American folk remedy for clarity was old and well tried and could be applied to any concern, be it the rise of fascism, the increasing disparity between economic classes, or the countless deaths from starvation and disease on the streets. A good night's sleep and these problems always faded into the background. That's all it took. A few hours of shut eye, and the mind was ready to crawl back into the comfortable shell it had made from the nightly news, old sitcoms, and the lies we tell ourselves.

Once more, I fished the vial out of my pocket and peered at the dark red powder inside. The riots and the drone of news anchors, whose concern would only become genuine when the rioters began devouring the rich and their enablers, had faded into the background. Nothing that blared through the television's speakers could hope to penetrate the broken steam pipe whisper of the little voice in my head. The voice that, at the provocation of all this Heavy, had begun to whisper maniacally upon the mountaintop and now roared behind my eyes. If I was to be damned, if I was to be forced to participate in this ghoulish and macabre exercise in the fluffing of some swine's ego and delusion - then it would be on my terms.

COYOTE WALLACE

Altenhofen had wanted Jimmy Wonderful, chaser of Truth, hunter of the Great American Clusterfuck, and voice of the Almighty Weird.

Well, he could fucking have him.

With an upward flick of my thumb, the black rubber stopper of the vial came free and fell silently to the countertop. The cap bounced once then rolled over the edge and onto the floor. For a moment, hesitation flickered within me, but among the damned and the puppets of the rich, hesitation had no place. It brought with it concerns about the capacity of my heart to endure the strain, the strength of my mind to withstand the vulgar inhumanity, and the distinct possibility of ending up licking a cactus while crooning about the ephemeral beauty of dreams.

If that didn't work, hesitation would resort to even more foul and underhanded tricks. These included, but were not limited to, thoughts of how your actions may affect your loved ones, memories of better times you could be throwing away, and (if it truly got desperate) professional integrity.

I had not paid for the Faerie Dust, and I was only there for a short time. Maybe that can account for why I poured it from chest height onto the countertop. Discolorations of pink, like hastily wiped away blood stains, formed on the counter's surface as the powder gathered in what might have been considered a damned fine approximation of the dunes of Mars. The dust was made from the bones of the Fair Folk, who claimed - though science was still debating this matter - that they themselves were sustained by a connection to a deep and mysterious universal consciousness, which we foolish humans mislabeled as flights of fancy and fantasy.

Pure imagination, uncut and unfiltered by the natural limits and safeguards that the human mind places on the "good stuff". There was a long litany of substances that man had made or harvested in his foolish hopes of replication.

These included DMT, LSD, psilocybin mushrooms, absinthe, and the bumpy asses of certain frogs, but they all came up short against the real thing. All of them pale imitations of what lay before me on the countertop.

Faerie Dust was the original track on scratching popping vinyl, and everything else was a cover on soulless digital.

I'd been down this road once and I'd sworn it off; both the terror and the wonder were simply too much even in the best of locations with a younger and less fractured mind. The last time I had been surrounded by kindly knowing souls, the likes of which I would not find within Altenhofen's high walls. This was not a good idea; this was not stoking the fires of inspiration or pretending to be some swaggering iconic rebel sage of the American Dream.

No, this was madness, and I knew it.

In a world where men like Altenhofen held the keys to everything and made prostitutes out of the wondrous, killers out of men, and toys of politicians - madness seemed much more appealing than it had any heavenly right to be.

The dignified way to set about the consumption of such a narcotic delicacy would have been to put on some relaxing music, move any sharp-edged furniture out of the room, and perhaps use a small spoon or straw to get it where it needed to go. Like any other powdery substance that will get you several years in a federal penitentiary, it was best dispensed in neat short rails laid out on any smooth nonporous surface. The effects would be almost instantaneous but continue to build. A roller coaster that got faster and faster with every beat of my heart. A doorway to a world without rules placed on the borders of the IS and the IS NOT.

Naturally, I buried my face against the counter and snorted like a hog seeking an apple core inside a pen that was ankle-deep with his own shit.

There was none of the fire into the numbing ice sensation that came with cocaine, none of the gathering bitterness in the back of the tongue either. No, the fire persisted in Faerie Dust without any sort of cooling loss of sensation at all. The dried-out remains of dead dreams roared their way up my nostrils and punched into the overworked vulnerable corners of my brain. They dug in, fastening invisible talons around the corners of my perception as tears streamed down my cheek and my body spasmed with hacking coughs. I felt as if I had just come up from the bottom of some great ocean depth and caught a last-second lung full of water.

My hands clutched the countertop so tightly that my knuckles had turned bone white. As I lifted my head, the tears lingering in my eyes transformed the world into bleeding shapes and running colors. My heart pounded in my chest and sweat began to bead on my skin.

Deep breaths. Deeeeeep breaths, Old Man.

"Nnrrrrrrrrrrgaaaaah!" I half-growled, half-shouted at the walls.

The walls remained silent. For now.

I entertained a fleeting, almost whimsical notion that I might reach a chair before things started to unravel. This notion was remarkably lucid for a man-wretch in my current state. However, following closely behind was a more fitting rumbling in my brain. My clothing was stifling the tiny mouths that would soon form on my skin, robbing them of precious air. That wouldn't do at all.

What if they suffocated?

I staggered into the living room, my knees buckling as I collapsed before the glowing screen of the television, like a man struck deaf, blind, and dumb by the revelation of his god. My hands tore at my shirt like frantic birds until the buttons popped, and I peeled it off my shoulders, letting it fall to the floor—a shed skin of some ancient and grotesque reptile that would knife its own mother for a headline and a very fast car.

"Eniws! Eniws! Eniws nmaddog yhtlif!" I roared at the television screen with the fury of a lion.

Wait a minute, did that come out right? Did any of it EVER come out right?

A blond woman with her hair cut into a neat bob and a bright red pantsuit stared at me from the screen, her eyes replaced by large, vacant holes. They weren't just missing; they had been gouged out, leaving grotesque voids. From them oozed not only blood but also the semen of countless unspeakable demons. Small tendrils of blue glowing light crept from the corners of the television, somehow less horrific than the fake, perfect smile that was as disquieting as white sheets in Mississippi.

"Former President Nixon's new invigorated state and message of 'Wolves or Rabbits' has really resonated with the American people who are desperate to make this country great again. We're tired of weak men who don't have the killer instinct to reach out and grab the world by the..." The television personality's words were so banal that hearing them was almost physically painful.

Despite the banality, I was too fascinated by the tendrils to care.

They had grown longer and thicker, composed of the familiar yet unnerving light of television snow. Lost signals. Incomplete relays of sight and sound. The kind of light that, if stared into directly by the naked human eye for too long, would cause sharp, dagger-like pain and wrap your stomach in a greasy, swaying hammock. The tendrils ended in large, flower-like bulbs, waving in the air around the edges of the screen as if belonging to a large but blinded octopus or other sea-dwelling horror.

"Anata wa machigatte iru!" I shouted at them though my lips did not move.

With wide-eyed horror, I brought my fingers to my cheek, passing over dry, chapped lips and hard, unyielding teeth. I screamed and laughed simultaneously, the sound reverberating with madness—pure madness.

I had grown another mouth on the side of my face.

The tendrils slithered through the air towards me, perhaps curious about the seasoning of my soul. The bulbous tips opened like flowers in bloom, revealing lamprey mouths glistening with sharp teeth. They danced in front of me in slow, trance-like rhythms—one came very close to my face, utterly unafraid. I reached out to grasp the tendril before my eyes and recoiled in disgust. It emitted a sick heat reminiscent of touching an overheated monitor or microwave.

The screen had transitioned from the blond with ugly holes for eyes to a man with a thick black mustache, glasses, and badly dyed hair with gray roots fighting through. His papery skin was drawn tight across his face like a foul mummified specimen. A centipede the size of a man's pinky finger tentatively poked its head from the corner of his nose. He was some manner of demonic zombie, a hollow man filled with bugs and crawling nightmares that burrowed under the skin and poisoned the heart. I might have stared forever at the cracks in his features, but a faint pinch at my side reminded me of Jenna playfully nipping at me in bed.

Another tendril had attached itself to my stomach over my navel and was pulsing. I couldn't tell if I was being fed from, filled full, or some horrid mixture of the two, but I was VERY sure that it was obscene. With a loud yelp of pain, I ripped it away, and it made a wet, suckling pop as it came free. Summoning all my remaining will, I dragged myself from the floor.

"Je dois tuer le monstre!" The mouth at the side of my face bellowed like an angry Parisian drunk.

I stood before one of the small, mostly decorative coffee tables, taking deep breaths and dabbing at the neat bloody ring around my belly button with my fingers. Half-hunched, I resembled an escaped lunatic, menacing some innocent poor soul in the old black-and-white horror movies of my childhood.

My hands seized around the small table's legs without conscious thought, my movements disjointed, resembling stop-motion frames of behavior that no longer guaranteed coherence. Empty distance fell away, and time took on a strange, record-skipping quality, consisting only of actions with no lead-up. Hoisting the whole damned little table over my head by its legs, I stalked across the room back towards the glowing tendrils and their hungry, disappointed lamprey mouths, back towards the monstrous faces and their poison words.

Fear gripped me. I imagined being pulled apart by the hungry tendrils, my bones given to the news anchors to gnaw on for scraps of marrow. My soul hollowed out and filled with dry white sand, my eyes empty and vacant—perhaps even forecasting the weather.

So, I did what any sane man might do in that situation...

...I beat the television to death with a small, goddamn table.

Sometimes I laughed. Sometimes I wept. Sometimes I did both simultaneously. I was foaming at the corners of my mouth, while the sinews in my arms and neck stood out like iron cables beneath my skin. I hammered and hammered until, at long last, the screen went dark, and glass glittered like lost diamonds on the floor.

What I was left holding was the stubby scraps of table legs and jagged splinters of wood—a hunched, heavy-breathing maniac whose mind had slid over the edge and into insanity.

"Fine mess we've made of this." a muffled voice drifted up, seemingly out of nowhere.

"Mmhmm. It's fucking glorious, man. The swine are sure to come running." a second voice chimed in.

I was so startled that I turned and dropped my makeshift club, unsure of how long it took to reach the floor. I no longer trusted time, I no longer trusted distance, but I was sure at that moment of the reliability of my hearing. I had heard voices, damn it! Male voices. I was sure of it!

I fell onto my knees, miraculously managing to not cut myself to ribbons on the shards of glass left from the violent assault upon the television set. There would be a door, a handle, a key, something that I would be able to use to expose what was surely a tunnel that Altenhofen had dug beneath the whole place, for purposes both nefarious and obscene. The tunnel would be filled with blank faced goons squinting against the darkness with clubs in their hands and malice in their eyes. A legion of soulless puppets too eager to prove their worth as brutes to notice the strings.

My cheek against the floor I listened, dragging myself like some strange animal from an alien world whose head weighs far too much for earth's gravity towards the source of the sound. I knew that it had to be there, this sudden mad obsession had swallowed everything else. The rationale blotted out as I was swept further up into the hunt. There was a truth that needed to be found regardless of cost. A secret that was in the dry dead earth beneath me, placed there by machinations I could not fully see, waiting to pull me down into the deep dark that every secret calls its home.

I felt the skin of my face stretch impossibly as my eyes widened when I found what I'd been looking for...

A crack between the wooden tiles.

I was on it in an instant, scrambling into a wobbling squat and hooking my fingertips into the thin line between the wood. I prepared to pull with all my might, to exert some tremendous effort, for surely it was fastened down tight. I yanked upward with all my might, completely heedless of the fact that had I met the slightest resistance, I would have certainly torn every muscle to shreds and sent my spine into a series of popping cracks. Fortunately, at least for the back of an aging journalist, there was absolutely no resistance at all.

I went tumbling back onto my ass, and while that lack of resistance was surprising, it was nothing compared to the slow dissolution of the plank in my white-knuckled hands into weightless greasy smoke. My excavation of the tile had left a square just large enough to fit one's head through in the floor, but rather than the thick darkness of shadow to suggest a crawl space or even the feared tunnels that I had known for such a certainty to be beneath me; I saw only a shimmering wet surface from which came a soft glow.

I crawled on my hands and knees over to the edge of the shimmering portal and peered down. I was helplessly transfixed by the unearthly shimmer, held fast for some inscrutable morsel of time at what I saw there. The best description that I have is that of one peering into a bathtub or swimming pool from a modest height while the sky rains stars down from above, a subtle distortion of light, depth, and dimension sloshing beneath my eyes that kicked back a myriad of prismatic colors.

In those depths, I could just barely make out the rough outline of men, some sitting, some walking around, or just standing and gesturing while in the midst of conversation. Their features, however, were too muddled and smudged for recognition. They looked as if someone had ground their thumb against the wet paint of their faces before it had been given time to dry or set. They were beings of smudged ink, smoky hazes, and light bent on trickery.

I needed to get closer to observe the truth.

I sucked down a deep breath as if I were preparing to leap from the side of a ship into storm-tossed waters and plunged my head down through the square.

There was a moment of surreal disorientation; perception shifted, and I discovered no substantive liquid existed beneath the thin veneer that had separated me from this small pocket of creation. On the other side, there was not just air, but air spiced with tobacco, whiskey, and pungent cannabis sativa. The space contained a hidden world that was situated between the imagined and the unbelievable but true. There were no walls that would have supported the ceiling; instead, there were these wide-open vistas of strange landscapes - dry ocean beds, immense forests, deserts where the painted stones looked as if they might break and float upward like the innards of a lava lamp - and the floor was no better.

The ground was a collage of the impossible, or so it appeared to a mind that was overloaded with imagination, bubbling insanity, and fear. The landscape stretched out in all directions and seamlessly transitioned from islands of hardwood and comfortable throw rugs to sudden hard-packed dirt roads and swaths of seedy bars whose shadows held thick beneath the dingy bulbs of overhead lights.

Neither the shifting nature of the floor nor the open vistas that mocked the very notion of walls could compare, though, to this strange Pocket of Nowhere's population. They were all the worst sorts and varied in terms of age from their late 20s to slightly older than me - late 60s or maybe early 70s. These beings, these madmen, this TRIBE of swaggering malcontents chewed cigarettes between their lips (save for the elderly who chewed the tips of cigarette holders instead) and cavorted amongst themselves as if it were a day of play in the yard of a lunatic asylum.

One was speeding about on a motorcycle that seemingly traveled from left to right without ever changing direction, as if he circled the entire world with each go. Another was standing with a glass of Chivas, sloshing it from the glass as he vehemently ranted while conversing with an old man who sat behind an ancient looking wooden desk. The desk was littered with papers and relics - not at all unlike how I'd kept my own - and an IBM Selectric, whose long journey out of the 1960s had left it faded of color but unbroken of spirit.

"Dispatches? Dispatches? Goddamn it, man! We have more important things to worry about than dispatches. Have you seen the state of the universe? It's a fucking pigsty! A swine heap! Why the Hell am I the one who has to cover time? Do you have any idea how boring time can actually be?" The Chivas Splashing Man said as he paced before the desk.

His features were hauntingly familiar, but I could not quite place them. He reminded me of a relative that I had never met but, through an obscene fluke in the game of genetics, one which could have passed for a brother. The Venerable Scribe did not look up from the Selectric; indeed, the pace at which his fingers drew across the keys seemed to quicken as cigarette smoke curled in the air over his head. His eyes, hidden behind dark aviator glasses, never left the page.

"Because you left before you accomplished anything, and I'm the fucking line editor," The Venerable Scribe growled between clenched teeth.

Their voices were the same but distorted by the weight of age, and I felt as if I was listening to someone doing a very good but not exact imitation of myself in both instances.

All at once, the typing stopped; the roar of motorcycles stopped; the clinking of ice cubes in glasses of Chivas stopped. A silence so heavy and wide that it settled over all of Reality like six feet of white winter snow had dropped all at once over every atom of this strange nexus. The stillness was so oppressive that I dared not even draw a breath.

The Venerable Scribe sniffed the air like a hound who had just stumbled upon the scent of a careless rabbit. Two short snorting inhalations went through his nose.

"What is it?" The Chivas Slinger asked with a solemn but fevered intensity.

The Venerable Scribe tilted his head back, and for one hideous moment, I saw the ancient reptilian eyes behind his glasses before the angle changed and only my reflection stared back from the mirrored lenses. He had fastened his gaze on me, and almost in unison, the others, who had all stopped whatever madness they were about, now craned their necks upwards as well. My reflection stared back at me in each of their eyes.

"Flattery," The Venerable Scribe spoke the word 'flattery,' but my spasming wrecked mind translated it, quite correctly I might add, into 'fresh meat.'

My heart stopped, and my balls curled up somewhere just beneath it in my stomach.

I screamed.

I was still screaming when I pulled my head back, found my footing, and ran like a mad bastard for the door. My mind, unable to make sense of or comprehend the full nature of what it had beheld, now defaulted to some primal and fundamental self. There was a pause in my escape as I fumbled with the doorknob, and had it been locked or jammed I may well have completely fallen to a depth of terror from which I could not return. Fortunately, it came open effortlessly, and I spilled out into the night, barely aware of my surroundings.

I continued to scream as I yanked my head back, regained my footing, and bolted for the door like a crazed lunatic. My mind, unable to process the incomprehensible sights it had just witnessed, reverted to a primal state of survival. There was a moment of hesitation as I struggled with the doorknob, fearing it might be locked or jammed. If it had been, I might have plummeted into a bottomless pit of terror from which I could never escape. Thankfully, it turned effortlessly, and I burst out into the night, barely aware of my surroundings.

I ran with the wild fear of a creature that had just witnessed lightning strike the earth, setting it ablaze with flame and smoke. I didn't stop or pause to consider my path, not even as Altenhofen's squat, armored abode suddenly loomed before me. I didn't register the pool lying between the structure and my frantic form, nor did I notice Moxley, lounging by the poolside, rising from his chaise lounge.

COYOTE WALLACE

We collided, and the world erupted into a kaleidoscope of colors.

Fade to black.

Time Is On My Side, Yes It Is

I was nothing, broken down to my core elements and scattered from one black horizon of oblivion to the next. Consciousness was not something I sought; indeed, I fled from it, hiding in the deep inkwells of the abyss, where troubling thoughts and terrifying visions dared not intrude. There was a peculiar heaviness to my nothingness, an out-of-place substance that troubled my feeble mind, which cowered from the prospect of awakening. To awaken would mean confronting the sharp-toothed beast of reality and facing the shame of my own inadequacies.

Out of the blackness came colors, swimming like exotic fish that had mistaken the night sky for the ocean's depths and now flaunted their bright scales for the whole world to see. Reds and blues raced from the corners, deep yellows and burning oranges cut their way through the center, and cooling greens rolled behind it all like the tide of a sea come to reclaim its errant children.

I was warm and safe, but the colors were digging in, pulling me upwards out of the darkness and replacing that sweet gauzy emptiness with troubling fragments of memory. I clung harder to my oblivion; it was comforting in its sweetness and ultimately reminded me of the lazy mornings when I'd once awaited my mother to awaken me for school. Many a morning I had lain in bed, dozing somewhere just beneath thought but aware, and in my awareness, dreading the knock at the door that would start my day. That dread forced the mind to savor the little scraps of non-existence even more.

"I'm tellin' ya, Moxy - If he doesn't wake up, I'm going to eat his fucking toes!" a petulant, almost bratty whine stabbed at my peace.

Wait, what did he say?

"You can't just bring a guy here and lay him out on the bed like that and not expect me to at least take a pinky toe, that's ah torture is what it is. Come on, he's got two!" The owner of this voice continued. Unfamiliar, gruff, and clearly sadistically insane were my general impressions, but I was still recovering from a nasty trip.

I paddled away from the shore of wakefulness, a groan escaping my lips despite my best effort. The sound was oddly distorted and flat in my ears, like I had a bad head cold or was wearing heavy earmuffs. Had it not originated in the back of my own throat, I might not have recognized it at all.

"About time, Jimmy. Hey, Jimmy - Wake up!" Moxley's voice this time, and upon recognizing it, I was pulled back into thought and all the horrors of wakefulness.

I immediately rolled over and tried my best to vomit, but my body simply refused. I wanted to spill my cookies all over the floor, but it was as if the inner mechanisms of my physiology had ceased taking commands. The realization that I was on a bed, crumpled sheets holding crumbs and a thin layer of cigarette ash, came only after this, and on its heels was the realization that I wasn't merely not in my own room - I wasn't anywhere that I recognized at all.

It wasn't the bungalows, that was for certain.

To be fair, at that moment, I would have forgotten my own mother had she been forced to compete with the view.

The window looked out upon not the Salt Flats, but some grand and magnificent harbor, the waters inviting in their warm blues beneath a sun that did its very damnedest to paint the world in gold. A township lay just beyond the harbor, the buildings made of rough lumber and not a scrap of concrete among them. The harbor was bustling with activity, both men and women in attire that belonged on the lifeless mannequins of a museum display. It was the ships, however, that stole my breath and forced my mind to come to a jarring conclusion: I was still deeply under the influence of the Faerie Dust, possibly forever, and my mind was not to be trusted.

They were schooners, cutting through the water with their sails slowly lowering or raising depending upon their coming or going. Their wooden hulls and gallant flags that whipped in the wind overhead had no earthly business being seen by my eyes. I was powerless to do anything but stare, struck dumb as if I'd come home to find The Pope sitting on my couch and furiously masturbating to German Troll Porn.

"Is it real?" I asked, and again my voice sounded strangely muted, but at that moment, I simply assumed it was a side effect from snorting enough imagination dust to bring C.S. Lewis back from the dead, appropriate distance from all schools and playgrounds notwithstanding, of course.

Something landed on the bed. I assumed it was a cat or perhaps a small dog jumping up to join me. I felt it moving along the sheets, but in my stupor, I paid it no mind—only the waters.

"Of course, it's re-Oscar! Get down! What do you think you're doing?!?" Moxley's alarmed tone made me turn my head at last.

As I did, my eyes must have widened to the size of saucer plates at the sudden weight upon my chest. There, standing upon my ribs, was a diminutive gargoyle. Perhaps a foot and a half tall at most, with slick amphibian skin that ran from green to black and two small horns on the top of his head. His lower canines protruded out over his top lip, and his wings, giant and bat-like, flexed and fluttered with menace. He was completely naked, and his absurdly disproportionate genitals, which would have been hilarious on some deeply juvenile level had he not been perched upon me, bounced as he scrambled up my side and wrapped one three-fingered hand in the thinning hair at the crown of my head. I shrieked in surprised pain, only to have the little bastard use his other hand to strike me across the cheek.

"The fuck!?!?" I exclaimed, thoroughly shocked and dismayed.

SLAP!

Once more, I felt the sting across my cheek.

"Snap out of it, ya sod dustin' addle pate!" the little creature barked in my face, its breath a horrendous mix of burning tires, Lucky Strike cigarettes, and the burning asshole of a three-day-dead possum.

Moxley stepped out to the side of the bed, pulled the little creature by the scruff of its neck, and hauled it off me. The gargoyle creature's legs kicked feebly, and when he released the little beast, the wings began to beat instantly. With an offended snort, it flitted across the room to land on the arm of an old velvet upholstered chair with cherry oak arms and legs.

"Sorry about Oscar. He gets overexcited, and I might have told him you tried to kill me." Moxley offered with one hand rubbing the back of his neck awkwardly. He had the expression of a schoolboy who had just gotten caught tossing bricks through a window.

My brain was still stuttering and tripping over the disconnect. I did not feel as if I were still in the grips of the Dust; there was no further sense of rushing madness. But the world seemed to refuse to go back to 'normal' just the same. The presence of Oscar the Gargoyle, to say nothing of the fact that I was clearly neither in Utah nor even the waning modern era, refused to let my tired mind fall back into the comfort of the ordinary. I was held suspended between sanity and madness by the hands of a purple-haired malcontent. That's all I knew for certain.

Moxley wore obnoxious green trunks, and only in this partially clothed state did I notice how utterly thin his figure truly was. The bones of his shoulders stood out like sharp peaks, and the lines of each rib pressed against pale skin. The bones of his hips rose up over the band of the trunks like smooth mountains worn down by time.

The tattoo I had noticed earlier on his hands and neck revealed itself to be a never-ending sequence of numbers, interconnected with strange, glyph-like symbols. The markings reminded me of the cheap necklaces sometimes sold in occult novelty stores, with the numbers making up the chain and the thicker glyphs spaced out between them. The tattoo ran from the center of the back of his neck, down either arm and both sides, curling inward at his thighs, and unless I was mistaken, it would have completed the loop by crossing the bottoms of his feet.

The pain and time invested in such adornment must have been staggering.

"Where the Hell am I? What happened?" I asked, rubbing the cheek where the small hand had struck me, eyeing Oscar warily.

"I'm not Flower-Girl, but if I had to take a guess, I'd say you got irresponsibly high and lost your mind. Faerie Dust leaves a sort of pinkish tint to your Veritas," Moxley explained, unsuccessfully fighting down a grin.

"My what?" I asked, pushing myself into a sitting position on the bed.

It was much nicer than the ones in the bungalow, Altenhofen's wealth be damned. There was an authenticity in its softness, and without looking, I knew that it would be stuffed with the downy feathers of some unfortunate flock of geese.

Moxley rolled his eyes and looked momentarily frustrated by my lack of understanding.

"The word for 'you.' Your personal Word, that which makes up who and what you are. It contains everything— your nature, your age, health, and even your fate. Yours looks like someone wrote on your soul with shit and cigarette tar stains. You know, in case you ever want to think about what sort of person you are," Moxley said, shaking his head like a teenager who'd come home early just to find his parents passed out mid-coitus on the floor of the den.

"Fuck me..." I muttered under my breath, there was nothing like waking up in a strange bed and getting lectured by a purple-haired Judas about the layer of filth on your own soul.

"Only on my father's birthday." Moxley said, jerking his thumb towards the bat-like creature perched on the arm of the chair.

"That's Oscar, by the way. I made him when I was twelve; he's sort of like..." The young Namebreaker began to explain.

"Your cat. If cats could talk and fly. Yeah, I got that. Ugly little bastard, isn't he?" I jumped in, Oscar was the one thing I didn't have questions about - mostly because I didn't want to know.

"You're no peach yourself, ya' prick!" Oscar grumbled and gave his wings a quick stretch before tucking them against his back.

Moxley laughed at this so deeply that he was forced to wipe a smudge of teardrop away from the corner of one eye.

"Something like that. I made him when I was twelve; my father wouldn't let me have a pet that I didn't make myself. If you think he's ugly, you should have seen my first dozen or so attempts. Some real quality traumas there." Moxley played off the recollection like a joke, though I wondered how much of that laughter only grew in soil watered with the pain of his youth.

Oscar tapped his chest with one claw-tipped finger.

"Three poodle hearts." the little creature beamed with pride.

I took a moment and did my best to gather my thoughts. The very act of thinking almost seemed to take too much effort, as if the signals fired in my brain were operating on a delay. I felt like a man recovering from a bad fever or a night spent pounding away at the keys until the sun and his own exhaustion drove him to seek the solace of sleep. The ringing of a ship's bell, clear and carried on the salted breeze that blew through the window, pulled my eyes back out towards the ocean and those seafaring craft. Moxley made a little grunting laugh as he followed my eyes.

"I have to be hallucinating..." I said more to myself than Moxley or his pet.

"Oh, you are. Believe me. You are tripping balls. Your consciousness has just been transferred to a physical representation of yourself that was plucked from a temporal deviation where you weren't. When this all ends, you will go right back to being the embarrassing fifty-something-year-old boomer, desperately trying way too hard to hold onto his 20s that pushed us both into the pool."

He threw me a wink despite the sharpness of his tongue...

I could only groan at the memory.

"What's out there though? That's not a hallucination," Moxley gave a little sly laugh and looked out the window before continuing. "My father built this house with his own hands and his own Word. Everything you see, every part of this place - it was all put together from different moments," he explained with all the patience of an older brother giving his kid sibling the rundown on Santa Claus.

"Dear God, man. You mean we're traveling in time?" Even as I asked, there was the realization that it was becoming increasingly difficult to be incredulous. Prolonged exposure to wizardry and general weirdness will do that to you.

"No, Jesus-fucking-Christ, that's a myth. A real one. As in, it doesn't happen. Do you have any idea what time is actually like?" The question flew from his lips.

"I think you've established at least five times that I do—" Not for the last time, Moxley cut me off and reminded me why I always bought teachers a drink at bars.

"It's like being caught in the biggest, nastiest, fucking river you can imagine. You can push forward and be carried easily, push back and it's nearly impossible," the bratty punk wizard explained as if he were talking thermodynamics to a very smart labradoodle. Moxley drew a swift line through the air with his finger as if to indicate the flow of this river. "It's easy to observe a river, goddamn near impossible to change the way it flows or fight your way back to the source." Moxley said before pushing a hand through his violet hair and easing his way over to the windowsill for a better view.

"So, what...?" I didn't get to finish the question. "Snips, instants, half a second here, an eyeblink there. Nothing big. Nothing that anyone notices or even thinks about. Time holds things together much better than cement or nails." he explained.

Though the young Namebreaker did his best to hide it when he spoke, I caught the barest hint of a wane smile reflected upon the glass of the open window. I doubted the line about cement and nails was one of Moxley's own; it had a certain parental ring about it, and the look on his face all but confirmed the nostalgic recollection.

It occurred to me there and then that this was an opportunity. Regardless of whatever strange temporal fuckery Moxley had worked, I was now alone with the man. I had a chance to speak with him, understand him, possibly even persuade him to change his mind about the task before him. I would have to take that opportunity if I could. Our chances were too slim to play it safe.

I'd taken a liking to the young man, and despite our vastly different backgrounds, there was an undeniable sense of camaraderie. This connection fueled an intense desire to understand why he had found himself on Altenhofen's twisted path. Not knowing was the journalist's excruciating Hell—a torture akin to the stomach-churning withdrawals and depraved cravings of a dope fiend.

Once you were hooked on the truth, cut with ink and injected with uncoated groundwood newsprint, you chased that fix. Just as surely as sharks navigated the seas and coyotes courted the moon, the truth seeped beneath your skin and soaked into your cells. The truth, a transformative stimulant, paradoxically beckoned and terrified.

You could swallow the little lies, occasionally wash them down with a glass of whiskey, or fuck them out of your mind with anyone but the one you were supposed to be fucking. Everyone you'd ever known had a preferred method of looking the other way; discussing the matter was thought too impolite for modern society.

But the big lies? Those became an intolerable affliction, demanding immediate treatment with a bittersweet elixir crafted from facts mined from the hidden recesses of the human condition. Empathy and understanding, fortified with the Truth, were the potent cure-alls concealed in the hearts of the misunderstood, misaligned, and outright weird.

"Why? Why would you help Altenhofen at all? Look at this place! It's like something out of a dream. You've got a fucking gargoyle sitting on your chair!" I threw a hand out towards Oscar unable to keep myself from becoming animated as I spoke.

"From everything I've seen you're even more familiar than Tek about this whole..." My mind struggled for the right word, skipping like a scratched record,

"Goddamned mess!"

I could have been more delicate in my questioning but being plucked from the normal flow of time and space by a purple haired punk does nothing for one's temperament.

"I'm not a fuckin' gargoyle! WHY WON'T YOU LET ME EAT THIS MAN'S TOES?!?!?" Oscar piped up before Moxley could answer, beating his leathery little wings with the fury of a barn owl who'd just sat down on a hot poker.

"Oscar, go to your crate. Now." Moxley reprimanded his winged companion, and I could tell by the cross expression on his face that he was going to give me an answer, but whether that answer was something I could use or if it was just more posturing, I couldn't know.

Oscar snorted and fluttered up from the armrest of the chair, his grotesque genitals bouncing unsteadily as he hovered. He bobbed in the air, prompting one to wonder if Moxley's 'pet' had been sneaking treats when his master wasn't looking.

"Meh, I'll get a bagel..." Oscar muttered with a despondency that rivaled the surliest of teenagers.

"It was nice meeting you." I said, unsure of the proper etiquette for homunculi, but opting for caution.

"Die in a fire, asshole." Oscar retorted, throwing up his middle finger as he flapped out the door like an overweight bumblebee with a five-pack-a-day habit.

Once we were alone, Moxley turned his attention to me. Leaning against the window frame, bathed in the golden light of the sun from that perfect day crafted from lost moments by his father, he seemed even younger than he had outside Altenhofen's bungalows. This was his sanctuary, where he felt most at ease, and where he spent most of his time. Despite his bravado about his father, he had retained this place and sought refuge here whenever he wished to escape Altenhofen's grasp.

"What? You'll believe that politicians will sell out their own country for some donations, but you can't wrap your head around a guy who can bend time needing cash? Maybe I'm like you, hopelessly addicted to many really REALLY good drugs, or maybe 'Temporal Dandy' doesn't pay the bills; ever think of that?" Moxley tossed the question at me before I had a chance to respond.

"I mean, that would be my guess, but I'm just the person you're asking about," he added with cheeky bitterness, the rapidity in his tone preempting further probing into his façade.

"I don't believe that." I told him.

I couldn't.

Swinging my legs over the edge of the bed felt like navigating a minefield, each movement a shaky step toward reclaiming some semblance of control. I had no clue where my pants were, but just sitting up and trying to stand sent tremors through my wobbly limbs. I'd almost convinced myself I was a spineless blob, but as my feet hit the hardwood, I realized I still had some bones rattling around in there. Attempting to stand was like trying to balance on two Jell-O molds strapped to my ankles.

"Oh yeah? Why's that? Let's hear it, Jimbo." Moxley said with a little roll of his hand.

"You burn through the money as soon as you get it, waste it on whatever makes you forget, and yet I'm looking around. There's none of those toys you had in the bungalow, no televisions or game consoles. You're not keeping any of it because it doesn't matter to you." I said, keeping my eyes glued to Moxley, watching for any reaction.

"Do you have any idea how big this house is? Oh, wait. You can't, because you only perceive space and time in a way that your sanity will allow so you don't freaking go mad. I could have every other room filled with the greatest pleasures known to man. What makes you think you know anything about me or what I'm doing at all?" Moxley pushed off the wall a little and took a few steps towards the edge of the bed.

"You put me in a room with a magic window." I replied dryly without looking away.

"What?" Moxley stopped, puzzled.

The faerie dust hangover might have been worth it simply for the fact that an observant old man had gotten one over on a young lad who could see the future. Foresight did not convey wisdom, only the opportunity for wisdom or an elaborately constructed bad choice.

"This place," I said, emphasizing each word, "you say that it's huge and held together by moments in time that are so vast a simple fellow like me can't hope to understand. Fine. That doesn't change that this is your room, that is your window, and if you were going to start changing things around here - this is where you would have begun because here is the only part that really feels like yours." I put it down for Moxley like Sherlock Holmes doing his best to make Watson feel like an asshole, as if it were all so transparent.

I was a bullshitter of the highest order, and I like to think that it went with the territory.

Moxley's good humor drained from his features, and I realized then how temperamental the young man was, how quick to sour on a situation he might be. When he was showing off, he could be a charming foul-mouthed bundle of energy. Now, he was feeling exposed, and the different sort of attention wasn't agreeing with him at all. His head cocked to the side just a touch, and he pointed a slender finger at me.

"You don't know anything about me." Moxley said with a sort of raw menace that reminded me of a dog that had been whipped so many times that it now bared its teeth at anyone who tried to offer it a kind hand.

"So, tell me why you do it." The words came out before my logic could remind me that Moxley could, with a whisper, turn me to dust or deposit me on some World War I battlefield.

I knew he didn't have to tell me, and on some level, he probably did as well. However, I had yet to meet anyone who boiled with anger and had been hurt so clearly they did not want, on some level, to tell their story. To be heard. To make sense and purpose from the wounds by way of telling.

Moxley turned away and walked with quick, heated steps across the room. He stopped before a poster of some skinny, androgynous figure whose fame had yet to reach my aging shores. All dark hair and skinny-legged jeans.

Conrad Allerton, my father, would have told you that Altenhofen was right," Moxley began, pausing only to look over his shoulder to see if I was still following along with the tale. "They knew each other; they were friends even. Roy didn't start out this way; he wasn't Hitler or Pol-Pot or the Devil," the young man spoke with a quiet steadiness that, until this point, I might have doubted existed at all within him.

Just a side effect of having more money than God?" I should have been gentler in my pushing, but sometimes you had to lay your foot heavy on the accelerator.

Moxley ignored the barbed question.

"They were friends after the war; they met working together on deprogramming the Namebreakers that had been used in conflicts. This was years before they figured out that Dynametrium would retard our abilities, much less figuring out tests to find us," he said, giving his head a quick shake.

"I can actually remember the old man telling me the stories of what a wild card Altenhofen had been when he was younger, I mean..." Moxley told the tale with the bitterness of a man who had something of great value stolen from him.

In a way, I suppose he had.

"What happened?" I asked, but my mind was having trouble imagining Altenhofen as a wildcard. It took the memory of the pictures on the wall outside of the dining room in Altenhofen's 'home' to prop up the notion.

I may not have understood all the finer points of mysticism and magic; Namebreaking was not in my wheelhouse. But I knew power. I knew the corruptive nature of unchecked indulgence, the heady warmth of self-importance, and the fiery armor of righteousness. These elements did not change a man; they merely ate away the veneer that he presented to the world. Power didn't make you evil - it just made you believe you were above the distinction.

For a moment, Moxley remained silent, his brow furrowed deeply and his bottom lip protruding in contemplative consternation. A tension gripped the muscles of his shoulders as he embarked on a familiar quest - the search for the right words.

"We're still people, you know? That's what the Informals and you Dead Tongues always forget. We have the same problems, the same fears, and the same bad reactions. We slip through the same cracks," Moxley spoke, his voice carrying a weight of introspection. He paused, chewed his lip, and glanced out the window at the boats slowly traversing the horizon.

266

I nodded, indicating my continued attention.

"Altenhofen's son was born around the same time as I was, and when he started displaying signs of having The Word, his father naturally sought out mine once more. Altenhofen didn't see it as a malady then; he saw it as an opportunity. Hell, I think he was proud of it. Quinten Altenhofen was quiet and weird, but I'd never had friends before, never knew any other children. My mother died having me, and Dad, well, Dad treated me like any other project. I was just happy to have a friend," Moxley reminisced, his smile devoid of mirth, tight and strained.

I waited in silence, cautious not to prod Moxley further lest he retreat into the devil-may-care persona he'd crafted for himself. In that respect, we were very much the same creature. It was better to play it cool, allowing the tale to unfold before me, waiting for the opportune moment to strike at a weakness. The story begged to be told, and I simply had to coax it along its path - all while ignoring details like my whereabouts and the potential consequences if Moxley were to catch on to my intentions. Nothing compelled careful consideration of one's words like the prospect of fleeing from a hungry T-rex in one's final moments.

Moxley met my gaze, and for a fleeting moment, a profound sorrow flickered in his eyes, compelling me to rise and place a reassuring hand on his shoulder. Deep lines etched their way across his face as he steeled himself, molding the downturn at the corners of his lips into a grin as bitter as it was defiant.

"I might talk a big game about watching the 'river,' but I didn't see it coming. Quinten, he'd say weird shit, but when you don't have anyone to compare it to, how do you know? My old man hadn't even completed tattooing this damn *Signum Tempus* on me," Moxley's tone grew angrier, his fist balling up at his side. Anger at himself, anger at his father, anger even at fate and the genetic coin flips that had led him to this point.

"You're losing me, kid. What's your fault? What the hell is a Sigma Tempest?" I asked as I eased off the bed, the sheet wrapped around my waist.

My pulse quickened as I saw a clear line of how to stop Altenhofen, even if there was no way to change his mind. The game might have been rigged, the dealer playing with a loaded deck, but if that loaded deck sprouted legs and walked off the table - in pure defiance of expected reality?

Well then, the whole game would have to change.

Altenhofen had weaponized Moxley's self-loathing, his guilt, and his shame - he'd turned the boy's heart into the very chains needed to bind him. I didn't know how, I didn't know when, but even without the much-vaunted Word of the Namebreakers, I saw it as clearly as if it were written in dayglo paint on Moxley's chest.

"We were painting; can you believe that? Ol' Conrad really liked to toss out that line about creativity being essential to magic. He also used to toss that out for mathematics, 14th-century literature, and two therapists worth of childhood trauma. He'd give us these abstract assignments and thirty minutes to just slap down what we could. None of them were ever good enough. Our subject was 'Real' that day. You believe that? Real," Moxley spat out the words like food that was too hot for the tongue.

"Sure, kid. Yeah..." I said with as much comfort as I could muster.

"He asked me if I thought they were real people, you know? If all of us were made by the Word, then were we any different than the paper and the paint? I just laughed. I was a kid; it was weird and stupid, but I didn't THINK anything of

it, and like I said, the Signum Tempus wasn't done..."
Moxley's voice wavered.

I wanted to offer comfort, but my mind kept rushing back to the dinner. Back to Altenhofen and that soup of his, the little story about how it had been his son's favorite, and he'd eaten it every day, even after growing disgusted, just to remind himself.

What had he been reminding himself of, though?

Love or hate?

There was a sudden new sinking feeling in my stomach, a realization that neither Tek nor myself had fully grasped what we were dealing with. The road ahead was turning treacherous, mean, and deadly, while our brakes were boneless beneath our stomping feet. I'd taken Altenhofen for a wealthy fool, a man addicted to triumph and victory, and who saw the weaponization of fear against the Shadow People like the Namebreakers and their ilk as a way of making a profit. Now, I was beginning to suspect that he was something altogether more worrisome.

The Righteously Mad.

"If I hadn't been such a baby about the stupid needles..." Moxley's jaw clenched tighter than his fist.

Looking at him, I suddenly understood, at least partially, what the Signum Tempus was. The strange tattoo that adorned Moxley's skin, a string of eldritch numbers and symbols whose meaning eluded me. That was the Signum Tempus. If Moxley's story was correct, it meant that his father had begun etching it onto his body when he was just a boy.

"Dear God..." The words escaped me before I could stifle them.

Moxley looked up, noticing my movement for the first time, and his defenses sprang back up. A quick snort escaped his nose, and I realized how close he had been to tears.

Speaking the Word and using it to alter the world around them may have ignited some internal fire fueled by the Namebreaker's very life force, but memory was a flame as well, and when it burned, it burned hot.

"Don't be too judgmental. The placement might have hurt, but it's also why I can see the river's immediate flow around me when I'm not stuck in an instant with an asshole like you." He fought down the emotional response, burying it beneath his façade of barbed wit and uniform hostility toward the rest of the world.

I just listened.

"It doesn't run on my words; it runs on my father's, so I'm not constantly running the risk of burning out. This was my pop's way of saying that he cared." Moxley managed to sneer as he said it, but the cloak of surliness he used to hide his pain now appeared transparent.

"What about Quinten?" I asked, though I already feared the answer.

Moxley couldn't meet my eyes and looked towards the door instead.

"He took his mother apart. Pulled her Word into all its base elements and then tried to bring her back again. The way a kid might take apart a vacuum cleaner or a toy. When Altenhofen tried to stop him, he shattered his legs. My father discovered them the next morning. Quinten had… been more successful than he should have been…" Moxley gave an uneasy shake of his head as he laid out the end of the story.

"How's that possible? Don't you get stronger as you get older? Shouldn't he have burned himself out?" I was horrified, but I had to know. Damn me, I had to know.

Moxley looked up at this question, his gaze meeting mine with a hardness born from his own encounters with the sharp edges of truth.

"There's power in madness. Maybe he was just a prodigy, whatever was broken in his head made him burn at a different rate than the rest of us. You'd have to ask my father, but that's not possible because he fucking took the little shit and left. There's your great mystery, Mr. Journalist. Conrad fucking Allerton bailed on his family and the Almighty Cause to run off study his new pet. Altenhofen didn't want anything to do with the boy, not after that. He recovered but his wife…" Moxley trailed off.

"That's awful, and I'm sorry you've got it in your head that you're to blame for all that, but you're not, and it doesn't make Altenhofen right." I tried to comfort him.

Moxley said nothing, his jaw clenching and unclenching reflexively as if I were pouring antiseptic on a fresh and ragged wound.

"That doesn't mean that it must be a slow death or a war. That's not the way the world works. There is always a better goddamn way than the one the swine try to shove down our throat!" I said, pushing on while silently thanking the gods for my own lack of children.

Moxley's eyes narrowed down to slits.

"The way the world works? What do YOU know about the way the world works? Why don't you tell me some good old homespun wisdom, hmm? Got a little insight into the American Spirit or how much fun it is to get loaded and cheat on your wife?" Moxley's eyes flashed as he spoke, and a stitch of light crawled across the *Signum Tempus*.

"You don't know shit! You can't see the river; you can't even conceive of how many little decisions and choices and instances of your own shitty nature subtly alter the flow. People like you say things like 'Butterfly Effect,' but if I told you the word for causality in Time - YOUR FUCKING EARS WOULD BLEED-." His voice escalated into a shout before simmering down to a menacing hiss.

Now he had me on my proverbial heels.

"You think that because you sniffed around the skirt of an Informal that you can tell me about the way the world works?" Moxley turned and took a step forward; our noses were almost touching, and his voice was like steam escaping a busted pipe.

I raised one hand with the palm out and kept the other clasped around the sheet over my waist. If I was going to have my atoms scattered across time or my skeleton yanked out of my body, I did not want it to happen with my manhood swinging in the breeze. That's the sort of death you only court at the Republican National Convention or on a ketamine bender deep in the heart of Amish Country.

"Hey, I didn't mean any offense, but you can't seriously think that slowly wiping out your own people is the right answer." I tried to keep my tone calm and steady, hoping to prevent any sudden outbursts. If I was good at it, I hoped at least, that he wouldn't turn me into an infant and give me to a smug Hollywood actress to raise for social media likes.

"The difference between me and people like you is that I don't have to THINK that I'm right. I can KNOW when I'm right." Moxley's sneer deepened as he turned back towards the window.

He gazed out at his ships and the jarring blue of the sea, standing there beholding an instant that had to be older than either of us, older than his father or even Altenhofen. A tremble ran through him, and I felt myself backing towards the bed until the rear of my knees bumped against the mattress itself. The air felt suddenly overcharged, as if ball lightning might at any moment begin leaping about the room and scorching flesh from bone.

"I am NOT like you, Mr. Wonderful. You cast your words out like messages in a bottle thrown into the ocean, hoping that somehow, they'll change things. They'll make you money, make you famous, or make you loved. Well, you know what I am?"

The air around us grew very still, and I had the strangest recollection of the sea pulling back in the moments before a great wave was to batter the shore.

"I -AM- *Homo Magus*. I am a Speaker of Time, A Weaver of the All-Thing. When I whisper a word, the sky trembles, and when I shout, creation itself quakes at my command. The way of the world? I'll show you the way of the world..." Moxley took a deep breath.

The Signum Tempus slithered across his skin like a serpent in the throes of an otherworldly dance, bestowed with an eerie life of its own, a spectral tattoo pulsating with an otherworldly energy.

He spoke, but there was no sound, none that I can repeat here in any quality that might help you understand. The sound of time itself is not properly expressed with the auditory comparisons of the physical world. If one wishes to try, then they must first imagine the breaking of a great dam of water and the rush and roar of that water as it tears across the face of Creation itself. Once one captures this roar in the jail cell of their mind, they must then replace all sense of liquid flowing with a discordant tick of every clock that has finally, at long last, unwound.

Moxley was right; my ears did bleed, and the pain pushed me onto the bed. I was still doing my best to cover my ears with the sheets and my hands, heedless of my nakedness, when I felt Moxley take me by the wrist and haul me up.

"Look! Look if you want to know so damned bad! Look!" He must have been shouting but I could barely hear him, I'd gone deaf, it was like my ears were stuffed with tightly packed snow.

I didn't want to, my head was pounding and now I just very much wanted to be free of this madness, but I was helpless against the pull of it. Gone was the peaceful blue of the horizon where the sea and the sky met like long lost lovers. Replacing the horizon was a new sky, one as gray as ash and spotted with black patches that may have once been clouds. The earth beneath this gray sky was muddy and in it nothing grew because the soil had been torn up and the roots of the grass destroyed. Squat ugly box-like buildings stretched their way across this muddy landscape, surrounded by miles upon miles of barbed wire and chain link fence. At the borders of these fences stood men in black uniforms, their faces hidden like the plague doctors of old behind gas masks and I realized then why the sky was gray.

They were not simply ugly boxes of industry.

They were factories of death.

They were an ancient and forbidden solution, one that mankind had always entertained in the darkest recesses of his soul. Once spoken, it spread like a virus through the hearts and minds of the desperate and the fearful. The strange, the weird, the mystical itself, lulled into a state of docility like a cow with its head stuck in a feed bucket during its ride to the slaughterhouse. The people were pacified by the comforts of the West Coast, where it was easy to bury one's head in the sand. They had been convinced by their own optimism and the perfect smiles of the entertainment industry that a new age was already upon them.

COYOTE WALLACE

The Shadow People would be like frogs in a pot of slowly boiling water. By the time anyone realized that humanity had no intention of sharing this world with anyone or anything that made him afraid, it would be far too late.

The smell hit me like a fist, and I had to turn away, moaning pitifully.

Moxley would have none of it.

"Remember this. Remember what you saw. THAT is the future without Altenhofen's cure. That's what happens if I don't do this. Now… FUCK OFF!"

Moxley's words echoed in my head like thunder. I was falling, falling through the floors, through the earth, through the long, endless dark until, at last, that endlessness proved to be an illusion and succumbed to light.

For a surreal moment, I realized I was hanging upside down over the pool and could see the water rippling beneath me. Moxley was just climbing out by way of the little silvery ladder on the pool's side as I hung there. My noticing must have been the gravest of insults to gravity, for it chose that moment to remember me.

I plunged straight down into the chlorinated but pleasantly warm waters of the pool, fought to right myself, and with a few kicks of my feet, swam to the surface. I broke the water, gasped for air, and doggy paddled to the edge. I didn't think I had the strength left to pull myself up onto the rough-textured concrete around the poolside, but I managed it and rolled over. The Faerie Dust was still doing its thing, and the stars glittered like the most beautiful diamonds ever stolen from the clutching fist of the earth.

Moxley was gone, but that was fine.

Just fine.

The world dissolved into the inky depths of the night sky, and if I dared to dream amidst that darkness, they were dreams woven of black smoke and swirling gray ash.

DAY TWO
Death.

"Laugh long into the night, drive fast, and never trust a faerie or a telemarketer with your true name. Not if you value your credit score." - Jimmy Wonderful, Terror and Poor Choices in Arcadia

Coffee, Shame, and The Cold Certainty Everything Is Fucked

As a rule, when it comes to matters of faith, I plant my flag firmly in the territory of the non-practicing agnostic. Demons, vampires, lycanthropes, the Fair Folk, and Namebreaking lunatics aside, the only thing I am certain of is that I am certain of nothing. This does not, however, prevent my imagination from flights of theological fancy. When, at 9:25 a.m., there came a heavy knocking upon the door of my bungalow, that imagination found it particularly easy to envision what it must have been like to be on the receiving end of a god's wrath.

I stumbled out of bed, nearly tripping over the pile of wet clothing that I'd left on the floor, and hastily wrapped myself in a bathrobe. My head hurt, my mouth was as dry as a stretch of Arizona highway, and I desperately wanted to hide beneath the covers until Altenhofen was forced to send his lapdog, the murderous Hawthorne, to break the door down with a fire ax.

BANG! BANG! BANG!

A fresh series of knuckle-reddening strikes on the face of the door summoned my stiff-jointed figure. Before opening the door, I paused with my hand on the knob to give one last look around the bungalow.

The television was destroyed, along with one of the small inn tables that I'd weaponized during my mania. The refrigerator was hanging open, and at least three bags of potato chips had been spread in a circle around what I could only assume was the floor panel that I had believed was a window into another world. I'd done worse on the Mystic Standards' dime, but not in a long time. Not since Jenna came into my life and the need to live with the throttle held wide open had abated to only the odd craving whenever I felt the walls closing in.

I opened the door just enough to poke my face out. The sun was blindingly bright and forced my eyes into a watery squint. Pain exploded in my head, and I squeezed down on the door's frame to keep from wilting in the light. No one tells you how fucking bright Utah is. How mercilessly the sun just jabs you right in the eyes every chance it gets.

Percy was standing there, already craning his neck to try to see past me. Sensing that if nothing else, when all this was over, he'd be the one tasked with cleaning up. The heat of the day clearly didn't agree with him, and his corpulent face was already glistening like canned ham. He dabbed away the sweat with the help of a cloth handkerchief and stared at me with all the humor of a landed catfish.

"Breakfast is to be served shortly." Percy said with a dry tiredness.

"I'm good, thanks," I told him and began to close the door. To Hell with food; what I needed was twelve more hours of sleep.

Percy jammed his foot in the door, and I watched as my hopes of going back to bed jumped the rails like a runaway train. There'd be no more blissful oblivion for me, no escaping the merciless sun either or the responsibility that was even then already barreling down on me. To steal someone else's line, 'It was time to face the music' - but at least the music would have some toast and coffee with it, or so I hoped anyway.

"Fine, fine. Let me get dressed, you fucking ghoul. Goddamn it!" I half mumbled and half snapped at Percy.

This was enough to mollify him, and he pulled his thick foot from the door's frame. I still had the smell of ash in my nose, and the sight of Percy's glistening face was too much for me at this early point in my day. I closed the door and stood there with my back against it, swallowing down my nausea and the overwhelming urge to scream. I was certain that if I began either one, I'd be unable to stop; and that would certainly do no good for the lie I was telling myself about the state of my sanity.

No good at all.

At a certain point, a man must realize when he's up against something that was larger than himself and his ability to stand against it. I had reached this point. Mentally battered, frightened, and faced with the fact that in the stark light of the day, I wasn't just a fool but a fraud. The swaggering bravado of my youth had given way beneath the weight of time, crumbling to expose a man who was much more comfortable writing about The Weird than getting down in the mud with it. I wanted familiarity, I wanted warmth, I wanted Jenna and a tall glass of something strong that burned on the way down.

I needed a shower, and by the time I was beneath the spray of the water, I was already rehearsing in my head the most honorable way to be a coward. The thought of participating in Altenhofen's obscenity - be it genuine or token, was grotesque. I was leaving. Damn them all. I would leave and go home and never speak of this place again. Our country was already going to Hell in a handbasket, and I was far too old to play the hero. Whatever Tek wanted me to be, whatever Altenhofen hoped I would be, and whatever I thought I would be all meant nothing in the face of the outcome that Moxley had shown me.

Altenhofen's son had been broken, damaged in some way that was unforeseen; as Tek and Moxley both attested, Namebreakers were, human - and like the rest of humanity, there existed within them potential for both great good and tremendous evil.

COYOTE WALLACE

I felt that Moxley might have been sugar coating the truth a bit when it came to how Altenhofen and his wife's fate played out. I didn't need the particulars, but the imagination had a nasty way of filling in the blanks. My troubled mind kept leaping to an old video I'd seen of animal testing, an old hound thrown into a pool and pushed away from the sides just to see how long it took to drown. Altenhofen had been that dog until Conrad Allerton had arrived and God only knows what sort of things he'd seen in that time. I had a feeling though that 'God' had particularly little to do with it.

A clean shirt and a pair of comfortable jeans later, I was already throwing the leftovers of my belongings back into their suitcase. My mind was steadily mapping out my escape and making quick work of the task at that. The little matter of my broken resolve was of surprisingly minor impediment to fleeing in cowardice and abandoning Tek. I wasn't a Namebreaker, and before this whole mad experiment, I hadn't personally known any either. I bore them no malice, but this was not my fight. In a few dozen years, when I was dead and Altenhofen was LONG dead (but not that black-eyed snake Hawthorne), there would come a tipping point; then The Word or magic or whatever the Hell you wanted to call it would be gone from mankind.

I'd buy a nice cabin in the mountains somewhere with what was left of my fortune, drink and smoke, and discharge firearms at the artifices of the ugly religion of Capitalism. I'd never write another word, and if the urge threatened to take me, I would stuff every manuscript into a barrel and light the whole thing on fire. The American Dream had turned vicious and sharp-toothed; its promise of fortune, freedom, and equality was a siren's song meant to lure in the unsuspecting and the foolish into its waiting jaws. America was a mad cannibal bitch, and she would eat you guts first while you were still alive to appreciate it if you were foolish enough to go looking for her.

The American Mystic was on his own.

A quick glance in the mirror, and I was almost aghast at what I saw there. My eyes were sunken and ringed with dark bags. I looked, despite the shower and clean clothes, like a coke fiend who was halfway through the process of drying out. The greasy hammock that my stomach swayed in was no better than it had been before the shower, and I opted to roll myself a joint. I doubted it would be enough for my nerves, but it might allow me to hold down some toast and the coffee that my brain needed to make coherent sense of anything but running away.

Sensing that Altenhofen would be there but hoping that Tek would forego breakfast so that I could slip out without the messiness of my shame, I stepped out into the bright morning. The joint helped take the bite off it all, and there was something beautiful about the sun peaking over the walls of Altenhofen's compound. A few good moments were spent lingering there outside the door of my bungalow. I left my suitcase propped against the door and proceeded to walk across the lawn that Altenhofen had spent so much money shipping out to this godforsaken stretch of nothingness.

There's a peculiar thrill to be had when walking across the expensive grass of a wealthy man's lawn that feels a bit like screwing his wife. I would have enjoyed it more and highly recommend it, but no matter how many puffs I stole from that joint, my gut was still in knots. The sight of Hawthorne enjoying his own cigarette by the entrance to the main house did nothing to help this matter. When one looked upon the man, it was impossible not to feel the same almost knee-jerk chill of the soul that one felt when they stumbled upon a rattlesnake sunning itself in their path.

Hawthorne was draped in the same drab, gray suit as the day prior, its color matching the desolation of his soul. The barrel of his pistol protruded from its weathered leather holster, a chilling reminder of the violence he harbored within. An ominous aura enveloped him, a spectral manifestation of the bloodlust and greed that fueled his existence.

Despite the supposed immortality that lent the man his eternal youth, there lingered a palpable sense of decay that emanated from Hawthorne, a decay steeped in the atrocities of the nation's past. He was not merely a relic of history; he was a living embodiment of its darkest chapters.

There was a perverse fascination in his presence, beckoning to the primal, untamed instincts within me, urging them to confront the depths of his depravity. How often does one come face to face with such a wretched figure, adorned not with riches, but with the blood of countless victims? Imagine having the opportunity to confront the last remnants of the Third Reich or spending mere moments with Pol Pot's closest confidant. The mere thought sent shivers down my spine.

Every encounter with Hawthorne ignited an internal turmoil within me – a battle between the desire to unleash a barrage of accusations and the realization that he had endured far worse. It was a sobering realization, more chilling than his capacity for inflicting pain – knowing that there was no insult or accusation that could penetrate the armor of his callused soul.

"Good morning, you humorless, dead-eyed son of a bitch." I greeted him with forced cheer, concealing my revulsion beneath a thin veneer of civility.

Hawthorne's gaze shifted towards me, the cigarette between his lips bobbing with each calculated movement. His stone-cold demeanor exuded an amalgam of contempt and revulsion, as though he could smell the stench of my disdain emanating from every pore. I could only hope the pungent aroma of the weed I carried offended his senses, though I doubted I was that fortunate.

"You remind me of one of those beetles," Hawthorne drawled as he pulled the cigarette from his lips and pushed a stream of smoke out the side of his mouth.

"Oh yeah? Ringo or John?" I asked with my left-handed cigarette dangling out of my mouth in my best impersonation of Marlon Brando in the Wild One.

"No, I mean the kind that's always pushin' a big ol' ball of shit everywhere he goes. An' lord to watch 'em you'd think they was mighty important but at the end of the day? They crunch under the boot just the same," Hawthorne said, his words dripping with menace, like oil slicks on a dark highway.

"Well look at you, stringing more than two words together without a grunt. You missed your calling; you should have been a writer like me. Just think of all the stories you could tell - The Time I Shot That Guy or It's A Fine Day For Ethnic Cleansing or just go straight for the award scene with 'Angry, White, and Armed: A Tale of The American Micropenis'," I was in fine and stinging form as I cut into Hawthorne.

I was leaving after all, and that realization infused me with a certain amount of courage where otherwise there may have been none.

Hawthorne made a snorting sound like a horse that had just caught wind of a mountain lion's passage on the trail ahead. He pushed off the side of the house where he'd propped himself and turned fully to look me up and down. Hawthorne was almost a foot taller, and despite being three times my age, he still had a form that exuded muscle and lean murderous intent. I could verbally slice apart his moral character and all that he represented, but there was no doubting that he would have cut a fearful image riding out of the sun on horseback, bringing poisoned progress and death with him.

"You like to think you're a smart fella, don'tcha?" Hawthorne's stoney voice had softened a little with pleasure, a chilling sound. His head cocked to the side, his lips tugging upwards in their corners.

I held my ground, knowing that I'd soon be fleeing said ground with the utmost haste was what kept me planted there as Altenhofen's pet rattlesnake tried to decide if I was worth a venomous fang or not. Yet, Hawthorne's smile and the malignant happiness that spread through his words were enough to make that ground feel a lot less stable.

Whenever men who think that the land can be tamed and mastered smile, it is never for any good or noble reason.

"Middling to average, I only appear smart when observed by the common idiot," I quipped from around the tail end of my joint.

Hawthorne took a sudden step toward me, his looming figure casting a shadow that swallowed the very sunlight. The scent of his tobacco hung in the air like a harbinger of doom; I would have bummed one off the bastard, but surrendering then would have been akin to capitulating to my own surliness.

Whatever dark mirth had pulled Hawthorne's lips upwards now drained away, leaving his countenance as barren as the desolate Salt Flats themselves, yearning for the embrace of oblivion since Altenhofen's invasion. His eyes, once filled with a twisted amusement, were now as dead as the wasteland stretching to the horizon. There was nothing there—no sadness, no anger, not even the mad gleam of lunacy that often haunted the eyes of those marked for lives of brutality.

There was only a void behind Hawthorne's eyes—a vast, yawning emptiness that had been carved out by the curse of immortality. No matter how many Words were poured into that abyss, it remained unfilled, a bottomless chasm where hope went to die.

"Mr. Altenhofen wished me to give you a quiet reminder that while no one here could care less about you sneakin' off to get a few humps in with Pocahontas..." Hawthorne's voice lowered to a grave whisper, his words punctuated by the flick of my joint disappearing into the grass.

"...If you keep gettin' the boy to waste his juice before he does the job, I'm to find a way to keep you in your room at night." Hawthorne's tone was quiet, but the gravity of his words hung in the air like a guillotine blade poised to fall.

"What makes you think that's even a concern?" I asked, half-expecting him to reveal some clandestine surveillance system hidden within the bungalows themselves.

The bleak emptiness in Hawthorne's eyes momentarily lifted, replaced by a chilling grin that seemed to slither across his face like a serpent. There is nothing that a stupid dog enjoys more than the performance of the one or two tricks that it actually knows.

"Makes my skin itch when one of them breaks a Name; feels like fire ants crawling all over me for just a second. Don't worry how I know beyond that; you just mind what I'm sayin' to you. You won't be asked twice." Hawthorne remarked, tossing in a little wink with his threat.

As his menacing concluded, he stepped back, and I realized that my heart, despite the mellowing effects of the pot, had picked up its pace. The fight or flight response was still functioning, and that was something; I'd be happy to be done with the fear altogether when I was back home, and this place was consigned to that little mental folder marked 'bad ideas that had not panned out as you wished them to, Jimmy.'

That folder, I noted with some dismay, was growing thicker with the passage of time.

There was a moment when I felt like saying more; cursing and holding my ground in defiance was a hard temptation to let go. One last tirade on my way out; my tongue practically dripped with venom, and inside, there was a raging wild horde of insults, sharp truths, and bitter cuts not only to the man but also to all that had spawned him.

He stood for both the perversion of the American ideal and, paradoxically, the instrument that had been used in the bloody business of the nation's birth. I may have sometimes trafficked in the strange territory where myth and man met, but Hawthorne was the living embodiment of a wrong done to a stranger for no cause greater than one's own advancement. Looking upon him was like reliving stealing money from your mother's purse but magnified a hundredfold.

"I don't think that'll be a problem." I told him, while trying to keep the tightness in my voice to a minimum.

Hawthorne gave a grunt but replied no further.

I stormed past the dead-eyed brute and barged into the bungalow, seeking solace from the scorching sun outside. However, the layout was a middle finger to my hopes, with every window magnifying the brightness to a blistering inferno. My head pounded with each step, courtesy of my encounter with Hawthorne. Nonetheless, I reminded myself of my empty stomach and pressed on towards the dining area, until those damned pictures of Altenhofen and his brood stopped me dead in my tracks.

Those cursed pictures held me in their thrall, whispering stories breathed to life by Tek and Moxley, connecting dots I hadn't even seen. When had Altenhofen known about his son's emptiness? Not the Namebreaker bit; that was obvious - but the void lurking behind his eyes, the one Moxley had rambled about. Could Altenhofen have been oblivious, blinded by paternal love? It was a nauseating thought; Altenhofen prided himself on reading people, on unraveling their deepest truths - how could he have missed this?

I longed to touch the photographs, to trace the contours of the boy's face with the haunting eyes that echoed the forlornness of Victorian-era children. However, a glance over my shoulder brought me face to face with Hawthorne, watching me like a predator sizing up its prey. I dared not touch the pictures, and it was probably for the best.

The pieces were beginning to slot into place.

Morning lacked the grandeur of the previous night's dinner, no servants, no elaborate spread. A stack of plates lay forgotten on the table, a stark contrast to the opulence of Altenhofen's estate. He himself was absent, but Tek and Moxley were already there, lost in their own thoughts. Tek poked at a sausage link with disinterest, nursing a cup of coffee as if the caffeine could ward off the impending shitstorm.

I focused on Tek, realizing that since the chance to slink away had evaded me, I might as well shoot for the righteous path. Skulking in the shadows would've been far too tame for my liking anyway.

If nothing else, I could scout out the source of her coffee. Best to steer clear of Moxley for now. You never knew how someone might react when their nocturnal revelations were brought to light in the harsh glare of day. I had no desire to conjure up the spectacles that lurked beyond his little slice of eternity. Delving deeper would only tempt me to linger, and I knew myself too damn well for that. It was smarter to play dumb now that I'd embraced the sensible, cowardly route.

"You look... refreshed," Tek remarked, popping a morsel of sausage into her mouth with a flick of her fork.

"You're a terrible liar; you'd never make it in American politics," I grumbled, pulling up a chair beside her, trying not to eye her coffee too conspicuously.

My retort earned a chuckle, but a glance into Tek's eyes revealed the weariness that had taken root overnight. I highly doubted she'd slept any better than I had, but at least she had a good reason. I'd been nosing around in the darker corners of the universe, picking up a scent that had me shaking in my boots. Tek, on the other hand, had real stakes. I'd faced vampires, demons, faeries, and the like, but none were as nasty as the pre-deadline jitters. For me, it was nerve-racking enough when it was just money and reputation on the line, but for Tek, failure meant a lifetime of regret.

And that, my friends, was a beast of a different breed.

"Not going to tell me I look like shit?" Tek, despite the weariness lingering in her eyes, managed to ask with a sly turn of her lips.

"I'm too old to go to a hospital and ask a young doctor to fetch a pineapple out of my ass. So, no, I don't think I will say that to you. Besides, I was hoping to butter you up and get you to tell me where you got the cup of joe." I replied with perfect honesty.

I realized then that my guilt over the plan to run had broken some inner dam, and now I was helpless but to tell the truth. I could no more have lied to Tek than I could have lied convincingly to my own mother. On the heels of that realization came another fresh wave of guilt: I hadn't felt that way about twisting the truth to my own ends when it came to Jenna. I was a bastard and a hypocrite; the truth was the only poor currency I had with which to pay penance for my sins.

However, I was just enough of a cad to cover that truth in humor.

Tek's laughter had a little more vitality this time around, and she seemed to enjoy it more than the food. For that, I was thankful at least. Tek wouldn't be bailing out, even if the attempt to convince Altenhofen to change his path proved to be nothing but the halfhearted eccentricity of a dying old man. If I could give her a little relief and a break in the tension before I ducked and ran like a dog with his tail between his legs, then that would be fine by me.

"In the back, no servants today. Go ahead, I've barely touched mine." Tek said as she slid the cup over to me.

I took it gratefully, and while it was just lukewarm, I drank greedily – I'd have mainlined the caffeine if I could. Though I had loaded my plate and had been hungry, most of my appetite had diminished when I'd been confronted with the burden of hiding my planned escape from Tek. Cowardice was an excellent appetite suppressant.

I pecked at my toast, tearing little bits off and dipping them in a swath of strawberry jam. My silence outside of the light banter with Tek was mostly a cautionary measure; I did not want to run the risk of her asking me anything about our little argument that we were to make for Altenhofen's amusement. I knew there was no swaying his mind, and even if it were possible, Moxley had already shown me the outcome. If she didn't ask, I wouldn't have to tell the truth, and the only boldfaced lie I would have to deal with was the one that I told myself about the act not being as rotten as it was.

Across from us and a little way down the table sat Moxley. He was wrapping waffles around links of sausages and pouring syrup along the center before taking huge bites. The syrup had run down onto his hands, and after every few bites, he would pop a finger into his mouth to suck greedily at the sweetness before resuming his meal. He paid no attention to either Tek or myself and seemed as content to avoid me as I had been to avoid him. Just looking at him summoned up the terror of the previous night.

The burnt smell was back in my nose, and it reminded me a bit too much of the smell of a hog roast. That moment when the swine is brought out from the fire pit at last and its tender flesh, blackened on the outside, falls loose and easy from the bone. The urge to vomit came suddenly, and I had to force down the mouthful of toast.

"Are you ok?" Tek asked, her concern only making it worse.

I didn't answer; instead, I called out across the table to Moxley.

"Where is everyone? Where's the Old Man?"

Moxley stopped eating and looked up. There was a shadow of small bruises along the side of his neck, and his eyes held a sort of reproachful glint. I suspected I wasn't his favorite person after spilling his guts. I had made him feel vulnerable, and something told me that with all the power at Moxley's fingertips, vulnerability was not a condition he was accustomed to.

He'd also clearly gotten a reprimand from Hawthorne, the same as I had. The bruise on his neck was owed, in part at least, to my own doings.

"Altenhofen always sends them off when he brings one of the Resonance Towers in. No idea where Roy is though; could go ask Hawthorne - he seemed so cheerful this morning." Moxley said, not bothering to gild the sarcasm that soaked his words as he dropped his eyes to his plate and kept on eating.

I stood up, realizing that trying to eat had been a mistake. Allowing myself to see Tek again had been another. I'd ventured into waters that were far too deep and filled with far too many hungry horrors. The notion that I could change anything or that those changes might even make anything better was a fool's errand, and I had reached my limit.

"Where are you going?" Tek called after me as I started towards the door.

"To tell Hawthorne to call his damned boss," I said, sweating. Behind my eyes, the image that I had glimpsed from Moxley's window - that moment from 'somewhere up the river' - a bend where Altenhofen failed to quietly erase the Namebreakers and the world descended into madness, fire, barbwire, and ash - kept swimming up.

Hope needed uncertainty to grow, and Moxley had scorched and salted that earth. I had no more fights left in me.

"Why?" I heard Tek's chair scoot against the floor as she asked.

"It's because he quit." Moxley said smugly, his mouth full of God only knew what. I hadn't the inclination to look.

"What!?!? Jimmy, wait a second..." Tek's confusion, for just one moment, had produced something plaintive in her voice. Any better man would have stopped then and there. Their courage, character, and moral fiber would have demanded it so.

I never slowed down.

COYOTE WALLACE

The Devil That You Know

I could hear Tek coming after me as I pushed out the door, the taste of toast and lukewarm coffee turning rancid on my tongue. Gripped by a suffocating, invasive claustrophobia, I needed to break free! All that remained was to confront Altenhofen and demand my release, or else I'd trudge through the Flats with my shirt tied around my head like a desperate wanderer lost in the Sahara.

"Jimmy, stop!" Tek's voice cut through the air behind me, halting my escape. My legs rebelled against my will, and my upper body surged forward with a momentum of its own, a strange sensation as if my body had been split in two. I spun around to face Tek, frustration bubbling up inside me.

"What the hell is this?" I barked.

Approaching cautiously, Tek regarded me as if I were a wild beast ensnared in a hunter's trap, ready to lash out at any moment. Despite my fear and anger, she remained strikingly beautiful, a reminder of a past I wished I could forget. Her dark hair swept back from her face, her eyes reminiscent of the petrified forest, weathered and timeless. Clad in a simple white blouse and jeans, she exuded a quiet elegance without effort.

She slowed her approach, sensing there was no need to rush after me now.

"Can you please explain what's happening? Where are you going? What did Moxley mean when he said you quit?" Tek's voice held a fading hope, her questions revealing her growing disappointment.

She could read the truth on my face.

"Let me go. This whole thing is useless; it's a fucking joke. A goddamn scam!" Words that I would have much rather swallowed down now came back up, regurgitated by the stress and fear.

Thoughtlessly, I carried on, half-shouting in my agitated state.

"There's no convincing him to let it go; he has no intention of doing that! He just wants to see if we'll beg. That's all! Besides, even if we killed the bastard, buried him in the desert, and burnt the whole damned operation to the ground, it'd only get worse. The kid showed me what lies up the river. I'll have no part in it. None of this fucking matters." I pelted her with words like a boy trying to drive away a stray dog that followed him by throwing pebbles.

"You're not making any sense. What river? What do you mean, it doesn't matter? We talked about this. We have to at least try!" Tek's confusion gradually gave way to anger, and her voice rose with that growing heat.

"Time. Moxley showed me what's driving Altenhofen, and worse, what would happen without him. You see? None of what we do here matters. It's already been decided. The bastards wrote the ending first. There were camps, cities of fire and ash! They'll hunt you, and not just you either! They'll hunt everyone who carries even the possibility. We're like Public Defenders; we're not supposed to win. We were never supposed to win. Now, let me the Hell go." I spat it out with such intensity, never pausing or halting for Tek to get a word in edgewise.

The words came with such furious and hurtful reproach that Tek took a step back and almost bumped into the wall.

"Jimmy, please..." Tek began, trying to throw water on the fire.

"I don't know what Moxley told you, but that's not how it works. Destiny is not set in stone; we aren't trapped. The

Word for the Future is always changing, always morphing and mutating because every day we're all changing it."

Tek paused, quickly gathered herself, and pushed her own panic and dismay down to the wayside. When she spoke again, her voice had taken the firm but calm evenness of one who was talking a distraught banker off the ledge of the New York Stock Exchange.

"Conrad Allerton has been gone for years; who knows what tutors or sort of crap Altenhofen has been spewing in Moxley's ear. We make our own fate, our own destiny, our own fucking time." Tek said with such conviction that for a moment the fear abated. When her lips soundlessly moved again, and my legs could once more carry me, I almost stayed.

Tek was persuasive because she believed every word, and there was nothing more compelling in a dire situation than a true believer. However, Moxley had laid before my own eyes a sight so terrifying and soul-wrenching that even Tek's words were brushed away by the sheer scope of the futility. I wanted to believe her, I wanted to believe that Moxley was wrong, and that life did not break down into simple binary outcomes. I needed there to be more to destiny than just a coin flip, more directions than simply left or right. Yet, no matter how I tried, the image kept coming back, surfacing in the black waters of my imagination with a clarity that I prayed would lessen with time, alcohol, and distance.

"Can you see the future too? Is that one of the Names you know, huh? You know that one?" I asked, battling back the temptation that some might have mistaken for morality, but I now knew it was just my pride.

I'd fancied myself a great champion when fighting windmills, but now that I had come face to face with a giant, I found myself lacking in the bravado of yesterday's battles.

For a moment, I saw Tek wrestle with her own temptation—the temptation to lie to me. I'd learned to recognize that look, having chased too many stories and listened to too many damned interviews. There was a pause and a moment where she chewed upon her lower lip. The woman who had not-so-subtly teleported me to the top of that dark mountain was strong and carried herself as if she had paid for every victory with blood, sweat, and effort. Never tears. Those were kept back like precious stones for her own treasure trove of hurt. Yet the possibility to help those like her must have been maddening.

In the end, she fought down the urge to lie.

"No, I don't, but it's what I believe, and even if I did spend the time learning the exact same things Moxley has, I still would believe that. Our choices matter, Jimmy. What we do matters even if we fail," Tek said with a softness that could only mean vulnerability.

Once again, I had to be the kid throwing rocks at the stray to drive it back, but this time, I chose a nice big one.

"If you don't mind, I'll just take the advice of the guy who was trained by someone who knew what the Hell they were doing. No offense, but you said it yourself - you can't do what he does. So how could you know? The rest of it? That's just the sort of thing they put on inspirational posters for the gullible to keep them flipping burgers instead of eating the wrong end of a hunting rifle." I hated myself for saying it, but I had to be free of this place. I had to leave. I could not stand to see what was coming.

"There a problem here, y'all?" Hawthorne drawled from the doorway. He'd half moved inside - only the cigarette in his hand staying outside the door.

Tek looked away from me at once, and though separated from Hawthorne by that open stretch twenty-five feet or more between the front door and the entrance into the dining area, one could see the blooming disdain across her features. Her eyes narrowed into slits, and every muscle in Tek's body seemed to bunch up at once. Her hands became tight little balls at her side. I watched her lips threaten to curl into a snarl, but she fought it down and instead looked at me with a mixture of betrayal and disappointment that felt like a cold dagger shoved into my guts and stirred around.

The slow dying that came with remembering the moment you became an absolute bastard and there was no going back.

"No," Tek said simply and stepped back.

I started walking towards Hawthorne, for once the miserable prick's presence was preferable to being alone; all it had taken was the defilement of my soul and the realization that I was some sort of bottom-feeding cowardly shit. At the time, at least, it didn't matter if I was a coward; my bravery or cowardice would not change anything at all regardless of my choices.

Time was going to play out as it would, and my involvement was simply a seasoning that neither added nor took away anything of substantive value.

"Where's Altenhofen?" I demanded and I suppose by the rapidity of my step and the look on my face that Hawthorne saw that I meant business.

He wasn't intimidated, if anything, he looked amused, but it was enough to make him flick his cigarette away. I like to think that considering he could have punched my head clean around on my neck, that was some small victory.

"He's busy," Hawthorne replied and crossed his arms over his chest as he blocked the door.

"To Hell with his goddamn busy! I am leaving. You can either take me to him and let me tell him myself or you can open the goddamn gate and I'll just walk. Take your pick," I shot with more heat than I had intended.

I was too angry at myself to be afraid, and it was very easy to take that anger out on an unrepentant sonofabitch like Hawthorne. I didn't like him anyway and found Altenhofen's keeping of the man on retainer even more grotesque after I'd learned what he was. It gave me the same feeling as when I'd read about the Nazi scientist who'd gotten themselves cozy jobs and pardons in the states by agreeing to work for the US government.

There were times it was simply better to do without.

"Hold your horses, just because you and the little Injun girl had some sort of tiff don't mean I'm goin' to disturb Mr. Altenhofen. Frankly, you should be counting your blessings; I haven't never stuck my pecker in one of them squaws that was worth the dirt I got on my trousers." Hawthorne said it low enough that I was sure that Tek hadn't heard it.

I had heard it, however.

I had never been a man of violence or dramatic action. I chronicled the violence, chased the dramatic action, and had, for the most part at least, only been an observer to that world. True violence rarely looked as clean and slick as it did on the television screens or when blown up to ridiculous proportions for the movie theaters. I had only a voyeur's taste for such things, and aside from a few scuffles in bars that had been neutralized by bouncers, who could read situations almost as well as Moxley could with his Signum Tempus, I was a stranger to violence.

Aside from the bloodying of Stanley McAlister's nose in grade school, I'd never had cause to even throw a punch.

As Hawthorne spoke, I thought of Stanley and did my own time travel through the magic of memory, recalling that day. Stanley had been whipping a dog that made the mistake of wandering onto the Latham Miller School for Young Boys playground. They'd hemmed the old copper dog with its mange-chewed furless back legs into the far corner of the playground, and with its back pressed into the chain-link fence, the beast had at last laid down to accept its fate. I'd been small and bookish, and my best friend, Rory Keebler, himself a pudgy bespectacled kid who came from a long line of pudgy bespectacled kids, perhaps read *Lord of the Flies* and understood too well the cruel smiles of other boys, had cautioned me against interference. I'd marched across that playground though, and when I had reached McAlister, I'd spun the cruel little sonofabitch around and hit him as hard in the nose as my stick-like arms had allowed.

He'd beat the shit out of me, but the dog ran away.

I'd counted that as a victory.

My fist was coming up just as Hawthorne himself was leaning back after his little imparting of carnal wisdom. It came up with all the burning fury that the last twenty-four hours of fear, self-loathing, and hangovers could bestow. I did not see Hawthorne; I saw every ignorant bastard that still flew the Confederate flag. I did not see a hired gun; I saw the bulging plastic scrotums mounted on the back of trucks. I did not look upon a cursed man; I saw the sweaty bleating faces of talk radio hosts, so much like the Southern Baptist ministers of my youth during their sermons, ranting and raving into their microphones and the swaggering white devil that was America's notions of its own innate superiority - *Da aut omnia mori* - Give Everything or Die.

He caught my fist as though I were a child, and I felt my anger turn into a quick sharp panic. Hawthorne's hand nearly engulfed my own, and I could feel the rough, sandstone quality of his fingers against the back of my hand, the gunslinger callused pad of his palm pressed up against the points of my knuckles. Nothing flickered in his eyes, not hate or surprise or even some mocking amusement - just the nothingness of the old dry desert beneath the timeless baking sun. His lips might have curled up into a smirk, but that smirk didn't live in that wasteland behind his eyes. Nothing did.

"Jimmy! Hey! Let him go!" Tek was yelling from behind me, too good to abandon me despite my efforts to drive her away.

I stared into the nothingness, and it held me transfixed the way a snake might hypnotize a bird.

"Why, lord have mercy. Since it means that much to you, pardner, I'll walk you out to the site myself. No reason to get all excited about it," Hawthorne's voice was like an old sarcophagus being pushed open, gritty and too old for trappings of the tongue that it still held onto.

His grip tightened around my fist and though I wanted to give no indication, the growing pressure and pain of his grip robbed me of that choice and pulled my eyes to the point of my ensnarement. Hawthorne's free hand came up, and with an open palm struck me high across the jawline and ear. My legs went out from under me instantly; my head rang as surely as it had the first time I had heard Moxley or Tek use their Namebreaking in my presence.

I hit the floor and found myself staring dazedly at the dirt around the edges of the soles of Hawthorne's boots.

The sound of Tek's shoes on the hard tile were felt through the palms of my hands more than heard in my ringing ears, and I looked up to see her plant two palms against Hawthorne's chest and shove him back. Putting herself between the brute and myself in case he decided to turn the slap into a beating. I might have been slightly rattled, but I could almost see the air around her shimmer, though it was likely the stars clearing from my vision.

"Touch him again and I swear I'll pull your fucking heart out your ass, you fuck!" Tek growled as she stood over me like a mountain lioness defending its cub.

She meant it.

"Oh, keep the fire out of your britches, Honeybear," Hawthorne taunted, his words cutting through the tension like a knife. "He's alright and besides, you know as well as I do that I'd just come back and snap your neck like a twig. Wouldn't be the first little half breed split tail that got it an' I don't imagine you'd be the last; might be the one that smells the prettiest though. Most y'all got a 'stank' about you but you smell almost like a white w-."

"Take me to him, you prick," I said from the ground and wiped my mouth on the back of my hand.

A thin trail of bright red blood stood out like a mocking grin on the skin just behind my knuckles. I shook it away and managed to get to my feet. There was some wild part of me that would have liked nothing more than to have another go at Hawthorne, but it was severely tempered now, having the taste slapped out of your mouth would do that to a person. No matter how angry I was, the shame was back and now stronger than ever, and revenge lost out to the desire to hide my face a few thousand miles away.

"Jimmy, wait a minute..." Tek said, and put a hand on my shoulder, but I pretended not to hear the worry in her voice.

"I'm going home. You should do the same thing, Tek. I'm sorry that all this has happened, but I'm not the one to fix it. If you had seen what I'd seen, you wouldn't even try. You're a good person, but this is too heavy." I said it all in one go, but I did not have the courage to meet her eye as I did so.

I pulled free of her, and she protested no further. Hawthorne's shaggy grin was worse than the slap had been, and I could feel Tek's eyes digging into my back as I walked for the door. I consoled myself the best I could that I wasn't a Judas, just a coward at worst, and too smart for Altenhofen's game at best.

Outside the door, I once again had to face the murderous sun, and I can assure you that getting slapped does not cure a hangover. I shielded my eyes against the brightness and followed behind Hawthorne sullenly enough as he neared the front gate that we had driven through upon my arrival.

"You know I actually respect you for this more'n I would if you stayed. A fella that knows his limits, well, the rest of us can work with that mighty fine. Lord knows I always cottoned to havin' young fellers that knew to pass me the rifle when their nerve broke. Yella dogs have their place, Mr. Wonderful." Hawthorne mused as he walked, knowing there was nothing I could do but listen.

Hawthorne stopped midway between the house and the gate; his boots half buried in that goddamn out of place grass that Altenhofen had imported. There was a little bolt of cold fear that ran up into my heart when his hand dipped into his coat; it occurred to me that if he wished to kill me for trying to strike him, getting me away from Tek would have been a wise consideration.

For a moment, I saw with absurd mental clarity Hawthorne producing some ludicrously large pistol from beneath his coat and blowing my brains all over the lawn. Bye-bye, Jimmy. Show's over.

Instead, it was his cigarettes, and he shook one out ahead of the others and offered it to me. I wanted to hit him again, right then and there - at least try. I also think I had never wanted a cigarette more badly in my entire life. I'd already traded in my dignity and last scraps of self-worth by succumbing to the urge to run; what was one more degradation now.

"Thanks." I said coldly.

He shook another out for himself, pulled it free with his lips, and lit it before tossing me the lighter and carrying on. Hawthorne was a bastard, but he had the easy languid gait of a lion that understood that nothing in its territory could provide a real challenge to his rule. That, in the Kingdom of the Tooth and Claw, his will was supreme and enforced with bloody efficiency.

"Don't be so surly," he said, taking a drag from his cigarette. "I was payin' you a compliment. A man cannot know what he truly is until he is faced with the certainty of his own damnation. That's how we find our paths in this world. Look at me - doin' mighty fine for a feller that the Pinkertons turned their noses up at. I know more about human nature than even Mr. Altenhofen does."

He stopped by the front of the gate and punched in a quick series of numbers on the keypad.

3282

My mind fastened upon the numbers and locked them away for safekeeping.

Just in case.

"Are you even human anymore?" I asked, feeling the itch of curiosity kicking up again, "Some people might think that the whole lack of dying thing precludes you from calling yourself that. Then there's the whole fact that you're a goddamn monster even without some curse."

Hawthorne turned slowly away from the small console on the wall by the gate and fastened those cold empty eyes of his upon me. The Nothing was back. That vast emptiness of self that had held me hypnotized before was chilling when Hawthorne let his token attempts to masquerade what he was fall to the wayside.

"I'm human, sonny boy," Hawthorne growled, his menace deepening with the insult. "You can bet the hide I'll take from you if you imply otherwise again."

"Don't let the little redskin bitch fool you," he continued, his tone laced with bitterness. "I was killin' white folks long before I was puttin' mud people in the ground. I served my country, and then when they had no use for me, I went to work for the railroad."

His voice carried the weight of his past as if it were a club with which to beat my modern sensibilities to death.

"I killed Chinamen that got notions of unions, I burnt coloreds with tar 'n pitch for the same," Hawthorne explained, his words dripping with not anger, but apathy. "You think that makes me a monster? Like one of them filthy blood drinkers or the gawldamn devilry spewin' Namebreakers? Well, who'n fuck do you think paid me to do it all?"

I should have been terrified, but I was strangely fascinated by the fact that such a beast could masquerade as a man. Behind him, the gate was sliding open, revealing the wide-open, clean savage beauty of the Flats. I could just make out the faint shapes of what must have been Altenhofen and a few of his men, arranging what resembled a small-scale Washington Monument carved out of black stone, though at this distance further details were lost.

Not to mention I still had Hawthorne to deal with.

"Are you really going to play the 'I was just following orders' card?" I asked, tentatively starting towards the open gate.

Hawthorne stepped in front of me and laid his hand on my chest, those dreadful nothing eyes peering down into my own.

"You take this knowledge with you when you run back home, Yella Dog. The men who paid me to spill all that blood are the men who built this whole wide world that you live in. All of it. Them fancy newspapers you write for?" Hawthorne canted his head to the side as he tossed the rhetorical question at me.

"They came here on the railroads. Everything you have, everything you enjoy, I want you to remember - you wouldn't have it if men like me hadn't been willin' to put heads on pikes or throw their little squirmin' brats off mountain tops to draw out the ones that wouldn't git in line. I'll never regret what I've done. Ever. Fuck the curse. I've seen all my kin die - no great loss. I've watched the country go to shit - no great loss. I've been killed more times than you've known the comforts of a woman - still don't regret it." Hawthorne's cigarette flared like some baleful eye as he spoke.

"I stand corrected then." I said, putting my hands up and looking down. "You're not a monster. I was not properly informed of all the details." I added, hoping he'd simply move out of the way so I could leave this nightmare.

"That's gawldamn right you were." Hawthorne, satisfied, began to turn to lead the way down to Altenhofen.

I do not know what possessed me then—some small bit of madness, some dying embers of the man I had been once in my youth or had hoped to be. Before Hawthorne could fully turn back to the gate, I pushed past him, my shoulder clipping his own.

"You're a goddamn obscenity that thinks it's a man," I said with the same resolve to take what came as a man throwing himself from a perfectly good airplane with just a satchel of silk between him and his maker.

This wasn't a newfound reserve of courage; to call it that would have been an obscenity all my own. I'd thought about Hawthorne waiting around out front of the house while Moxley, Tek, and myself glutted ourselves on coffee and the morning chow. The way he'd lingered there instead of following Altenhofen out to the site, and there was a little whisper that had suggested that there was no way that such posting could come without a little reminder from Altenhofen to keep an eye on us. Slap me? Sure, it had hurt my pride and ground my immediate anger out like a cigarette crushed beneath a boot heel.

But a worse outcome?

Well, I wagered that the invisible leash that Altenhofen kept Hawthorne on was strong enough to hold him.

I heard him fall in behind me as I stepped beyond the gate, exhaling blue-gray smoke into the air like an offering to the unyieldingly bright sun that hung over the Salt Flats. Would he shoot me? Crack open my skull with a swift and brutal strike from the butt of his gun while my back was turned? If he was in a hurry, he might simply twist my head around backwards on my shoulders.

I felt like a reckless high roller in the heart of Vegas, squaring off against a seasoned cardsharp armed with nothing but a pair of deuces, a tumbler of whiskey, and a feverish dream.

In that fleeting moment, the suffocating grip of fear that had shadowed me throughout this wild escapade eased, if only slightly. It was an odd twist of fate that a lungful of cancerous smoke brought the first taste of liberation. The tsunami of terror began to recede, leaving behind only faint ripples at the edges of my consciousness. Though the main narrative remained elusive, the marginal notes came back into focus.

I may have been a scoundrel, but I refused to be caged like some exotic bird, a spectacle for the amusement of those who seek to imprison the untamed and the beautiful.

I was going home.

COYOTE WALLACE

The Man, The Fear, and The Answer

A ltenhofen's fortress was the only thing, aside from the distant mountains, in the Flats that wasn't actually flat. The grotesque architecture and naked arrogance of its placement were a monument to the louche dreams of the filthy rich. There was an untouched newness to the place that no amount of pomp or posturing ever really banished, and even the paved downward incline that I found myself walking along was still fresh and smooth. I could just make out the small mouth-like holes that were being eaten out of the blacktop by the wind, the salt, and the rare but intense manifestations of rain over the Flats.

Even Altenhofen's wealth couldn't entirely dull nature's fangs.

Hawthorne was behind me, and I could hear the steady clock of his boots. He kept to himself like a sullen child who had been sharply reprimanded. The fear that he would shoot me or beat me or slowly disarticulate my limbs from their sockets. He would doubtlessly do this while musing about the transformative nature of murder and its necessity for men to find the true north of their character. I thought I might just welcome the bloodier outcomes far more happily than I would another glimpse inside of Hawthorne's head. Dying might have been frightening, but listening to some bad parody of Hemingway was a damnation that was a step too far.

Fortunately, I'd yet to encounter a Hell that I couldn't talk my way out of.

309

COYOTE WALLACE

Midway down the incline, one of the three men who was helping Altenhofen set up the Resonance Tower, a pale-faced young gentleman with a scruffy goatee and thick glasses that gleamed in the sun, pointed at us and called attention to our approach. Altenhofen had been standing amongst them, his hands shoved into the pockets of his black suit as he admired the ebony monolith before him. A moment later, he turned and fastened his awful blue eyes upon me; I knew then that I would have rather faced a thousand of Hawthorne's ilk than stand in Altenhofen's presence.

Hawthorne was a butcher, a killer, a rapist, and a brute. Altenhofen, however, was something else, something worse. A manifestation of a sickness that had hidden behind the dollar and grown like a malignant tumor in the mind of our country. He'd spread, taking over the systems and the controlling interest that might have opposed him; fashioned them instead into instruments to further his means and then kept right on rolling. Hawthorne would put you in the ground, but Altenhofen would put you to work as a cog in his machine. He'd make you another part of the assembly line dismantlement of all that was strange and beautiful in our often-mixed-up country and do so with a smile.

I pretended not to notice the submachine guns that two of Altenhofen's little helpers kept hanging from straps around their shoulders even as they worked. I couldn't help but steal a glance at the Resonance Tower. The device, with its strangely broad metallic bracings near the bottom, reminded me of some eldritch version of a Christmas tree, but I was too focused on Altenhofen himself to overtly indulge my curiosity.

Besides, I was leaving.

"Ah, Jimmy! What a surprise this is. I suppose I should have known that you'd be curious about what we're doing

310

out here. The mechanics of it. The WORK of it." Altenhofen said with an almost youthful exuberance that was utterly out of place coming from his decrepit form.

I did my best not to look back at the Resonance Tower, to pay no mind to the dark shape of stone and inscrutable craftsmanship. My gaze remained steady and locked on Altenhofen himself. To do otherwise would have invited my mind to start pulling at the threads, to start digging and scratching at the surface as if I were a hound dog in search of a buried bone in his master's backyard. My curiosity had always been a little stronger than my fear and a great deal stronger than my good sense. I had no desire to test my resolve when it had already so recently failed me.

This time I was firmly on the side of fear.

I wanted out.

"I'm afraid I've got some bad news for you," I said, keeping my tone nice and even, more measured than when I had first spoken to Moxley or Tek. Not every power that could destroy you took the form of magic or eldritch horror. Some were quite mundane and no less lethal for it.

"Is that so?" Altenhofen asked, dismissively gesturing to his crew to continue with their work.

Roy Altenhofen was many things, and most of them I would have said with the sort of venom that others reserved for the swear word of choice they used to describe a cheating ex-lover. He was an unrepentant mad capitalist, a dark architect of the erosion of the American soul, a killer of magic, and worst of all - the sort of swine that would have voted for Nixon.

In other words: a wealthy, covertly genocidal prick.

He was not a man that missed the little details, though. He'd gone rich on the little details, and in a way, so had I. He used those often-overlooked facts and connections to build an empire, and I used them to build a myth. I sold stories of the Weird and the Wild, while he sold a future where the American public blissfully worries about nothing larger than what some stupid celebrity said on social media. A warm and comfortable descent into fatal normalcy as America in her last painful moments of life coughs up her soul on the living room floor.

The old bastard did not miss a beat.

He studied me as he approached, narrowing his eyes and scrunching his lips. Try as he might with his greeting, it was clear once I'd said that I wasn't here to appreciate his little doomsday device with him, that he had defaulted back to 'not having time for this'. His eyes darted to what must have been Hawthorne's handprint still stinging and hot on my cheek and then looked beyond me.

"Mister Hawthorne, would you be so kind as to return to your post," Altenhofen requested with a tight dry politeness.

"I was just makin' sure he got here is all," Hawthorne replied, his voice carrying a remarkable amount of worry for a man who supposedly could not die.

"Yes, you felt the need to leave your post so that you could walk our guest down to the one discernible point of interest within miles. I'm well aware of your intention," Altenhofen dryly remarked, the corners of his mouth barely twitching.

Hawthorne could only grit his teeth and take it.

"I'm sure you'll have a very good excuse for why you've left the young mister Allerton alone with a Namebreaker who can manufacture every known naturally occurring venom on the planet - and probably a few that do not exist," Altenhofen remarked, his gaze fixed on Hawthorne as if he had just scraped him off the bottom of his shoe. "Who, might I add, already has killed at least one man that we know of. I am sure that your excuse for leaving them unsupervised will be positively thrilling to hear."

Hawthorne's retort hovered on the edge of his tongue; a wild beast held back by the looming shadow of Altenhofen's authority. Yet, like a caged creature resigned to its fate, he swallowed the words. A nod replaced his intended response, his gaze falling to the ground in deference.

"Right away, Mister Altenhofen." Hawthorne muttered, a fleeting glance directed my way before he averted his eyes.

He blamed me.

Good.

"I apologize for any unpleasantness with Hawthorne," Altenhofen's tone carried a veneer of sincerity, though it lacked genuine remorse. He didn't seem to regret the pain or the risk to my person, but rather the loss of control over the situation.

He wasn't sorry that Hawthorne had hit me; he was sorry that Hawthorne had hit me without his express orders. For Altenhofen, and men like him, there was nothing worse than a loss of control.

"I hope you know that he will be disciplined accordingly," Altenhofen remarked with a hint of severity. "Part of the reason that I employ him is that there is not much in this world that he has not seen. Therefore, it is very rare that anything provokes him to act without my saying so. You must have really gotten under his skin," he added with a sigh, his apology tinged with a sense of resignation.

It was unsettling to hear his apology, knowing the looming consequence for Hawthorne's actions. The tension in the air seemed to thicken with each passing moment, reminding me of the precariousness of my situation.

"I'm not sure discipline takes with men like that. Did the ol' 'corrective reinforcement' take with your son?" I blurted the question out before I could stop myself.

Altenhofen made a faint clucking sound with his tongue against the roof of his mouth and folded his hands behind his back. I'd landed a blow before he could get his armor up, and for a second, just a second, he did not know how to respond. He had not counted on Moxley opening up to me. The satisfaction from seeing that was so sweet that it began to eat holes in my fear, the same way that the elements had already begun to erode Altenhofen's hideously self-serving castle.

"What is this bad news you have for me, Mr. Wozynski?" Altenhofen asked, shedding any pretense of affection or charm.

Good.

It was better to be hated by swine than loved by kings.

For a moment, I reminisced about my father in the old days when 'Jimmy Wonderful' hadn't yet been molded from the scraps of my imagination. Back when Jimmy Wonderful was simply James Wozynski, and he had to break the news to his dear old dad about his plans to attend university and pursue a career with his words. Altenhofen's expression mirrored my father's own when he realized I wouldn't be joining him in the Tennessee tobacco fields. He braced himself against the impending disappointment, a trait passed down from men like my father and Altenhofen's generation. It was as though they followed a mysterious and secretive creed where outward displays of emotion were considered sinful, and facing adversity without flinching was a form of reverent devotion.

"I'm leaving. I'm done. You can keep your money, and if you want to sic your lawyers on me or the Standard, that's up to you," I told him plainly, with no embellishments of manners or room for misunderstanding.

Altenhofen's gray, bushy eyebrows lifted upwards, but I sensed this was more a practiced response than a genuine display of surprise. His hands remained folded behind his back, and for a moment, he looked down at the ground, studying the baked white earth and the thin layer of dust clinging to his expensive Italian leather shoes. In that moment, he could have been mistaken for an old schoolteacher preparing to shoot down a tiresome child's incorrect answer. I recognized the expression well; disappointment being inwardly trimmed down so that its true depth and scope would not be visible to outsiders.

"Oh? I'm very sorry to hear that, Jimmy. I was truly looking forward to hearing your thoughts on the whole matter. I'd hoped you would use one of those lurid and catchy taglines you're so fond of - 'The Preservation of Humanity: A Tale of Treachery, Woe, and Determination' - how's that?" Altenhofen asked with a paper-thin smile.

I recalled thinking that he could barely move that first night at dinner, that he was a man staring down his own mortality. However, now, as I looked upon him, his black suit matching the hideous stone from which the so-called Resonance Tower (and the very walls of his 'fortress') were made, I sensed a terrible vitality. He was like some vile modern mummy, a man who had been hollowed out and had all his warm, wet bits replaced with the hard soil of the Flats and clean, crisp hundred-dollar bills.

"Yeah, that's great. Don't quit your day job. Now, do you want me to start walking, or are you going to give me a ride back to the airport?" I managed to ask Altenhofen with the queer bravery of a man who might have feared the future but was soundly unimpressed with the men who made that future.

The workers paused, and the one with the menacing-looking firearm hanging from his arm like some strange alien black beetle shifted his weight uneasily from one foot to the other. I supposed that they were unaccustomed to anyone speaking to their master in such a manner, and I took a small amount of pride in that. Defiance can be contagious, and while the fabulously rich worry very little about plagues or famines, they fear defiance the way dying old men fear for their souls.

"Oh, I'm afraid that won't be possible," Altenhofen said with a lightness of tone that, for him, must have been amusement, but for any other living soul would have just been bitterness smeared like cigarette ashes over the memory of joy. "Not until after Moxley has finished his task, at any rate. Besides, most of the staff have already been sent home. You are welcome to stay, however, and I hope that during that stay you might reconsider your position."

He turned back to his men, and even the gunman averted his eyes, their spirits withering under the intensity of his gaze. It was perplexing how such an aged figure could instill such fear. Hawthorne might have epitomized brute force, but Altenhofen, despite his frail appearance, exuded authority through sheer willpower rather than physical strength. The answer was as ordinary as it was profound: money.

"What about them? Why can't I just leave when they do?" The fear was back, seeping up into my voice. There was no panic quite like the panic that set in when a man realized he was trapped.

Altenhofen's tone, though even and measured, had the weight of industry behind its every word as he said, "I'm very sorry, but that is simply out of the question. These men have all been vetted. They've worked for my company or one of its subsidiaries for years, and most of all, they understand the consequences—the consequences of making what I'm doing known before it is done, Mr. Wozynski."

He paused, his gaze steady, before continuing, "The margins for interference are slim, but I will not take that chance. After tomorrow night, unless your friend is very convincing indeed, there will be enough Dynametrium to fuel a cure for the whole sad lot of them." This thought produced the slimmest of smiles on his lips.

With a dismissive wave of his hand, Altenhofen said, "Then it is simply a matter for the marketing and the distribution branches to deal with." His attention drifted back to the black monolith his men were securing into the hard-packed dead earth of the flats.

"I understand the consequences," I offered, almost numb with anger and the crawling panic that came with the realization of my confinement.

"Do you?" Altenhofen asked, turning to look back over his shoulder at me.

In the pregnant pause that followed, the silence enveloped us like a shroud, punctuated only by the rhythmic clinking of tools and the mournful sigh of the wind sweeping across the desolate landscape. In the distance, only the far-flung peaks where Tek and I had sought refuge bore witness to our confrontation. It was then, gazing into Altenhofen's eyes, that I truly grasped the depths of his madness. He was beyond reason, a runaway train hurtling down a track of his own making, heedless of any obstacle in his path.

COYOTE WALLACE

As Altenhofen's gaze dug into me, I couldn't help but marvel at the audacity of his arrogance. Here I stood, goddamn Jimmy Wonderful, and yet even my quasi-fame seemed insufficient to deter his machinations. His appreciation for the challenge of facing the consequences of his actions was palpable in the glint of his eyes behind that impenetrable facade of his black suit.

"I just want to leave. What do you say, guys? You can fit me in the back of the truck that you hauled that monstrosity here in, can't you?" I appealed to the workers, bypassing Altenhofen.

I hoped to reach the common man in them, appealing to their fear of being stuck here as witnesses to the birth of a beast that would likely spell the end for the Namebreakers, slowly erasing them from the American fabric itself.

They ignored me, sharply disappointing but oddly fitting. That's what Altenhofen did to people – his 'power' was money in exchange for blind eyes and diligent work, without the fuss and mess of morality.

It's strange when a man remembers that he's late on his own union dues.

"I don't think you understand the consequences, Mr. Wonderful. I don't think you have even the faintest respect for them," Altenhofen remarked, his tone dripping with contempt as he emphasized the word "Wonderful."

He turned his back to me, his gaze fixating on the distant mountains to the west. "Your whole mythos is based around framing yourself as an anti-authority figure, perpetually curling your nose up at anyone or anything that presumes to tell you what to do. In your own way, you're just as predictable as Hawthorne, even as predictable as Moxley or his father. I find that terribly disappointing." Altenhofen's voice was almost sorrowful.

Almost.

"I don't give a raven's wet shit about what disappoints you. I'm leaving," I snapped angrily.

Now it was my turn to pivot sharply on my heel and stride away. Fury surged through me, propelling my steps across the flats. I saw no reason why that fury couldn't carry me out of this forsaken place. True, I knew I would change my mind after just a few hours in the scorching sun, but I would be damned if I intended to give Altenhofen the satisfaction of locking me down. As I stormed off, I half wondered if the goon with the gun would sneak up behind me, yank my arms back, and zip-tie my wrists. Perhaps he'd drag me back to the posh bungalow Altenhofen had arranged for me, like the world's luckiest terrorist. But he didn't, and in that moment, I felt liberated, a surge of energy refueling me just by spitting in Altenhofen's eye.

Let him send Hawthorne; I'd throw stones if I had to.

I was free, and when Jimmy Wonderful was free, nothing could stop him.

"You'll not be able to stop wondering what it was like, this moment. You'll lie awake at night wondering what the quaint native girl said or what it looks like when we bring their end into this world. The shame of looking away will kill you slowly," Altenhofen retorted as I stormed off, his words carrying the weight of the devil's own ugly truth.

Earlier, Tek had used the Word to all but freeze me in my tracks. Now, Altenhofen wielded an eldritch magic just as ancient and dangerous—a weapon far deadlier than anything the Namebreakers possessed: the truth.

"Fuck you," I spat into the emptiness without turning around.

I wanted to flee this place—the vision that Moxley had shown me, Tek's earnest strength, Hawthorne's murderous eyes, and Altenhofen's goddamned pre-purchased omnipotence were all too much. I longed for my bed, my wife, a tall glass of fine whiskey, and dreamless sleep. Yet Altenhofen had set the hook, and now I found myself lacking the strength to yank it free. I was being reeled back in, and though I knew this, though I could feel it, I could not escape it.

"You know that I'm right. You know it in your bones. You've spent your whole life chasing the big moments, marking the high tide of The Shadow People in our country. Some guilty little part of you that you'll never admit in front of others or your peers or your silly little fans is that you've known all along what was coming. That one day this would happen, one day there would come a time when all that lives in the dark would bow and bend to those of us who live in the light." Altenhofen's words were as inescapable as the turning hands of a clock.

"You've known and you've waited and now here it is at last, and it scares you, so you try to run but deep down we know, we both know, you'd always look back." Altenhofen's implacable smugness dripped from his words as he spoke.

320

Something clicked inside my head, and I turned, squinting against the sun. Altenhofen stood in front of the Resonance Tower now, admiring it. He must have drifted there as he was talking when I'd turned my back, and though he'd just been speaking to me, he paid little actual mind now. I was no competition for the black stone, and I'll admit that even my eyes were drawn to it. The longer you stared at the smooth black pillar, the more your eyes could almost make out upon its surface—strange markings that swam in and out of focus like one of those 3D pictures that you sometimes find in malls. I realized if I stared too long, my head would begin to hurt, but Altenhofen had no problem with it.

"You said that I was predictable like Hawthorne or Moxley and his father. According to Moxley, it was his father, Conrad, who fled with your son. That's how he ended up in your custody, but that's not entirely true, is it? You didn't lose Conrad Allerton or your son, did you? Moxley's father didn't abandon him either." I could almost see it; saying it aloud just made it clearer.

As my accusation hit him, Altenhofen was reaching up to lay his hand on the Resonance Tower. He stopped abruptly, as if he'd just been admonished by a stern parent to stay away from the stove. His fingertips hovered scant inches from the stone's surface before they curled back against his palm, and he let the hand fall limply back to his side.

"Do you know what you do with a dog that has learned that it can bite the very hand that feeds it?" Altenhofen asked. Though I knew the answer, I don't think he wanted to hear it from me.

"I'll tell you, Jimmy. You kill it. Even if it pains you to do so, even if it is the hardest thing that you ever do. Conrad Allerton stole my son and robbed me of making right what was done to the boy's mother. Did I find them? Eventually.

Time itself was on Conrad's side, and time is a formidable adversary, but like all things in our country, it bends to the whims of wealth," Roy Altenhofen explained, his intensity quietly growing as he spoke.

The reaffirmation of his goals infused him with a vitality that might have otherwise been stripped from his weary flesh by time long ago.

"You killed him." I said before I could help myself. It was as plain as the nose on Altenhofen's face.

"He fooled me into believing the answer was to train them. That we could school them and fix those who were too broken to handle the power that had been laid at their feet by God," Altenhofen's words were filled to the brim with contempt.

"The truth, Mr. Wonderful, is that they cannot reliably be taught, and they cannot be trusted to police themselves. The lie, the one that I bought into, cost me my family and allowed my... son... to become a monster when he should have been suffocated in his crib," the contempt in Altenhofen's voice became cold and hard.

For only a moment, that contempt lingered before fading back into his implacable demeanor.

"Though if you're asking me to confess..." Altenhofen trailed off as he turned to face me.

He didn't need to confess; it was in his eyes, in the way he regarded me then.

"I'm afraid that's a step too far, but no, Conrad Allerton did not escape paying his debt, and now his son is helping me correct this world. I've given him the opportunity to restore the world to how it was meant to be," Altenhofen declared with a chilling sense of contentment, his voice carrying the weight of conviction.

"Imagine how glorious our history might have been without them. No one is afraid of monsters or horrors in the shadows, no one wasting their time chasing miracle cures or setting themselves above the rules," he continued, spreading his arms wide as if to unveiling a utopia free from the shackles of fear.

"No one but men like you, you mean." I countered, my voice struggling to rise above the low howl of the wind that swept across the desolate Flats.

Altenhofen's smile sent a shiver down my spine, igniting a surge of primal rage within me. In that moment, I entertained a dangerous fantasy of wrapping my hands around his withered throat and squeezing until the very life drained from his wretched body. The cure for debauched and ridiculous wealth, I mused internally, is a merciless strangulation by way of a chronically neurotic journalist. You heard it here first - the cure for income inequality is the merciless strangling of the rich with our bare goddamn hands.

With a faint shrug of his thin shoulders, Altenhofen responded, "I suppose we shall see."

COYOTE WALLACE

The Magician and The Doctor

I stalked my way back up the drive like a dog that had just been pelted with rocks to run the mutt off from upturned trash bins. One foot in front of the other, and my hands crammed into my pockets. Jenna would have called this brand of sulking my 'surly teenager impression,' and I suppose that was fitting enough. After all, I was grounded in a manner of speaking, and there were no two ways about that fact. The odds of my escape or being provided with means to leave were, if I was to make a generous estimate, floating somewhere between campaign finance reform and a snowball's chance in the part of Hell that is Arizona adjacent.

It had been a long time since I'd lost a scrap of wits, but it seemed as if everything I tried simply brought me back into Altenhofen's orbit. If I wanted out, I'd have to play his game. The panic had given way to a steady restless ache as I walked back through those gates. My mind was already doing the gymnastics needed for the acceptance of the fact that I would be here till the ugly end. My belief that there was any way to convince Altenhofen at all was now even lower than my belief that I could outsmart the man, and the terrible weight of that inevitableness had sunk deep into the stormy waters of who I was.

I'd been afraid before; every man has. But now, the fear had teeth, and the battle had a new importance. This led to a strange alchemy within my very bones; a shifting in gears beneath the hood of my heart to something better suited for the uphill battle. Some people, when the strange ride that is their life gets scary, close their eyes and just hold on tight. However, a special few thrust their hands up towards the sky and scream out – FASTER! FASTER! FASTER!

You can guess which of those I was.

Hawthorne was waiting by the door exactly where he'd been that morning. He had returned to his post at Altenhofen's orders and was now watching me with sullen, hateful attentiveness. I had a feeling then that if the situation provided for it, and it still might, Hawthorne would take no small pleasure in breaking every bone in my body. His eyes promised this outcome, hard flints that followed a man much like a coiled venomous serpent will keep a man before it in case the serpent decides to strike and give him one of nature's special lethal cocktails. I did my best not to make eye contact. I just pushed ahead towards my bungalow.

We still had a few hours before Altenhofen returned, and we were called upon to play out the sad farce of trying to convince him to stop his plans. There was no sign of Moxley or Tek, and for that, I was grateful. There was nothing quite so bitter as abandoning a beautiful woman only to find yourself crawling back because your plans for escape blew up in your face

My bungalow was still a wreck, and I supposed I should have expected no less with Altenhofen's little helpers taking the next few days off. I still had a generous supply of 'creative stimulants' (read: illegal and controlled substances) that had been provided for me, but when a man faces the certainty of watching a great wrong be done to a people, it is only hard alcohol that can be summoned to the fight.

Once inside, with the door locked firmly behind me, I took down a whiskey glass and threw four fingers worth of Chivas into the bottom without thought or care for ice. I took the first glass without pause or cessation; high-quality booze ran from the corners of my mouth and down my chin, pattering like dirty raindrops onto the countertop as I stood there in the kitchen, thoughtless amidst the spinning of my tires. The heaviness of the situation had driven the fear like a railroad spike into my heart, and now that it had been yanked out, only anger could rush in to fill the void.

By the second glass, I was able to get a grip back on my nerves. The Fear and The Heavy were relegated to somewhere in the back of the mental train, and seething anger had slid its skinny butt into the conductor's seat. I was trapped, this was true, and there was no escaping what lay before me. The turmoil bubbled into defiance, and if Altenhofen thought that he would get his way with me, then he would be sorely mistaken.

Maybe Tek had been right, maybe Moxley's 'river' wasn't set in stone, but was I willing to risk it? How does any decent man even make such a choice? A slow and peaceful demise was the reward for inaction; an end not only of life but of wonder itself. A suffocating demise that would culminate in succumbing to all that was mundane and neatly defined was just what Altenhofen had planned for the world.

The reward for successful action, if Moxley was to be believed, was horror that should have been unimaginable. Unfortunately, humanity had already familiarized itself with the notion of "unimaginable horror" long ago in Germany. America herself had been damned handy some eighty years prior, and it was on these foul pages of history that Altenhofen would write his name if not stopped.

I want to believe that any sane man would have chosen as I had initially. That opting out had been no more despicable than asking for a nice long drag from an ether-soaked cloth before having your foot amputated by a chimp with a power saw.

The voice of reason, the ghost of James Wozynski, kept screaming that the risk was too high. The kind of man who would risk so much of the world out of a blend of anger and hope would have to be a true wretch. Lower than swine, shameless, and unrestrained. A fool, a lunatic, and a selfish bastard all rolled into one. The kind of self-serving person who could stand in front of a room and claim to pour his heart and soul into a cause, when really, deep down, he just craved glory.

He'd have to be goddamn Wonderful, wouldn't he?

I left the Chivas on the countertop, wiped the back of my mouth on my hand, and stalked across the living room. My shoes crunched broken glass underfoot, but I barely heard it. My mind was elsewhere, grasping onto the thread of an idea I'd only caught when propelled upward by that surge of emotion. The alcohol pulsing through my veins was like high-test gasoline, yet I remained steady, not sloppy, not yet. The Truth wouldn't allow sloppiness, not then. If I could jot down all of it, lay out the facts on one of the steno pads I'd brought with me, I'd be able to see the weak points more clearly.

I was going to do it. Fight back. The consequences of success or failure be damned.

I had to believe there were more than just set-in-stone outcomes looming large on the horizon. That our actions could make the world better. That there was something out there, even in a world of men like Altenhofen, bigger than percentages and more important than math. I glimpsed this intangible once or twice as a young man, always on the move on highways or beneath the surface along the coast. Something in whose wake I'd traveled and sailed into some measure of success. An ideal, a notion, a dream, or just a promise broken one too many times that we still clung to like children with unreliable parents. Our American birthright, paid for in blood, guaranteed each of us the pursuit of our own destiny and the shaping of our own futures.

Did I believe in Fate? Perhaps.

Did I believe in The American Dream, tattered, bloody, smeared with the shit of a million atrocities from lifetimes of misuse at the hands of men like Altenhofen?

You're damn right I did.

I tore open my bag, hauled out the steno pad, and fumbled with the small pack of pens as I tore open the plastic wrapping. Stories may flow effortlessly from fingers to keys of a sleek computer or trusty old electric typewriter, but I've always believed that sorting thoughts worked best in longhand. You had to snatch ideas, little slivers of truth, from the fast-flowing stream of your own consciousness, and it was the kind of work one needed to feel in their hands.

I yanked the pen cap off with my teeth and spat it out onto the bed among its fellows, serving as a warning that I might come back for them. Always keep your pens in mortal terror of you; otherwise, they become prone to mutiny. Nothing gets you in trouble faster than an unruly pen that refuses to take orders.

I scrawled Altenhofen's name at the top of the page and drew two quick, sharp lines beneath it.

Roy Altenhofen and Conrad Allerton had joined forces—two men on different paths that they believed would lead to the same destination. One, a Namebreaker who wished to heal the lost disparate souls, broken rogues, and shattered orphans for whom The Word was more curse than gift. The other, a man with a fortune at his fingertips who wished to fix the world, rebuild the burnt homes, and safeguard the imperiled future. Peers? Definitely. Friends? Likely, at least on the surface.

At least at first.

I walked through the bungalow, scribbling as I did. So deep was my concentration that, had I been without my shoes, I would have cut my feet to ribbons on the broken glass that used to be the television screen. The Chivas glass pulled me back, as if I was following some invisible tether, and I settled back down on the stool by the counter without needing to take my eyes off the steno pad. My penmanship was the wild, slightly too large, variety of a man who might only have a passing familiarity with a scribe's work.

The two agreed on certain issues, and that bound them together. When they met, the most common cure for being a Namebreaker would have been what? A lobotomy followed by a glossectomy? Drooling tongue-less mutes in filthy asylums and aging sanitariums certainly was as good a cause as any. A worthy dragon to be slain by good men armed with sterling ideals. The Doctor and The Magician working together to clean and stitch an old wound in our culture that had gone foul with infection. Cigars were smoked, brandy drank, debates had, and world views exchanged.

Another two quick lines beneath The Doctor and The Magician.

Dynametrium had been introduced to Altenhofen by way of Allerton. Still friends then, still working together, still trying to find a way to fix those who could not or would not control their abilities. I had to wonder though if, just maybe, this was where the first cracks began to form. Was this where the strain began to bend and buckle their relationship? For Roy Altenhofen, this was the lord's work, but at a certain point, with abilities so similar to Moxley, Conrad would have seen where it was going.

For Conrad Allerton, this glimpse would have made it not the Lord's work but the Devil's deeds. Conrad Allerton had been an outspoken advocate for the fair and ethical treatment of his people; he was 'The American Merlin' and widely regarded as a master of his craft - but he was still human.

He still made mistakes.

COYOTE WALLACE

When had he realized what he had done? Had it been the thought there was, at the time, only a limited amount of Dynametrium that kept him still? I thought it might, I couldn't be certain, but I was leaning towards a 'strong maybe' on the matter.

My hand shook as I picked up the Chivas, and I almost missed my mouth. Splotches of the high-priced booze spread out on the steno paper like ghostly continents on an old map. The shakes didn't matter, though if those trembles were brought on by pushing my aging prison cell with its aching lower back and sharp stabbing pains in the knees that grew worse with each morning, then I would endure. If it was brought on by fear and nervous energy, then I would simply persist. The body belonged to James Wozynski, and he knew damned well his race was nearly run, but I am Jimmy BY GOD Wonderful, and I don't quit. If I were to lose my life and find myself thrust into oblivion, then I would leave this world on terms that I dictated.

Leaning over the handlebars into the screaming wind and shouting for more.

I circled the question.

The crack might have formed with the harnessing of the Dynametrium into a cure by Altenhofen, but the break happened with the children. That was certain. Conrad had the ability to see the future and all its permutations, and what father, upon hearing the first cries of his son, would not look out into the future that lay ahead of his boy? At the same time, Altenhofen would have been thinking the same thoughts. When Altenhofen found out he'd sired a Namebreaker of his own, he'd suddenly realized how many of the horrors that he'd seen stuck with him.

What were sons if not the future that fathers wished for the world?

Did Altenhofen even try? I pondered this question, wrestling with conflicting emotions. Despite his despicable nature, there was a part of me that wanted to believe he tried. There are no monsters more formidable than those who have faced monsters themselves. Altenhofen, standing beside Conrad, had seen the darkest depths of the Namebreakers. He aided in curing the afflicted, but the haunting memories lingered within him like a dormant poison, awaiting activation by an external catalyst. Quinten Altenhofen became that catalyst. In him, Altenhofen didn't see the future Conrad envisioned with Moxley; instead, he saw the fear of being replaced.

But why reveal the truth to Conrad? Why not intervene at the first sign of trouble? Why not keep it a secret? Hadn't Altenhofen confessed his wish to have suffocated the baby in his crib?

As I set aside the pen, I surveyed the chaotic steno pages. The second glass of Chivas lay empty, its contents consumed. A feverish warmth enveloped me. Glancing at the phone mounted on the counter, I briefly considered calling Jenna. She owned an insight I lacked, especially concerning the motives of the affluent and our fellow man. While I pride myself on understanding the American spirit my readers look for, my cynicism often blinds me to certain nuances.

The thought of Altenhofen or, worse, Hawthorne eavesdropping on our conversation felt repugnant. The idea of deceiving Jenna, with our exchange recorded, would push me into realms of madness. My love for her burned fiercely, transcending my identity as James or Jimmy. The thought of lying to her, even for her own good, revolted the part of me that still clung to James Wozynski's integrity.

I couldn't bear that. I cherished her deeply.

Then, like a bolt from the blue, it struck me: Love.

Love is why he didn't keep it a secret. Love, despite the fear, had led Altenhofen to ask for Conrad's help. Love had made him believe there was hope and that the boy might grow up to be like Conrad. That the dangers were hysteria, that with proper training and mentorship, the boy could have not just a good life, but a great one. Conrad would have volunteered to help, been glad of it, because he was a good man? Maybe. Good men were only often described as such because their interest aligned with the common interest. Conrad must have known that at a certain point, Altenhofen would want to try to make more of the Dynametrium. He would need to create a larger supply to "help" others; he was a man of numbers and calculations. A man of science, business, and medicine - timetables were something he understood intricately. Conrad Allerton had to know that, eventually, Altenhofen would try to use a Namebreaker to make more.

Quinten Altenhofen was going to be the mechanism through which his father changed the world, and when the boy had broken, when that terrible emptiness inside of him had shown itself, Altenhofen's world had been rocked. Had he taken it as a failure by Conrad or a betrayal? I couldn't know. The death of his wife, the unimaginable pain of what he'd endured - deserved or otherwise were beyond my fathoming.

Conrad had vanished with the boy; he'd known what Altenhofen's response would be, but he hadn't had time to get Moxley. Once in the wind, a man who could dart between the passing moments would be almost impossible to catch, wouldn't he?

Outside, I heard shouting. Moxley and Tek were having an argument, and I intended to rise from my stool and go see what the Hell was going on, but a second thunderbolt hit me, and my knees nearly buckled. I'd been trying to puzzle out how Altenhofen would have even gotten the drop on Conrad Allerton. How he could have ever caught up to him, even with that murderous fuck Hawthorne helping him. He hadn't needed to find him though; his location hadn't mattered. Altenhofen had his son, and even a father who knows that rushing into a burning building will surely mean his own death might still charge headlong into the inferno for the sake of his offspring.

Roy Altenhofen hadn't used his extraordinary wealth or his Cursed henchman. He hadn't needed to uncover some old charm that rendered him immune to the Namebreakers' abilities nor did he need a weapon forged by some strange eldritch means. In the end, Roy Altenhofen had used the fact the Namebreakers were us and we were them, to trap and, I believe, kill, Conrad Allerton.

Even a wizard might be bound by his heart.

I dropped my pen and ran to see what all the fighting was about.

COYOTE WALLACE

The Wrong Tree

"You really don't think you're doing anything wrong? Really? That's your position? You don't see that you're helping him wipe your own people out?" Tek hurled questions like stones as she stood squaring off against Moxley.

"You are not that vile; I just can't believe that." Tek spat on the heels of her own questions before the purple haired Namebreaker, who had quite neatly shattered my will like the old soda bottles I threw against the rear brick wall of the Piggly Wiggly when I was a boy, could even answer.

Moxley was taking it swimmingly for an ill-tempered, smart-arsed little prick. Two fingers were pressed against the little space between his eyes, and his head hung in a weary bow, his chin almost touching his chest. He looked to me like a man suffering the onset of a terrible migraine or the certainty of an oncoming embolism. I'd like to say that I sympathized, but the boy had nearly driven me mad, and I had to admire Tek's gumption. Altenhofen might have been a dead end, his heart a dry, dead thing in his chest, but I had sensed a degree of kinship with the boy and hoped that meant there was a chance.

Unless, of course, that kinship was of the Selfish Bastard variety.

Damn it.

"We're not a fucking people, you twit!" Moxley snapped, his posture straightened by the anger like an electric current had just been passed through him.

He looked as if he was going to say more, but then he saw me coming out of the door, ceased the train of thought, and instead spat out.

"Look, your boyfriend is here; now you can go ride the old man's pogo stick and leave me alone. Isn't that swell? Now, very nice talking to you; I really hope the whole crazy bitch thing works out," Moxley snarked, whatever he had been going to say discarded in favor of this jab instead.

Tek looked over her shoulder at me and narrowed her eyes before turning her attention back to Moxley. I briefly wondered how her opinion of me was holding up after the disgraceful showing of my true colors. Maybe she would be understanding or hyper-empathetic to my cowardice; she was, after all, a Namebreaker of considerable talent.

Weren't the sorcery types supposed to have a genetic predisposition towards enlightenment? Surely, there was a Word glowing upon my chest or forehead or hovering in the air above me that indicated I was remorseful and had suffered a moment of weakness. She'd get that. She had to.

"He's inconsequential, just a washed-up relic of the past, but you, you matter," Tek asserted, her voice carrying a sense of urgency. "Listen, Moxley. There are barely five thousand of us left in this country, who knows how many more in the world. And that doesn't even account for those they consider 'cured'—those who might still return if not for the Dynametrium in their systems."

Tek paused, swallowing her pride for the sake of the dwindling remnants of wonder in the world.

"We don't have to fade away like this. We don't have to perish because of someone else's fear," Tek pleaded, fighting not against Moxley, but against the deep-seated wound that left a scar on his heart.

For a fleeting moment, Moxley averted his gaze, his resolve wavering in the face of Tek's earnest plea. Despite being the most formidable trained Namebreaker in the free world, the heir to his father's legacy, Moxley's cultivated cynicism began to crumble under the weight of Tek's sincerity.

"You possess the Words of time. I possess the Words of life," Tek gently reminded him.

But then, like a snapping rubber band, Moxley's surly punkish exterior snapped back into place. His defiance returned in full force, his eyes narrowing with reproachful fury as he fixed his gaze on Tek. It was a look that spoke volumes, filled with a mixture of heartbreak and betrayal.

"You've made it this way and ruined the world for people like me, people like my father. Those of us who tried to make life better," Moxley seethed, his words dripping with bitterness.

"We used to be in the courts of kings, you know that? I mean, does that compute? But no - it wasn't good enough. We needed people like you running around with no training and no self-control. Do you know what that got us? That got them to fear us. We're not people to them; we're bombs that can talk!" Moxley's voice trembled with emotion as the words took hold in his throat.

"Do you ever think about that when you're out there thumbing your nose at the government? Why the hell do I even have to explain myself to you?" There was a defiant cant to the side of Moxley's head as he finished, a challenge in his question.

"You want me to tell you who I am?" Tek's voice was a velvet-wrapped blade in response to Moxley's challenge.

"Oh, that'd be just grand. Positively splendid. Faaaan-fucking-tastic. Give it to me, go on. Let's see what the little urchin girl has. You've already been plotting to kill me, or did you think I wouldn't see that possibility swirling around you?" Moxley's eyes widened as he spoke, and while I wanted to believe he was wrong, the look on Tek's face killed any doubts I had.

Tek's brow lifted upward, and for a moment, no longer than a single heartbeat amidst this madness, her lips fell soundlessly open. Moxley took it for what it was: an opportunity. I saw his chest swell with the sharp intake of air. The hair on the back of my neck stood up. The sudden realization that he was going to use the Word, that it was going to come to that, chased by the mad dog of fear that Hawthorne and Altenhofen would see this as cause for action of their own. Not giving up in the face of a lost cause was one thing, but dying before you even got a chance to throw the first punch served no one.

I had to do something.

"He killed your father!" I shouted out, heedless of consequences. Future be damned.

Moxley stopped, the strange gathering energy in the air that compelled the hairs on the back of my arms to stand up suddenly ceased as if an invisible lever had been thrown, cutting all power from the air. Moxley looked over Tek's shoulder at me in struggling disbelief. His purple hair lay messily upon his head, and he seemed like a little kid who had been caught playing dressup in his father's clothes. His eyes were bright and wide in their startled surprise. How long had it been since anything had honestly surprised Moxley? How long had it been since he was reminded that it was impossible to know everything? How long since he was reminded that the limits of our knowledge are made known to us with every passing year of our lives?

He froze completely.

Tek's expression morphed into one of incredulous wonder, her face a tapestry of disbelief. In contrast, Moxley, accustomed to foretelling the future, found himself in unfamiliar territory. While his visions left little room for surprises, Tek, versed in the Words of life, navigated a world brimming with unexpected twists and turns. Unfortunately, her encounters with surprise seemed to lean towards the unpleasant, the unsavory, the unfortunate.

"What did you just say?" Tek asked me, the fact I was a coward momentarily forgotten

"No, that's bullshit..." Moxley added.

"When he stopped me. When I tried to leave..." I paused and did my best to apologize to Tek with my eyes though she was too focused on my words to spare a care for any apologies in my gaze "...He all but spelled it out. When your father took Quinten, his boy, when he fled with them after the accident; he knew that Altenhofen would kill the boy. So, he stole him away."

"Liar." Moxley muttered but he took a step back as if he had been struck by a physical blow.

I pushed on.

"Altenhofen used you as bait. He knew your father would come back for you, that you were a constant. Conrad could exist between moments, flee into little pockets of time but there was always one place that Altenhofen could be sure he would return to."

"His child." Tek said under her breath in horror.

"No. This is bullshit; part of some scam you two are running. A trick. Mr. Altenhofen took me in; he gave me a good life. I've been doing what my father should have done if his pride hadn't gotten in the way... I've been... helping." Moxley could foresee potential futures, but only if he knew where to look.

If he trusted them or underestimated them, then he was as blind as the rest of us.

Tek sensed her opportunity and turned back to Moxley, her eyes bright with fresh hope.

"Do you see? You can't go through with this. You can't listen to him. This is your chance to do the right thing and make him pay for all the horrible shit that he has done, Moxley." Tek believed me, her voice echoing the same sentiment I would have expressed if she hadn't spoken first.

Moxley shook his head fiercely.

"No. Both of you fuck off!" Moxley trembled as he shouted the words.

"You're barking up the wrong goddamn tree! No, this is sick. Just sick. Don't speak to me. Don't bother me. Just...Just fuck off, okay? Fuck off." Moxley's words revealed the depth of Altenhofen's manipulation, leaving scars in his mind that would fester and linger far longer than any physical wound.

With Moxley's departure, any hope of salvation went with him.

"Well, don't I just miss all the fun?" came a growling drawl from behind us.

Hawthorne stood with his arms folded over his chest, a lit cigarette dangling from between his lips. I couldn't help but wonder if maybe he used every opportunity he stepped outside as an excuse to smoke, like a twenty-something working fast food with dead-end prospects. He seemed like the world's oldest and surliest corner-cutting slacker. Wishful thinking, though; nothing about Hawthorne really seemed like he was much for cutting corners. His posture was one of readiness, his jaw set, his eyes hard flints that dug into your skin like sharp volcanic glass.

"What the fuck do you want, you goddamn ghoul?" I'd had enough of Hawthorne and his master. If he thought the earlier slap was enough to cow me, he would find himself sorely mistaken.

"There's no scraps from your master's table out here, Hawthorne," Tek said as she put herself between me and Altenhofen's hired monster.

Vanity would have said she did it because she liked me, but I had a feeling that she simply hated Hawthorne more than she was disgusted by my cowardice. I didn't think that Tek could use her Word before Hawthorne pulled his gun and shot her down like a dog, but she didn't put on as if she knew that. Shoulders squared and chin slightly raised, she all but dared him to make trouble with her, and given the mood she was in, I would have almost felt sorry for him if he had.

Almost.

"Look at you, Fuzzy Britches, gettin' all hot and bothered every time you see me. I just came here to tell you and Shakespeare over there that Mr. Altenhofen is ready to hear you out now. I'm only here to fetch you," Hawthorne said with a grin that would have shamed the Devil himself.

I stepped up to Tek's side, and she glanced over at me before looking back to Hawthorne.

"Well then, lead the way, you son of a bitch."

Unspoken Questions and The Damned Souls Who Ask Them

You'd be surprised what rolls through your mind when you're walking behind a powerful sorceress and a man who, by all accounts, could not die. Oddly enough, whatever panic I'd previously felt had receded, and I was able to stroll across the bridge of sanity into the land of the mad with remarkably little hindrance. Hawthorne was out in the lead, and Tek was just ahead of me. I should have been trying to ask her out of the corner of my mouth what the play was, but I kept silent, even if in that silence the doubt was deafening. Altenhofen wasn't going to listen, not to me and certainly not to Tek, but she was going to try, and if she failed...

...Well, I suppose she might just kill him.

No detours to the dining room this time; once through the doors of Altenhofen's little fortress, we button hooked right and ascended the stairs. I was thankful, if nothing else, that Hawthorne had kept his gloating only to the ugly knowing grin on his face. If he hadn't, I'd been too focused on him to notice how sparse the home became in terms of its personal furnishings as we pushed deeper into Altenhofen's sanctuary.

Hawthorne pushed open the double doors of Altenhofen's office, revealing the space where the man spent most of his time. It was a study in minimalism, with a single imposing desk standing defiantly against the sleek modernity of the room. The polished black marble floor contrasted sharply with the chrome accents and the large, polarized glass windows that offered a commanding view of the desolate flats beyond. Two chairs awaited, one for me and another for

Tek, while what initially appeared to be a transparent tanning bed revealed itself as a hyperbaric chamber upon closer inspection.

Not a single ornament adorned the walls, and Altenhofen's desk was conspicuously devoid of any clutter. It was just him, us, and the imposing figure of Hawthorne, who watched with the cold dark eyes of a Great White shark doing a poor impression of a man, holding the door open.

"Here they are, I think they upset the kid though." Hawthorne's rumbling tone lacked any hint of faux concern for Moxley, bearing instead the surly contempt of a small-town cop catching you smoking a joint behind the local Baptist Church.

Altenhofen sat behind his desk, his back to us as he gazed out over the Flats. The view was extraordinary, as I mentioned earlier, but I doubted he truly appreciated it. No, Altenhofen had cast his eyes not towards the horizon, but towards the culmination of his work. The tipping point of the Namebreakers' existence in this world had been reached. Another five years, perhaps another ten, and there would be no turning back. Another ten after that, and we wouldn't even remember them except in the conversations or musings of old men like me.

Turning in his chair, Altenhofen sighed, but there was no anger in the sound of that air pushing out of his tired lungs. No, anger would have implied some small victory or advantage that Tek and I could have exploited. Instead, Altenhofen simply seemed resigned, tired, and bored. Like Moxley, he was a man who was sure of how the future would play out. Not because he'd seen it in some mystical glimpse forward, but rather because he'd built the whole thing, paid for it, and probably still had the damned receipts if it didn't turn out the way he planned.

I stole a glance at Tek, but she wasn't looking at me. Her eyes were focused only on the two men before her. I couldn't help but admire the certain degree of bravery in her. A young woman, at least twenty years my junior, stood before what might have been the wealthiest bastard in all the world, clad simply in a black sleeveless t-shirt and jeans. She met the King of Swine with her head held high and dark eyes that would not flinch or look away. Her blood was seeped into the soil from which my American Dream had grown, her story - not as well known to me then as Moxley's and splotched with the deep shadows of her own guarded past - had borne the hard scrabble pain of a life that even my well-compensated imagination could not comprehend.

That tale, with all its ups and downs, hurts and moments of despair, had led her here. Was she really a murderer, as Altenhofen had implied? I'd known her for just a few days, but I didn't think so. The problem lay in the act of knowing - which had always been the curse of my ink-smeared ilk.

"Oh, don't worry about Moxley," a wane smile pulled across those old lips. "He'll be sullen for a time, but all that any pain they've caused him will do is make him dig his heels in deeper. He's a good boy, unfortunately afflicted with any number of unsavory tastes, but that is in the nature of what he is," Altenhofen spoke with the steady confidence of a man who had planned for all his eventualities.

There was no doubt that he'd anticipated any effort to subvert Moxley.

I wove myself around Tek, slipping towards Altenhofen's desk while Hawthorne waited by the door and Altenhofen postured behind his words. I pulled out one of the chairs and sat down, regretting only that I had no cigarette to light up in defiance of Altenhofen's disdain for personal destruction. He turned his attention from Tek to me, and there was a momentary pulling of his lips from his teeth in a look of disgust that only the rich can ever properly manage to manufacture when confronted by the audacity of those they see as their lesser.

"I did not invite you to sit down, Mr. Wozynski," Altenhofen said with a cultivated dryness that would have shamed a world of disappointed fathers.

"The name is Wonderful, at least when I'm on the clock, and if you don't like my manners then I guess you should have let me leave, huh?" I said, as if I wasn't awaiting Hawthorne to pistol-whip me from behind until the only words I made again were of the 'inspirational' variety for people recovering from head trauma.

"He's got a point," Tek added, and though she did not take a seat herself, she moved up closer to the desk and laid a hand upon the back of my chair.

"I suppose you're right," Altenhofen conceded, and the sneer faded into a mere contempt-laden smile.

"Whatever happened to you that made you this way, whatever made you think this was the path - it isn't too late. I understand wanting to help people, I understand getting lost trying to do that. If you don't, if you do this, if you make Moxley do this, we'll be I-" Tek began without prompting from Altenhofen, those first words as sincere and passionately honest as any I had ever heard.

Altenhofen cut her off.

"Excuse me. That's very nice but on the cameras, when you were trying to turn Moxley against me, you used the word 'please' and I think I will insist that you use it now."

"What?" I asked, feeling my own anger rising up.

Hawthorne laughed by the door, his chuckle slicing through the air like the gleeful creak of a gallows in the wind.

"Even if you had turned Moxley..." Altenhofen's voice oozed with the same affection a banker might display while explaining how he now owned another man's home.

"...There is still enough Dynametrium stockpiled and already processed to see my dream accomplished. I am the one with the power to change the situation, not a Namebreaker, not a monster - me." Altenhofen's hands slammed onto the desktop as he spoke, his demeanor subtly leaning forward to cut into Tek with his words.

"So, she will begin by saying 'please,' just as she said to Moxley. That is the problem with Namebreakers. They refuse to acknowledge us as the owners of this world and set themselves above the rest of us." His demand for Tek's degradation resonated with ancient tones, akin to priests demanding confession and fathers insisting on evidence of virtue.

Bow to me. Bow to me, and you may have some measure of comfort in knowing that you tried and lost fairly.

I glanced at Tek, and my heart shattered just a little more.

Her head had bowed, and her black hair, as black as raven's wings, spilled around her face. Her cheeks had darkened not with embarrassment but with anger that warred now with the desperate need to avoid the bleak promised futures that Altenhofen and men like him had made for the Namebreakers and the rest of us. The final sands of countless hourglasses had delivered her here on this day and at this moment in the room with this man who embodied so much of what the American Spirit had become.

A wild-eyed lunatic tearing out his own heart in a desperate attempt to rid himself of all that made one unique for the sake of manufactured acceptance.

I looked back at Altenhofen; even his weathered old face was preferable to watching Tek decide if it was worth murdering her pride for the sake of a long shot that almost certainly didn't exist. The game was rigged. The system was corrupt. Tek would beg, and Altenhofen would refuse. She would lash out, and Hawthorne would kill her where she sat.

I saw it all with brilliant, awful clarity.

So, I did the only thing that a red-blooded American can do in this sort of situation; the only thing that MY American Dream, my American Spirit, all the keepers of the Strange, those curators of the weird, wild, and categorically obscene would have me do in this situation. The only thing that I felt I could do to keep Tek from losing her soul and maybe, just maybe, a step towards buying mine back.

I leaned across that desk, and as the sun blazed in its brilliant painted setting splendor, I punched an aging white billionaire directly in his filthy goddamn Nazi jaw. I hit him with all the furious might of a man who spent far more time getting sloppy in dive bars and book signings where I marveled at my own luck. I may not have been to Hawthorne's measure, but even a booze-soaked old newshound can engage in the despicable act of punching an elderly man so hard he falls out of his chair.

I've tried most drugs known to man and a few only known to the Shadow People. I've engaged in carnal acts that involve painted-on honey and nameless shapes in the dark. Of all the divine pleasures of this world, including true love, nothing had ever felt as good as punching a goddamn billionaire parasite in his face. As if all the frustration and that sense of having the goodness choked out of me day after day had finally culminated in this one act of defiance.

If you ever get the chance, I highly recommend it.

Altenhofen let out a shrill cry of startled pain; he hadn't anticipated that (the fucker) and he slid out of his chair and onto the floor. I turned my head, and my eyes met Tek's own; I saw the ringing of tears there around the rich browns of her eyes.

"You idiot. I was going to do that." Tek actually managed to smile in the face of impending ruinous oblivion.

If it was to be the end—if Tek and her people, along with all the other Shadow People, were to be erased—then they would not kneel. They would not, at the moment of their accounting, be remembered for cowardice, shame, or groveling for scraps from those who deemed them unworthy. They would not leave this world as obedient captives of a society that had cast them aside. Magic, The Word, Namebreaking, Mysticism, or Wizardry—whatever you called it—was like the weird, the wild, the outlaw, and my own white whale—the American Dream; a thing that could not bow but only rise. Destruction was the only weapon of those who opposed that dream, for though it could be swindled, manipulated, or tricked, it could never be enslaved for long.

"What do you expect, I'm Jimmy Wonder—"

BANG!

I'm sure you know the rest of the line. I am Jimmy Wonderful, the last sage of the forgotten highway, a consumer of much whiskey and a teller of tall tales. My first cousin is Mr. Coyote, and where the strange goes, I go. I scream 'Faster! Faster!' barreling down the highways, mad on chemical cocktails the likes of which would send a God-fearing DEA agent into the lunatic asylum from which I had no doubt escaped.

I had been shot.

Interestingly, I do not initially remember the pain. I do remember the falling though, the slow erosion of my balance, and the upward rush of the black marble floor to meet my face. Warmth, terrible awful warmth, spread throughout the low of my belly, and for a moment, I realized that all the other aches and pains of my life were gone. If I survived, this would be the end of my writing career; I would revolutionize the healthcare industry with a brand-new cure for everything from aches and pains to seasonal depression.

What more fitting American cure-all exists than a gunshot?

"I told him what would happen." I heard Hawthorne drawl from what might have been across the room or a galaxy away. I wasn't sure.

There was a great deal of dark red liquid coming out from between my clutching fingers as I rolled onto my back. A troubling amount.

What happened next was terrible to behold.

Tek's attention tore from me where I lay and settled onto Hawthorne with a quiet fury that had been building up since we had arrived. Hawthorne was no slouch, however, and in the dreadful slow motion bestowed upon me with a .45 caliber kiss, I could see the hammer on his pistol drawing back. There was a lethal promise in the steadying barrel with its faint whiff of gun smoke curling from the bore.

There was a flash, and whether that flash was real or my mind playing tricks on me as I bled to death on the floor is as questionable as the existence of a banker's heart.

The 'light,' if that was what it was, seemed to gather in the throat of Tek and dust her lips with a glow that had been no doubt stolen from the stars. The pain had come now, a stabbing hot poker that twisted in my guts, and despite this, despite the blooming agony, I was unable to avert my eyes. Even death could not compete with a Namebreaker who had made up her mind.

Every vein that was visible in Hawthorne's body abruptly stood out against his skin, bulging and dark as if the blood had been drained from them and instead replaced with motor oil. His flesh had gone hot pink and then deep purple in the matter of an instant, one eye hideously rolled up in his head as white foam flew from between clenched teeth. Hawthorne's left leg buckled beneath him, and a strangled, muted curse choked in his throat. The lips and eyelid on that left-hand side drooped like melting wax.

Interestingly, I do not initially remember the pain. I do remember the falling though, the slow erosion of my balance, and the upward rush of the black marble floor to meet my face. Warmth, terrible awful warmth, spread throughout the low of my belly, and for a moment, I realized that all the other aches and pains of my life were gone. If I survived, this would be the end of my writing career; I would revolutionize the healthcare industry with a brand-new cure for everything from aches and pains to seasonal depression.

What more fitting American cure-all exists than a gunshot?

There was a great deal of dark red liquid coming out from between my clutching fingers as I rolled onto my back. A troubling amount.

With the detached horror one can only properly pick with long-term coverage of the American political scene (or a bullet in one's guts), I realized that Hawthorne was being boiled alive on the inside. Attached to that realization, by a thin thread of journalistic habit, was the notation that it would seem that a Namebreaker's use of the Word manifested in more ways than the auditory. Here, with my guts full of death and my ears rendered deaf by America's most dreadful of manufactured thunders, I was perceiving more than I had any earthly right to.

Somehow, impossibly, and with mad triumph gleaming in his lone good eye, Hawthorne was still able to keep the gun in his outstretched right arm. The barrel wavered up and down but remained loaded with the same murderous potential that had cut me down. Hawthorne fired again. In horror, I thrust one bloody hand outward as if I might somehow stop Tek from being shot in the face. But I needn't have worried - the bullet passed by her head and struck the polarized glass of Altenhofen's windows.

Hawthorne fell onto his side, and his gun finally dropped from his hand onto the black marble floor.

There was no sound. The gun had been too loud. No sound, just the slickness between my fingers. I was cold, colder than a banker's heart, and had only the vaguest sense that cold was a bad sign. Not good at all. I looked up, and the glass of Altenhofen's fancy-ass windows had begun to crack. A jagged line in the glass, like a psychedelic light show mocking my impending demise.

I was dying, but hell, at least the light was beautiful. All of it was beautiful. My cozy little love shack with Jenna, the clickety-clack of the keys as some half-cooked idea sprouted from my whiskey-soaked brain, the ghosts with their tragic tales, the fairies with their wild-ass dreams, the vampires sneaking through the darkness like horny teenagers in a horror flick. All the weird shit, all the strange corners, all the damn secrets.

There was something coppery in my mouth. Pennies had a bad habit of showing up where you least expect them - but blood? The realization of blood oozing into your mouth from a bullet wound was about as pleasant as a porcupine in your underpants.

"I think the filthy swine finally got me," I wheezed, surprised at how much like a scared little kid I sounded.

"You're okay, Jimmy. You're okay. This is bad, but I can fix it. I'm going to fix it. Just hang in there, okay?" Tek's voice was a frantic lifeline in my hazy consciousness as she knelt beside me.

Her gorgeous dark hair had streaks of gray now, and her face looked like she'd just wrestled a grizzly bear. I could see, even through the lens of my foggy state, the hollows in her cheeks and the way her clothes hung on her frame like they'd given up on life. How much of herself had she given to take down Hawthorne?

I didn't want to die, but the weight of it was getting lighter by the second. I didn't want to see the blood, the death, the final gasp of America's wild spirit. If all the weird, the mystical, and even the damned Wonderful were about to be snuffed out, was it really that hard to let go?

Who the hell would want to live in a world without magic? Can you even picture it?

"Jimmy?" Tek's voice sounded a million miles away, like she was yelling from the edge of the universe.

I could hear Jenna strumming a tune that I didn't recognize just down the hall. The melody was warm and inviting, maddeningly familiar but it just wouldn't leap to the front of the mind, like trying to hold the sea in your hands. With some mild amusement, I discovered that I could not answer Tek. There was no darkness; everything seemed a thousand times brighter and more colorful - more vivid than it had ever been before.

Dying was like waking up from a long and fitful dream, and I knew it was as easy as letting go, as easy as allowing the colors to swallow me up and carry me away. The only hindrance to this being the end of our story was that Altenhofen had begun to find his way to his feet, half leaning over the edge of the desk for support. I could just see one hand thrust into his pocket, and while I wanted to scream, while I wanted to warn Tek that he was behind her - I could do nothing.

A syringe. Dynametrium. Tek was too focused on me, searching for the right Words to put my ruined body back together again. I fought the warmth, fought the colors, fought the easy sweetness of death, and tried to scream.

I felt the bloody bubble pop on my lips, but there was no voice behind it.

Tek's eyes widened in horrible surprise when Altenhofen thrust the syringe into the side of her neck. I watched, helpless and sinking into the brightness of it all, as the silvery-blue liquid pushed its way into Tek's veins. Her brow knitting together in determination against the voice, the True Voice, dying in her throat.

"JIMMY!" Tek screamed, and the colors themselves shook.

The pain went away, the heaviness of my body was all at once gone, and I dissolved into the light.

Even the Weird could die.

Day Three
Rebirth

"America had always had an obsession with blood. It was the currency with which we traded with the world and only sacrifice that gun manufactures will take. The best of the harvest just doesn't count it, it has to be blood. Blood for the dollar, blood for the bullet, blood for the filthy insurance salesman. With this kind of obsession with the red stuff is it any wonder that a vampiric Richard Nixon would rise to the top of the swine heap?" - *Jimmy Wonderful, Stakes and Garlic on the Campaign Trail*

COYOTE WALLACE

The Compass of the Weird

I was surprised by just how much dying felt like plummeting into a bottomless swimming pool. Despite the muted details of the world around me, as if overhearing a distant conversation down a long hallway, I felt weightless, floating in an upward trajectory countered by a gentle yet insistent downward pull. Light and color enveloped me with such intensity that even with my eyes shut tight, the vivid hues penetrated my consciousness, painting an otherworldly scene that bordered on madness.

Great swirls of green, which looked like the limbs of some ancient bottom-dwelling octopus, lashed the space before my eyes. Explosions of violet that reached heights only dreamed of by the angriest volcanoes rained down upon me from the heavens. There were tidal waves of the very paint, used by whatever mad deity ran this world to color in the sunsets, that rolled me in their clutches as if I were a piece of driftwood. I was spat out into great chasms of indigo blue bleeding into ivory whites and sun-dazzled golds.

Always moving through the color, floating through beauty that had no rhyme or reason.

All at once the color fled, rushed away as if I were a magnet whose polarity had suddenly been reversed, and with a start, I awoke to find myself sitting at home on my couch with Jenna curled against my arm. She wasn't quite dozing, but familiarity told me she was close; she was in that warm comfortable place where one can only linger when they feel safe and loved. Gray sweats and an oversized NOFX t-shirt that had survived both the painting of the living room and ten years of wear and tear could not dim the warmth of her against me. Whatever impossible odds I might have ascribed to my returning to her side were forgotten completely with the first breath that carried the smell of her hair.

"Bad dream?" she asked me and nuzzled in close, her breath tickling the side of my neck.

The television, its volume low but not quite muted, was showing a great many police officers and armed men escorting what appeared to be various members of congress out of their offices in handcuffs. Nixon himself, smoldering as he was pulled into the sun, thrashed and fought in his chains. The head leech, who made literal what his underlings had only the courage to take as figurative, was at last getting what he deserved.

"The worst. Christ, I'm an idiot for thinking about leaving here," I muttered into the soft sweetness of Jenna's hair.

"You're an idiot but it's only because you're too hard on yourself. Even you know that deep down you deserve to cut yourself some slack. That's why you're here," Jenna mumbled against my shoulder.

"What?" I asked, but there was a small bloom of horror in my heart that was taking root despite how badly I wanted to forget where the seed came from.

Jenna looked up, and her face was not the peaceful sleeping countenance that I had been curled against me on the couch where we had watched *Stand by Me* and *The Dark Crystal*. Erased was the woman to whom I had made wild love fueled by tequila and hope when Obama had won. No, her face had aged a decade in an instant, and her eyes were ringed with the redness of tears. My sweet love was broken, pained, and yet already healing.

355

"You knew that you wouldn't come back, that you would choose being Jimmy Wonderful over me. You knew, down deep in that little compass inside yourself that it would happen, that it had to happen," Jenna's voice grew heavy with the aching hurt of mourning.

"No, that's not true. Don't say that, baby. That's not..." I started to plead my case, but Jenna laid a finger against my lips.

"You're *wonderful*." She whispered.

Those colors were back, gathering at the window, brighter and brighter. Their glow threw everything into the stark silhouettes that only those who had been at ground zero for atomic fire could know. As they grew in their intensity, and the world began to give way, Jenna pressed her lips against mine and once more I shut my eyes against the color. I held her, I held her as tightly as I ever had, and I kissed her as fiercely as a man who, desperate in his own heart for his love to persist, might believe the fates can be swayed by something as small as a kiss.

The colors rolled back like the tide, and I suddenly plunged downward a good six inches into something soft that molded itself to my form. With a start, my eyes came open, and I realized I was no longer sitting on my couch. I was instead sitting on one of the god-awful bean bag chairs of Tom Mulkey's office back at the Mystic Standard in Chicago.

The city, in all its old ugly glory, stood waiting for me to conclude whatever banal tasks with Mulkey that had summoned me back to The Mystic Standard. The bars and dives with their neatly ordered promises kept on shelves in beautiful bottles. The cornucopia of sights, sounds, and smells that was the streets. Music. So much music and good times and unfettered wildness.

"Now, what I'm thinking is that we rewrite the ending. I mean - I love you Jimmy, look at this face, I LOVE you. You're my applesauce surprise - I just don't think that if you end the story that way that the demos are going to go for it," Tom said with a smile so big it barely let his lips move.

His tanned boyish face and six-hundred-dollar haircut looked all wrong; the features were too loose upon his skull. Minor detail. Rewrite the ending? That dirty little sonofabitch wanted me to rewrite the ending?!?!

I was Jimmy GODDAMN Wonderful, and whenever I ran across sniveling sprats like Tom Mulkey out in "The Wild," I casually reminded them that until a paternity test proved otherwise, I might well be their father.

"The fucking demos? I don't give the wet shit that a raven wouldn't spare on your Porsche, you smarmy little bastard! That's how the story ends, that's the truth and you can't change the truth! You just follow the goddamn Weird wherever it goes and try to carry the truth back with you, even if it's burning you to hold it. You don't change it just because it makes someone happy!" I shouted, rising out of the bean bag chair in my righteousness.

"Jimmy, Jimmy, Jimmy... Calm down. We're all friends here at the Mystic Standard. We sell the world a window into the strange, a glimpse into the weird and odd - perception is reality. How does it look if the protagonist, the hero, is lying there dead on the ground?" Tom explained as he slid around the desk.

His lips still couldn't move for the size of his giant smile.

Over Tom's shoulder, I could see the Chicago skyline slowly beginning to sink. The buildings gradually dropping one-by-one into the ground. The rumble could be felt all the way up in Tom's office through the soles of my feet. History being erased and consumed by something that I dared not let my mind linger on for a moment longer. My eyes flitted back to that horrible artificial smile, and I reached up, grabbing Tom behind his ears. He let out a terrible awkward squawk like a chicken that had just found itself seized by the neck, but I held on, and I pulled with all of my might.

Tom's face came off in my hands with a sticky wet SCHLOOP! I stared at it in my hands, horrified for a moment at the fleshy interior and the vile mucus-like substance that glistened with the promise of grotesque unnatural origins.

"For some sort of American sage, you're rather slow on the uptake aren't you, Mr. Wonderful?" Roy Altenhofen, his face wet with the leftovers from his "Tom mask," said as he adjusted his tie.

"FUCKER OF GOATS!" the scream tore out of my throat before I could stop it.

I pushed Altenhofen back onto the desk and squeezed as Chicago continued to crumble and sink, the death cry of the city rattling the ground upon which I stood. For a mad instant, I glimpsed up and there were only a few traces of the very tips of the highest skyscrapers remaining. They sank two at a time beneath the hard white earth of the Salt Flats that extended as far as the eye could see towards the horizon. A lifeless dead place in which all was dry and hard and lacking in the most basic qualities for anything but miserable survival.

Altenhofen looked positively gleeful beneath my strangling hands.

"Girl! Girl! Please come in and set Mr. Wonderful ablaze. He's always wanted to burn out rather than fade away like his much-vaunted rock 'n roll stars. It seems the least I can do for him," Altenhofen called out, unimpeded by the fact I was midway through the act of murdering him.

I bore down harder, and I could feel the tendons straining against my skin as I pressed my thumbs inward.

"Kill you and eat you! Kill you and eat you! Kill you and fucking eat you, swine!" I ranted while frothing mad with murderous fury.

I was so invested in Altenhofen's strangulation that I did not immediately turn to face the girl that he'd called for, even when I heard the click of the office door. My investment in crushing Altenhofen's windpipe with my bare hands in a fit of what can only be described as a primal caveman-like rage at meeting the source of all absolute darkness in the universe. The strangulation of billionaires, even in the hallucinatory realm of death, was simply much too all-consuming for distraction. The colors were back, gathering at the window, brighter and brighter. Their glow threw everything into the stark silhouettes that only those who had been at ground zero for atomic fire could know. As they grew in their intensity, and the world began to give way, Jenna pressed her lips against mine, and once more, I shut my eyes against the color. I held her, I held her as tightly as I ever had, and I kissed her as fiercely as a man who, desperate in his own heart for his love to persist, might believe the fates can be swayed by something as small as a kiss.

Then came a splash of something wet upon my back; the air suddenly heavy with a high acrid smell that could only be gasoline. The gas filled my nose, blotting out everything else. It was enough to cut through the rage, at least for a moment. I turned my head, startled, half drenched in flammable liquid, and found myself looking at what must have been Hell's own version of Tek.

She was partially slack-jawed, her once-willful brown eyes flat and unknowing. Her long black hair had been shaved down to only stubble, save for an ominously bare patch on the right-hand side of her skull where the ugly raises of old stitchwork remained. The hospital gown that her bone-thin frame was covered by, if you could call it that, was filthy and tattered by neglect. She'd just dropped the bright red gasoline jug onto the office floor where it lay like some surreal breed of lethal squash when I turned to her.

She was fumbling like a child with a book of matches.

"Tek?" No matter how softly I spoke, it couldn't hide the horror.

She didn't answer, just kept striking at the match she held. When the match failed to take light, she simply dropped it and moved onto the next one. If she recognized me at all, there was no sign of it that I could detect.

The rage returned.

"You bastard! YOU FILTHY BASTARD!" I screamed until my throat hurt.

I wasn't just choking Altenhofen now; I was shaking him and screaming. Not words, just sounds. Language escaped me, and now all that spewed forth was mad incoherent disgust and curse-laden revulsion for not just my demise, or even the wrongs done to those I knew, but all of it. All the horror. All the machines built by all the men in service of death, be they mechanical monstrosities or institutions of wealth. The systems of hateful oppression and the small men with big bank accounts who ran them.

Woosh!

I was burning—flames had spread across my back, arms, catching in my hair and splashing over my cheek. Agony, agony beyond all knowing took me, and I let go of Altenhofen. Lost in my pain, I ran screaming towards the window as the fiery colors came. It had to end. My sanity was now crumbling away completely. This was madness—not Hell, not Heaven, just the awful certainty that my mind had finally fallen completely apart.

The colors broke through the glass, washing away Altenhofen and the horrible future's parody of Tek. The flames persisted, but so did I. My being was too solid for the colors to move, too heavy for them to rip free as they had done before. The pain was more than anything I can put to words—I was burning to death, yet death would not come. The brightness of the color, the vividness of it, was such that I would have looked away or shut my eyes if I had the power. Even the hurt could not persist in the face of such color without being muted and dulled for the audacity of the attempt.

Yet, even my most token ability to resist was now gone; my eyelids, like my hair, lips, and fingers, were burning away. I saw, with the most hideous clarity, a figure approaching from out of all that swirling madness. At first, he was nothing more than a silhouette, but as he approached out of that tempest of all the colors of creation itself, his details came into being. Though I burned, I could not look away; though the agony tore scream after scream from my body, I could focus on nothing else.

The figure was a man, tall and broad-shouldered, his dour face covered by a beard that had long ago begun to succumb to the march of white hairs. The hair on his head was similarly afflicted around the temples, though time had not yet found the boldness to reach further. He wore blue robes, and upon them were the same pattern that I had seen tattooed on Moxley's skin.

I would have greeted Conrad Allerton with a bit more respect if I wasn't on fire and either in Hell or the grips of insanity. He seemed to sense this, and though he took his sweet time (what felt like an eternity to a burning man) looking me up and down, when he spoke it was with the calm authority of the man who had once fought for the best, and not merely against the worst.

"There's something you need to know going forward, Mr. Wonderful. Something that I hope gives you some small

comfort. Consider it a reward for trying to reach Moxley."
Even the fires that consumed me could not dull my ear to the
sound of parental pain cracking the stoic façade of Moxley's
father.

"Dying is, once the fuss has concluded, very easy. Living
is the painful part." Conrad Allerton said with gentleness
that belonged only to the best teachers dealing with the
unruliest of students.

If there was more, I did not hear it.

The hungry flames had consumed me at last.

R.I.P James Wozynski

I wish I could tell you that I came to myself with a sudden gasp of sweet air or that my eyes popped open to the radiant vision of Tek standing before me. I wish I could tell you those things because it would make for a better story, but waking up from death was nothing like the stories. I was cold and craved the warmth of the colors, the nothingness of swirling kaleidoscope oblivion, the way a child yearns for his mother. Fitfully, I slapped my head, feeling something pushing against the top of my skull - the inconvenience of it finally forced my eyes open.

I immediately regretted that choice.

My, for lack of a better word, corpse was lying propped against Altenhofen's desk, exactly where I had been shot. The color had faded from cheeks that I knew from countless mornings hunched over the bathroom sink with my mouth full of toothpaste. The eyes that had squinted over the very manuscripts that had pulled me from obscurity and provided me with the means to feed and clothe myself, now stared blankly ahead.

All around me on the floor was my own blood, and I had only the vaguest realization that I was sitting naked in the sticky mess. The scream that tried to bubble out of me was stifled only by the clamping of my own hands over my lips. For a moment, I could do nothing but stare at the corpse, wondering if I was a ghost; returned as one of the living dead from my own murder to roam the earth. It was only when I tried to stand and slipped in the blood, banging my knee against the floor as I did, that I realized the truth.

I was alive.

Once I found my feet and carefully navigated my way out of the pool of my own blood, I took stock of myself in the cracked glass of Altenhofen's windows. The heaviness of night was upon the land, but I could see my reflection well enough in the glass to be both amazed and terrified. My hair was full and thick, the lines of age upon my face had been all but erased. The body that I had poured years of bourbon, cigarettes, and numerous other illicit substances into, was lean and freshly hewn from youth. I was once more a young man of maybe twenty-five, the rogue that had ridden with the faeries, the dreamer that grinned from the posters kept on the walls of those who yearn for a return to the margins where freedom was fast and deadly.

Hawthorne had killed James Wozynski, so Tek had, in her last desperate act before her heart could pump the Dynametrium through her system, not saved herself or even the aging old writer who had struggled with the burden of being a myth. Instead, she had saved me.

Jimmy -fucking- Wonderful.

How much time had passed? The full dark suggested hours. The fact that Hawthorne and Altenhofen were gone was second to the fact that I had no clue where Tek was either. I was covered in blood, naked, and possessed with a wild vitality that came from adrenaline shooting through an unencumbered system. I was unarmed, unarmored, and lacking in any meaningful combat experience.

Naturally, I stole the pants off my own corpse simply because walking around in some dazed state of half madness trying to prevent an unspeakable horror, and hopefully the death of a friend, is always best attempted with pants. No great hero has ever saved the day with his flaccid penis swinging in the breeze. Well, maybe they had, and I just didn't know it. My sanity was tethered together by the barest of threads, and stripping my own older dead body for his pants wasn't helping.

I left Altenhofen's office as if I were Hell on Earth, calling out for him among the finery and pomp as I made my way towards the stairs.

"Altenhofen! Hawthorne! You bastards! Where are you??!?" Despite all my fury, my voice found only the walls.

When I made it to the front door, I saw the compound's gate was open, and felt my heart sink into my belly. If they were outside of the compound, they could be burying Tek in the Flats, and there would be nothing I could do about it. I ran, heedless of the fact that I didn't have any shoes, towards the gate. The night sky above me was black and starless; even the moon had hidden its face. The wind had picked up somewhere out of the north, hard and cold, the sort of wind that moaned as it spread itself across the shadow-drenched landscape of the Salt Flats.

When I crossed the threshold of the gate, I realized it was much worse than that.

Altenhofen had accelerated his timetable considerably. It may have taken them a few hours to get everything in order, but what I saw before me at the foot of the small artificial hill was enough to momentarily chill my blood. Moxley stood with his hands pressed against the Resonance Tower, his head slightly bowed and his lips furiously moving. Altenhofen stood back several yards away and appeared so captivated that he didn't even seem to mind Hawthorne's smoking. Hawthorne, for his part, looked remarkably well considering I'd seen Tek boil him alive from the inside. That is to say - still surly and ugly as a bulldog licking piss from a pinecone, but otherwise alive.

Tek lay at their feet on her side, her hands bound behind her back in tight black plastic ties that bit into the flesh of her wrists. My eyes saw with a precision that had not been dulled by years staring at screens or bent over pages. Tek's left eye had swollen shut, her nose pushed to an awkward leftish angle, and I could only guess at what other injuries Hawthorne had bestowed upon her as repayment for the smiting she'd given him.

Thunder cracked overhead, and the Resonance Tower began to light up. All along its black onyx surface began to appear script in the most brilliant of glowing blue lights. Each marking was as beautiful and unique as a star, and Moxley Allerton was bathed in that illumination. His head still down, his palms still thrust against the surface as he chanted.

"SWINE!" I bellowed out into the night, into the storm, into the face of Altenhofen's future, and into the eye of fate itself.

Moxley ceased his chanting, and the light of the Resonance Tower dimmed. He turned and looked at me in stunned surprise, but it was nothing compared to the look on Altenhofen's face. The old man's jaw had swung open, and his eyes were bright with startled wonder at my resurrection.

"It can't be..." Altenhofen said, and despite his age, he sounded remarkably like a boy who had opened his largest Christmas gift to discover it contained only wool socks.

"The bitch snuck one by ya, sir. Ain't nothin' I can't correct. Just got to make sure she doesn't do it again," Hawthorne said as he unholstered his pistol. His savage smile revealed his intent, yet it was clear he had no immediate plans to use it on me.

A more noble man would have fixated on the gun threatening the captive woman. A righteous man would have paused to offer a prayer for divine intervention. However, I possessed neither nobility nor righteousness, and I harbored no desire to feign either.

I had always been a traveler on the strange, lost highways of America, a vagabond and a rambler who eked out a living with a pen. Through this, I had honed my ability to read the world around me almost as well as the Namebreakers did.

My focus remained on Moxley's face.

His eyes widened in surprise, and as he processed the unfolding scene, conflicting with whatever narrative Altenhofen and Hawthorne had spun, his brows furrowed. I observed the subtle shift in his posture—a faint squareness of his shoulders, a burgeoning anger that raced across his features with greater clarity than in his aged form. He resembled a man unexpectedly accused of a scandalous act, too stunned to articulate his indignation properly.

"You said she killed him trying to kill you! That Hawthorne had to subdue her. You lied to me, Roy," Moxley's voice cut across the empty space, and though he did not take his hands from the tower, he craned his neck to look up at me.

Fear. Real fear. That was what flooded Altenhofen's eyes then, and he turned away from me, breaking away from even Hawthorne; walking as fast as his enfeebled legs could carry him towards Moxley. The stern guardian routine had crumbled away, and now he was all but pleading.

"Moxley. Moxley, my boy. This is all a very big misunderstanding, and I am more than willing to untangle this whole mess, but first, you must finish what we've started, boy. Our work is too important," Altenhofen coaxed.

"He killed your father!" I screamed.

Hawthorne put his foot down a little harder on Tek's throat, and she began to kick and writhe beneath him. If I had been able to in that moment, I would have jumped upon him and pulled him apart with my teeth if I had to.

"Shut your gob, Shakespeare!" Hawthorne growled.

Moxley looked at his surrogate father, the man who had been obscured from Moxley's "vision" by the wound left behind by his own blood. Conrad Allerton's supposed abandonment had left a hole in Moxley, a hole that Altenhofen had exploited and filled. The boy had been his puppet, and the loss of Moxley's father had been the tool used to hollow him out for Altenhofen's hands. I can't be sure of that explanation, but it feels righter than any other.

Without ever taking his hands off the Resonance Tower, Moxley shifted his gaze to Hawthorne and myself.

"You are one unimaginable prick; I hope you know that." Moxley said with just the barest hint of a smile, then whispered something into the wind that I could not hear.

Honestly, I'm not sure which of us he meant, at least until Hawthorne vanished with but a single word from Moxley's lips.

"Get her and move! I'm not sure where he'll land!" Moxley yelled. For a split second, I didn't understand what he meant.

Where he'll land?

Then it hit me, and I ran down the hill as hard as I could. My legs pumped, my new young heart beating away in my chest. The hard soil of the flats cut my feet, yet I didn't care or stop. I wrapped my arms around Tek and hauled her up and forward, letting the momentum I'd built up with my run down the hill carry us both. I'd just gotten her up and out of the way when Hawthorne returned - from a fall that must have been more than a thousand feet straight up. He landed with a loud crack and a wet thud, very much dead and bursting upon the unforgiving soil like a bag of spoiled meat thrown out a high-rise window.

I'd seen what Tek had done to Hawthorne and knew instantly that this would be no more effective in stopping him. Not for long.

Tek groaned in my arms and looked up at me with her one good eye.

"Wasn't sure that I got that one off in time. You died," she said through broken teeth and split lips.

"Yeah well, thanks to you, I got better," I said, praying she couldn't see the damage Hawthorne's fists had inflicted on her in my eyes.

I didn't know what else was to come, what else this world had in store for me, but I did know this - Whatever new life had been given to me by Tek's efforts would not be squandered in the hypothetical. I had lived between the pages of James Wozynski's work, inside of him, part companion and part alter ego. That was done. I was Jimmy Wonderful now, through and through. I'd passed through the valley of the Weird and been reborn.

Moxley and Altenhofen were another matter.

There were still reckonings to be had; the storm was rolling in from the north. A powerful and invisible beast lost within the blackness of the night sky that bellowed thunder and summoned flashes of lightning against the distant mountains. The air itself seemed alive with power; every trace of reality infused with a tremendous static electric charge.

"Moxley, listen to me. You need to conserve your energy. I know you're angry, but we can talk about that after you make more of the Dynametrium. After we save EVERYTHING," Altenhofen pleaded, nearly beside himself in desperation.

There was a reckoning to be had.

Old Man Time

The storm howled across the sky above our heads like some mighty cosmic deity dealt a killing blow. The wind, pushing against us, blew with such force that small loose bits of earth skittered by my feet. Behind me lay Hawthorne, a crumpled heap, his limbs twitching as life slowly seeped back into his broken body after the fall.

However, my attention was primarily drawn to the Resonance Tower, its strange glowing eldritch script, and the two men who stood before it.

"Tell. Me. The. Truth." Moxley spat each word from his mouth as if dipped in molten brass.

"Moxley, you have to understand..." Altenhofen's pleading voice cracked against the wind.

"I HAVE to understand? Do I? Tell me again what it is I must do; we'll see if you can fly as well as Hawthorne!" Moxley snarled, withdrawing his hands from the Resonance Tower for the first time.

"He abandoned you!" Altenhofen moaned as the lights on the eldritch script began to fade.

Moxley seized Altenhofen by the front of his suit, hauling him forward until their noses almost touched. From where I stood, they looked like a terrible "Before and After" photo, America's youthful rebellious future nose to nose with the man who held the present in iron gauntlet-covered hands.

"Liar." Moxley said so softly that I had to strain to hear him against the wind.

With a great push, Moxley sent Altenhofen tumbling to the ground, where the old man landed with a pained cry.

Moxley stood over him, the Resonance Tower to his back slowly losing the last of its glow. Altenhofen's desperation at long last gave way to the truth of what he was; he looked up from the ground at Moxley like a viper that had been struck only by a glancing blow. His eyes were full of black hate and menace, of spite that was so old and strong that it had been fashioned into a cell for the American Spirit; hammered into a blade for the bloody work of the removal of our soul by way of surgery.

Behind me, there was stirring, and remarkably, Hawthorne had risen to his hands and knees. His face, as pale as a sheet of paper, was streaked with crimson from his own blood. I broke from Tek then only to retrieve Hawthorne's pistol from his grasp. His fingers spasmed in their attempt to hold on but failed in his half-crushed state. Amidst the flickering illumination of the lightning, I watched with horror as Hawthorne began to regrow his teeth and most of his chin.

"You ungrateful little faggot! You are a miserable, spoiled, degenerate wretch! Yes, yes, I killed him because he stole my revenge and it was you, Moxley! It was you who I used to lead him here, you who I used to decipher his studies, you who he tried to call out for after Hawthorne opened his throat. There's your truth!" Altenhofen shouted in the face of the angry young god, his pride would no longer allow him to beg - not when the game was finally up.

Not at the end.

"Fucking...cocksucking little punk..." Hawthorne croaked from behind Tek and I before coughing up what might well have been a kidney.

Moxley had his confession, and behind his eyes, I saw him decide to kill Roy Altenhofen then and there. His lips drew into a thin, hard line, and as the first droplets of rain fell to the starving earth, Moxley drew the breath that was to deliver his vengeance.

Altenhofen had stolen Moxley's youth, and the piper was to be paid at last. There was no creature so fierce in its retributions as those who danced with the Weird and had known the cold bite of the collar. No hate has ever burned as deep as that which is ignited by the attempts of the powerful to domesticate in men and women the parts of themselves which must never be tamed.

Time itself buckled like a sheet of tin pressed upon by a giant, invisible hand. I could feel it dimpling at the edges, and the stormy night sky broke in places into rays of sunshine, then winter gray, and finally clear but slightly askew stars. Nature itself was coming apart in the midst of Moxley's fury. The very windows of time itself opened up like the eyes of some great beast to look upon the boy who claimed to be its master. Next to Moxley, what was Altenhofen but the man who had foolishly thought himself enough to scrub the birthright of creation itself from the blood of those who dared carry it?

Thunder, only this time I heard it in my head instead of my ear and felt all the way down in the pits of my soul. The realization that it was not thunder at all, but was the tolling of some unimaginably large clock, the striking of some invisible hour that had finally come around at last, left my mouth dry in fear so large it overlapped with awe. Moxley's lips moved in the dark; neither Tek nor myself could look away as Altenhofen, already an old man, began to gasp like a fish out of water on the ground at Moxley's feet

Unfortunately, Hawthorne was nowhere near as awestruck as Tek or me.

Hawthorne tore up from the ground; his body still in the process of reknitting itself like a ghastly video played in reverse. He barreled through Tek and myself with such force that the gun was knocked from my hand and the air from my lungs. He paid us no mind, though; his murderous eyes cared only for Moxley. He had crossed the distance between them and us by the time the younger man had even looked up from his work on Altenhofen.

Hawthorne hit Moxley with a low tackle at a near full sprint, lifting the young wizard up on his shoulder as he did and driving his spine first into the unyielding corner of the Resonance Tower. Moxley gasped in pain and surprise, the air no doubt driven from his lungs as I scrambled to find the gun.

Hawthorne gave him no quarter; he brought the back of his head up in a sharp arch that struck Moxley in the bottom of the chin and rocked his head back, then drove his knee with cruel, merciless intention into the boy's groin. When Moxley began to double over, Hawthorne caught his throat in his hand and shoved him back against the Resonance Tower.

"Can't 'port me into the fucking sky when I'm holding you and I don't age. That means your fucked, sonny-boy. Nice and hard just the way you like it." Hawthorne's fingers dug into Moxley's throat as he spoke.

No air meant no use of the Word.

The scene was chaotic, with Tek already rushing into the fray by the time I retrieved Hawthorne's gun from the ground. Her face was a swollen mess of bruises and lacerations, and God only knew how many more injuries she bore beneath her torn clothes. Yet, she charged forward, unencumbered by pain or fear, hurling herself onto Hawthorne's back and clawing at his eyes with her nails.

"Let him go! Let him go right now, you bastard!" Tek snarled like a lioness as Hawthorne grunted in pain beneath her weight.

"Stupid bitch!" Hawthorne screamed, frantically trying to dislodge Tek from his back.

In a desperate move, Hawthorne swung his elbow backward, colliding with Tek's jaw and sending her crashing to the ground in a dazed heap. Meanwhile, I moved closer to the unfolding confrontation, intending to shout Hawthorne's name like a gunfighter in an old Western calling out his rival, but the words died in my throat.

As the chaos ensued, the Resonance Tower regained its eerie glow. The strange symbols and words, their meanings unknown to me, once again radiated with an eldritch aura.

Moxley, taking advantage of the distraction caused by Tek, pressed his palms against the tower once more, his bloody lips curling into a snarling grin of defiance.

In the midst of the turmoil, Altenhofen, who had appeared old before but now seemed ancient, with his once white hair reduced to mere wisps upon a piebald skull, and his sunken eyes and liver-spotted hands resembling those of a desiccated mummy, thrust a trembling hand toward the Resonance Tower. The gnarled fingers, like twisted branches of a long-dead tree, quivered with an eerie anticipation as they reached out, as if beckoned by some unseen force.

"Stop him! Crush his throat! Stop them, Hawthorne! Kill them al-"

The world transformed abruptly, echoing with a deafening boom and bathed in a flash tinged with gunpowder.

Altenhofen collapsed onto the earth, his gaze fixed upon the celestial canopy above. He looked down at his chest, unbelieving, and it was not till the paper-like skin of two fingers touched the bright red flower blooming to the right of his heart that reality set in. I did not know if he was dead, and at that moment I did not care. All that mattered was that he had finally fallen silent, relinquishing his hold over us like a master releasing his pawns.

Hawthorne's gun had gone off in my grip before I even realized I had aimed it at Altenhofen. For a moment, he looked down at his chest, unbelieving, and it was not till the paper-like skin of two fingers touched the bright red flower blooming to the right of his heart that reality set in. Altenhofen collapsed onto the ground, his eyes fixed upon the stars.

Hawthorne had descended into some sort of focused psychotic mania. Both hands were wrapped around Moxley's throat, squeezing the life out of the boy. Moxley's eyes had already begun to bulge, and small trickles of blood escaped the corner of his mouth, yet he still did not release his hands from the tower. Electricity crackled in the air once more, and the rain burst forth with a deafening roar, assaulting the parched, lifeless soil of the Salt Flats.

"You should have spent more time learning to kill and less time dreaming about what you could do, boy. Give up...Give in...Let it happen..." Hawthorne cooed as if he were putting a child down to bed.

"Let him go, Hawthorne. Let him go or I'll shoot!" I yelled, the gun back out in front of me, so much heavier than my pen ever was.

Hawthorne didn't care. He didn't even seem to hear me, and Tek was still finding her senses on the ground. The frigid rain cascaded down, its furious deluge threatening to engulf everything but the Resonance Tower. Moxley looked not at the face of his potential killer, but at the sky, at the source of the pelting rain and the thunder and the lightning.

"Magic is about fixing the world...not breaking. Fixing..." Moxley said with what might have been the last bit of air in his lungs.

COYOTE WALLACE

A light of the purest blue erupted from the top of the Resonance Tower and rocketed into the sky. Altenhofen had placed other Resonance Towers across the world, intending to magnify Moxley's ability to create a fresh supply of Dynametrium, and whatever effect Moxley had unleashed now followed that same path of magnification. A force that can only be described by the likes of me, as a slow rolling but invisible explosion of force - shoved myself, Hawthorne, and Tek back onto the ground while Moxley was flung in the opposite direction.

After a moment I found myself and Tek lying amid upturned hard-baked earth, the rain was still pelting down and though I tried to sit up it felt as if my body had been dipped into molasses. I was stunned in the same manner that a fish in a pond might be stunned by a blasting cap tossed in by a redneck angler. Helpless and immobile. I could only imagine that Tek, having received a beating and not given the privilege of a brand-new body, felt much worse.

That unstoppable bastard, Hawthorne, was on his feet before I could even remember that I still had feet. He staggered over to me and put his boot down on the inside of the wrist connected to the hand that held his gun. My fingers convulsed in pain, and he plucked the firearm from my grasp, checked the chamber, and gave me a swift kick across the jaw for my troubles. Blood filled my mouth, hot and coppery, and my head rang like a bell.

"What? You thought you could just fix the curse? Is that what you were going for? You little shit. You little fucker," Hawthorne muttered as he shuffled towards Moxley's prone figure on the other side of the Resonance Tower.

He paused once as he passed Altenhofen's still body and looked back at me. He would be back for me. My debt would be paid. There was no mistaking that, but first Moxley had to be dealt with. Moxley, who in the end had betrayed

Altenhofen and Hawthorne by believing in the most painful truth of all: that sometimes those who say they care for us do not have our best intentions at heart.

Hawthorne stood over Moxley and drew back the hammer. There was no missing at this range, and while I could not see any movement from Moxley, I assumed that even if he was dead, Hawthorne would still put a bullet in him. Hawthorne was nothing if not thorough.

"You're going to need a bigger Word, boy," Hawthorne's words were punctuated by the rotation of the cylinder and the click-click of the gun's hammer.

"Didn't try to fix you. I turned. Oh Jesus, that hurts. I turned all the Dynametrium into water. I reversed it all." Moxley's words, pained and weak beneath the storm, nevertheless managed to sound triumphant to my ears.

The gun in Hawthorne's hand dipped, and I saw the look of confusion wash across the haggard face of Altenhofen's hired killer. I suspect that he had spent countless years at Altenhofen's side, learning and listening in the way that one casually picks up the craft of a loved one or any father figure. He looked like a man who had just discovered his wife of twenty years was having an affair with the pool boy.

"You couldn't. That's too much. It would kill you," Hawthorne said, almost in a daze.

"Yeah. That part sucks, but on the upside, I get to watch Tek kick your fucking ass," Moxley said, even as the whites of his eyes began to slip into the same shade of blue as the Dynametrium he'd just banished from existence.

There came a whisper from my right that sounded like flowers blooming, that reminded me of the tumble of old stones down a mountain, that bubbled and swam in the ear like the waters of the great rivers that carved their way across the face of America. Tek had risen to her knees, and with a quick shake of her head, the wounds upon her face were gone.

Hawthorne must have realized the ramifications of what Moxley had done in that instant, or perhaps he really could smell it when someone used the Word. He whipped around, still standing astride Moxley's form, and the gun was suddenly on Tek. Hawthorne would kill us all and leave us here to rot; I doubted he cared about the loss of Altenhofen too much, but the loss of money and purpose had, no doubt, sealed our fates in his eyes.

Another whisper from Tek's lips, and in it, I heard the silent beat of paws beneath the underbrush. I heard howls at the moon, and in it, I felt the great primal fear that followed every man when he ventured into the woods, the sea, or any place where his position on the food chain was forfeit.

Hawthorne's hand and the gun that it held fell to the ground, and a bright gout of blood sprayed out into the dark and the rain. Hawthorne staggered away from Moxley, clutching his stump in a macabre mixture of disbelief and pain that would have haunted me for the rest of my days if not for the true horror that came next.

Tek was rising to her feet.

"I thought about what to do with you. For a while, I even thought there might be a way to break the curse and kill you, but you're right, Hawthorne. I can't kill you; maybe no one can. You like to pretend that the curse laid upon you was a mistake by my people, but I think it was a riddle, just not one for you to solve." Tek's tone was reasonable, even, and measured. No fear or anger tainted her now.

"You stupid red cunt! I will tear your heart out and eat it! Do you fucking hear me!?!?! No matter what you do to me. No matter what you think you're going to do, I will come back! I WILL ALWAYS COME BACK!" Hawthorne would not plead as Altenhofen had; he would not pretend. Not even now.

Tek approached him slowly as if he were a wounded animal caught in a trap.

"I am not 'a stupid red cunt,' Hawthorne. I am The Old Magik, I am the sister of Coyote, Raven, and Bear. I am a daughter of the Sky, and I promise you on the blood you've spilled - you will not leave this place." Tek, who had been beaten and chosen by Altenhofen as the patsy, who had learned her Namebreaking piecemeal from a world that men like Hawthorne had tried to grind to dust beneath their feet, said to the undying monster before her with what to a fool's ear might have sounded like compassion.

It was not.

"Goddamn you!" Hawthorne pushed himself towards her, the same mad charge he'd thrown at Moxley.

Tek held the ground she stood upon without so much as a thought of retreat.

Lightning split the sky, and Hawthorne had made it three steps before Tek spoke the final word, bracing herself against the pain that was to come as she did. I cannot be sure of the Word's meaning, I cannot be sure of its purpose, but to my ears, it sounded like the branches of mighty trees groaning in protest. The sound of all things that grew green and wild beneath the sun cried out to answer Tek's call.

Hawthorne fell to his knees, gargling and choking, and his arms thrust themselves outwards to the side at a downward angle. What appeared to be long, thin ropes tore themselves from first the stump of his missing hand, and then from the tips of his fingers on the one that remained. These "ropes" dug themselves into the soil even as Hawthorne's belly began to swell. His head thrashed from side to side wildly as his jaw first dislocated and then locked itself open.

"I can't break the curse, Hawthorne. You may well live forever, but since you refuse to learn to become a better man, I can't let you go on hurting anyone. That's the thing you taught us, Hawthorne. The lesson learned only after you'd been made." Tek explained with tears in her eyes. Her dark hair had begun to go gray as The Word fed upon her for the change it would make.

Hawthorne's head ceased moving, and the gurgling pushed into the realm of choking. All at once, Hawthorne's swollen belly erupted in a spray of gore upon the ground. What I had thought were ropes before now revealed themselves to be thick, vine-like roots. They dug into the ground even as Hawthorne's eyes ruptured in their sockets, pushed out of place by the sharp, pointed tips of the branches growing inside of him. A final wheeze came from lungs that no longer had room to expand, and the trunk of his new form ripped itself from his mouth, sending his teeth scattering out on the water-starved earth. There was a wet ripping sound as the last of his body gave way, and when Tek was finished, what had been Hawthorne was now the lone green shade tree in the middle of the Salt Flats. The soil would be poison and would have killed any other tree in less than a day, but this one would, due to Hawthorne's curse, endure forever.

Tek stood for a moment, swaying on her feet, and then she collapsed, and I ran to her in the rain.

The Return of the Wild American Unknown

The worst part of any accident is never the crash; neither the sound nor the fury, or even the violent tossing of the physical form, can claim that title. The worst is always the cleanup; the moment after the whole world falls apart when you're left scrambling to save whatever you can is always the worst. There is no soul more wretched in its own misery than that of a man or woman who, with the memory of their life before that crash still lingering like a phantom limb, struggles to find what had been lost. In these moments, even those of us who have been made atheist by the pinch-faced, miserable fucker of a teacher that is life, may find ourselves compelled to call upon our gods for favor and mercy.

I muttered a prayer as I reached Tek's still form on the ground and sank to my knees beside her. When I rolled her over and discovered she was breathing, I realized that I'd been holding my own breath. Her black hair was now streaked with white, her lips chapped and broken. She looked as if she had walked across some pitiless desert and had only survived by luck or stubborn nature. The Word peeled the nutrients and calories from a Namebreaker's system, and I was neither a doctor nor a Namebreaker, but I was uncomfortably sure that Tek had pushed herself to a place that part of her might not ever come back from.

"Hey, come on. Wake up! You gotta talk to me, okay? Just wake up, alright?" In the rain, I could not tell if I was crying as I said the words, a horrible fear that Tek would die, and I would be left alone in this dead place gripped my very soul.

For a moment, there was no response beyond Tek's shallow breathing and the rolling of raindrops down her cheeks. My heart skipped a beat, and then her eyes opened, dark, wide, and startled with her own survival.

I should have fixed your face. Fuck, my head..." Tek groaned as she sat up, her movements sluggish and groggy, like someone emerging from a long and fitful sleep filled with nightmares.

"Next time you get me killed, you can fix my face." I tried to sound solemn, but my relief at her survival kept breaking through, causing my lips to curve into a smile despite my efforts.

"Deal. Where's Moxley?" Tek asked, touching her fingers to the side of her skull tentatively and wincing at the pain the touch brought.

I glanced towards the Resonance Tower. Even in the darkness of the storm-battered Flats, I could make out both Moxley and Altenhofen. They lay like the hands of a clock that had stopped at three, motionless and silent amidst the chaos of the storm. I looked back at Tek, feeling guilty as I tried to find the words to tell her that Moxley had given his life for us. That his final act of defiance against Altenhofen had cost him everything, taking from the rich bastard the only thing he valued as much as Moxley valued his own father: his legacy.

"I don't think he made it." I said, and if there was any hope or goodness in those words, it was only that in the rain, Tek might not see the shame I felt at being alive.

"No, he's still alive. I can feel it. Help me up, Jimmy," Tek commanded, sounding like the battlefield medics from old World War Two films, never giving up despite the odds or the dimness of the spark.

I helped her to her feet, and we limped our way over to Moxley. In doing so, we were forced to pass Altenhofen's corpse. I had never killed a man and personally found even the idea of hunting distasteful. Something in me was unable to look away, though. I expected to feel some wave of disgust or remorse, but in all honesty, all I really felt was relief.

Altenhofen was responsible for all of this, all the hurt and the pain and the blood. Spite and greed had taken his noble ambitions and wrapped them in a foul corporate caul that served as a womb for the monstrosity he'd become.

I was alive, and Altenhofen was staring at the sky with that final grimace on his face like everything else that died in the Flats.

"Jesus, God Almighty!" I recoiled in horror when we got close enough to see Moxley clearly.

Moxley's colorful hair had fallen out, and his gums receded back on his teeth. He was thin beyond human comprehension, just bones with skin stretched across them, and his eyes, frighteningly vivid and lucid, had sunken back into his skull. He looked like one of the figures pulled from the camps at Bergen or Auschwitz, a human being pushed beyond the limits of starvation into some realm of wasting that lay beyond. Every vein in Moxley's body stood out bright blue, almost iridescent beneath his skin, and that faint glow was spreading into the nearby tissues at an alarming rate.

Tek covered her mouth to stifle the gasp when he, with what was no doubt great effort, turned his head in our direction. The capillaries of Moxley's eyes had begun to rupture, and amidst the dark blood, one could see tiny pinpricks of glowing blue - clusters of his cells already converting themselves to Dynametrium.

"You can't blame me for giving it my best shot, Hawthorne. I should have known that it'd come down to you, but you better hurry. I think you're going to miss the chance to kill me." Moxley rasped with a gallows' humor that made me once more grateful for the rain.

I could lie to myself that I wasn't crying.

Tek slipped out of my arms and eased her way to Moxley's side.

"I got him. Hawthorne's not a problem, okay? You stopped them. You hear me, you little shit? You stopped them. Just hold on, and I'll fix you," Tek's voice cracked and buckled beneath the horror her eyes showed her.

"Don't be…stupid…You're burnt, and I stopped being able to see the future ten minutes ago." Moxley uttered with more courage than most men would have mustered. Only when he mentioned not being able to see the future did his voice threaten to break.

The unknown would always have sharper teeth than death.

I joined Tek by Moxley's side and took his hand in my own. I had no idea what good the gesture might do or even if he could feel it; his hand felt like a loose bundle of sticks in my own, and after a moment, the fingers closed around mine. Moxley squeezed my hand and fought back what might have been a sob.

"I got you." I murmured, and of all the many words that I have made over the many years that I had made them, these felt the hollowest and useless of them all.

Moxley's body jerked and stiffened, and for a moment, I thought he would succumb to a seizure. Then, his eyes opened once more, and though I felt certain he was blind, they fixed themselves upon me.

"I was wrong. I forgot the purpose of the Word. When all the choices are bad, we make new ones," Moxley said through the pain, as if these words were more vital than those with which he'd bent time itself.

Tek gently wiped his brow with her hand.

"I did it, Tek. Truly. No more Dynametrium. Not in the food, not in the medicine, all the people it silenced… Tell me it worked… I can't… I can't see how it plays out anymore… I'm…" Moxley's dignity might have wavered at the end, but Tek silenced him with a kiss on his forehead.

"It worked. I promise. You saved everyone. You made it right." Tek comforted him as best she could, and I squeezed his hand a little tighter.

Then Moxley Allerton, son of "The American Merlin" Conrad Allerton, seemingly satisfied with this answer, gave a final sigh and slipped from this world. For a moment, he remained as he was at our side, and then the Dynametrium's growth accelerated tremendously. I felt his skin harden and crystallize beneath my fingers, and for one surreal moment that will burn and linger in my mind for all of my days, he was a perfect blue crystal statue of the young rebel I'd met three days prior. The transformation rendered his boyish features into a work of bitter natural art, a disconsolate shell that bathed Tek and me in its soft glow.

Without warning or heraldry of its own end, what had been Moxley obeyed the same spell that he'd woven in the moments before his death and turned to water, the glow lost the moment it joined the rain.

Later, I would have time to piece together how Moxley had accomplished the feat, how he'd not only erased every trace of Dynametrium from the face of the earth but also changed the very rules of its existence. Moxley had previously used the Resonance Towers to create smaller fields of Dynametrium, but he'd been using them one at a time. When Altenhofen had aligned all three across the earth in his plan to create a limitless supply of the stuff (without the need for the 'Namebreakers' themselves as an ingredient), he'd left the door open for Moxley to do something that I think all of us who have traveled the deep valleys of American strangeness and hard concrete paths of the margins have always dreamed of.

He'd undone the mistakes of his father.

The implications of what Moxley had done, however, could not penetrate the anesthetized sensation left behind by the shock in the moments of his death. They did not outpace the sudden need to be out from the rain and away from the death and the Resonance Tower. The implications of what

Moxley had truly done didn't reach me as Tek searched for keys to fit any of the vehicles left behind in Altenhofen's garage, nor did it bother to notify me at all of its presence when she was successful or while I was busy stealing an ill-fitting suit from a dead billionaire's closet like the psychologically damaged fiend the night had made of me.

We left out in the limo that Hawthorne had picked me up in, Tek eating a bag of pilfered corn chips in the passenger seat beside me while staring out the window. This was a final indignity thrust upon us by Altenhofen, that we were to ride out of the Flats in his gas-guzzling motorized instrument of phallic compensation. Despite the horror and the blood, I felt a mad thrill as we drove through the gates and left Altenhofen, the Resonance Tower, and his fortress in the middle of all this beautiful nothing in the rearview mirror.

The implication of what Moxley had done as his last act of defiance against a world that told him that he should not exist did not make itself known to me until, simply to break the silence and quiet the voice in my head that cried out for me to make haste back home to Jenna, I turned on the radio.

"This is a TOX News Special Report. We have unconfirmed reports coming in now that President Nixon has been killed by his own Secret Service agents when he tore open the throat of Vice President Gingrich and began sodomizing the corpse. Witnesses say that President Nixon was hissing, baring his fangs, and ranting uncontrollably about being worshiped as a blood god." The newscaster's voice warbled with the sort of panic that only comes to men who read the news when their ears are full of the oncoming traffic of ever-mounting surprises.

Honestly, it could have been worse; imagine what sort of world we'd have to live in where we might choose a disgraced reality television star or even a career politician. Moxley hadn't just broken the chemical chains that held down his fellow Namebreakers; he'd shattered the masks and facades that had been used to hide the truth.

Tek leaned over and changed the station, and the air was flooded with the sound of Little Richard's "Rip It Up" beating its way out into the night. Satisfied with her work, she flopped back in her seat, and out of the corner of my eye, I saw her nod her head approvingly. My foot pressed down on the accelerator, and the limo's engine gave a throaty roar of approval. The road was all straight out here, all open, all flat, and it led away from the pains of our new future's birth.

The sort of road that begged you to run ever faster towards tomorrow.

"Little Richard," Tek said with a voice too tired to do more than remark.

"I can swing with some Little Richard," I added, too excited to be tired and too determined to escape for small talk.

Moxley had opened up a brand-new world; he'd taken the first impossible step towards repairing a wound that had nearly left our country spiritually bankrupt in the name of fear. This world would be overflowing with new Namebreakers, new instances of strange, new possibilities for those who had so desperately needed anything to alter the course of their own destiny. No more were we to be bound by the choices of the past and the terrible momentum of history; we had the opportunity to set right in our now what had long ago been told to us was written into our very nature. Those stories that would grow from this righting of the ship would need telling; they would need a "Jimmy Wonderful," but more importantly, they'd need the woman who rode beside me out of the nothing and into the wide-open tomorrow.

I glanced over at Tek and grinned.

They'd need their American Mystic.

COYOTE WALLACE

Epilogue

I know it may sound like a bit of self-flattery, Tom, but I like to imagine that after finishing all of that, you started furiously masturbating at the sheer idea of just how much money you were going to make. I mean, come on, picture the headline: "Crazed gonzo journalist shot dead at the estate of an eccentric billionaire." That's a hell of a headline, isn't it? My God, man! Take control of yourself! Dump that awful "healthy soda" you lie to yourself about down the drain and have a stiff drink if it makes it any easier for you.

What a damn shame it is that there were so many juicier stories back in those early days, huh? I don't think I lasted an entire news cycle. Nothing is more humbling than your own death and seeing that it doesn't rate higher than America's morning dose of cat videos and squirrels riding skateboards.

But here you are, reading this, and wondering what you're going to do with it. Maybe I've picked up a few tricks from Tek on the road, or maybe I just know how spineless corporate lemmings like you think when confronted with something that you cannot explain.

Here's what you'll do, Tom: You'll see it all in print. Every damn word that your eyes have touched will find its way onto a page. I don't care if you have to run it in the Mystic Standard while shedding tears as your boss pours molten shit down upon your head. If you make it into a book, you will ensure that Jenna receives every dime that would have otherwise been mine.

Welcome to the brave new world, Tom. It's weird, it's wild, and it's gonzo, baby!

Without the test, I hear the government is going to have to even let the people afflicted with lycanthropy go. Those who wanted to go at least. Maybe they'll do something about all the deer that keep pilfering my garden? Most of the vampires have fled back into the shadows or Los Angeles (the fact that LA is filled with blood-drinking ageless undead surprises absolutely no one), and even the faeries are beginning to return.

I didn't think that it would work. In the chaos of the early days, I thought we would descend into the Hell that Moxley showed me. The first wave of Namebreakers coming into their abilities have, in some cases, no doubt been every bit as worrisome as we'd feared. However, others, like Latisha Green, who endured her trial and the badgering of an angry DA without an ounce of Dynametrium in her body and the system - filled with people who now understood that the Namebreakers could be them - upheld.

I drank myself silly in joy when they let her walk free.

The fight isn't over though, Tom. There are still those out there in the hidden places of our country who feed The Fear, who whisper lines of division between us and The Strange, hoping that one day someone will come along and take up Roy Altenhofen's mantle. Having seen the things that I have seen, having watched the price that was paid for this new world be paid by a young man who had all of time before him while someone like me was given a new lease on his existence - I can no longer sit on the sidelines. I cannot wait until the next Altenhofen puts his boot on the throat of someone else.

All my love to Jenna, but the man I was really did die in Altenhofen's office.

I'm Jimmy Wonderful, now and forever, and we're going to change the world one Word at a time.

With bootlegger blood running through his veins, Gonzo fire in his belly, and folk punk-fantasy percolating in his brain, Coyote Wallace spins up genre-bending tales that draw on the spirits of Appalachia as well as fantastically imagined pasts, presents, and futures of the American Spirit. Creator of the MEDIUM series THE DISPATCHES FROM APPALACHIA, contributing writer for RUNESCAPE: SHATTERED PARADISE, and BOOK OF WYRM: COMPANIONS, and the first twice-selected (in one call) novelist under the Nightmare Press banner.

Coyote's debut novels, AMERICAN MYSTIC: THE LIFE, DEATH, AND REBIRTH OF JIMMY WONDERFUL and SARAH CORBIN'S BLOODY REVENGE, promise readers a double-barreled dose of the wild, the weird, and the wonderful.

Thank you for reading! If you like the book, please leave a review on Amazon and Goodreads. Reviews help authors and publishers spread the word.

To keep up with more Nightmare Press news, visit us at:

Nightmarepress.net
Facebook
X
Instagram
Nightmare Press Network on YouTube

To interact with authors and other readers, join the Nightmare Press Fans & Authors group on Facebook